DARK WINDOWS

(or The Death of Godard)

By Neil Coombs

To Lisette, My best student.

Neil Coombs
x

DARK WINDOWS

Published by lulu.com

http://www.lulu.com/content/3283287

ISBN 978-1-4092-2129-6

First Edition 2008

Copyright © Neil Coombs, 2008

TO CINEPHILES OF THE WORLD

All organisations, institutions, places and characters appearing in this work are fictitious. Any resemblance to real persons, living or dead, is purely coincidental.

Chapter 1:

The Death of Godard

The body of Jean-Luc Godard sat hunched in a partially melted white plastic garden chair, his lifeless eyes regarding the partially tended garden of a rest home for the elderly in Penmaenmawr.

ıı

Shot / Reverse shot.

▸

If he was watching from art-house heaven, he would be asking…

Why, of all places, have I ended my days here? What is the significance of this – that a famous European filmmaker should die in the anonymous garden of an anonymous Victorian manor house in an anonymous part of the United Kingdom?

Perhaps he would have known the significance of his death – only he knew what was left in him at the end – what unfulfilled plans faded with his ebbing consciousness.

⏮

One scant hour earlier, Godard's rented Toyota Yaris had been heading west towards the edge of a new Europe that was joined as never before – a Europe that had never been as integrated or stretched as far as this, from the Bosporus to the North Atlantic - that had expanded without any apparent invasion or war. It was a Europe for the workers, it was a Europe for the capitalists, it was for the Socialists and Fascists, the nationalists and internationalists, the conservatives and radicals – it was a human endeavour that contained all of humanity and all of its future. It was a web spun by invisible spiders, Godard knew that the spiders would soon appear and he knew that it was imperative for him to be one of them.

He turned off the A55 expressway, the sea to his right, the mountains to his left and the fading sun illuminating it all through the fast moving clouds of the late March afternoon. He thought little now – he knew too much and one of the things that he knew was the reason for being here – incognito, in secret: Money – he needed money again, this time more was needed for a plan that had to remain hidden. He had been wooing easily flattered financiers with his cultural prestige – collecting small sums of money to fill the large pool of finance required to create his masterpiece. He knew that he was back, that he had a vision again – his muse had taken an interesting route to this point in time but the determination was there now – he had decided to open the windows and let the light of Godard illuminate the world.

He had developed a concept – a high concept linked to a revolutionary intent. His next film would be the most important he had ever made – a rallying cry for dreamers and revolutionaries – entertainment for the masses, using the juggernaut of the motion picture industry to change the world, to foment revolution and alter the political landscape forever. Godard was not wrapped in such hyperbole – he just knew: He knew that his life was moving inescapably towards this subtly messianic goal, he knew that the corporate elite would not allow him to carry out his revolution easily and he knew that after the revolution no one would care.

For the past eighteen months, he had been visiting television executives around Europe. He was collecting money like the producers of *Springtime for Hitler*, seducing the little old ladies of the media world with his aging prestige and pocketing their money on a promise that would never be fulfilled.

He was returning to the United Kingdom to find finance for the first time since his *British Sounds* project was banned by 'independent' British television for being too radical. That was a time when England had at least a little credibility. Then, in that decade, he had made *One Plus One* – re-titled and re-edited it was released and disowned, he was naïve back then. Polanski, Antonioni, Truffaut – they had all made movies in England in the sixties. No one of note had any intention of associating themselves with this flabby isle nowadays – intellectual, artistic, political, culinary flab. The world did not like the United Kingdom and Godard represented the world.

The covert nature of Godard's project ensured that he was travelling alone and would return alone to his reclusive and secure home in Rolle, in Switzerland – a void at the centre of the web. He was here, in Wales, to meet Huw Pugh of S4C: Film Commissioning Editor of the United Kingdom's Welsh language television channel. He was here to secure the final piece of his financial jigsaw puzzle – the money that would allow the production and distribution of his populist rallying cry – a film that would not be esoteric like *Notre Musique* or obliquely deconstructive like *Eloge De L'Amour*. It would follow on from where *Alphaville, Breathless* and *Le Mepris* left off and its effect would shake the world as much as a fictional feature film can. His cultural capital and place in the history of the twentieth century was already ensured but no one expected Godard to change the twenty-first century. He felt ominously like John Lennon walking out of the lobby of his hotel in New York, knowing that he was back and about to say something to a world that was ready to listen. He had allowed the Dark Windows to restrain him for too long and now he had nothing to lose.

▶▶

A chill washed his aging frame as he turned into the entrance of *Plas Coch* and parked discreetly at the foot of the long drive. The mountain breeze in the spring leaves masked the noise of the dual carriageway that cut the village off from the bright expanse of sand below and the Irish Sea glittering blue to the horizon. The fresh sea air cut lightly through Godard's lungs as he exhaled the last of his stale cigar smoke. He still smoked the cigar of his cinematic heroes: Hitchcock, Welles, Ford, Hawkes but could never admit to it...

perhaps it was the cigar of Belmondo – he made Belmondo – fuck Belmondo – he was Godard – he was the icon and he knew it.

He ambled up towards the aging garden where Huw Pugh was waiting at a white plastic table. As Godard ascended the drive and turned one corner, his doppelganger turned another – walking through the lower gates, sporting the same shabby intellectual air and smoking the same cigar. Godard's identical twin opened the hire car door and sat calmly in the still warm driver's seat, waiting.

Reaching the top of the drive, Godard shuffled around the edge of the garden, sticking to the raised path and flower borders that skirted the apparently deserted Victorian house. The house and its location resonated with a dead Europe – an enlightened utopian Europe where the patrician classes cared for the workers – it felt like his family's summer house on the banks of *Lac Léman* – it smelt of his childhood. It reminded him of the mental institution that his father had sent him to for stealing his grandfather's first editions of Valéry... As he considered the stolen books, he took a book of his own – a slim black notebook, full of tightly written notes and carefully dropped it, kicking it underneath the bush that he was examining. The sleepy bees on the spring blossom brushed against his worn raincoat and headed off towards an uncertain summer. A hush descended on the enclosed garden, the silence of green lawns, high hedges and privacy. The wind tugged at the very tops of the tall trees. Where life touched the skies, a battle was raging and its faint rustling cast a blanket over this quaint British seaside scene. As he strolled along the border, he avoided Pugh and considered the flowers; dead-heading was one of the few pleasures he allowed himself and as he circled the periphery of the damp lawn, he carefully pinched the spring blooms from their succulent stalks. His pleasure derived from the feeling of his fingernails cutting into the soft flesh at the neck of the plant and removing its head – he was a god in this universe – decapitating with a remorseless pinch, restoring order and allowing new growth – he was at peace now and ready to meet his financier.

He walked over to Pugh and sat heavily on a plastic chair that gave slightly beneath him, the legs spreading out to distribute his mature weight – a weight that had always been measured in kilograms as one day all people would be measured. There was a moment of silence as the two men regarded each other.

"Mister Godard..." The reverie was disturbed by Pugh's gratingly obsequious and parochial enthusiasm. His formal business attire appeared to come straight off the peg – laundered in such a way as to look brand new – he obviously had someone to iron his shirts and press his trousers. His aviator's watch hung heavily on its thick bracelet as the scent that he wore hung on his portly frame. Hairs protruded from nose, ear and neck, the smile and firm handshake revealed a starched collar, cuffs and cufflinks that kept his hairy body framed and contextualised. He was a businessman and Godard was here to do business with him.

"Mister Godard..." he seemed to roll the name around his tongue, delivering it in the attractive and musical accent often parodied but always distinct. "I'm glad, we at S4C are glad, that you have elected us to help fund your new project Mr Godard. I'm sure that our channel will be ideal for the British terrestrial premiere of your film and you will recognise that, at this point in time, we share a mutual distrust for the English, their language, their colonial, empirical, Victorian superiority... I am hoping that your choice to work with us reflects your understanding of the depth of Welsh culture and tradition; that you share with us a distrust for the purely visual – for eye candy – that you share our love for the literary tradition, for music, land and language... we, at this point in time, Mr Godard, have much in common and we intend to support your project with no questions asked..." His speech trailed off as had many of the others that Godard had been subjected to over the past eighteen months.

Godard had very little interest in English culture and no awareness of Wales, the Welsh or their traditions. Like most Europeans, he assumed Wales to be part of England like Cornwall or Yorkshire. He was here for S4C's offer of hard cash, to fund this project that was nothing to do with Wales or England.

Huw Pugh had exuded slightly less confidence and more sophistication at their only previous meeting. It was at the Sarajevo Film Festival in August 2005 and Mr Pugh had said very little, cowed by a land that, despite a communist regime and civil war, appeared more cultured and civilised than Rhyl on a Saturday night. He realised that North Wales would never attract international celebrities or hold a significant film festival. The highlights of the movie map of Wales featured such classics as *Carry on up the Khyber*, *Tomb Raider 2*, *Holiday on the Buses* and *Inn of the Sixth Happiness*. The centre had moved away from the United Kingdom and Wales was at the periphery of the Kingdom. In Sarajevo few people spoke English on the streets and no one spoke Huw's mother-tongue. Godard's Switzerland may have given us the cuckoo clock, Wales had given even less of cultural significance outside of Wales. A World War had been triggered in Sarajevo and perhaps the events of the next few minutes could cause a similar chain of events to emanate from a small village on the North Wales coast.

Godard had remained mute, he had come to collect a cheque, not to discuss history – he made history, he didn't have to talk about it.

"*Paned*?" Huw asked enquiringly "…cup of tea Mr Godard?"

He nodded in reply and from the shadowy interior stepped a tall figure carrying a tray on which sat two steaming mugs of strong tea made with milk and sugar. The man carrying the tray resembled an elongated owl, his eyes sunk into deep sockets, prematurely bald with his hair rising in two tufts from behind his ears and his small nose slightly hooked – his physiognomy was hard to place in the catalogue of human facial types. He quietly placed the tray on the stained table and stepped back into the dark parlour beyond.

Godard raised the mug to his mouth and grimaced as he swallowed the disgusting concoction, he gulped the warm liquid down quickly to avoid the taste – he had had worse in other locations – in other countries. As the intoxication of the drugged tea swept across Godard, he realised that he would never make his film or any other film – his last vision would be of England's green and pleasant lands (in Wales) and it would be an empty vision.

"Magog... get out here now" Huw was swift to call his accomplice, "at this point in time, I must leave – you know what to do…"

He rose immediately and strolled down the drive to his car, pointedly ignoring the man in the driving seat of the adjacent Toyota. As Huw headed back to Cardiff, Magog was systematically and efficiently removing the contents of Godard's pockets... a passport, a wallet, some papers, keys, cigars and matches – very little for a man of such cultural significance. He took a small bottle of methylated spirits from the pocket of his brown tweed jacket, poured it into Godard's mouth and over his slumped body, the remainder he poured into a half-drunk bottle of cheap wine that now sat on the stained table. Taking a single match from a box of *England's Glory*, he placed the box on Godard's lap and struck the red head on the underside of the table – he dropped the flame into Godard's soaked lap and the symbolic immolation commenced. He immediately turned his back on the scene and swept down to the Toyota, climbing into the passenger seat. He handed Godard's property to the doppelganger in the driving seat and they left as inconspicuously as Godard had arrived.

Magog and the new Godard sat in silence. The rain began to fall as they joined the A55 expressway, this time heading east, to John Lennon Airport, to the centre of the web.

Chapter 2:
Dark Windows

This is the story of what a man's memory can endure, and what his perseverance can achieve. If the machinery of the modern media could be depended on to investigate every case of suspicion, and to conduct every process of inquiry, with only moderate assistance from the lubricating influences of oil or gold, the events which fill these pages might have claimed their share of the public attention in a film or television series.

What follows is an extract from the script for a short documentary film produced by Larry Went for a BBC Television strand on conspiracies in 2001. The programme has never been aired.

DARK WINDOWS
By Larry Went

SYNOPSIS

Throughout the Twentieth Century a battle has raged between the Realists and the Surrealists — between the realists and the dreamers. On the surface this may seem a superficial conflict for creative or stylistic dominance — a mere polemical debate. This argument between reality and fantasy is an eye peering from behind a political and cultural veil. At the root of this conflict lie a series of secret organisations that control Western society through the overt and covert use of propaganda. This documentary film attempts to reveal how far these fantastic theories reflect a reality and to what extent they are imagined conspiracies.

Through contact with a number of key players and analysis of key texts — Larry Went attempts to reveal what lies behind the Dark Windows of the Twentieth Century.

FADE IN:

SERIES OF SHOTS:

   A) MONTAGE: London at night, reflections in the windows of semi-occupied office blocks, cars passing by. Filmed using time-lapse photography.

   B) MONTAGE: Extracts from daytime television shows, dramas, comedies and news reports.

> LARRY WENT (V.O.)
> (staccato)
> A shadowy organisation controls our thoughts by planting secret messages in our minds. Everything that we watch on a screen or listen to through the media is arranged to control and brainwash us — all of this is controlled by a secret organisation known as <u>Dark Windows</u>.

INT. OFFICE — DAY

> VENDOR BUSCH
> Dark Windows is a secret organisation created by a conspiracy of secret organisations.

EXT. PARK BENCH — DAY

                  MIKE WAR

They have a dream — to control the world by controlling our thoughts and desires.

INT. OFFICE — DAY

                  VENDOR BUSCH

I believe that the highest members of Dark Windows are the descendents of aliens — of non-human beings.

SERIES OF SHOTS:
  A) MONTAGE: Stock footage of crowds around the world: commuters, sports events, music concerts, demonstrations, political rallies.

                  LARRY WENT (V.O.)
                     (melodramatic)

Dark Windows are in control of the media, the cultural and publishing industries. They have a grand plan to dominate and control the world.

INT. OFFICE — DAY

                  VENDOR BUSCH

I challenge the Dark Windows to come forth — to open up and show themselves.

                    LARRY WENT (V.O.)
                Just what is 'Dark Windows' to
                provoke such fear and such anger?

TITLE SEQUENCE
SERIES OF SHOTS:
   A) MONTAGE: Fast cut series of stills, graphics
       and moving images from a range of media
       products. Theme music: "In The Dark" by The
       Violent Femmes.

                "He's in the dark
                And the night is his friend
                He's on a mission that can never
                end
                He has a heart that was broke long
                ago
                He has more women than you'll ever
                know"

EXT. LEICESTER SQUARE. LONDON — NIGHT

LARRY walks through the crowds in Leicester Square,
talking to the camera and pointing at the film
posters on display.

LARRY WENT

Dark Windows are everywhere — in everything we watch on television — in every film we see and in every magazine and newspaper. Perhaps this film [points at poster for Pearl Harbor] or that one [points at poster for The Mummy Returns] contain secret messages. That one definitely does [points at cinema screening Harry Potter and the Sorcerer's Stone]. These films control not only our actions but also our thoughts and dreams.
(pause)
Or is it all a myth?
(pause)
I am going on a journey to find out just how true any of this is.

SERIES OF SHOTS

A) MONTAGE: Series of general views of Liverpool (Waterfront, Cathedrals, Museums, St. George's Hall, Lime Street Station, Sefton Park) using dissolves between shots.

LARRY WENT (V.O.)

The journey begins in Liverpool: Hotbed of political activity — land of the Beatles, possibly the

>   European City of Culture 2008 and
>   also home to Mike War —
>   Communications theorist and number
>   one Dark Windows hunter. He
>   broadcasts on Liverpool Community
>   Radio from where he attempts to
>   reveal the true extent of the
>   media's influence on the world.

INT. RADIO STATION — DAY

>   MIKE WAR
>   They think that they've got
>   supreme power, right? But we've
>   got more power mate… we have the
>   power to inspire and mobilise
>   ordinary people… we're the
>   audience — the consumer, right?
>   We're the ones who have to buy
>   into the dream to make it all
>   work, if we refuse to buy into it
>   — it won't work, right?

SERIES OF SHOTS

   A) MONTAGE: Series of library and archive shots that synchronise with LARRY's voice-over. Using Ken Burns effect to move between still images.

LARRY WENT (V.O.)

Dark Windows theorists would have us believe that this organisation was born at the start of the Twentieth century with the development of the modern mass media. As soon as the power of cinema was understood — a battle commenced for the control of its language. One of the best-known organisations involved in the development of cinematic language was the Surrealist movement in 1920s Paris. The theorists argue that 'Dark Windows' was formed in 1929 by French writer, Georges Bataille after he split from Andre Breton's Surrealist group.
(pause)
I wanted to find out more about Dark Windows and how the idea has developed since the 1920s. MIKE WAR has sent me to Osnabrück in North West Germany to meet an expert on this mysterious organisation. VENDOR BUSCH's view of Art History fits perfectly with the conspiracy theories espoused by MIKE.

INT. OFFICE — DAY

> VENDOR BUSCH
> These messages are there for a reason — there's no such thing as random coincidence, it's all synchronicity — you should read Carl Jung, his work on Archetypes and the Collective Unconscious. What Jung didn't realise is that his ideas would be scientifically applied as a control mechanism — that a system could be developed to control humanity through control of the Collective Unconscious — do you understand what I am getting at here? Art, Film and the Media can be used to plant 'shadows' in the human psyche — these can have a positive or a negative effect — whoever controls this system can control humanity — and this is why the organisation must remain secret — the Dark Windows are a one-way street my friend. You will find that all of this started with the Surrealists and their revolutionary ideas — they thought that they could use these techniques to make the world a better place — they wanted to

liberate the subconscious — to free the world and fight against the kind of culture that had created two World Wars. It started there but it has ended here...

LARRY WENT (V.O.)
Okay, that's a start — now I go back to Liverpool to meet Mike War again — it seems like it all began very positively but how did it all go wrong?

INT. RADIO STATION — DAY
MIKE WAR
What you've got to see mate is that this technique — this idea that Breton and the Surrealists developed — needed power — it needs capital to create control systems — to create big movies and media systems. That is why they signed up to the Communist party — Breton, Dali, Bunuel — and they set up sister groups in Belgium, Czechoslovakia, Mexico, England... right?

> LARRY WENT (V.O.)
> Every time I think that I have grasped the concept, I see it from a different angle…

SERIES OF SHOTS:

B) MONTAGE: Series of shots showing Larry travelling across Europe — back to Osnabrück. Music Bed: "Darklands" by The Jesus and Mary Chain.

> LARRY WENT (V.O.)
> So far we have an angry Scouser and a mad German telling me that the man who painted melting clocks is behind a terrible conspiracy to control us all through Hollywood Blockbusters…
> (pause)
>
> Somehow it doesn't all ring true — perhaps VENDOR can explain how this all works…

INT. OFFICE — DAY

> VENDOR BUSCH
> Yes, perhaps I can explain to you with a model… Dark Windows operates in a pyramid structure: At the top there is a leader — a co-ordinator — this person can be

traced back to Bataille — the original leader. Below him are a limited number of very wealthy and powerful owners of media groups. These people have control over politicians and celebrities through the ownership of large news organisations and media production companies. At the bottom of the pyramid we have writers, actors, film-makers etc. — these creative people are allowed free reign but are not aware of the system that they serve. Anyone who becomes a threat — anyone who produces dangerous work is either bought out or killed. The system is really self-regulating it just needs a few people at the top of the pyramid to make sure that there are no cracks… that the windows remain dark. My belief is that they are trying to conceal a terrible secret - I believe that the highest members of <u>Dark Windows</u> are the descendents of aliens — of non-human beings — and that there is some kind of deeper meaning to this control system… what that is

— I cannot possibly guess my friend.

LARRY WENT (V.O)
There seem to be so many arguments and some of it seems a bit — well — crackpot.

Chapter 3:
Dreams That Money Can Buy

Christ was the Worde and spake it
He took the Bread and brake it
And what the Worde doth make it
That I believe, and take it[1]

Walton-on-Thames is a wealthy suburban town in Surrey, thirty minutes from the centre of London by train. An attractive and conservative town that grew slowly around the River Thames from Roman times when the first empire expanded through Europe. It is said that Julius Caesar forded the Thames at Cowey Sale on his second invasion of Britain. Walton village went on to be part of Henry 8th's estate - its 12th century church sits on an ancient royal ley line that runs from the centre of London at Charing Cross through Buckingham Palace South West to Walton.

The town developed extensively in the 1960s with a new pedestrianised shopping centre and a Woolworths replete with abstract tiled mural. There was a brave new modernist white concrete town hall bordered by paved formal gardens, their openly stocked rectangular goldfish ponds challenging future hooligans to disturb the order of this controlled environment. A small area of parkland surrounded the formal gardens – picket fences enclosing a

---
[1] Poem attributed to Elizabeth 1st from St. Mary's Church, Walton-on-Thames

cricket ground with a neat weatherboard clubhouse painted black – tall horse chestnut trees surrounded the area and enclosed the adjacent housing estates. These were no ordinary estates, they were private roads with large detached houses – homes to stockbrokers and businessmen – powerful people lived in these unassuming mock-Tudor lawned villas. Despite this wealth and influence, the town centre had always seemed vaguely tatty. A strange modernist sculpture rose like an alien fish from the plaza, next to the Le Corbusier influenced Campbell and Booker's department store ('your Harrods in Walton') its large square plate glass windows and blocks of primary colour seemed like a Mondrian painting in three dimensions. An early example of a Safeways supermarket sat opposite the department store – in the 1970s they introduced new and exotic food – yoghurts, avocados and Laughing Cow cheese triangles – all of these could be purchased and carried home in large brown paper bags. Car owners could even use the new innovative multi-storey car park on Hepworth Way.

This road that loops around the town centre was named after a pioneer of cinema, Cecil Hepworth, who crossed the river in 1899 to develop one of the first film studios in the world – by 1923 he was out of business, the stars of Hollywood usurping the theatrical, pastoral, historical themes of British cinema. Nettlefield Studios in Walton continued to be used for B Movies and television work up until the 1960s. One of the last big productions at Nettlefield was 'The Adventures of Robin Hood' – the television series that famously gave work to scriptwriters who had been blacklisted by Hollywood.

In nearby Weybridge, British film and television stars lived in Saint George's Hill, the exclusive private estate with its golf course and gated entry. Tom Jones had a private zoo there, Cliff Richards had a secluded retreat and John Lennon had written 'Lucy in the Sky With Diamonds' while living in a mock-Tudor mansion that he owned there. The town's celebrity status was marred by the 'Walton Hop' scandal... revelations, extended newspaper coverage and court cases linked the children's disco on Hepworth

Way with celebrity sexual abuse... the town got tattier and by the 21st century seemed to be just another part of London's extended suburban sprawl.

▶▶|

On the south bank of the Thames you will find Walton Lane, an uninhabited road that links the marina at Walton's Cowey Sale with Weybridge town centre. There are large islands on the Thames here where mysterious boathouses float - out of the reach of roads, mains electricity or gas supplies. As you head out of Walton, just before you reach the temporary bridge that crosses to Shepperton, a left turn takes you down to Walton Lane; the broad Thames to your right, to your left a large flat green with standing stones in the centre, *the Seven Witches of Cowey Sale*. Legend has it that seven witches were turned to stone on the green after breaking a pact with some kind of higher force...

It was dark now and raining, Larry Went was driving his 850cc orange Mini Traveller down to Walton Lane. The small windscreen wipers struggling to keep up with the downpour as the headlights weakly attempted to pierce the heavy rain. Larry was alone in the car, a cassette player screwed into the functional minimalist interior blasting the Cure's *Lovecats* into the empty dark night. It was 1984, Larry was heading to Weybridge – to a hot date with his new girlfriend – all crimped hair, perfume and promises. He was smoking a big joint laced with 'Red Leb'. The road rushed close to Larry's feet, the old Mini felt like a sardine can hurtling along, inches above the tarmac at 40 or 50 mph. Suddenly the car lurched over an obstacle barely visible on the lonely dark track – he felt it scrape under the bottom of the car, pumped the brakes and slid to a halt. Silence descended on the unlit lane... Larry heard the river – the wind in the tall trees and his own shallow breathing.

What was that?

Larry thought that he had seen a sack in the car's beams just before the bump... a sense of dread engulfed him, should he go back and look at what he had hit? Should he just drive on? He slowly opened the door and grimaced as the cold rain dispersed the smoky comfort from his enclosed tin box.

"Shit!" He walked back up the road...

"Fuck!" It was a body – barely recognisable but - a body.

The low chrome-plated steel bumper of the Mini had peeled back the flesh from the face and chest revealing a viscous combination of blood, sinew and bone that 18 year-old Larry couldn't bear to look at. He turned away and leant on his car – should he just go – just leave? Larry was 18 years old and stoned – his life could be over – no polytechnic for Larry, no generous student grant and student lifestyle – fame and fortune eluded him here and now. This decision, taken in the next few moments, before another car came down the Lane, this decision could affect lives here and lives yet to be. The weight of each future moment, each place and time held Larry rigid and fixed...

Then, from nowhere, a course of action began to unfold. Larry got back into the car and reversed it up to the body, he got out, swung open the two rear windowed doors with their external hinges and grabbed hold of the corpse by its sack-like clothing. The body was small and light – like a child – no specific gender but surprisingly light. The disfigurement rendered the body alien or reptilian – Larry couldn't look. He placed the body in the back of the car and carefully shut the doors.

He could hear something coming – some sort of a high-pitched whine clawing through the night air. A solitary lamp rounded the corner and temporarily blinded him – blind panic rising in his chest as the Yamaha FS1E moped raced past him, the rider's face hidden behind a dark, mirrored visor.

There was no turning back now, Larry knew that it was stupid but he had made a decision and he always followed his decisions through. The fresh November air smelt of death now – death sounded in the riverside trees that swayed back and forth as the autumn wind rippled through their broad leaves. He started the engine – first time – and quietly edged the small orange vehicle across the road and over the rough wooden bridge that led to the large island that bisected the Thames between Walton and Weybridge. Suddenly a Hitchcock film flashed through his stoned mind – suspense on a pleasure island, in the dark – the tunnel of love, a murder – a tennis match and a man standing in the dark calling "Guy, Guy"... the call mutated into "Larry, Larry"... guilt, sweaty, palpable guilt.

Larry pulled himself together, he sensed his immaturity – his inability to make a rational decision enforced by his dazed, drugged state of mind. He looked at his carefully aged jeans with their artistically bleached patches and intentionally worn knees and thought –

"What a stupid, self-obsessed prat. Why am I so obsessed with how I look... how this would look to someone else – how this would look in a film or... why can't I just do something about this?"

The course of action evolved – Larry jumped out of the car and dragged the body to the edge of the bridge – he pushed it lightly and completely into the pitch-black waters of the fast-flowing Thames.

That should wash away any evidence

He kneeled down and caught his bare knee on the head of a protruding rusty nail. As the blood seeped from the small wound, Larry prayed, he prayed for rain and he prayed for time.

▶▶

Time passed. Larry was now 40 years old, he was sitting at the table in his quiet suburban house, he opened the newspaper – a headline screamed at him:

New Clue For Thames Body: Police re-open case as family push for new enquiry. DNA discovered on rusty nail.

His heart sank – technology had caught up with him – they were bound to track him down now. Then his spirits rose - at last Larry could confess. He could finally be at peace with himself – he could confront the guilt that had been eating away at him for 22 years.

Then the crying began – from another room, another place - Larry began to drift into consciousness – the crying – the guilt – the killing – the police – he was struggling to make sense of what was real and what was not. He worked his way slowly through a hierarchy of realities:

First...

That wasn't a human being that I hit – it was some kind of alien, some half human being.

Then...

There's no way the police could trace me – I'm not on a DNA database, they can't know me.

Then...

They could never prove it – how could they link me with the death – unless the moped rider recognised me – or if I had left traces on the body, in the car, on the bridge... no, they'd never make it stick in court.

Then...

That newspaper story wasn't real – it was a dream – they couldn't really find me out now, after all that time, after all that has passed. I'm lying in bed in North Wales – they couldn't find me here, not now with a career and a family. They wouldn't put that in a newspaper – I'm dreaming it all – they'll never find me.

Larry felt comforted by these arguments; in his semi-conscious state he felt that he had organised reality. A small alien knee planted itself in his throat and he choked. His weeping 3-year-old child crawled over his neck to reach the comforting bosom of his wife lying next to him in their over-warm and rickety double bed. At that moment a motorbike engine whined past his bedroom in the dark and cold spring night... a night that still smelled of death.

As his son settled quietly in the bed next to him, Larry lay half awake – scared and disturbed. He was awash with guilt – guilt at the dim-distant killing on a quiet riverside road – guilt that his whole life was a lie – it shouldn't have happened this way – it wouldn't have if he had just kept driving that night in 1984. Then, finally, as began to wake fully – he realised that none of it had happened. The death, the alien body, the motorbike, the guilt – it was all a dream – yet somehow it seemed like a real, suppressed memory – a small dark window at the back of his mind. He had dreamt that dream many times before, different every time but always the killing, the guilt, the body and the nagging doubt. There was something about that dark road – that grassy patch – that 'Cowey Sale' that left a queasy feeling of uneasiness in Larry's waking mind.

Chapter 4:
Little Caesar

"Crime is a fact of the human species, a fact of that species alone, but it is above all the secret aspect, impenetrable and hidden."[2]

A shaft of light cut through the darkness of Freddie Foulke's office, playing on the projection screen that had descended mechanically from a discreet metal box attached to the wall. Freddie stood to the left of the screen, partially obscured in the shadows around the bright animated screensaver that acted as the room's only illumination. Freddie Foulkes was the Chief Executive Officer of the Bland Corporation, a tall, thin man who was just starting to show his fifty years. He was dressed in designer jeans and a black roll-neck shirt, his greying hair close-cropped and receding but his body tanned, lithe and muscular – his money bought him a personal trainer and time to look after himself. Freddie's Swiss office was in Berne on *Enffingerstrasse*. He had similar offices in other countries: The London office in *South Kensington*, The San Francisco office on *Folsom Street* and the China office in Kowloon on *Chun Choi Street*. Each office had an identical *meeting room*.

The meeting rooms are ten metres square with three dark leather walls and hardwood Venetian blinds on the one windowed wall; they are quietly air-conditioned and furnished in a layout specified by Freddie: An Eileen Gray

---

[2] Georges Bataille

Double X table sits by the projection screen with enough room to pace back and forth between the wall and the large modernist table. Five black leather reproductions of Mies van der Rohe's *Barcelona Chair* are lined up facing the table and screen at a distance of precisely five metres from the wall on which the screen hangs. The single, wide, dark hardwood door is in the centre of the wall, behind the five chairs. Each of these offices is modelled on the idea of a projection room, the audience sits at a low level, sutured into the organisational apparatus – the CEO stands at the front – his eye on the door and the crowd – he has a high angle viewpoint of the assembled audience who number no more than five.

Magog sat expectantly in the third Barcelona Chair – in the Swiss office, he was alone with Freddie – waiting for him to begin. He had been given presentations like this before. It seemed strange to be spoken to as if he were a class of naughty schoolchildren or a lecture theatre full of sycophantic employees but this was how Freddie felt comfortable communicating - everything was a keynote speech. This mode of address distanced him – it set him apart from the rest of humanity and made him feel important.

Freddie used bullet points, pie charts and Venn diagrams to convey the simplest information in the most convoluted way. Conversely, he also enjoyed simplifying complex issues with lists – all life was homogenised into a series of points – sequential steps to an identifiable end result. Magog imagined Freddie's home life with his beautiful Russian partner, Eva Slopnick – how did they choose their evening meal? He imagined him drawing a branching diagram of the possible food combinations with their resultant effects on his digestive systems and emotions – using a projected presentation to illustrate the advantages of various menus and a laser pointer to highlight his favourite puddings. He looked as if he were about to begin his routine – his presentation to an audience of one. Magog realised that he should sit back and be quiet – it would soon be over with – there was no point prolonging the tedium by contributing. Freddie interrupted Magog's musings with a surprising new technique – questioning – bringing the audience on board. He fired a question at Magog from the shadows:

"How do you think it went Maggy?"

"Sorry?"

"Did the disposal of Godard go according to our plan?"

Magog nodded in response...

"I don't think so Maggy – shall we try phoning the North Wales Police... shall I explain?"

Freddie clicked his remote and the first bullet point appeared – typing itself across the dark screen:

Click

1: Eliminate Target.

"You succeeded in this first task using the poisoned draft – the drugged tea."

Click

2: Remove Target's Identity.

"You just about managed this one but..."

Freddie used his laser pointer to erratically underline the word *identity*.

"but... you didn't account for the rain Maggy. The rain put out the fire before his face was destroyed."

Click

3: Cover Tracks

" You did okay here Maggy – I think you were anonymous enough *and* you have enough identities to keep everyone guessing – even I'm not sure what to call you..."

"You can call me Maggy..."

Magog had a number of different names, faces and passports – all fully customisable for the job in hand. For someone who was striking in their peculiarity, Magog seemed to be able to blend effortlessly into most environments – his strigine demeanour containing elements of all human society – it was as if his unusual face was the original face of mankind – a mirror that reflects whatever the viewer wishes to see. Freddie continued...

Click

3a: Avoid Investigation

"Fortunately I have enough influence to keep this whole thing quiet – the papers won't publish anything and the police already know that the body belongs to a poor local homeless drunkard – a nameless man who appeared in the village some weeks ago – the man that we sent there and the man that you drove back to the airport with... which leads me to..."

Click

4: Replace Target

Freddie started to get evangelical.

"It's a great feeling to have this power – to be able to swap people, to move them around on the chessboard... you too are one of our pawns Maggy... remember that next time you cause me extra work... Do you know about Anne-Marie? – She knows all about us – Godard's friend you know – and our friend too. Why don't I just call her now?"

Squinting with excitement from behind his lightweight rimless glasses, he turned on the speakerphone that sat on the Double X table and dialled a number. The speakerphone crackled – *dial-tone – speed-dial – Swiss ring-tone* – a relaxed female voice answered with a Swiss accent;

"Hello!"

"Oh hi, Anne-Marie, it's Freddie here... how's your new Jean-Luc – has he settled in okay?"

There was a pause – the voice over the speaker changed tone – the English less assured...

"Fuck you Freddie! – Isn't it enough that I've gone along with... with. Without your gloating – I bet you are on your loud-speaker – giving one of your stupid keynotes talk – you are, are you not...? you!"

The telephone was slammed down in Rolle. Freddie looked slightly crestfallen as the dial-tone gnawed around the darkened room. Magog was embarrassed by this melodramatic performance – was this man really head of the Bland Corporation? As he began to comprehend that the two of them were completely alone in this room, Freddie's expression switched to one of psychotic and destructive self-assurance.

"None of that matters Maggy – it's all tied-up now – she's on board and you're back here with me…"

Freddie walked over to the third Barcelona Chair and stood behind Magog – stroking the tufts of hair that protruded from behind his ears…

"The books are balanced now Maggy – there'll be no disruption to our plan…"

Chapter 5
Groundhog Day

"What would you do if you were stuck in one place and every day was exactly the same, and nothing that you did mattered?"[3]

Larry Went had been working for the past six years as a lecturer in Film Studies at a quiet, provincial college in North Wales. He had always thought of his life in terms of films and quotes from films, for the past few years - especially during term-time - he had often wondered whether his life was closest to The Truman Show or Groundhog Day. Most days were an amalgam of the two stories: Every morning he woke up to the same scene and wandered through the world – the centre of his own narrative in which very few things changed – or if they did, the change was at a painful, imperceptible pace - his life had become enclosed in a small community from which there seemed to be no escape – it was very different from his youth in London and the South of England, when the world was full of possibilities. As he walked the few hundred yards from his home to the college where he worked, Larry couldn't hear his footsteps – *it was the walk of a dead man* – he started the same internal dialogue that chomped around the inside of his consciousness like a tiny Pac-man, eating up time and energy. 'Mid-life crisis' was too much of a cliché for Larry – but that's probably what it was:

My life is just controlled from the outside – I have no control – it's like 1984 – it's like the Truman Show – this place has a very limited cast and the

---
[3] Groundhog Day (1993)

same actors are being circulated through a range of roles. My ex-students are now my managers – accounting for my life through computers, flow-charts, spreadsheets and bar graphs. I suppose it would be no better elsewhere – in a University or whatever, you would still have managers – and... you can only become a manager if you are stupid enough to buy into all the bullshit or thick-skinned enough to not give a toss. Let's face it, Larry – you've reached 40, you've spent 20 plus years working in different versions of wage slavery – the same job in different places or the same job in the same place – you just don't want to work for some system or some guy that you don't believe in anymore but there's no way out. You look around and you think... 'Why has he got a flash car and a big house and I've got debt and a rust-bucket?' You'd be happy to clean the floors for LockeArts now – perhaps you should have networked with the big shots when you had a chance when you had youth on your side. But perhaps you never were a big shot – perhaps the problem is your self-perception – if you were capable of doing it, you would have done it instead of coming up with half-baked, half-formed concepts. Continuity, that's what you need – keep doing the same thing over and over until someone notices or you become good at it – you can't just pretend that you're a polymath, because you're not – why are you learning the piano? You'll never be any good... It's a shame that we can't use our hindsight to do it all over and see if it would have been any different. What would have happened if I'd stayed in London – if I hadn't moved out – if hadn't been drawn back to suburbia

Then Groundhog Day hit him:

"I... fuck face, cut me some fuckin' slack fucker"

Every day, Larry listened out for sentences containing the word 'Fuck' – he was interested in how many times it could be used in one sentence and in the different ways the word was used within that sentence. This was an engaging communiqué but he was sure that the unattractive teenage girl in the pink velour tracksuit could have done better if she hadn't stopped to take a deep drag on her cigarette. Years ago – he would have said something to her – he would have told her to mind her language – but he'd lost interest in discipline. As he walked into the college through the light, modern main-entrance, his second Groundhog Day experience hit him:

Every morning the same slack-jawed teenager stands in front of the same chocolate machine – staring into the fluorescent light that makes the chocolate look so different, so appealing – Larry had never seen him buy anything but he hovers there, forever deciding, an imaginary string of drool extending from his enlarged bottom lip, his eyes fixed somewhere inside the machine. It felt like a dream to Larry but... he didn't have time to think about it – he's got a 9 o'clock class.

Larry reached his office at 8.30 it was a cramped room with no windows and six desks, the walls were covered with shelves full of dusty files that no-one ever took down – there were 'teaching packs', 'course files', 'tutor files', 'session files', out of date text books, boxes of leaflets and student work: piles of paper that had between them taken years of various lecturers' working lives to compile and collate – all of it for no real reason or to no real effect. The room was dark and cramped and crowded, the only noise in the room was the whirr of six computers – so much for the paperless office that these depressing devices had promised. The only consolation that Larry had was that the office was small – *there's a general belief that if a man has a large office, he must be an idiot*. Larry sifted through the stack of white A4 sheets on his desk to find the lesson plan that he had prepared on Friday – ready for Monday morning's session.

II

Time:	*Monday, 9.00*
Duration:	*2 hours*
Aims:	*To enable students to develop an appreciation of the history of British Cinema and the development of cinematic realism.*

Objectives: *Students will demonstrate knowledge and understanding of realism, the history of British Cinema – its economic, social and cultural contexts.*

Content: *Students will be shown extracts from a range of British films to illustrate the concept of realism and 'Britishness' in cinema. They will be asked to discuss and analyse the sequences shown.*

▶

He gathered together his resources – video extracts, photocopied notes, whiteboard pen and eraser – and took the short walk down the unlit, windowless corridor to the small third-floor classroom with its single skylight projecting the rising sun into the gloom. Light footsteps scraped across the window in the ceiling as the shadow of a strange creature was projected onto the wall in the pink haze of the early morning light… for a second Larry thought about robots – electronic surveillance devices crawling through ducts and up walls, spying on his every move with cameras that record his thoughts and actions – he shook the paranoid delusion from his early morning thoughts and looked up to see a seagull's webbed feet scrambling to grip on the double glazed window before skittering down the slates and flying off looking for something to scavenge. He checked that the empty room was ready to receive his class –eight of them if they all turn up, he adjusted the lighting, turned on the large television, cleaned the whiteboard and then headed back to his office to make a cup of tea.

When he returned five minutes later with his steaming mug of tea, he had a full house – all eight students in various stages of solipsism were scattered around the curve of desks in the cramped room – all looking expectantly at him. After a few minutes small talk, Larry began – he made a fresh attempt to achieve the morning's objective – one objective of many that make up the year's curriculum… what was this one again?

To develop awareness of the economic, cultural and social contexts of British cinema.

Where to start? At the beginning is usually a very good place so Larry tried to explain how the British Film Industry developed...

"Well the British Film Industry has its roots in the work of the early cinematic pioneers from the age of silent cinema. When cinema was first developing as an industry – as a *form*, it wasn't dominated by Hollywood but by a series of entrepreneurs, magicians and inventors who set up small studios to attempt to find a use for this new technology. One such pioneer was Cecil Hepworth who set up a studio in Walton-on-Thames in 1899 and made a dog into a film star with his 1905 short *Rescued By Rover* – right I'll, err show that to you now..."

Larry fiddled about with the remote control for a while before showing the six-minute long silent film. He attempted to persuade the students that the film involved dramatic editing and fast-paced narrative as the dog (Rover) rescued a baby. The students weren't convinced. Larry continued to head for his objective...

"The First World War effectively destroyed the European film industry – whereas the industry in Hollywood could develop free from the economic and physical effects of the first modern war. The great American film-making pioneer D.W. Griffith was strongly influenced by Hepworth and was able to develop this new film language while British films were excluded from the American market..."

There was a question from the class and the aim started to go off target...

"So who were like the enemy in the First World War? I mean who started it?"

Larry paused for a few seconds before responding,

"Hmmm, good question, thanks for asking – it is commonly agreed that the assassination of Archduke Ferdinand in Sarajevo was the catalyst for the war but it all developed out of a series of pacts and rivalries... there are even some theories that suggest the USA instigated the first world war specifically to undermine the European film industry – to destroy its power and take control of the collective unconscious."

Katie had glazed over but she responded nevertheless,

"Right - but do Germans, like, look Japanese?"

"Not really Katie, what are you getting at?"

"Well right," she shuffles about a little and starts to become animated, "in *Pearl Harbor* – all the Americans are fighting these blokes who look like Japanese or Chinese, but they're Germans right?"

"No, that was a different war and they *were* Japanese..."

"How come?"

Larry tried to get back on target, to focus on his objective; he ignored the question and pressed on...

"So, anyway British cinema has certain genres, certain types of films associated with its national identity – can anyone name them? Can anyone think of the types of films that we associate with British cinema?"

The students call out a few suggestions.

"like Gangsters"

"and err like comedies and Carry-ons"

"yeah and there's James Bonds"

"what are those well-boring old stories from, like, books called?"

Larry tried to encourage and organise these nuggets of knowledge,

"Very good, all of these British genres; the Gangster film, the Comedies, Thrillers and Period Dramas all have, at their root – they all have an element of *Realism* – so what is Realism?"

He attempted to define Realism using the whiteboard to outline his key points:

1: *Psychologically rounded characters.*

2: *Settings, locations and costumes that appear to be based on real life.*

3: *Dealing with social or political issues.*

"Now one of the key figures in the roots of British cinematic realism is Humphrey Jennings whose films such as *Spare Time, Listen To Britain* and *A Diary For Timothy* are seen as crucial moments in the development of a specific British Cinema."

At this point Larry intended to show the students an extract from *Listen To Britain* – he tried to put it into context – to explain the importance of the film before he played the extract – but he knew what will happen, it's obvious really, not many people are interested in it – Larry was – he was fascinated. This was the only chance he got to watch these films – it's his treat to himself; he didn't get time to watch them at home. His excuse now was that they are educational, they're part of the curriculum, he's *'learning'* the students… *'they won't learn themselves'* as he is wont to say. The voice-over begins,

"This is the BBC Home and Forces Programmes, here is the news"[4]

Larry looked at the students' faces and realised that he's lost it already – they were drifting off, falling asleep or sending surreptitious text messages – there were two keen students who were straining to make sense of the shots of tractors, aeroplanes and cottages – to no avail.

Larry adjusted his worn jacket. He had planned to move on to explain how Humphrey Jennings was involved with the Surrealists (he had been on the selection committee for the International Surrealist Exhibition held in London in 1936) and how there wasn't really a battle between Realism and Surrealism – how the battle was between the forces of reaction and revolution – a battle of ideology not style or technique. Larry wanted to explain and enthuse but the blank faces scared him, the challenge was too much for him. He wanted to influence them but he worried that they might not be ready for him to explain about the *Dark Windows* – it wasn't really easy to understand and even Larry wasn't sure that he could get his head around what was real and what was fantasy. He gave in, he decided that it was time for a coffee

---

[4] Extract from soundtrack of "Listen To Britain", Humphrey Jennings (1942)

break – it's only 10.00 and Larry had given up on the next generation already (or maybe he'd given up on himself).

They all shuffled out of the classroom and Larry headed down to the student lounge where he bought a hot *espressochoc* in a polystyrene cup and sat with his notebook – attempting to structure the next hour – hoping to get back on track for his objective… He was joined by his line manager; Rhodri Hughes, Head of Humanities. Rhodri stood over Larry, his hair and suit sharply cut, his cuffs gleaming white.

"We've got to have a meeting Larry, I'd like to see you over in my office now…"

"But I'm in the middle of a lesson"

"Then set them some work"

"It's not that easy – we're just looking at Humphrey Jennings and I've got to…"

He gesticulated at his notebook.

"Look Larry, I've got a *quality and standards* meeting at 11.00 – then I'm off to *strategic planning* this afternoon, I'll see you in my room at 10.45 – OK?"

Larry dashed back to his classroom and attempted to excuse himself – he didn't bank on one of his students actually wanting to talk to him. Matt Black was one of the keen ones – he wanted to be a journalist or photographer, or maybe an artist – he reminded Larry of his own youth: The world ahead of him, no ties – just an orange mini traveller and a girlfriend – infinite options – infinite confidence, where had it gone? Matt was really excited about something, Larry tried to tune into the present again as Matt started to speak,

"Larry… you know that like tramp who was all sort of burnt up?"

"Sorry Matt, I've got to go – I've got to go and see someone,"

"No, you know, in Pen' – that tramp who was all burnt – well I saw him, it was well disgusting and I got a photo of him with my mobile…"

"Sorry Matt – it does sound a bit disgusting – I'm not really into that sort of thing."

"No, you know, it's all like Media and News – do you think I could sell it to like the news or something? You used to do stuff with the BBC didn't you – can you sell it for me?"

Larry hadn't really grasped what Matt was talking about,

"What is it you want to sell?"

"Well right, there was this old tramp bloke who burnt himself all up with meths and stuff and it was right near where I live in Pen' at this big old house where like old people live."

"Is that Plas Coch?"

"Yeah, that's it – you been there?"

"I went to some sort of Summer Fair there last year – you can walk up to that mountain from there – what's it called?"

"Dunno, do you want me to send you the picture – you could sell it for me."

"Look Matt, I'm sorry, I've got to go – it's not really *my* thing and I don't think it's the sort of thing that *any* newspaper would be able to publish – okay?"

Larry left the class some questions to answer on the history of British Cinema and the definition of Realism – they seemed to like comprehension exercises.

He headed off to Rhodri's office thinking that the meeting will be about some wrongly completed enrolment form or some pointless student complaint. He entered the large windowless room and sat opposite Rhodri on one of the brown plastic chairs that indicated that this was an educational establishment. Rhodri turned and looked beyond Larry as he absent-mindedly fiddled with his cufflinks.

"I'm sorry Larry, you're a bit late – it's 10.55 – I've got to go to this quality thing. It's nothing sinister – I just wanted to catch you to flag up a few changes that might effect you. I wanted to give you the nod but I'll, errr... I'll trickle them down to you later. We'll be having a meeting to discuss them next week – got to go now, see you next week."

Rhodri stalked out of the office and left Larry on the brown plastic chair wondering what that was all about. He was not exactly sure why he'd been so urgently summoned and then abandoned without being told anything. His paranoid tendencies told him that there was some deeper meaning to it all – some strategy to undermine him. Before he could get too deeply embroiled in that line of self-delusion, his mobile phone vibrated against his chest. He took the phone out of his jacket pocket – someone had sent him a text message – he didn't recognise the number. The message read: *"can u sell it 4 me?"* Attached to the message was an image – Larry knew it was going to be the 'well burnt tramp' and was just about to delete it when his morbid curiosity got the better of him. He opened the image file and his heart sank as thoughts flashed through his head – flash: he knew this man – flash: it was a relative, a friend, someone he knew well, someone he knew personally – flash: it was someone else, someone famous – someone he knew very well but had never met. He knew then, somehow he knew, he knew despite the low resolution and the tiny screen - that this dead tramp was Jean-Luc Godard.

Chapter 6:
The Servant

Magog stood outside the Berne office, his head pressed against the hardwood door. He had just settled into a warm relaxing bubble bath in his hotel room when he had received the summons from Freddie.

He felt that he was starting to lose his focus – his motivation – he was starting to wonder what he had been put on this planet for. He had always felt like an outsider – he had always seen himself as David Bowie in *The Man Who Fell to Earth* but perhaps he was flattering himself. He had managed to forget his past – he had closed down his memories – but he did have them, they were there somewhere. Despite his chameleon-like nature, Magog was sick of his appearance – he was starting to show his age and had decided to try something different, he had been to the hotel barbers to have his trademark tufts trimmed – hopefully Freddie would be confused by this small change. He wasn't sure if he like the way that Freddie had been treating him – he felt pigeonholed by this ineffective bureaucrat. Freddie may be in control of the Dark Windows for the moment but nothing lasts forever in this cutthroat world. Freddie knew little of Magog's background – the Dark Windows survived through secrecy; people only knew what they needed to know. For all Freddie knew, Magog could be the man who fell to Earth.

So here was Magog, his forehead pressed against the entrance to Freddie's domain. In a world of air-conditioned, centrally heated hotel suites and offices, the wood was cool and natural – a link to the real, organic world that ultimately supplied the Dark Windows with their power. Magog was getting into character – preparing himself to be the subservient sidekick – controlling his anger and self-righteousness. He would bide his time my pretties – he was waiting for an opportunity – but for now it was time to enter Freddie's lair and listen to his orders. He gripped the reproduction Bauhaus chrome handle and quietly pushed the heavy door open.

Freddie was standing in the shadows of the cool, hushed room. He adjusted the blinds, allowing *noirish* shadows to project across the interior – he seemed fully aware of the dramatic nature of the scene he was creating. Magog moved silently to the first Barcelona chair and lowered himself carefully into the soft leather seat. Freddie sat on the table facing Magog, his smile restrained, the teeth betraying a deep tension.

"I'm concerned Maggy…" he paused, distracted "you look different…"

"I've had my hair cut"

"I didn't realise that it grew…"

Magog thought of a number of sarcastic responses but held on to them – it wasn't appropriate. He had learnt that silence created a more powerful mystery. He quietly nodded at Freddie, inviting him to continue.

"I'm concerned Maggy – we may not have complete control of the events emanating from Plas Coch. I dealt with the Police and the Media – then I thought to myself: Is there anyone in that back-water likely to make a connection between the corpse and Godard? – I thought to myself: Perhaps – what if the coroner was a conspiracy theorist? – You know how those bastards operate independently sometimes – and a lot of them read trashy conspiracy fiction – it goes with the job. And then I thought to myself…"

Magog could imagine the bullet points and was glad that Freddie hadn't treated him to another audio-visual presentation – this time the clicks were all in Freddie's head.

"I thought to myself – we'll have a little trawl around for any local conspiracy theorists – and…" he paused for effect, "we're a bit worried about this one!"

Click

The projector flashed into life as Freddie clicked the button on his laser pointer. Magog had been lulled into a false sense of security, he reverted to type and settled back into the comfortable chair, taking a small bag of mixed nuts from his jacket pocket, he started to nibble them as if he were in a cinema eating popcorn.

"You still eating that bird-food Maggy? – You need some proper food – I'll treat you to a steak later, I know a great…" He trailed off again - he appeared to be losing his grip. Freddie was the sort of man who had reached his position in life by wearing the right clothes, using the right language and reading books about how to develop the right handshake. He had no life - the Dark Windows were his life. He was a steak-eating salesman and Magog felt like a nut-nibbling misfit. Magog knew that he was useful to the organisation but they'd never let *him* rule the world like this *yes-man*. Magog crunched on a brazil nut and nodded again – his wide eyes fixed on the face that was being projected onto the dark wall. Freddie continued:

"This is Larry Went, he's a small-town conspiracy theorist – the sort of idiot who could ask the wrong questions if he got wind of anything. He's a failed artist and documentary-maker who works in a small college near Plas Coch. He's just started wrting a small book about Surrealism and the links to Dark Windows for some small 'independent' publisher that we own – I'll let you look at the first thirteen chapters if you're interested."

Click: Larry Went

Click: Conspiracy book

Magog couldn't hide his surprise – the face on the screen was a face from his past – someone that he hadn't seen for many years. The face took him back to another place, another time – to Walton-on-Thames: The Walton

Hop, Coke in bottles and 10 Rothman's King Size. To a modernist apartment in a modest high-rise block clad in blue panels – to a Cherry Coke made in a Sodastream – a living room lined with vinyl records and a black leather sofa – to rare roast beef sliced thinly and served on its own – the pink flesh alone on a large, flat plate. It took him back to a room that was dark now – someone in a leather jacket had thrown themselves out of one of the windows in the 1970s – there were no windows in the apartment now. The memories that flooded back through Magog's head were starting to overwhelm him; he focused back on the wall in Berne – on the projected face...

"Are you following this Maggy?"

"Intently – I know this, this Larry..."

"Personally?"

"I know his brother very well"

"An interesting coincidence"

"Jung would call it synchronicity"

Freddie asserted himself again, "Let me finish now Maggy, before we stray too far from the point."

Click: BBC Documentary

"He made a short documentary for the BBC five or six years ago, pulling together a few of these conspiracy theorists – they know bits and pieces about our organisation. He got some of it right but he missed the real point. We had trouble getting the BBC to pull it, but eventually they did – in September 2001. They own the rights to the programme and they've put it in their archive – it will never come out now, it's past its sell-by-date." Freddie paused for effect to take a sip from a glass of iced water. "Anyway, Larry seemed fairly sceptical about the whole thing – especially some of our friend Mr War's more outlandish claims."

Click: Darkwindows.co.uk

"Then this happens – he's set up a website trying to breathe life into his daft documentary and to publicise his new book. It means nothing really – in fact the more of this tosh that's out there, the better – he's even got a video of Princess Diana up there – it all acts as a smokescreen to obscure what we're really up to..."

Magog raised one eyebrow and remained silent.

"As long as he doesn't make the Godard connection – we can leave him be... if he does – you'll have to visit him Maggy. Perhaps you could travel back to Wales with his brother – is he one of us?"

"Very much so – Chris Went is virtually owned by the Dark Windows"

"Interesting – you fascinate me Maggy... I'd like you to look at this copy of Larry's documentary" he handed a slim envelope to Magog, "and, err, get in touch with this Chris Went – you two may need to pay Larry a visit."

Magog returned to his hotel, sat on his bed and played the video. He skipped through to the end, you only need to watch the last five minutes of this type of film – these documentaries always string out a few slim facts and then summarise their sparse ideas at the end.

Further Extract From:
DARK WINDOWS
By Larry Went
#

EXT. MOUNTAINSIDE — DAY

> LARRY WENT
> Well, this has been a strange and disturbing journey. It all started with the development of a new technology — cinema — and has led to an alien race that control human society for some dark and mysterious purpose… It seems that not only are film makers and film stars involved — but also governments and business leaders.

INT. STUDIO — DAY

> MIKE WAR
> There's this secret meeting they have in Switzerland every year mate — at Davos. Forget your Bohemian Grove and your Illuminati — this is where the real power is.
> [PAUSE]
> It's at this meeting on a mountaintop — in a Swiss ski resort that they meet to plan your dreams and desires.

> LARRY WENT

So my dreams and desires don't come from me? They are created for me?

MIKE WAR
Right mate — you are, we all are — the one-dimensional man that Marcuse wrote about. Your depth as a person comes solely from your participation in the collective unconscious — and this collective unconscious has been hijacked by dark forces in order to control you.

LARRY WENT
Are you sure there's anything wrong with a 'dream factory' — that's what your getting at — isn't it - a Hollywood-run 'dream factory'? It seems to me that it's just a development of human society — storytelling traditions and shared myths taken to a global — technological level…

MIKE WAR

That's right mate — the only problem is — that it's all corporate propaganda — and it all emanates from the Dark Windows.
[PAUSE]
There used to be dissenting voices right? There were movements with manifestos — Futurists, Communists, Surrealists right? There's no manifestos now mate — there's no organisations, movements, collectives — it's all individualism now — and individuals are easy to pick off. These dissenting voices have been silenced by a neo-Stalinist style system that allows, that encourages any opinion — as long as — and this is the crucial point mate — as long as no-one's listening. If anyone starts to have an effect that challenges the Dark Windows' collective ideas — they are silenced!

LARRY WENT
(disbelieving)
Right... And how is it that they are 'silenced'? — I mean, you must feel in danger?

MIKE WAR
I'm being watched — I've been threatened, phone calls in the night — messages — you know mate? They've got me on their little list.

LARRY WENT
But how do they do it? How do they 'silence' people? I mean you can't silence everyone — you can't silence the BBC can you?

MIKE WAR
Right — well... generally any dissent — any challenge to the Dark Windows' ideology comes, ultimately, from an individual — an author of dissent — and they have two basic options: either assimilation or death of the author.

SERIES OF SHOTS:

    A)   MONTAGE: Images taken from throughout the documentary are repeated — shots of famous historical figures and anonymous crowds shown in a fast edited montage using a range of distorting and colour-shifting visual effects.

              MIKE WAR (V.O.)

        If the authors of dissent don't want to be assimilated into the organisation, the Dark Windows have assassins who carry out carefully planned executions using untraceable poisons. They also have an army of trained doppelgangers to replace the dead 'authors' — some even say these doppelgangers are alien shape-shifters.

              LARRY WENT (V.O.)
                  (ironic)

        So there we have it — the Dark Windows are all around us — controlling us and watching us. I haven't met anyone who admits to being a member of the organisation but — I have seen some strange things on my journey — and maybe those dreams we have aren't our own… Maybe someone else is

planting these dreams and desires
in our subconscious — controlling
us from behind the Dark Windows!

Chapter 7:
Being There

"the birth of the reader must be at the cost of the death of the author"[5]

The dead man looks like Godard – it was a crazy idea but Larry couldn't throw it off. *The dead man looks like Godard* – but why would a seventy year-old Franco/Swiss film director be in North Wales unannounced – and why – if he had been killed – had no one recognised or identified him?

After his brief encounter with Rhodri, Larry had finished with work for the day – he had put a sign on the classroom door for his afternoon session, explaining that he had a doctor's appointment and directing the students towards an on-line learning environment that didn't exist (he was confident that they would never attempt to look at it anyway). He had taken his battered briefcase, walked home, got into his rusty Toyota estate car and headed up the A55 to Penmaenmawr – to Plas Coch – to the scene of the crime.

He wasn't sure what was compelling him to follow this ridiculous idea – it was something to do with his sense of paranoia: The inconsequential meeting with Rhodri, the student with the photograph – if his life was an artificially created Big Brother type world – then why not follow the lead? Maybe someone was writing the story of his life for him and they'd decided to make it more interesting. He knew that all of these idle thoughts were hypnagogic illusions, but it comforted him to invent these fantasies. Perhaps he could

---

[5] Roland Barthes, "Image, Music Text"

create an artwork from them – some sort of film, installation, story, animation... he could always add it to his Dark Windows website – to expand and develop the conspiracy theory. Maybe he *could* get the BBC to screen his documentary. He was generally cynical about all of this conspiracy rubbish but these idle, unstructured thoughts were a useful way to pass the time when driving. The thoughts were going nowhere but they were an effective coping strategy.

As he approached Penmaenmawr, he began to think logically again. He parked at the top of the village and changed into his muddy walking boots and old waterproof. He looked the part of an inconspicuous rambler and headed up the road to Plas Coch. On his way up to the imposing house, he passed no one – it seemed a strange coincidence that one of his students had happened to photograph the dead body – but it was a small world around here. He walked up the drive, following in the footsteps of the dead man. There was a little police tape around the scene of the fire but no policeman on duty, no surveillance cameras; the windows of the house were dark and unoccupied – dead quiet.

Larry took the same route around the garden that Godard had taken – past the flowers that he had dead-headed. As he walked up to the taped-off area, he didn't notice the slim notebook concealed beneath a bush. His interest in the whole idea was starting to wane – he was feeling guilty about abandoning his class – about the changes to his job – his income: He had commitments – he was attached to *this* life in *this* place – he couldn't just dive off this hill into the distant sea and be reborn immortal – he had responsibilities. He began to think that the whole dead Godard concept was crazy in every way – he didn't want to have to explain himself to the police – his job was comfortable – he could adjust to whatever new situation Rhodri was hinting at – it wasn't exactly difficult to adapt. He turned and headed back, resolved to drop this Godard illusion and focus on his job – his book – his family. Then, just as he had decided to go home and focus on his mundane existence and was heading back round the garden to get on with life, his muddy boot kicked Godard's notebook and his life changed forever – there would be no turning back now. Larry swiftly picked up the book, looked nervously around and slipped it into his pocket. He knew that it was something important but he didn't know what yet.

He strode down to the beach to consider his discovery. The tide was out and a vast expanse of sand spread before him. The noise of the Expressway racing behind his head distracted him. There were very few people about: In the distance there was one man and his dog, in the car park there were a few empty nondescript cars. One car was facing out to sea – an overweight old man was lying back in the driver's seat with his mouth open. If it wasn't for his wife next to him – alive and reading the Daily Mail – Larry might have thought that someone had killed Alfred Hitchcock and left him in the car park at Penmaenmawr beach – but that would be ridiculous – wouldn't it?

Larry headed down the beach, savouring the expectation of studying the slim volume that he was gripping through his pocket. He began to question his bourgeoise terms of reference; the thoughts planted by his exposure to twentieth century Western culture: He can't walk on the beach or in the mountains without thinking of Andy Goldsworthy and Richard Long – his terms of reference related to the canons of fine art and cinema – he saw a flock of seagulls and thought of Alfred Hitchcock's *Birds*; walking down to the beach reminded him of Truffaut's *400 Blows*; British seaside resorts like Llandudno remind him of *Quadrophenia* or *Carry-on* films. Even here – out in nature with the sea breeze and the evening sun, everything was referenced in the filing cabinet that was his brain – everything was referenced to a film – even this image of his brain came from Svankmajer via Cronenberg and Kubrick.

It was time to get the book out and start to think logically again. He carefully took the slim volume from his pocket – its pages were damp and warped – he must be careful not to damage them. He gently removed the elastic band that secured it and opened the illicit notebook. It was full with closely written text – in French. The sevens were crossed – there were sequences of numbers – small diagrams and words... the majority of it meaningless to Larry. Some of the words were names – they jumped out at him: *Anne-Marie, Colin, Luis, André, Claude, Ingmar, Andrei.* Larry's school French was not good enough to read any of the prose – odd words stood out. Then there were the occasional sets of numbers. They looked like precise co-ordinates, postal codes or telephone numbers. Larry was excited – it was a mystery – something that he could work on. This looked like Godard's book, Godard's writing. The photograph had looked like Godard's face – but it was all too crazy... Maybe it was a set-up, an elaborate hoax like *The Hitler Diaries* or *The Dead Sea Scrolls* (or were they real?). Larry didn't understand but he knew that something was happening and that the answer lay somewhere in the history of cinema and in this notebook.

He sat on a rock for a long time – watching the sunset before he headed back to his car and back down the dark road to his home.

Chapter 8

This Happy Breed

The full moon lit the broad expanse of Penmaenmawr beach – the night air was chill as a perfect Martini, a slight breeze rolled off the lapping waves with the scent of salty olives. All along the promenade night fishermen stood sentinel in bright red waders with black hooded jackets, their white faces skeletal in the moonlight. Their rods sat before them on wire rests, reaching out across the rocky breakwater. Their lines suspended over the blue sand, their hooks baited, waiting for the incoming tide.

Larry walked to the shoreline – the ranks of fishermen silent behind him – the sea stretching before him to the horizon. There was a shape floating in the sea – down at the shoreline – a bloated, white figure. Larry strained to see it, his socks wet on the sand. The waves carried the shape towards him and it became clearer – it was the dead body of Alfred Hitchcock. Larry wanted to run but couldn't, he edged slowly sideways along the shoreline – away from the blue mist that was starting to engulf the figure. The bloated corpse began to rise out of the sea – floating, levitating above the lapping waves. Suddenly Larry realised – it wasn't Hitchcock – it was a toad, a huge bloated toad blinking at him through of the mist. Larry was frozen to the spot, he could sense the fishermen behind him but couldn't turn his head – his eyes fixed on the giant toad rearing out of the mist. The toad began to speak, repeating over and over:

"It's nothing sinister Larry, it's nothing sinister…"

It was then that the fishermen began to chant,

"I'm on the edge... I'm on the edge,"

"I'm on the edge Daddy..."

"DADDY... I'm on the edge..."

Alfie, Larry's three-year-old son was balanced on the edge of the mattress, a few inches from Larry's face – playing some sort of roll-off-the-end-of-the-bed game. There were two Alfies initially but, as Larry pulled himself back to consciousness, he brought his eyes together to focus on the one child.

"Where's Lilly, Daddy?" he called, "Daddy, Where's Lilly?"

Alfie's joy and energy abounded but Larry hadn't quite reached full-charge yet – half of his consciousness was still on that beach with the Hitchcock toad and the hooded fishermen. It was 6.15 a.m. – a bit too early, but time to get up. Larry croaked at Alfie, - "Shhhh... your sister's still asleep... Let's go down and get some breakfast." All that Larry could think about was coffee – steaming hot coffee. He had been woken at 6.30-ish nearly every morning for the past seven years or so; he had not stayed in bed beyond 8.00 and had never been out of debt. He had worked continuously in the same job at the same place and all that he owned was either someone else's rejects or bought with someone else's money. He had reigned in his own ambition – perhaps this was for the best as he had very little talent. All he had of value in his life were his wife, two children and a mortgage on his dilapidated semi-detached house. At 6.15 on a wet Welsh Wednesday it was difficult to see the value...

"Can you put them back in for me-ee-ee-ee-ee" Alfie wanted Larry to help, "can you put the driver in the helicopter for me? Oy-oy-oy-oy-oy?"

"I put the winchman in the helicopter yesterday and he's still there..."

"can you put the driver in the helicopter for me? Oy-oy-oy-oy-oy?"

"I can, just hang on a second" – Larry was trying to fill the kettle.

"why aren't you doing it then? Oy-oy-oy-oy-oy?"

The only answer is to make a pot of coffee and another cake. Larry had become an expert at baking gluten-free cakes since his body started to disintegrate... first he had wrecked his ankle playing five-a-side football, then it was his stomach and the gluten intolerance, most recently it was the panic attacks and flashing lights. *When a guy has children, he asks for trouble.*

Casey smelt the coffee and came downstairs, blonde and beautiful, Larry watched the shape of her body – her soft feminine figure in tight combat-style trousers and white cotton t-shirt – perhaps family life wasn't so bad...

Lilly had got out of bed and gone straight to the computer in the living room, Alfie was mooching around talking to himself and the world in general. Then everyone started talking at the same time:

"What? What, no what, cuckoo"

"Do you want to go to the supermarket after work Larry? I..."

"Mummy, whenever I save something, I get two things – it's like totally weird..."

"To the supermarket?"

"Yes..."

"Daddy, cuckoo, I want to help you cook..."

"You can, you can – get up on this chair... Anyway, Casey?"

"Yes?"

"This dead guy... I've got to do something about this notebook and then there's the photo'..."

"Can I mix it Daddy?"

Larry poured some sugar and buckwheat flour into a bowl of melted butter, he broke two eggs on top.

"Yes Alfie, just mix this up for me. Anyway Casey – what do you think I should do about the book and the photo'?"

"Look – are we going to the supermarket after work?"

"Yes but... this thing with Godard – it looks like... no! Don't eat that Alfie, it's got raw eggs in it... it looks like Godard – will you at least look at the picture for me?"

Larry went over to his jacket and took his 'phone from the pocket – he turned it on, fiddled with the buttons and started to get irate.

"Have you had this?"

"What?"

"Have you been playing with this 'phone?"

"No, I've been in bed…"

"It's not there, the picture's gone. Fuck, I don't believe it!"

Casey gave Larry a withering *'don't swear in front of the children'* look.

"Larry, there's no time for all this now – I'm taking the kids to school in fifteen minutes and Lilly's not dressed – can't you help?"

"But Casey, I need to speak to *someone* about all this – the photo', the notebook… and then I had this dream about Hitchcock and there was this toad that said 'it's nothing sinister' – and that's exactly what Rhodri said to me – and now the photo's gone from my 'phone – you can't say I'm making it all up can you?"

"Can I put it in the oven Daddy?"

Casey started to get angry. "This is typical of you Larry – you came home late – you don't want to talk to me – you're muttering about some dead tramp and how everyone's got it in for you at work – how you've found a book that was written by Jean-Luc Godard – and now you're talking about toads and Alfred Hitchcock… You need to get all of this straight Larry… you're mixing up dreams with reality and your little misconceptions about other people…"

"But *this book* is real…" Larry brandished the slim notebook.

"Look Larry – dreams will always be dreams. You've spent too long confusing dreams with plans. You need to forget about the dreams and focus on reality. This – Alfie, Lilly, Me – we're reality… if you're unhappy with your job – if you want to make a plan to create a new reality, one that you're more happy with – go ahead." Casey softened a little – still practical but more sympathetic, "Look Larry – a plan creates a new reality – a dream runs away from it."

That was her last word. She turned her attention to the children; pulling them together and sweeping out of the door while Larry sat at the kitchen table with his notebook and his cold cup of coffee – wishing that it was still steaming hot.

Chapter 9
The Blue Lamp

Larry didn't like it in Colwyn Bay town centre. He had thought about Casey's comments and had decided to skip work for the morning. He had realised that perhaps he *was* too much of a dreamer – that he needed to act. For some reason he felt that he had to take action to atone for some nebulous sins – the guilt that haunted his dreams – the dead bodies that he felt responsible for – the one in the melted chair and the one on the dark road. He had decided to go to Colwyn Bay police station and tell them about Godard – his suspicions about the dead body. He didn't feel that there was much more he could do – he didn't have the time or resources to get to the root of this all by himself.

When he arrived in Colwyn Bay, parking at the mall in the town centre, he had had second thoughts. So now, here he was, standing in *House Bargains* – aimlessly browsing the shelves – feeling guilty, while he considered what he should do next. He was looking down his nose at the other shoppers – the type of strangely British societal mis-shapes that inhabit these stores on weekday mornings. He didn't really like to think of himself as a bourgeoise snob – but that's what he is. All of these overweight people with no control over their mouths or their emotions. A Dickensian grandmother in casual sportswear was threatening her threadbare grandchildren (who should be at school)...

"Fuckin' get here – quit fuckin' cryin' ya little shites!"

Larry was wondering how these 'little shites' will relate to people as adults and how the tattooed grandmother with her gold chains had reached this stage of social de-evolution – how had she come to the conclusion that it was normal or acceptable to act like that in public? Larry began to wonder who it was that had turned 'shit' into 'shite' – he never used the latter term and was reminded of an incident at nursery last year, when he had gone to collect two-year-old Alfie.

⏮

The over-enthusiastic and out-of-breath nursery assistant had pulled Larry to one side and said, "I need to speak to you about Alfie – we were all singing 'one, two, three, four, five, once I caught a fish alive' – and when we got to 'this little finger on my right' – Alfie sang 'this little finger on my shite' – *and* when I told him to stop, he kept repeating the word – it isn't really appropriate behaviour"

Larry only ever said 'shit' and he seldom used it front of the children, he was affronted by the assumptions of the nursery assistant and decided to apologise, "I'm terribly sorry - I expect he was playing around with sounds – he doesn't know the meaning of the word – and we certainly don't use language like that at home. It won't happen again – I'll twat the little shite when I get home!"

⏭

Larry emerged from his shite reminiscence to find himself still in *House Bargains* – staring at the shelves of tat – and there, nestling between microwave popcorn and a *'chairobics'* DVD was something that caught Larry's eye: It was a VHS video cassette of a film by Luis Buñuel – *The Milky Way*. In this store that seemed to epitomise everything that Larry thought was wrong with the modern world; waste, exploitation, shoddy, dumb culture and pointless products; he had found something that, to him at least, was the height of all that was good about Western Culture: A film by Luis Buñuel – a film about a pilgrimage to Santiago, a film that explores Catholic orthodoxy and narrative conventions in a way that no contemporary film-maker seemed able to do – a film that can make you think *and* feel – that occupies the space between dream and reality. And – it only costs 59p.

This discovery on the shelf of *House Bargains* activated Larry's paranoia again; someone must have placed this remaindered video here for him – it was too personal to be a coincidence – it was too much. He decided then and there that he *would* go to the police after all and see what evolved. He also decided that he would keep the notebook to himself – it would be his secret and perhaps it would be of some use to him. Maybe it was a book with some of the cultural capital that he lacked.

▸▸

Larry stood in the reception of Colwyn Bay police station. He had rung the bell on the counter and was waiting for a policeman to appear on the other side of the scuffed plastic window. A man appeared, "how can I help you?"

"I want to speak to someone about a death – about the tramp that died in Penmaenmawr."

"Another one, eh?" He turned and called over his shoulder, "Dave, there's someone coming through." He turned back to Larry, "Just go through that door…"

Larry was led into a small interview room. He was invited to sit in a plastic chair and wait. A few minutes later, Dave came in - "Alright Larry – what you doing here? Come to give me my *Pulp Fiction* CD back?"

Larry suddenly realised that Sergeant Dave Williams was one of his ex-students – a jovial ruddy-faced man who had taken Film Studies five years ago while he was between jobs. Larry's paranoia increased but he pressed on…

"Hi… err… Dave… it's, well it seems a bit daft really but…"

"Steve said you had some information about the dead tramp – how's your book going?"

"It should be published in the summer, hopefully –it's taken a lot longer than I thought."

"Yeah, right, you were just starting it when you were teaching me – when was that? Five years it must be – you still got my CD?"

"I don't know what happened to it but, erm – I should have given it back." Larry was adding more guilt to the waves of paranoia. "Anyway Dave – it's this tramp. Now this might sound stupid but – do you know who he is?"

"Well… One; It's not my turf, two; It wasn't a suspicious death and three; I wouldn't tell you anyway. So – what is it Larry?"

"It's just that I – this might sound a bit daft – I thought that this – erm – tramp – that he might be Jean-Luc Godard."

"What Larry – are you serious? You think this dead bloke was the captain of the Starship Enterprise – 'make it so' – and all that? My mate at the counter there is a Trekkie – we call him 'Data' – he's fuckin' ace with computers."

"No Dave – that's Picard, not Godard – Jean-Luc Picard is a fictional captain – Godard is a famous film-maker."

"I've never heard of him – he can't be that famous."

"Don't you remember – we did that New Wave module – that film with the girl selling the New York Herald Tribune – you said she reminded you of Casey – my wife?"

"Fuckin' hell Larry – you've got an odd memory – I'll believe you but I don't know what you're on about – was it one of those black and white French films? – Are you okay?" Dave looked concerned, "I mean – are you serious about all this? Isn't that Godard bloke already dead – I mean he must have made those films about fifty years ago at least…"

"Of course he's not dead – he's only just released *Notre Musique*!"

"Sorry Larry – if he's not dead – what are you here for? Have you got something to show me – some evidence or something?"

Larry gripped the notebook in his jacket pocket. "No, I just – it's just this photo' of the dead man – it looked like…"

"What photo'?"

"Well – a student sent it to me and then it, er, it vanished…"

"Look Larry – I think you need some time off work – we've got plenty of photographs of him *and* the melted chair – he was *wrapped in plastic*... And – I shouldn't tell you this – the body has been formally identified by a relative; Mr Monod – he came from Switzerland – and he's paid for a proper cremation"

Larry was adding sheepishness to his feelings of guilt and paranoia, "I'm sorry Dave, I..."

"Think about it Larry - is there anything in the news about this Picard guy going missing? I mean, it would be all over the papers – wouldn't it? Perhaps he's just got one of those Gallic faces?"

"When is the – the cremation?"

"It's at Mochdre on Saturday morning – but I didn't tell you."

"I'm sorry about all this Dave, I – I mustn't have been sleeping too well recently – I've been having these dreams..."

"Right Larry – well I've got work to do," he called to his assistant; "open the door for Larry – *make it so* Data..." Larry stood up to leave – avoiding eye contact with Dave or Data. Dave had a last parting shot.

"Larry?"

"Yeah?"

"Nothing sinister but... Leave death to the professionals."

"Right Dave, I'll use that line in my next book."

Chapter 10
Friday the 13th

"I'm out for a good time - all the rest is propaganda!"[6]

Larry spent Thursday and Friday at work honing his plan, fine-tuning his options. Rhodri was avoiding him, the students were behaving themselves and, at home, Casey was busy with the kids. It was all settling back into a comfortable routine. Larry still had the Godard notebook and was quietly considering its possible meanings or uses – he was making a half-hearted attempt to translate it, to see if it *was* anything more significant than a notebook written in French. There had been one additional strange occurrence but Larry had tried not to read too much into it, he was attempting to suppress his paranoid fantasies.

He had received a phone call from his brother, Chris. Now, this might not seem strange, but Chris normally only 'phoned once or twice a year. He had already called Larry at Christmas – a March 'phone call was unheard of. That was not the end of it – he had told Larry that he wanted to come and visit this weekend; that he would be in Llanberis on Friday with a friend and wanted to come over to see him. Again, this might not seem strange, but this would be the first time ever that he had come up to Wales to see Larry. Chris was based in London where he worked as a photographer for a publishing company dealing with extreme sports. His job meant that he was always travelling the world to somewhere exotic or mountainous. Back home in the UK, however,

---

[6] Saturday Night and Sunday Morning (1960)

he usually refused to travel North of Watford. Today – out of the blue and out of character - he was visiting Snowdonia with a friend called Dewi to cover some kind of extreme-jumping-off-mountains-type 'sport'. This was the sort of thing that Larry couldn't really see the point of. He was more interested in endurance: long walks, cross-country running, cycling – but adrenaline junkies were something else, something that he couldn't fathom. He applied the same values to the films he watched; he'd much rather watch a seven hour Hungarian film about a group of imbeciles on a collective farm than sit through some punchy, high-octane disaster movie.

Larry didn't mind the general disinterest in visiting – Chris lived a different, high-profile life; a life of parties, book launches, airports, cocaine and beautiful women. North Wales and noisy children was way outside his comfort zone. The real problem with the visit was Casey's distrust of Chris. For some reason, she had never liked him, didn't trust him and didn't want him around the children. She had never appeared able to explain these feelings – putting it down to feminine intuition. Larry thought that she was just being petty – or maybe it was something to do with her sister, Sandy. Call it masculine intuition but Larry had always thought there was something unspoken between Casey, Sandy and Chris – some kind of secret they were keeping from him. It was difficult because Larry had secrets of his own in that regard...

So, the problem was that Chris was coming to visit and wanted to stay on Friday night – Larry wanted to see him, to catch up on old times, to maintain a link with his previous life and his roots. The solution was offered by Larry's colleague and bridge partner, Ian Thompson.

Ian was an angry Politics lecturer from Canada who had worked at Larry's college since Margaret Thatcher was Prime Minister. He had only just got used to the fact that some of the new students weren't born when he started at the institution. He had also got used to the complete disinterest in politics that pervaded the youth: Never mind party-politics; they weren't even interested in issues any more. Ian had therefore, over the years, been drawn to the same Dark Windows theories that informed Larry's documentary. He was interested in the way that vested interests use thought-control techniques in 21st Century democratic societies.

The last Friday before payday was 'bridge night' for Larry and Ian – so it was all arranged: Larry and Ian were going to play bridge against Chris and Dewi. They were meeting at Ian's cottage – up the valley in Penmachno.

▸

Larry's Toyota was firing up the A470 from Glan Conwy, through Llanrwst and past Betws-y-Coed. At night, there is just the road, snaking along the route of the river – heading inland – into the mountains. The lights of the rusty car illuminated the white lines and slate walls – the road was empty. He had to keep looking ahead, into the meandering cat's eyes. The clear night skies above him formed a dark canopy – mountains loomed on the distant horizon – dark against dark. Although he knew the route well, at times he felt that he didn't know where he was – he knew the points, the nodes – but not the lines that connect them. He knew not what lay stage left or right – he headed straight onwards, into his own experience – the limitations of his own memory. He was driving at speed, thinking of the recurring dream again – the dark road, the standing stones and the alien body. Suddenly, a rabbit leapt into the headlights and was extinguished. As the frail body was ripped open by the underside of the car, Larry's guilt resurfaced and was carried along the narrow winding roads, across the single track bridges to *Ty Gwyn* – Ian Thompson's white cottage in the middle of nowhere. He drove slowly up the pot-holed shale drive and parked alongside the two other cars – a battered white Renault 5 and a shining black Audi sports car – Chris was already here.

Ian was waiting in the porch – enthusiastic but slightly dazed – a powerful endorsement for the destructive power of cannabis. His detached cottage was ancient with thick stone walls and small decaying sash windows. The front porch was painted in a warm yellow and, from outside, it looked like a typical ivy-clad, run-down rural retreat. As they walked inside, the interior was a marked contrast – the cottage had been gutted and restored with a defiant minimalism. White walls met stripped oak floorboards, recessed wall lights illuminated political posters: Peter Kennard's CND *'Broken Missile'* collage; John Heartfield's anti-Nazi photomontage *'Hurrah, die Butter ist alle!'*. The main kitchen/dining room was open to the full height of the building – strip lighting was fixed to the exposed roof beams. In the centre of the open-plan living space sat a circular glass-topped dining table about 1.5 metres in diameter. Chris Went was seated opposite a strange-looking character with a stony face whom Larry assumed to be Dewi. The two were engaged in a light-hearted debate about the merits of Welsh mountains while sharing a slim joint. The smell of quality weed and cheap incense filled the air – Chris turned round and faced Larry, a wry smile on his face.

"Alright Larry, how's it going? Nice pad your mate's got here."

"You two haven't been here before have you? How do you feel about this card game business?"

Ian and Larry played bridge in a way that would be deeply disturbing to most traditional club players: Firstly they kept a 'crutch' on the table - a brief outline of the bidding system in case they forgot how to play; secondly they talked, smoked and drank while playing; thirdly, they wrote 'us and them' on the score sheets instead of 'we and they'. They played the Nottingham System of contract bridge – Larry liked the idea of a system based in Nottingham, it reminded him of *Saturday Night and Sunday Morning,* the British realist film with Albert Finney's classic *"Don't let the bastards grind you down"* line – a city with Robin Hood's reassuringly radical credentials.

Chris assured Larry that they have digested the rules of play – he invited Dewi to explain - which he did in a faltering East European accent.

"An interesting game – Nottingham is an interesting system. I have played bridge before, many times Larry. My partner and I usually play the Nightmare System – I have explained this system to your brother – he is not my usual partner – but we, Chris and I – if you are happy – we will play the Nightmare against your Nottingham and," he paused for seemingly sinister effect – "may the best men win…"

Ian chipped in with his broad Canadian accent as he bustled around the kitchen preparing drinks and snacks, "Fucking hell Larry, your brother and his mate were like stiffs when they arrived – I've given them a joint to loosen them up but they're still a bit uptight – come on guys let's cut for deal."

The good thing about an evening centred around bridge is that there is no need for small talk – in fact, it is actively discouraged. These four grown men were able to suppress any desire to discuss issues, relationships or life and could focus instead on the numbers. The wine was poured and the four sat, quietly studying the cards, avoiding any meaningful eye contact or conversation throughout the first four hands.

Larry made the first conversational gambit as they started to play the fifth hand…

"So, err, Chris – where have you been today then?"

"We were up *Tal-y-Fan* taking some photographs of boulders and stone circles – are you in hearts?"

"Yep – five hearts – err… that's just South from Penmaenmawr isn't it? Have you been here before Dewey?" Larry attempted to get more conversation from his brother's friend.

"It's Dewi, not Dewey – hmmm – Penmaenmawr - I have been reading in your paper…" he gesticulated towards a copy of the North Wales Weekly News… "A man was burnt to death – yes?"

"Well it's funny that you should say that – I was just about to…"

"Your fucking lead Larry, quit yabbering" Ian was getting frustrated – the points had been building up above the line but no one had made their contract yet and Larry's bid was enough for a game. Larry was pleased that Ian had interrupted – he had been about to launch into a speculative rant about the dead body and his Jean-Luc Godard theory – but he had suddenly become distinctly paranoid. He was uncertain about his brother and Dewi – he put it down to the effect of the cannabis. He knew that he shouldn't really smoke it – it does nothing for him except feed his suspicions and dull his senses. Larry felt vaguely justified in his current paranoia – he had kept quiet about his suspicions since his visit to the police station and yet, here was his brother's peculiar friend mentioning the dead man out of the blue – as a seemingly idle, throwaway comment.

They played the hand and Larry lost the contract. Chris dealt the next hand and opened the bidding with 'one club' – all four were slightly drunk and stoned – the bidding got slower and more desperate moving from Chris to Ian, to Dewi and Larry. Chris was at four diamonds, Ian passed and Dewi considered his options, fingering the cards and intently focusing on the combination he held – he began to speak, "five..." then the telephone rang.

Dewi answered his mobile 'phone, he appeared to become even more grave – even more serious. Larry only heard one side of the conversation as Dewi intoned a few bland acknowledgements,

"Yes... mmm... I understand... It's all over? That's it?... Yes... five minutes..." He finished the call and turned to his host. "I'm dreadfully sorry Ian – I have to leave for a short while – I'll be back to complete my bid in thirty minutes or so... forgive the disruption please – it's to do with work."

The others watched in dumbfounded silence as Dewi stood and left the room. Larry studied his dark attire as he disappeared into the night. He was wearing black combat trousers with a black shirt and a dark grey body warmer – he seemed to be covered in zipped pockets that stored all manner of useful devices; he had produced his 'phone from one pocket, a cigarette lighter from another and a third contained his car keys which he was absent-mindedly jangling as he left.

Ian turned to Chris, "well so much for your fucking partner – is this some kind of European gamesmanship? I suppose you cheese-eaters will want some food while we await Huey's return."

"It's not Huey – it's Dewey"

"To be precise, it's Dewi."

The cheese and crackers were served and the three remaining players struck up a conversation of sorts...

"So, how are the kids Larry?"

"Oh they're fine Chris – just fine..."

"And – err – Casey, how's she getting on?"

"Oh she's okay – run off her feet with the little ones... Have you seen anyone I'd know recently – do you ever see Sandy?"

"What – no – erm, I saw that Locke Brother the other day – you know that one you were at college with. They're doing alright you know – they've got a new exhibition on Cork Street soon and the British Film Institute are releasing some of their short films. It's a shame you couldn't have got into all that celebrity culture – that's where the money is - I don't know how you ended up here of all places..." Chris seemed to be attempting to provoke some sort of response from Larry.

"It's just the cost of living in London – I'm an economic migrant – this is about the only place I could afford to live..."

Ian butted in again "Have some more cheese boys – talking of creativity – how's your book coming on Larry?"

Larry was pleased to avoid the issues again – he still felt stoned and he didn't want to discuss anything too meaningful – especially why and how he came to be in North Wales. "I'm – er – I'm on chapter 13 now but I'm trying to combine some kind of biographical material with a sort of fictional adventure, but I'm getting a bit confused about what's real and what's fantasy..."

"That way lies madness Larry my old mate – that way lies madness..."

He struggled to repress the waves of paranoia that were borne upon this nascent conversation, he started to contemplate the nature of memory, celebrity and coincidence - his thoughts turning round as they sat listening to BBC Radio 1…

…are these ubiquitous celebrities part of the Dark Windows conspiracy - even the ones that I knew when I was younger like Joe Locke? – That would be ridiculous…

He went to the kitchen to take a knife from the drawer; the DJ was playing *Mack the Knife*. The track finished and, as Larry started to spread his cracker, the DJ said "while we're in the cutlery drawer…" and played *Daydream Believer* by Shonen Knife – Larry doesn't like that kind of synchronicity – he was starting to feel uncomfortable trapped in his own circular thought processes. The spiralling paranoia was interrupted by Dewi's return. No one asked where he could possibly have gone in the middle of the night – in the middle of nowhere; they just got on with the game. Dewi sat down and continued as if he had never left…

"five… no - make that *four no trumps* – enough for a game."

The game continued through one extended rubber – Dewi and Chris were eventual victors. Larry got up to leave almost immediately, Ian complained…

"Where you going Larry – don't you want to catch up with your brother – chew the fat?"

"Sorry guys – I've got a busy day tomorrow, I've got a funeral to go to."

"Who's dead?"

"I wish I knew…"

"You're a fucking weird one Larry – look, just take care on the road mate… and if you need anything, you can always rely on your mates…"

II

Larry headed home, back down the snaking road – nothing was said that night – nothing was discussed, even the game seemed somehow fractured and unresolved. All the way home Larry thought about Dewi, worried – for some reason - that this strange character might have tampered with his brake pipes. He imagined a camera fixed to the underneath of his car, a low angle shot of brake fluid dripping from the pipes below him - the same pipes that had killed the rabbit – but it was all in his head.

Chapter 11
Funeral in Colwyn

It was the type of sunny Spring Saturday morning that heralds a change of season. The cold winter winds of the previous week had been replaced by a warm sun that was tempered slightly by the chill air drifting off the distant sea. Larry was heading briskly down the tree-lined avenue that leads to Mochdre crematorium. The crematorium and municipal graveyard lie between the railway and the expressway – sandwiched between allotments and a recycling depot. The whole area is zoned off on the local council map as 'compost corner' – a place to dispose of that which is no longer required. You take your rubbish there to throw in the skip and, on the other side of the high brick perimeter wall; the mortal remains of your loved ones are cremated.

Larry was without a car – he had woken up late after the excesses of the previous evening to find that Casey had taken it and the kids to a party involving a bouncy castle, jelly and ice-cream. He wasn't entirely certain what was compelling him down this path but he had washed, shaved and dressed in a white shirt, black trousers and black tie. He had downed a cup of strong coffee and strolled swiftly down the two miles to Mochdre crematorium – hoping to catch Godard's funeral. Sergeant Dave Williams had told him the day but neglected the time – Larry was taking a gamble that mid-morning would be about the right time for a Saturday cremation. It was a nice day for a walk anyhow.

He approached the main crematorium and chapel – a single-storey functional institutional brick building shrouded by trees - it was all the more creepy for its lack of gothic extravagance. There appeared to be no obvious entrance for pedestrians, the building designed for arrival and departure by automobile. There were two main doors, one for arriving and one for departing mourners. As he walked to the left of the building, he stumbled into a large group of people dressed in black, milling about the exit – smoking cigarettes and chatting in hushed tones – he overheard two arguing.

"Look jughead – it was your job to bring the music"

"I did – I did, it's not my fault they chose the wrong track…"

Larry spotted two council workers having a break in the adjacent smoking shelter: A tall skinny teenager was addressing his short, fat mature colleague. They both wore the same size embroidered council sweatshirt that fitted neither of them, they were just finishing a conversation and lighting a new cigarette as he approached them…

"He only looked about seventeen."

"He won't make eighteen."

When they saw Larry, they turned and smiled, he asked them about the mourners.

"Are these for?"

"Young lad, wrapped round a lamp-post. It's all over now – are you here for the mystery man?"

"How do you mean"

"The – err – are you a relative?"

"No."

"A journalist?"

"No."

"But you're here for the Swiss fellow?"

"Yes"

"He's – err – laid out in the chapel now – you can go through round that way…"

The older man pointed towards a large hardwood door on the other side of the building.

II

Larry hesitated in the doorway of the chapel of rest – he could see a heavy wooden coffin resting on a metal trolley at the front of the aisle. There were pews on both sides of the artificially lit, windowless room. Eric Satie music was crackling out of concealed speakers. A silent, shadowy attendant was standing outside the door – he was the only other living person about – Larry felt that he had better check that he'd got the right dead man.

"Can you tell me – who's the?"

"Fellow called Monod"

That was the name that Williams had mentioned, Larry's instinct about the time was right. Uncertain of what to do next, he progressed down the aisle, towards the open coffin.

The body was covered except for the bloodless head that rested on a plain white linen cushion. Larry stared in fascination at the waxy Monod's face for several minutes when he suddenly sensed that he was no longer alone in the room. He turned and saw Sergeant Williams sitting in the back row, his head bent in thoughtful reverie – a slight clipping sound coming from his general direction. Larry turned and sat on one of the front pews – the mournful Satie music seeming to increase in volume.

It's not a very large turn-out is it? – didn't Monod have any friends? – If he'd have died in bed, he wouldn't even have me – if I hadn't gone to the police he wouldn't even have had Williams – at least he knows how to behave at funerals…

His thoughts were disturbed by the creaking of the chapel door as a figure in a dark raincoat entered the room and walked slowly up to the coffin. As he looked down at the corpse's face – he sneezed loudly, took a large handkerchief from his pocket, blew his nose noisily and turned to face Larry. Larry muttered – "bless you!" – and then recognised the man – it was Vendor Busch! Vendor recognised Larry, looked vaguely surprised, staggered to the back of the chapel, looked at Williams and sat down. At the same moment, a familiar figure entered the chapel and swaggered down to the corpse. He held a mirror over Monod's mouth and croaked, "Arrivederci Brother Donkey".

This is ridiculous he's obviously dead – what's this charade all about – is it aimed at me?

As the man turned to face him, Larry saw that it was Mike War. Mike walked over to where he was sitting and whispered, "It shouldn't have ended like this Larry..." Before he could reply – a third man entered the room – Larry began to panic...

I've seen all this before – I know what's going to happen next!

The third man walked up to the corpse, took a long pin from his lapel and jabbed it into the cadaver's bloodless cheek. Larry's mounting panic was making him dizzy – the room was starting to spin – he was beginning to feel nauseous...

If I don't leave soon, someone will tap me on the shoulder and give me a letter.

He tried to get up and leave – he felt dizzy – lights flashing – he needed fresh air. As he stood to leave, he realised that the third man was Dewi Winkle! He must get outside – into the light, into the air – he ran out without looking at anyone. Dewi, Vendor, Mike, Williams, Godard – it was all too much. Larry ran over to a bench, leant on it and vomited onto the flowerbed behind it. He sat down on the bench for a while, alone - his heart pounding – the birds and the breeze singing in the trees. He tried desperately to wake up – but he couldn't - it wasn't a dream. Ten minutes or so later, he sensed someone approaching and looked up to see Sergeant Williams.

"Like a lift home Larry? I've got a car here..."

The short drive home passed without event, Dave told Larry that the service had been brief and the cremation followed with little ceremony. Larry kept quiet – he was still trying to wake up – he knew that somehow he was implicated in this whole charade – and that it was something to do with the notebook. Something very strange was happening, but… as long as no one knows about the notebook, he should be safe for the moment – or at the very least he might remain sane…

Chapter 12
Whiteboard Jungle

Larry had gone home after the funeral and spent the remainder of Saturday in bed with the curtains closed and the light turned off. He was trying to get some silence, some peace – he told Casey that he was nauseous and had a splitting headache – in reality he was numb.

All day Sunday he hid in bed, developing his numbness into self-indulgent pain and mental anguish. He had opened the curtains and from his bedroom window he could see the sea, the golf course and the roof-light of his office. He began to think that he lived his entire life in a small, enclosed geographic area – he stared silently out of the window and remembered how he had attempted to take up running every morning before work. From this high vantage point, he could trace the circular route that he had traversed on his morning jogs: Down to the sea, along the promenade, up past the golf course and back up the main road, past the college where he worked to his home. He pictured a high wire fence along the route – with him caged in and pacing the internal perimeter – wearing away a track around the inner boundary like a sad and shaggy caged tiger – pacing round and round, not quite sure how or why he had become trapped in this enclosure.

After the strange staged funeral, Larry felt almost certain that some sinister force was holding him in this existence – in this semi-detached, semi-rural, suburban life. His house was overlooked on all three sides, double-decker buses passed by his windows, allowing the passengers privileged views of his living-room, bathroom and bedroom. He thought back to the time that he had taken his students to see John Lennon's house on Menlove Avenue in Liverpool, before the National Trust took it over - when it was still an ordinary, privately owned house. He thought about how the students had acted – peering through the windows, digging up pieces of turf, urinating in the back garden – obsessed with the tenuous link to fame… *"I pissed in John Lennon's garden!"*

He thought about how similar to his own house that anonymous semi on an average through-route was; how John had left suburbia as a child, whereas he had settled, as an adult, in this semi-detached utopia. As he ruminated on these relatively disconnected events, he heard music playing from his daughter's room – Lilly was singing along to a track from the soundtrack of Disney's *Beauty and the Beast* – something about how *"there must be more than this small provincial town"* Larry supposed that it was a very common theme.

The whole of Sunday was spent in this self-imposed isolation – Larry retreating into his bedroom with his fantastic notions and conspiratorial theories. He took time to try and be creative – ignoring the notebook that was burning a hole in his comfort zone – he took out his Random Poetry Generator – a surreal game that he had invented, allowing players to create their own individual or communal works of poetry. He managed to generate one verse that he was happy with:

Archaeology of the memory
Lights a message
to the civilized world

"That way lies madness" – Ian had said it all.

▶|

Monday morning, Larry was in work again – he could cope with the routine there – he didn't want to get behind with his classes and today he had a slightly more formal lecture to give – in a proper lecture theatre, with mature Art students who were supposedly more engaged, interested, involved. They were waiting for him as he arrived with his notes, videos and pens piled in a box file. He unlocked the door and the students filed into the back three rows of the tiered seating – leaving a gap of five rows between the students and the lecturer. There were about twenty students in total; reformed housewives, intense ceramicists and retired water-colourists. The room had no windows and the air-conditioning wasn't working, it was too hot and the air was stale. The room was, however, equipped with all manner of pointless electronic gadgets aimed at improving the 'learning experience'. Today, Larry's aims and objectives were less complex – he was going to use a few film clips and a presentation with projected bullet-points to outline one of his pet subjects: *Surreal Cinema and Ideological Liberation*. Larry was already starting to sweat in the artificial heat – he could see a couple of the more mature students starting to nod off as they settled in their seats – it would be interesting to see what sense they made of it all as they drifted in and out of consciousness.

He started his lecture by giving a selectively potted outline of film language and theory. He explained how film can be considered as an art form – not merely a commercial venture, but a new universal language. He described how the magic of cinema was recognised early – its specific power being the way that it records reality, as Godard later wrote, *"cinema is truth twenty-four times a second"*. In the development of a social function for moving pictures – there was a battle between those, like Edison in America, who saw film as a peepshow – an individual communications device or a way of generating money - and others, such as Georges Méliès in France, who saw film as cinema - as a communal experience – a magical entertainment. Méliès died in poverty whereas Edison helped to electrify America – he even created the electric chair by killing an elephant called Topsy... Larry realised that he was starting to go off-target again and decided to introduce his bullet points – attempting to explain the key concepts from scratch:

Click

1: The Camera.

"Right then – what do we need to make a movie? First we need a device for mechanically recording movement with the lens replacing the human eye"

Click

2: Mise-en-Scène.

"Next, we put something in front of the camera; this can be the 'real world' or a constructed, theatrical setting. Into this setting we can now direct sources of light and place people or objects. Much of this is common to other arts such as painting and theatre."

Click

3: Mise-en-Shot.

"We now have to decide how we are going to frame and record this constructed world. We now begin to utlilise the new language of film to impose meaning on this world - so what choices can we make when we have a camera at our disposal and a scene that we have constructed?"

Click

3a: Framing.

"We can decide how much of the scene we want in the frame – and from which position we are looking. If the camera has replaced the eye – we are controlling the viewpoint, the perception of the viewer. We can look at one detail – for example a human face – in close-up to the exclusion of all other elements of the mise-en-scène. Or... we can choose to record the whole scene in a wide shot with deep focus – with all elements, near and far clearly in focus for the viewer." Larry used two still images to illustrate this contrast – a close-up from *Battleship Potemkin* and a deep-focus shot from *Citizen Kane* – obvious choices but they did the job.

Click

3b: Camera Movement.

"We also have the option to move the camera – we can decide to keep the camera static and record the scene from a number of different angles with the actors replaying their gestures over and over again. The camera can look from high in the air or low on the ground – it can move: track, dolly, pan, tilt – the possibilities are infinite but the viewer has to make sense of the images presented to him... so that – err – brings us to..."

Click

3c: Continuity Editing.

"Right, well, this is – errr – this is the name that we give to the process whereby all these pieces of recorded reality, these captured fragments of space and time, are ordered together – are sequenced – to create some kind of coherence. Continuity editing utilises a series of rules that allow the film maker to imitate our perceptions of space and time – continuity editing tends to be invisible to the viewer as spatial and temporal continuity is preserved by using techniques such as creative geography, the eyeline match, shot/reverse shot and the 180 degree rule."

Click

3d: Montage.

"Montage is often seen in opposition to continuity editing – Montage is the sequencing of shots to create associations – shots are put together to create symbolic meanings, these symbolic meanings cause a response in the viewer... you can see montage editing used in advertising, propaganda, political broadcasts..." Larry was sensing that the students were starting to lose interest – was he stating the obvious or was he going too fast? He thought perhaps that he'd better ask them some questions to check... "Right – so here we are in a hot, sweaty lecture theatre in North Wales – this is our reality this morning, this room is our Mise-en-Scène, I am the star – the main focus of attention and you are all extras... So – how could we film this world that we inhabit – how could we film this lecture? He points at one of the more jolly and engaged female ceramicists – how would you direct this scene if you were in charge? Would you use a wide shot with deep focus, allowing me to drone on, or would you shoot the whole thing from a range of different angles and create a montage? What would your montage sequence suggest – what message would you convey and how would you do it?"

The student looked around at her classmates for support before replying "Erm… I don't really understand the question - this is your lecture and you want me to?…" Suddenly the fire alarm rang and drowned out any hope of a response; the students started to file out as cool air wafted in. One man stayed slumped in his seat. Dressed in very clean, smart casual clothing, he was about sixty-five years old and fast asleep – he had a concerned-looking friend squatting next to him – Larry shouted to the friend over the noise of the alarm, "What's the matter – is he asleep? My damn lecture put him to sleep?"

The friend shouted his response over the intensifying alarm, "He's not asleep Larry!"

"What do you mean, he's not asleep!"

"He's dead Larry"

"Dead!" Suddenly the alarm turned off – Larry was alone in the silent lecture theatre with two students; one dead and one alive – he lowered his voice as he continued, "What do you mean – he's dead? How can he be dead? I'd only just started the lecture… I didn't hear anything – did you hear anything?"

"Not a thing – he probably didn't want to disturb your lecture Larry."

▶▶

For the second time in less than a week, Larry was sitting in Rhodri's office – this time Rhodri was staying put – he seemed genuinely concerned about Larry and the events of the day.

"I just came from the boss's office – they've taken the stiff off-site, we're keeping it all as discreet as we can. Weak heart - did you know the... err, did you know him?"

"No, he seemed like an interesting old chap though – very clean..."

"It's a first for the college Larry – death by lecture – you're quite a man."

"Thanks – I fancy a cheap drink"

"How would you like a 10 day cut in your holiday entitlement?"

"How would I... do I laugh now or wait for the punch-line?"

"I'm serious Larry – I've been talking to the boss. There's too much paper piling up on my desk - too much pressure on my nerves. I spend half the night lying awake in my bed. I've got to have an assistant. I thought that you..."

"Me? Why pick on me?"

"Because I've got a crazy idea you might be good at the job."

"That's crazy alright, I'm a lecturer."

"Yeah, a teacher – a bore – a whiteboarder. You're too good to be a lecturer."

"Nobody's too good to be a lecturer..."

"Phooey – all you guys do is open doors and dish out someone else's theories – what's bothering you – it's that dead guy isn't it?"

"Which one? - I mean death would bother anybody..."

"Look Larry. The job I'm talking about takes brains and integrity – it takes more guts than there is in fifty lecturers. It's the hottest job in the business."

"It's still a desk job – I don't want a desk job."

"A desk job. Is that all it means to you? Just a comfy chair to park your arse on from nine to five – just a pile of papers to shuffle around and forms to fill in – with maybe a little doodling on the side? That's not the way I see it, Larry. To me, a manager is like a surgeon, and those on-line quality systems are like scans of the human body – and those papers aren't just strategic plans and minutes of meetings, they're living, breathing documents – packed with twisted hopes and crooked dreams. A manager, Larry is a psychiatrist, an academic, editor and confessor all in one."

"That's fine Rhodri – but I think I've heard it all before – I'm happy as a pseudo-academic, I can't buy into all that bullshit…"

He'd had just about had a gut-full of this – why was Rhodri suddenly offering him a management job? Last week, he wouldn't even give him the time of day – Larry had other things on his mind; the notebook, the funeral, the dead student – it was all stacking up. He decided to take it one step at a time – first he would investigate the mysterious notebook. He went to his office and scanned the entire book – he saved the files and then printed them out on A4 paper, he punched holes in the papers and put a treasury tag through them. He thought how he quite liked paper – perhaps a desk job wouldn't be so bad after all – some people's idea of heaven is a desk job. He gathered together his pile of papers and headed over to Gerard Lopez's office. Gerard was a French teacher and European film buff – if anyone could help Larry understand this notebook – it would be Gerard. He knocked on the office of Mr Lopez and waited – the door creaked slowly open and Gerard began to speak with his attractive French accent, "Hi Larry, it's good to see you – I heard about the – err – the death in your lecture – are you? Did you know the err?"

"I didn't really know him – he seemed a nice old man, very clean."

"And what were you talking to them about when he… You weren't showing them one of your shocking film sequences were you? You didn't give the poor old guy a heart attack?"

"I was just getting started – just giving a little of bit of basic background – you know about film language, editing…"

"You talk about Bazin and Eisenstein? About the Formalists and the Realists?"

"I didn't really get round to all that but I was leading up to some ideas about control – about thought control and the moving image…"

"Ah! That old one – are you still working on your silly book idea – don't you think it's all a bit passé?"

"It's not that silly – look I was thinking – somehow I wanted to work this into the book – I was going to try it in the lecture today but the fire alarm and the dead student stopped me…"

"Here, sit down Larry, you wanted to work what into your book?"

"Well – I've been working an a big 'What if' I've been thinking about the effect that the moving image has on children – I mean they all watch screens for a lot longer than we ever did right? What if the government had a positive censorship policy? What if, instead of Fireman Sam and the Simpsons, children were forced to watch the great animators and filmmakers from 6.00am – 6.00pm? Svankmajer, the Quay Brothers, Len Lye, Buñuel's Robinson Crusoe, Norman McLaren and the modern equivalents. What if television programmers' only considerations were art and revolution instead of profit and education for compliance? What dreams and nightmares would the children have if they weren't being constantly sold cheap plastic products and cynical ideas – how would they change the world? What liberations would take place?"

"Well – it might fuck with their minds a bit."

"We're already doing that with the dross that they watch now."

"You're just a cultural snob Larry – forget about it. You didn't come here just to tell me about that crazy theory did you?"

"No – I've got something for you," Larry glanced over at Gerard's bookcase – one book stood out; *Human Sacrifice in History and Today* – a strange choice for a French teacher… "I was wondering Gerry – if you would have a look over this for me?" He pulled out the photocopies of the Godard notebook, "would you read this through for me – in strict confidence and tell me what it's saying, I mean if there are any interesting ideas, concepts, theories?"

"Sure Larry – I mean - you are a killer now? I should be scared – are you in league with some dark order?" he looked over to his bookcase, then back to his desk. He took a padded envelope and passed it to Larry. "There are some films here that you might like to watch."

"Thanks Gerry - and – it might be nothing. I'll be in touch if I need you – if you could just keep it safe for me – if that's okay?"

"Killer Larry – no problem…"

Chapter 13
The Intruder

The evenings were starting to get lighter now. As Larry left work, he looked over towards the distant mountains of Conwy – the shape of sleeping beauty lying in the rocky horizon, bathed in a warm salmon-pink glow as the herring gulls hovered overhead – calling. Starlings appeared in hallucinogenic spiralling swarms – more and more joining by the minute as they swept across the sky, preparing to roost – to tuck themselves up for the night under Colwyn Bay pier. From the golf course, curlews called their distinctive 'peewit'. He wandered slowly home through the peaceful warm spring evening – considering his second brush with mortality.

As he approached his front door – he immediately recognised that something wasn't quite right – it was a subtle disjunction: The porch door was shut but the handle wasn't pulled fully up into place – through the glazed porch he could see that the red front door was slightly ajar - nothing too unusual – but not quite comfortable. Casey should be out now – she's taken the kids swimming, the car isn't there – the house should be empty and the door should be shut. Larry started to get angry…

Why has she left the door open? It's asking for trouble – it's lucky that we live in a quiet part of the world – the sort of place where you can leave your shed open and your car unlocked overnight… but the front door?

Larry tentatively approached the porch door – it creaked loudly as he slid it open…

I should oil that.

He began to mentally catalogue other faults in the structure of his house – he noticed cracks in the plaster and the twisted doorframe that indicated the house was slowly subsiding into the soft ground on which it was built. The deformation of the building was most apparent in the stained glass of the porch, whose soft lead was slipping out of line – out of synch with the rest of the house.

He walked through the door and remembered to check for signs of burglary – he struggled to get into the mindset of a burglar...

Now then, what would a thief want? The television – that's still there but nobody would want that old thing anyway. No one would want the toys that are strewn across the living-room floor... it looks as if someone has trashed the living-room, but with two small children, it's difficult to tell – it usually looks turned-over like this – mind you it does look as if someone's been throwing books all over the floor.

Larry called out, "Hello? - Casey? – Anyone home?" There was no response, he was starting to feel uncomfortable – the house creaked...

Is that someone upstairs or just a creak?

He pushed open the door and stepped into the kitchen – there were more toys and books scattered across the floor. The large kitchen table and all available vertical space was covered with dirty dishes, old newspapers, piles of opened letters, magazines, craft materials, pens, sauce bottles, shoes and plastic bags. The kitchen drawers had been left open with the contents dishevelled – half hanging out and half spread around the room. Larry was starting to suspect that the house had been ransacked – that he had been burgled. It was difficult to tell – it was possible that Casey had left in a hurry – that she had been frantically searching for something, for some swimming goggles or something, and didn't have time to tidy up... He decided to run upstairs and check his office – he'd know if anything had been moved up there.

The door of his office was open, he peered in – everything seemed out of place. One mess of books was piled high, another pile was tipped on the floor – papers and memorabilia were distributed artlessly across the desk and shelves – he picked up a framed picture of a spider and placed it back on the shelf. Where once everything was carefully placed, displayed, organised – now everything was scattered and random…

I'm sick of symmetry – all this junk has no substance anyway – it all looks fine when it's neatly indexed and organised on shelves, but it's all visual clutter – there's no substance to any of it. Look at these books – I've hardly read any of them – I've not paid for all this cheap, tatty furniture. It's all shoddy. It's no wonder the burglars couldn't find anything worth taking – it looks as if everything's been turned upside down but nothing's been taken…

He began to think about how his sense of self was defined by collections – not of spiders, postcards or stamps – but collections of books, music and film… all of them neatly categorised and alphabetically organised: Films by director (except for box sets with multiple directors – they come under 'v' for various), Books by subject and size, Music by genre then date. It mattered not if they all remain unwatched, unread, un-listened – they were all there, lined up and categorised. Larry's collections had been shuffled but not stolen – his desk had been rifled but merely left dishevelled – none of it really seemed to…

The door creaked open downstairs and Larry heard Casey, Lilly and Alfie entering – she called out.

"Larry! Are you there – what's all this mess? I've only just cleared up down here – Larry?"

He walked slowly downstairs and started to talk in a low, calm voice.

"It looks like we've been burgled Casey, did you lock the door?"

"We've been… is there anyone here? Have you looked around – how long have you been back? Of course I locked the – are you alright?" She seemed genuinely worried.

"Daddy, daddy was it a burglar – was it?" The children had picked up on it straight away.

"He better not have taken my toys!" Lilly ran upstairs – Casey glanced at her and looked to Larry for reassurance.

"She'll be okay – I've checked upstairs – whoever was here – they've gone now. They let themselves in and… they've gone now."

Larry seemed too calm – too relaxed about it all.

"It better not be one of your stupid games Larry – you're not cracking up are you? You haven't done this to the house yourself because you feel trapped have you? You better not be pissing about – what do you mean – *they let themselves in* – who are *they* Larry?"

"Look Casey – let's have a cup of tea, call the police and get the locks changed. There's not much else we can do – at least we're all safe. Someone died in one of my lectures today…"

II

Casey called the police – they only seemed interested in finding out how the 'burglars' had gained entry and in what (if anything) was missing. They promised to provide a crime number if she phoned back tomorrow. She called a locksmith who assured her that he would also come tomorrow, he advised her to bolt the door for security. Cars, lorries and buses wheeled past the windows, nobody called at the door, nobody walked past the house - hours of the early evening passed by. The sun set and nothing seemed very different – they both felt that they should feel devastated, scared and threatened – but Larry was too wrapped up in his recent unusual experiences and Casey was too concerned with the everyday realities of life.

"Larry – go up and read them a story, they're a bit quiet – we'll talk about this when they're tucked up – I've got an idea."

He found the two children playing happily with the piles of books that had been thrown off the shelves by the mysterious intruder. They had built houses for their toys from the books; sorted structurally – they made interesting towers of Babel. Larry ushered them onto the bed.

"Choose me a story Alfie..." Alfie climbed off the bed and randomly selected a paperback that was forming the roof of a fire station. "Are you sure you want this one Alfie? It's one of my books."

"I want it."

"Okay then, I'll try it," Larry opened the book and read the opening lines – adjusting them slightly for his audience, "Once upon a time, there was a moocow coming down the road and this moocow met a nice little boy named baby tuckoo – now baby tuckoo had a hairy face, and err, the moocow came down the road where Betty Byrne lived, and err..."

"Daddy, I don't want that story – can't we have a proper story – that story's boring"

"Well – I don't think I'm doing it justice Lilly – do you want to choose a different one?" Lilly got down and chose a book that was forming one half of a tent for a sleeping fox. "That's better – right, are you both sitting comfortably? – Then I'll begin: Burglar Bill lives by himself in a tall house full of stolen property..."

⏭

When the children had been read to bed – Larry came down to find that Casey had cleared a space in the cluttered living room, lit a fire and poured two glasses of cheap red wine.

Larry's paranoia caught up with him as he threw himself down onto the chewed leather Chesterfield, "I've been thinking Casey, this – this, break-in... I think it's to do with – I think they were looking for the notebook..."

"What happened at work today then - someone?"

"They died – in my lecture – it was some old guy – but that's not all, Rhodri tired to offer me a management job – and I think they're trying to buy me out..."

Casey laughed, "Larry don't be so ridiculous – if there *was* some conspiracy involving all of this – do you think they'd buy you out by offering you some tedious desk job? You're making fictional connections between real life – your little book and the films you watch... I've been thinking – you need a break – you need to sort this all out and get some kind of perspective on it – what exactly has happened to you? I'm listening if you want to try and explain it."

She took a delicate sip of her wine and looked directly at him, he saw their history in her eyes – their life together – their children. Outside of the intensity of life, in this quiet space, Larry briefly gained control – became aware of the tensions coursing through his existence – he briefly relaxed and sank into the sofa.

"It's just – I've started writing this book and then I think that I've found the dead body of Godard and *his* book, then there was Chris and his strange friend... and the funeral – he was there..."

"Chris?"

"No, I told you – his friend, Dewi, and I'm sure that Mike and Vendor were there..."

"The guys from your documentary?"

"Yes and then there was the dead man in the lecture and Rhodri and now the break-in – you can't tell me it's all a..."

"...coincidence – yes – of course it is. Don't you think that makes more sense Larry than this crazy idea that you are at the centre of some dark conspiracy. You're starting to lose touch again. Like I said – you need a break. They won't miss you at work, you can use all of this as an excuse to take a week off. I think you should go down to London, get some perspective on the whole thing – meet up with some old friends, discuss your ideas with them and see if they can help you with your book – you'll need some publicity if anyone's going to buy the thing when it's published."

"We can't afford it – how can I afford to go and stay in a hotel in London? And what about you and the kids with the break-in I'd be worried."

Casey seemed unconcerned – unflappable – a realist, "Don't worry – I'm not bothered, they're not coming back are they? There's nothing here for a burglar is there - and I've got a telephone – what are you going to do to stop anyone anyway?"

"But where am I going to stay?"

"You can stay with Sandy – it's all sorted. I spoke to her when you were upstairs reading."

Larry started to get excited, waves of desire and guilt swept over him...

Sandy... she wouldn't want me to stay with her, not after – she hasn't wanted to see me for at least ten years...

"Are you sure she?"

"Yeah, I know you two don't really get on any more – but she'll leave you alone – and she's still friends with some of your old crowd..."

The two spent the rest of the night talking: Larry speculating about connections between random events – real and imaginary; Casey planning the logistics of Larry's journey to London. Larry was getting quietly excited about leaving this perceived mess in order to follow a plan whereas Casey was getting ready to tidy up the mess and tie up the loose ends.

Chapter 14:

Two or Three Things I Know About Her

⏮

Central London in the early evening was warm and stuffy; the odour of decadence and car fumes stagnated in the still air as pigeons cooed around the overfilled wheelie bins that sat outside the terraced houses. Sandy Banks lived on the top floor of a tall, thin red brick terrace in West Kensington. She was also tall and thin, her straight dark hair tied back in a slim ponytail. She looked younger than her thirty-eight years, maintaining the pale, clear complexion and defined features of her youth. She was pedaling slowly uphill on her exercise bike when the phone rang, a long-sleeved tee-shirt and designer jeans hugged her lithe figure as she slowly dismounted and picked up the receiver of a restored Bakelite telephone.

"Hello?"

"Hi Sandy – it's Casey…"

"Alright sis' – sorry I haven't…"

"I understand – look – I haven't got much time but I want to ask a favour…"

"Do you want to borrow a bit more…?"

"No – it's – it's Larry…" there was silence in London, "…he's – he's getting a bit down here – there's – there's a lot going on…"

"Have you two fallen out?"

"No – it's difficult to explain – it's work and life – he doesn't seem happy – he needs a break. Do you think you could put up with him for few days while he sorts some stuff out in London?"

"What does he think? He wouldn't want to stay here with me – do you want me to book him into a hotel or something?"

"I haven't asked him but it will do him good to catch up on old times –if it isn't all water under the bridge now between you two, then it never will be…"

Sandy perked up a little, "Look love – it's fine by me – he can have the run of the place – I'm busy – we've got a big start-up next week and I'm going to be out, out, out. And… there's a private view for Joe's new show this week, Larry could catch up with some of the old crowd…"

"Yeah, it'll do him good to get away from me and the kids for a bit…"

"How are they?"

"Oh – they're fine… maybe you could come up?"

"I know, I know – look I'm busy earning a fortune here Casey and I will – I will, will, will come up to see you but…"

"Yeah, I know – you're too busy making money… I'm going to send Larry down tomorrow – he'll tell you all about it."

"What?"

"Look, got to go, got stuff to pick off the floor – I'll, err, speak to you soon?"

"Tell Larry to ring first – I might not be home."

"Okay – no problem – take care of him will you?"

"Sure will."

Sandy placed the heavy black handset back in its cradle and flopped her soft perfumed body onto a soft white leather couch. She writhed about a little until her physical self was attuned with its supporting cushions. She loosened her hair and ran her slim, pale, manicured fingers around her face and through her subtly styled layers.

It's been a long time. We've never really cleared the air – Casey, Larry, me – none of us know the full picture – I don't know if I even remember it right... it'll be good to see him again, it's about time I thought about something other than work and money...

She closed her eyes, slipped her hand across her firm stomach and down into her expensive fitted jeans...

It's about time...

⏮

Sandy had known Larry since they were teenagers in Walton-on-Thames. They had been close before – before Larry had got close to Casey - it was a long story.

Sandy and Larry were teenage sweethearts – teenage lovers. Casey knew this and accepted as much. The emotions may have been complex at one time but twenty years later, there were other things to worry about: Kids, mortgages, sleep... the histrionics of youth were in temporal perspective. But love was still there – lust – emotion – whatever it was, it was the root of the communications problems between the three of them. Casey was being brave to push Larry back into Sandy's life; in his present state of mind, he was bound to see Sandy as one of his missed opportunities: The wealthy, independent sister, with no ties and a flat in London. It happens all the time: reunited friends – midlife crises exposed on daytime television – divorcees electronically searching for their past loves. Maybe Casey was testing the limits of his loyalty and their relationship. Sending Larry down to Sandy was brave... perhaps Casey could work out the psychology of it all but she felt as uncertain about her motivation as Larry and Sandy. They had a shared, triangular history consisting of three different memories that between them held the facts that would never be one.

Larry had loved Sandy: They were inseparable teenagers with shredded sleeves on their black gothic tee-shirts as they crimped and back-combed each others dyed black hair before falling into the clean white linen sheets of beds in their family homes – to make love as only teenagers can – fumbling, uncertain - full of energy, hormones and confidence – engulfed in the experience of inexperience.

Then they went their separate ways to different polytechnics, to study Art and Film in Thatcher's Britain... they were the last of England and their love felt like the best and last of their lives... That was one of the memories, but there were others, seen from other angles.

II
Shot / Reverse Shot
▶

When they moved away, they stayed friends and shared friends – Larry in East London, Sandy in the West. After three years, Larry's final project at Polytechnic was a film – shot on 16mm – it was some kind of sub-Godard, pseudo political naive attempt at a comment on Eighties Britain and the Miners' Strike[7]. Larry had got Sandy to act in the film; she looked stunning on monochrome celluloid in her black eyeliner and crimped youth. She played a journalist from Surrey (although she was no actor) attempting to cover a strike at an East London sausage factory. Larry had borrowed a Nagra tape machine and an Arriflex camera – synchronised. They used black and white Ilford stock to film Sandy in close-up. Her beauty was inter-cut with general scenes from the everyday life of a sausage factory. A voice-over told the story of how the boss had been taken hostage by angry factory workers when he had banned Union activity. Sandy was given lines that made her look stupid – pretty but stupid... she wasn't stupid and she didn't forget easily.

---

[7] Inspired by Godard's 'Tout va Bien' (1972)

Extract From:
EVERYTHING'S FINE (1989)
By Larry Went & Joe Locke

\#

EXT. LONDON STREET — DAY

JOE LOCKE and SANDY BANKS are walking down an average terraced street in East London. JOE strolls purposefully ahead, SANDY skips along after him.

>   SANDY BANKS
> Do you love me?

>   JOE LOCKE
> Yes — I love your face, your ears, your hair, the back of your knees, the nape of your neck — your fingernails, your toes.

>   SANDY BANKS
> You love all, all, all of me?

>   JOE LOCKE
> Yes — but do you love me?

>   SANDY BANKS
> I love your furrowed brow, your chest, your cock, your shoulders — I love your lips.

>   JOE LOCKE
>   So - you love me totally?
>
>   SANDY BANKS
>   I love you completely...

INT. TERRACED HOUSE — DAY

JOE is sitting in the small bedroom of his messy house. SANDY is trying to force her way into the room, the door is blocked by a wardrobe.

>   SANDY BANKS
>   (hysterical)
>   Open this door you fucking male
>   chauvinist pig!
>
>   JOE LOCKE
>   (calm)
>   Wait a minute...
>
>   SANDY BANKS
>   (hysterical)
>   No — you wait a minute!!!

FADE TO BLACK: Voice-over continues over black screen with very brief shots synchronised to the narration.

A) MONTAGE: Shots of: Exterior of factory; sausage production line; a group of workers; a group of farmers; a grocer's shop; a group of businessmen.

>SANDY BANKS (V.O.)
>What is happening?

>LARRY WENT (V.O.)
>There is a factory in London… a sausage factory. There are workers… farmers… shopkeepers… professionals. And you and Joe are placed in the factory — you are journalists. And here there are workers who work and professionals who profess.

CUT AWAY TO: EXTRACT FROM TELEVISION NEWS BROADCAST: MARGARET THATCHER is speaking in Bruges.

>MARGARET THATCHER
>"We have not successfully rolled back the frontiers of the state in Britain, only to see them reimposed at a European level, with a European super-state exercising a new dominance from Brussels."

>   SANDY BANKS
>   (enquiringly)
>   Professionals who profess??
>
>
>   LARRY WENT
>   Under the surface — everything is
>   changing…

[End of extract]

There were tensions on set, the film was completed and had its premiere and only screening at the 1990 BP Film and Video Expo in Hammersmith. What shone from the screen was Sandy's innocent presence – her youth and beauty trapped forever – the reality of her reflection in the lens recorded 24 times a second in series on a long strip of celluloid. Larry's feeble attempt at political montage and radical polemics lost out to the chemical recording of Sandy's youth. After the screening, what was left of their relationship turned sour.

But there were other memories and other reasons…

II
Shot / Reverse Shot
▶

It was at the Film and Video Expo, funded by a multinational oil corporation, that Sandy's life took a different turn. She was spotted by MTV Europe and signed up to become one of the first *VJs* – her career progressed as she formed an Indy band and took full advantage of the *Britpop* phenomenon. She made money from the music market and when the market lost interest, she got involved in financial consultancy and Internet businesses – just at the right time. In a few short years she gravitated away from Larry, taking his friends and leaving him to get involved with Casey. Larry was not quite bright enough, not quite advanced, dynamic or ambitious enough. He was upset when Sandy abandoned him – his immediate response was to produce a jilted rant on video. He recorded extracts of happy smiling Sandy from MTV, removed the soundtrack, slowed the shots down and froze frames. He created a dislocated montage from these sequences - like an obsessed jilted stalker, he tried to make the personal political. He recorded a long harangue entitled 'Letter to Sandy' which was used as the soundtrack for this montage. Sandy didn't speak to him again for a long time – and when Casey got involved with him – Sandy didn't speak to her either. She wasn't angry with them – she just had more interesting things to do.

Extract From:
LETTER TO SANDY (1990)[8]
By Larry Went

SERIES OF SHOTS

A) MONTAGE: Series of still frames and slow-motion shots of SANDY BANKS taken from off-air recordings of MTV Europe.

          LARRY WENT (V.O.)
     Dear Sandy, in the press release that we sent out with our new film, "Everything's Fine", we prefer to use a picture of you appearing on MTV.
     We would like to discuss the problems raised by "Everything's Fine" that are highlighted by these images of you.
     We do not wish to avoid talking about "Everything's Fine" but believe that your act of shacking up with Joe and the military industrial complex that MTV represents is an act of betrayal against all those whom Thatcher has trampled underfoot.
     I would like spectators and journalists to analyse these

---

[8] Inspired by Godard's 'Letter to Jane' (1972)

stills from your work as a TV presenter — to compare them to your appearance in our film. To consider your pose, dress and attitude and to consider what is being sold in these images. These images that you look at now sum up the theme of our film more clearly than the film itself. For a very simple reason: It asks the question that is by no means new, but is still relevant at the start of the 1990s:
(pause)

    "What part should intellectuals play in the revolution?"...

[End of extract]

Larry had believed too many of the radical pamphlets and Crass lyrics that he read as a teenager and subsequently wasted years – waiting for something to happen instead of making it happen. Sandy had lived a full life and she was still only young – she was bored now – bored, bored, bored – and Larry reminded her of something. There was another part of this story that had affected her more than she had ever admitted, and now that Larry was coming back into her life, she had a floating feeling in her stomach and a lightness in her head that made her want to reclaim something that they had both lost in those early years.

Chapter 15:
Stolen Kisses

Joe Locke was a comrade of Larry's from the first days at North East London Polytechnic. They had shared student accommodation in a Canning Town tenement block; sandwiched between the Imperial Chemical Works and the Mattessons Sausage factory (that was to later feature in Larry's film).

The student estate was grim – very different to Larry's childhood in the stockbroker belt. It was a time of AIDs, unemployment and heroin; 1986 and Thatcher was wreaking change in the world – just 'ask Sid'. None of the changes seemed to help Larry – none of it was aimed at helping art students. The power of imagery was being used to sell ideologies and products – but they were the wrong products as far as Larry and Joe were concerned. Surrealism was being used to sell cigarettes and photomontage was being used by the Saatchi brothers to sell Thatcherism. Charles Saatchi was buying and collecting art in order to fill a disused paint factory that would eventually help support the 1990s *'Britart'* phenomenon... this was all anathema to Larry and Joe as they sat in their late-eighties dirty student flat, eating cheese on toast and plotting the revolution that they thought their art would inspire.

The two travelled daily to the art school at Greengate House in Plaistow where they each had a small studio space and were left to their own devices. Joe sat in a corner, absorbing theory – reading books by Lyotard, Debord and Benjamin. Larry knew the names on the covers but never read the books – he played about with technique: Superficially replicating other artist's work without really understanding it. In retrospect, Larry could see that Joe was studying the market; preparing for a time when he could seize the opportunity. Joe was serious - Larry was playing. When Joe finally produced a work of art, it had a clear concept and an intent that was fully formed – it fitted neatly into the conceptual structure of the art-world.

The two shared each other's food, record collections and ideas and, after the first year at Poly' and the summer break, they moved into a squat in Upton Park – close to West Ham's football ground. Larry's perception of his partnership with Joe was blinkered – he was obsessive and only saw relationships from his own viewpoint (it was the same with his love affair with Sandy). He didn't realise that Joe was close to his brother or that Sandy could think for herself.

In 1989 Joe assisted Larry on *Everything's Fine*, offering to act and help form the script. Joe saw it as a little bit of help – he was patronising Larry. Larry saw it as a collaboration without realising that, in collaborative terms, he wasn't even the equivalent of Andrew Ridgley to Joe's George Michael.

Joe had a pet rat and, at the end of the third and final year, the rat died. Larry heard it in the night – speaking English plain as day, "Joe!" it cried pitifully as it slipped away to rat heaven. The rat died the night of the BP Expo in 1989 – the night that Joe went off with Sandy – the night that they made love for the first time on an unmade mattress in a dirty squat.

It was the end of Larry's course, his friendship and his love.

▶▶

Joe and Sandy's relationship was short-lived; to them it was nothing but to Larry – to Larry – it ate away at him for twenty years. It was always there, just under the surface of his seemingly placid disposition, a sadness connected to disappointment – a sadness based on an emotional immaturity that he hadn't been able to admit to. There was something intangible that they had lost and, somehow Larry's recurring dream of death was linked to that disappointment.

Joe moved back to his hometown of Brighton where he joined up with his twin brother, John, to form an art collective: The Locke Brothers. The Brothers were tall, enigmatic and intellectual. They were well-spoken, upper middle-class boys with fashionable working-class pretensions. John was quiet and almost invisible, Joe was the voice of the Locke Brothers; his mood-swings and aggressive attitude consistently employed in the support of his art practice. The Brothers fine-tuned their image and developed a plan to invade the stuffy art establishment. They both took to wearing black and keeping their hair closely cropped. They blended effortlessly into the art-world where they furnished high-class galleries with their carefully constructed minimalist automatons.

Larry faded back to Surrey and watched the careers of others develop and grow as he sank back into fantasy – into the arms of Casey - Sandy's realist sister. Casey - who became his support, focus and burden. He had tried to stay in contact with Joe but the Locke Brothers were too busy – too successful. In the end it had become embarrassing for him. Larry the failed filmmaker, moved to Wales with Casey to become a schoolteacher and parent, he was far away from the world of the international art superstars. The ideology of the late Eighties had shifted and it had taken people in different directions; Larry had moved to the periphery, Sandy and Joe were at the centre.

Somehow Larry believed that this Godard affair might help him move back towards his old friends – they must have contacts, they must still be interested in ideas and faces from the past. He felt that he had an excuse now – an excuse to dive back into the world that had left him behind ten years ago – the death of Godard and the surreal events surrounding it were enough to shake him out of his self-imposed exile. He could create his future from this and Casey had pushed him in the right direction – he had to go to London and get help from his old friends.

Chapter 16

Tonite Let's All Make Love in London

Larry was standing on the platform of Colwyn Bay station, it was 6.30am and he was escaping before anyone was awake. He had left the family at home in bed, his students and colleagues would be sleeping too – unaware of his elopement. The station was quiet and dark; lorries and coaches from the Holyhead ferry were streaming along the A55 expressway that runs parallel to the railway line – an informal convoy trailing along an otherwise empty highway. The cool wind whipped silent black dust towards him, a small particle lodged in his eye, as he was trying to remove it, the rails started to sing and the new Pendolino train pulled into the station. He was travelling light, the Godard notebook weighing most heavily on his mind. He stepped up to the train, absorbing the peculiar scent of diesel, disinfectant and defecation that emanates from modern locomotives. He found a vacant double seat and sat next to the aisle so that no one could easily join him. His students would be turning up to an empty classroom again in a couple of hours and he was relieved that he would nearly be in London by then. He was hoping that, with his escape to London – his escape from the little enclosed world that he inhabited, his paranoid ideas and fanciful notions might fade away and he could start to focus on his future. Casey had promised to telephone the college and tell them that he was going to be off sick all week.

"Look Larry – you hardly ever take time off sick. Go away for a whole week, stay with Sandy. You can sign yourself off for a week - and when you

come back, nothing sinister will have happened, nothing will have changed... except maybe you..."

He settled back into the warm seat and stared idly through the window for thirty or forty minutes – absorbing and integrating himself with the rhythm and sound of the train. After stirring and partaking of a reasonable cappuccino from the buffet car, he woke a little and settled down to peruse the mysterious notebook. He carefully laid his own slim black notebook on the small folding tray in front of him along with a black disposable roller-ball pen. He donned white cotton gloves, slowly removed the Godard book from his bag and, with the care of a museum curator, started to leaf through it. He disregarded the majority of the closely written text as he searched for patterns – for some kind of structure. He trawled through the book for some time until he noticed names that were repeated throughout the text – names that were noticeable because they were faintly underlined in pencil. He wrote a list down in alphabetical order:

Luis Buñuel, Jean-Claude Carrière, George Cukor, Alfred Hitchcock, Rouben Mamoulin, Robert Mulligan, Serge Silverman, George Stevens, Billy Wilder, Robert Wise and William Wyler.

A few of the names were well known to Larry, some of these people were responsible for some of the greatest works in film history, and others were less well-known. He made a mental note – he would have to research them and what might possibly link them. Perhaps they were all dead, perhaps they had all been killed by some dark force...

At the back of his mind, he felt that he had seen these names together before – that there was some significance to this cinematic roll call. Next, he slowly re-read the notebook, carefully listing the six numerical sequences, hoping that he could make some sense of them starting with *322/00:15:04(1)*. By the time that he had organised all of this information in his own slim notebook, the train was approaching Watford and he had just enough time to carefully repack his bag before arriving at London Euston having made no sense whatsoever from the lists of names and numbers.

He took no real notice of the other passengers in his carriage as they shuffled and bustled each other down the aisles and onto the platform. He stayed seated and stared idly out of the window... then, amongst all of these strangers from his train, he saw a familiar face. The peculiar features of Dewi Winkle were purposefully heading along the platform. As he looked, Dewi appeared to glance directly at him... was he looking through the window or at his own reflection? It was difficult for Larry to tell. He started to panic again – subtly - but deep in his gut, he began to panic.

Why was Dewi on the train? Is he following me? Did he see me with the notebook?

Just a few days ago, Dewi had been a complete stranger – yet now, this strange looking character was linked to his brother, the funeral, his trip to see Sandy... Maybe he was involved with the burglary and the deaths. He seemed to have invaded Larry's life and dreams and it didn't feel comfortable. He sat back in his seat as the passengers dispersed, took out his 'phone and was about to call Sandy when paranoia swept over him, *"I'd better use a payphone"* he thought, in the naïve belief that this would somehow offer him security from the dark forces that were trailing him.

He made his way up to the crowded concrete concourse where a large group of people stood, rooted to the spot, staring just above his head as he aimed for the nearest 'phone box. The crowd of fixed humanity was standing, turned to stone like the *Seven Witches of Cowey Sale* – staring up at the huge Telescreen that stood centrally above the 'phone box. Perhaps all of these people had broken a pact that they'd made with a superior power – or maybe they were just waiting for their trains to arrive.

He called Sandy from the payphone but there was no reply.

She'll be at work... I'll have to kill some time... it was stupid to come so early.

Instinctively, Larry headed for the South Bank. He felt drawn to the Royal Festival Hall, the Hayward Gallery and – most of all – to the National Film Theatre. This was the place where he had first fallen in love with cinema – where he had seen *Breathless, Blow-up* and *Belle de Jour*. He had come here with Sandy, later with Casey and often on his own. He recollected seeing *Alice in the Cities* there without subtitles – not needing to understand the German dialogue as the universal language of film spoke to him. Here he fell in love with people that he would never meet and places that he could never visit: Jean Seberg is alive and beautiful, London is swinging and Catherine Deneuve is a young woman. In cinema – the dead are immortal, history is trapped and youth is eternal.

He could have taken the tube to Waterloo but; partly through fear of terrorism, partly through a desire to retrace the steps of *his* youth, mainly to get some air and feel the warm spring sun on his face; he headed off on foot. His route took him past the British Museum, Covent Garden, The Embankment, over the Thames and down to the National Film Theatre. London hadn't changed much. He passed the same pubs and cafés, the skyline seen from Hungerford Bridge had an additional gherkin but otherwise remained the same. The Royal Festival Hall was being excavated and refitted – London doesn't stand still but the pace of change is fairly glacial. The city's film culture had changed: The London Filmmakers' Co-op had gone, along with most independent cinemas and midnight movies... *The Scala, The Everyman, The Ritzy* – they had been the cinemas to go to in the late Eighties. The NFT was still there however, a reassuring reminder of the canon of cinematic excellence. Whatever they were showing would be good enough for Larry, he had decided to watch a film for old-time's sake before attempting to meet up with Sandy.

As he entered the glass-fronted bar of the NFT, he glanced around – half expecting to see faces from the past scattered around the modernist interior. He recognised the serious attire and demeanour of the bar's inhabitants but the faces had changed. Time had passed – in his head Larry knew that he had moved on, but his heart remained in that brief period of time when he thought that he could do anything – that he had the power and intellect to change the world. With age had come cynicism, regret and the slow entropy of his neurons.

Must fight against ... it... a film will help re-connect my neurons – a film will heal my chaotic confusion – give me new hope – re-connect me... I wonder what they're showing?

Larry walked into the foyer, scanning the posters and listings,

The Cinema of Pavel Juráček – I've never heard of him but it must be good stuff.

He looked at the screening times and chose *A Case for the Young Hangman*, a Czech film from 1969. He had an hour to kill so he returned to the café and took a strong black coffee to one of the outside tables. He decided to sit opposite an attractive young woman and ask her for a cigarette... why not – he's not really trying it on – he's nearly twice her age. She looked in her early twenties, had a Louise Brooks bob, was reading a slim volume of poetry and smoking a French cigarette.

"Err..." Larry caught her eye and smiled. "Would... er... would you have a spare cigarette that I could...?"

She looked up from her book and stared directly at him, her eyes lingering for slightly too long and he fell in love – like that – straight away – no question – like Cary Grant and Eva Marie Saint on a train. It was the type of brief, intense passing love that vanished with the encounter.

"Sure..." she had a North European accent, was beautiful, intelligent and behind the reach of Larry. He had travelled through time to reach this stage of his life – she could be any one of a number of missed opportunities from his youth; girls that he met at parties, in clubs and bars – they had all sailed by leaving regret and yearning in their wake. She passed him a cigarette, got up to leave, leant over and lit it for him. He noticed her vanilla scent and the title of her book, '*Nudisme*' – he wanted to ask her what was in it but he couldn't or didn't and she was gone. He watched her stroll away and fetishised the elements that made her a woman for him – the hair, the legs, the sandals. He thought about her feet, her toes – he longed to hold her feet and stare at her naked toes – but he was left sitting under Waterloo Bridge on a sunny spring morning – alone and suddenly feeling that he hadn't a care in the world. A coffee and a cigarette – separately they are good, but together – together they soak through your body and lift your soul. They kill you, yet they give you a glimpse of immortality. He killed his hour drinking coffee, thinking about the girl and forgetting his suburban life before heading away from the sun, down into the dark depths of the sparsely attended matinee screening of *A Case for the Young Hangman*.

Two hours later, he strolled out onto the South Bank of the Thames – light, reborn by the cinematic experience. The real world seemed somehow more real than before. He had shed his paranoia and called Sandy from his mobile 'phone – this time she answered.

"Hi! Oh Larry, Larry, Larry – I've been expecting to hear from you… Look I'm right in the thick of it now – busy, busy, busy… I'll meet you at Joe's *opening* tonight – it's on Cork Street…"

"When?"

"Oh – about sevenish – look – I can't really speak now…"

"Where?"

She hung up. He bought *Time Out* magazine to find out where exactly this *opening* was, then scanned the current exhibitions and planned a quick cultural fix to kill the rest of the day.

▶▶|

Sevenish soon arrived and Larry strolled from Piccadilly, down to Cork Street with a little trepidation. His cultural fix had made him feel like a fish out of water – he hadn't seen a familiar face all day, the soles of his feet were sore from traipsing around galleries and he was suddenly desperate to feel as if he belonged – to see Casey and the kids again. He had come from a place where there were few people – where too many people knew his business, to a place where there were thousands of unknown and disinterested faces. He almost felt as if he'd liked to have bumped into Dewi again.

The last light of a London dusk spread around the stuffy town. City life was heading home or out for a night that smelled bad – an early evening befuddled, half-drunk and stinking of fags – a human mass staggering back towards cramped trains, crowded buses and pokey accommodation. As he turned the corner into Cork Street, his urban negativity was swept away by the sight of Sandy. She was standing outside the LockeArts gallery wearing a short black linen dress, black tights and pinstripe Converse All-Star boots. He paused momentarily and watched her from the corner – she looked so young, her body seemed slim and untouched by time. She smiled and threw her head back, her dark straight hair falling over her shoulders as she talked to a small group of young art students and sipped from a glass of white wine. He started towards her, she turned, their eyes met, she smiled and his heart melted again…

"Larry – Larry, I'm so, so, *so* sorry for leaving you hanging around all day – but I did tell Casey I was going to be…"

"It's fine Sandy, I've been…"

"Oh Larry, she's a fool to let you come back to me like this – I might just want to keep you!" She threw her head back again and chuckled a low, sexy chuckle from the back of her soft throat.

He wasn't sure how to take her – *is she serious?* In a few fickle seconds, he had again distanced himself from Casey, from his parochial job, his anonymous house and even from his beautiful children. Like an amnesiac who can remember nothing of the past decade, he was back in the 1990s art-world. Familiar faces surrounded him, summoning him smilingly back to another place: A world of comfort, supported by the reassuring subsidies and sponsorship of multinational corporations. The Locke Brothers' new

'Gilgamaze' exhibition; supported by Unilather, a subsidiary of the Bland Corporation.

Sandy put her arm in Larry's and led him quietly towards the bustling exhibition. He felt all too fickle but – like his love for the girl in the café – he imagined that he could give up everything to be here and now with Sandy forever. He knew that life wasn't that easy.

They entered the gallery to see that an animated mise-en-scène using models from the Locke Brothers' latest film had been installed in the large, white, box-like space. Roughly based on the Gilgamesh epic; the thirty minute animated film had been a critical and commercial success, with a two week run at London's Institute for Contemporary Arts, followed by a DVD release from the British Film Institute.

The exhibition had developed from this short film and was displayed on a two metre square plinth that sat in the centre of the gallery. At eye level on the tall plinth was a cardboard maze, apparently created from 1950s packaging and paraphernalia. Small robotic creatures travelled around the maze; they appeared to be constructed from Meccano with chicken bones and feathers attached to their bodies and small rodent's skulls for heads. The creatures were carefully constructed and articulated, moving in apparently random patterns, each with their own internal logic. The whole was controlled by a laptop computer inside the glass case that enclosed the maze. The screen of the laptop displayed a retro-style tracking device that appeared to control and chart the movement of the six robots. The maze was lit by a single spotlight suspended from the ceiling where there was also a series of brass mechanical armatures that were causing five hundred pairs of rusty scissors to rotate slowly two metres above the heads of the crowd. The subtle metallic sound of the rotating scissors complemented the murmuring crowd gathered below – talking the type of arty small-talk that you only hear at openings and private views.

The majority of the assembled group were either dressed in the prerequisite black and grey garb of the art intelligentsia or the vintage clothing of art groupies. At the centre of attention were the two brothers; Joe and John. Joe towered above most of the crowd, his shaved head scanned the assembly over the top of a crowd of surrounding sycophants. John was beside him, quietly chatting to his wife, his head hanging low. Suddenly Joe spotted Larry and started towards him, the crowd parted to allow passage through the throng. He seemed genuinely pleased to see Larry,

"Hello you – you enjoying the party?"

"As I've always said Joe… 'The prettiest sight in this pretty world is the privileged class enjoying its privileges'…"

"I think I've heard that line before somewhere – you haven't changed have you? You and your bloody quotes… Look, we're going down to a little Japanese place after…" he turned to Sandy, "you know the place?"

"That noodle place we went to last time?"

"Yeah – see you in a bit – we won't be long – got to speak to Juan again before we finish, but…" he was distracted by someone else in the crowd and moved off apparently floating through the parting crowd.

Sandy and Larry spent a few scant minutes taking in the exhibition before wandering out onto the pavement again. Art students who had come for the free drinks were sitting on the kerb outside, smoking up the atmosphere with hand-rolled cigarettes. As they headed over to the Soba Noodle Bar they said little to each other, each contemplating the past and their own internal reminiscences. They took a table for four at the back of the narrow restaurant and ten minutes later, Joe walked in. He had managed to lose the throng and was in good spirits. When he is in good spirits he is like a northwest wind whipping across Snowdon, the staff became animated at the sight of him and led him to Larry's table. Joe was refreshingly down to Earth and appeared genuinely interested in Larry, he had the type of charming and self-deprecating demeanour that sets one at ease. His thin, well-cut face had a touch of beard growth, a pleasingly angular nose and freshly minted blue eyes that offered empathy as they pierced through Larry's insecurity.

The three spent an enjoyable evening reacquainting themselves until all the past trauma in their relationship had become a strong glue binding them together. Joe agreed to meet up with Larry later in the week, it was too early to discuss the Godard affair, but Larry had managed to drop some hints as he was keen to discuss it with his influential friend. At the end of the evening, Sandy and Larry headed off to West Kensington on the Tube while Joe hailed a taxi and headed East.

Chapter 17
Life Stinks

Larry woke slowly, trying to work out which bed he was in and why it was so uncomfortable. Across the room he could see an unusually large LED clock...

8.30 – I've overslept... where are the bloody kids? Why hasn't Casey got me up? Why am I on the sofa? Why aren't I at home? Where am I?

For some reason, it was taking Larry longer and longer each morning to work out who and where he was. He exhaled, straightened his vision and then his thoughts. The memories from last night were coming back to him now, the exhibition and his reunion with Sandy and Joe. Somehow it was all a bit sketchy, he was feeling that it should have been a major event; a night of passion, or maybe an argument, perhaps a night of high-flying decadent excess... Somehow it had boiled down to a couple of glasses of wine and a bowl of fish soup. There had been a cosy chat, a firm handshake and a peck on the cheek but, for some reason, he had expected more. He recalled how he had travelled back to Sandy's place feeling slightly frisky and hoping for some teenage-style sexual fumbling... but they were both older now and tired, they didn't even speak about their relationship last night. She seemed to want to keep him at arm's length, had poured him a glass of wine and headed off to bed, leaving him in front of the television. He had fallen asleep on the sofa and when he woke, Sandy had gone – this much he knew.

Perhaps I should have just walked in on her and made love to her then and there – maybe I wouldn't have been able to, maybe she wouldn't have wanted me to. She always used to do this – disappear – maybe I should have known she wouldn't stay with me...

He wandered into the quiet, child-free kitchen of Sandy's sleek and modern apartment. The kitchen was clean and uncluttered yet retained her personality through carefully placed tokens from the past and present. He noticed the lack of dust or grease as he stood and absorbed the hygienic silence. Somehow the atmosphere seemed overpowering, he turned to the radio for salvation and searched for a BBC station to suit his mood…

> 1: Too young
>
> 2: Too old
>
> 3: Too reverential
>
> 4: Too smug
>
> 5: Too much banter
>
> 6: Too chummy
>
> 7: No music

None of them seemed to suit so he turned to Sandy's collection of music – for some reason it was all trapped in a particular time; a past when she felt in control, sounds that filled her with the light and life of times gone by. He chose *'Talk Talk Talk'* by the Psychedelic Furs and the music instantly revived him. As he stuck the kettle on, a smile crept across his face and as the boiling temporarily drowned out the music, he studied the photographs stuck to the fridge with plain white magnets: Sandy with crimped orange hair, Sandy in a photo booth with Joe, Sandy on an ugly couch with red eyes, a dog, someone's cat, Casey and Sandy together in school uniform and – hidden behind a Captain Sensible postcard – a picture of Larry with hair and lots of it. He took the faded picture from the fridge and looked at the back:

I♥U… L…XXX

He remembered how he had burnt all of his photographs of Sandy when she went off with Joe – but, before he could begin to get too morbid, the kettle clicked off and 'Pretty in Pink' started to blast around the kitchen.

"Caroline laughs and
It's raining all day
She loves to be one of the girls"

He found himself dancing around the kitchen, reminiscing, a few lines in and he's lying face down on Sandy's empty bed, trying to find a scent that he remembered. He inhaled deeply.

"She doesn't have anything
You want to steal
Well
Nothing you can touch" [9]

As he caught her illusive aroma, the telephone rang – an old black analogue telephone from a 1950s American movie, with a dial and loud bells that rang around the bedroom – the sound of that old 'phone transported him back to the 1980s…

"Phone! Phone!"

He rushed into the living room and lifted the heavy receiver, a familiar voice mumbled from North Wales…

"Larry?"

"Oh - hi Casey!"

"Are you alright?" She seemed to be preparing him for something – he could sense that she was about to confess to something purely from the way she intoned 'alright'… "I… Larry, it was Alfie, he wasn't well and I – I forgot."

"You forgot what?"

---

[9] *Pretty in Pink* by the Psychedelic Furs

"I forgot to call the college for you and... err... I was out... and Rhodri – that's his name isn't it?"

"What's Rhodri got to do with it?"

"He... Rhodri left messages on our 'phone and he seemed to be getting angrier with each one... but I didn't pick them up until, and then..."

"That's great Casey – there's one thing you promise to do and you can't even..."

Her attitude changed... "Look Larry, you're living it up in London and I'm here dealing with head lice and vomit... just 'phone him today – okay?" She slammed the 'phone down and left Larry pondering...

Why is nothing ever finished? Conversations, card games, journeys – why do I have this desire to tie up and finish everything in some kind of... I mean, I'm the master of not finishing anything... Sisters, bloody sisters – I've got Casey hanging up on me and Sandy leaving without even...

He spotted a bright orange Post-it note on the table next to the 'phone.

> *Larry – didn't want to wake you... here's the key – don't forget to call Joe... see you tonight, tonight, tonight!!! P.S. Here's the key – make yourself at home, XXX Sandy.*

Why the bloody repetition? – She even does it on her notes. What is it about tonight and why has she written 'here's the key' twice? – Am I reading too much into all this?

He sat down with his cup of coffee and made a list of his own – black pen on orange paper.

1: Phone Rhodri – explain!

2: Phone Joe – arrange...

3: Phone publisher – check?

4: ???

133

He soon ran out of ideas for his list, it doesn't seem quite enough to fill a day but these things can be taken slowly – strung out to fill the available time. He even had the option of spending the whole day avoiding these three meagre tasks. Before starting on point number one, he took a swift hot shower, opened the small sash window in the living room and stuck his hot head out into the cool morning air. The streets below seemed fairly quiet, he could hear the sounds of people in the neighbourhood going about their important urban business – sirens, traffic and shouting merged with birdsong and the drone of a nearby extractor fan. He relaxed into the soft leather sofa, naked except for a fragrant white towel, and made the first telephone call:

"Oh – hi Rhodri, I…"

"Larry – where exactly are you? I was trying to get in touch with you all day…"

"Yesterday - I know but…"

"It's bad enough that you left your Realism class hanging around with nothing to do – again!" Rhodri wasn't usually quite so direct – he tended to develop the back-story first. For some reason, this time he was getting straight to the point. "I'm sick of this Larry – you're going to have to explain yourself to the Human Resource Director – I can't condone your behaviour any longer…"

"Look Rhodri, I'm not a fucking resource…"

"I might agree with you there, you're certainly not an asset, and don't swear at me – we've got a policy about that… *and* we've got a policy about sickness and reporting sickness; if you're sick, you leave a message with your line manager and set work for the students. You don't just put a note on the door and piss off home – you don't just not bother to turn up. I want you to speak to Trudy and explain yourself to her!"

"I'm not explaining *anything* to *anyone* who can't tell the difference between a human being and a desk. That Trudy's just a hatchet woman – it's the only reason she was given the job!"

"Well – it's funny that you should say that, I'll skip to the end if you like. It looks like your job might be on the line – and you're not helping yourself with this attitude."

"What? What are you talking about Rhodri?"

"Well, you know I wanted to tip you the nod about some changes?"

"Mmm…?" Larry was starting to feel less powerful in his own little self important *job-for-life* world…

"There's been a change in policy towards Film Studies; you're being moved in with the Computing department and we're going to have to drop most of that academic crap that you've been delivering. We're going to concentrate on New Media Production."

"What the hell is that?" Larry was being shifted into a zone of discomfort.

"Well – we've been in consultation with industry and we've had some sponsorship for the Computing Department. The Bland Corporation have decided to pay for a new hi-tech media suite for us, on the proviso that we provide new training courses that suit the modern cultural industries…"

"How do I fit in with all this?"

"It's an ideal opportunity for you. You'll be able to drop all that research bollocks and get into production – that's where your background is, isn't it? You'll have to apply for one of the new jobs – we want to make sure there's a level playing field for all of you – we can't guarantee anything of course – but you stand as good a chance as anyone. New Media is where it's at – you've got to embrace change… even your hero, Godard, knew that…"

"What do you mean, *knew*… I mean are you saying I've got to apply for my own job?"

"What I mean is – if you don't come in and see Trudy today, you'll be on a disciplinary. And *that* will be taken into account when, and if, you apply for one of these new posts…"

"Fuck you Rhodri! I'm in London – how can, how can I come into college? – I'm busy all week – I've got to see Joe Locke tomorrow, you *do* know who he is don't you?"

"So you're not sick? Look – if you don't come in to work tomorrow, then you won't even be considered for one of these new posts – we've drawn up a policy to make the decision fair. You'll be waving goodbye to your secure little job round the corner, your pension and your holidays – you'd never survive in the real world Larry."

The provocation was starting to get to Larry "You know your problem Rhodri – you know your problem? You've got too many policies and not enough principles, what about my current post?"

"It's tomorrow or nothing Larry, tomorrow or nothing – what have you got to say about that Larry?" He was goading him in a way that seemed alien. He had misjudged how far Rhodri could be pushed and how he might react. Their relationship had shifted – all the certainties had gone. Suddenly, here he was, 250 miles from home, in his sister-in-law and ex-lover's flat, about to lose his job.

His focus shifted momentarily as he considered the implications of all this; he looked at the low glass coffee table sitting aligned with the pattern of the oriental rug, he spotted a round stain on the hardwood floor, a small fruit fly crawling into a red wine bottle and drowning in last night's dregs. He had made a decision – he spoke with slow certainty into the heavy receiver…

"I have nothing to say Rhodri… You attend to your business and I'll attend to mine." He slammed the 'phone down and rubbed the bare soles of his feet vigorously on the rough woollen rug. He had pushed and pushed for the last few years and now he had a result. Confident in the security of Sandy's wealth, he had decided to recklessly throw away his little career.

Now was the time to indulge himself again, time to take another good strong coffee into a steaming hot bath and play with Sandy's toy U-boat as he planned his second phone call. Joe will help him. Joe has to help him…

Larry soaked for a full hour in the warm freedom of his redundancy; idly contemplating Sandy's body, considering the future stretching ahead into the night of his newly discovered highway.

Joe will help – how can I ask for help – what do I need help with? If I can find out how Godard was killed and who killed him, if I could...

He dived below the surface of his bubble bath as he considered his options.

Firstly, if this Dark Windows conspiracy tosh is real – someone high-profile like Joe will offer me protection, a way into the cabal. Secondly, if it isn't real – I'll need Joe's help to publicise the death and find out the real reason, the real cause of it all... It all rests on one thing; I've got to convince Joe that the dead man was Godard.

For the second time in one morning, he entered Sandy's quietly organised living room, steaming wet and naked beneath a soft towel. It was time to get dressed; he rummaged through his small backpack, extracting crumpled t-shirt, pants and socks – all black. He tightened a broad leather belt around his slim waist and headed out to make the second call of the day. As he lifted the receiver from its cradle, his own 'phone vibrated in his pocket – a text message, most likely an 'opportunity' to buy or upgrade something - no, it's from his publisher, *Genre Books*. He had been working hard to reach chapter 13 of his fictional book on Surrealism and the Dark Windows; it was to be published this summer.

Larry – sorry to let you know like this but we're going to drop your book. You may be able to get someone else to publish it – but we're restructuring the company. Our plans for a fiction imprint have gone out of the window. It's a dark day for Genre. Sorry again – it really is out of my hands. John R.

Larry was temporarily punctured,

All that work, all that time and effort, wasted?

He wondered why John had scrapped the book today, the same day that Rhodri had given him the boot. If he was still back at home in Colwyn Bay, his response to these setbacks would have been different: He would have sunk back into the depressing routine of his academic year – he would be tidying up his paperwork and fighting for one of these new jobs, he would have dug deeper down into his rut. Here, however, geographically and emotionally removed – ensconced in a temporary respite – he felt that he had a different motivation, one that was forcing him to carve out a new path to who knows where?

Another publisher – that's the one – Genre weren't offering me anything anyway, that small-town publisher was just indicative of my limited ambition. Sandy and Joe will know bigger and better people... why didn't I stay in touch with them? Why didn't I come down here to sort myself out sooner?

It was getting on for mid-morning now. Larry considered his orange note momentarily, took his black pen and carefully drew lines through items one and three. It was now time to address point two, time to 'phone Joe. Larry knew why he hadn't stayed in touch – his ego wouldn't let him go cap-in-hand to his rival; the man who stole his love. But now – now he didn't care; he knew that he could trust Joe and that the water had flowed so far under the bridge that he could ask for help without losing face – he had no face anymore, it was all gone, gone, gone, and trust was more important at the moment – he was sure that he could count on Joe's discretion. He slowly dialled the number that he'd been given last night.

"Good morning, LockeArts gallery, how may I help you?"

The voice was English, female and public school. There was no need for bilingual response here – it was Larry's mother tongue – he felt comfortable as he contemplated the power inherent in the English language and his own implication in that power structure. Its universality approached that of the language of film – but somehow English always falls short.

"Oh hi, could I speak to Joe?"

"Mr Locke? – I'm sorry the artists cannot be contacted on this number. Could I pass on a message?"

Larry left his name and number, hoping that Joe will get back to him – suddenly he had a lot riding on his relationship with Joe – a mere ten minutes later, the 'phone rang.

"Hi Larry, it's me."

"Joe, it was good to see you again last night…"

"What are you actually down here for? We didn't really have an opportunity to discuss…"

"I'm not great on the 'phone – could we get together later today?"

Joe seemed distracted, "Yeah, I know… busy Larry – what about tomorrow morning? 10.00 in the V&A – the William Morris room – you know it? It's a café now, not an exhibit."

"I know the place, that's fine, I want to…"

"Have you got an idea for a new project? Maybe you could come up with a proposal that you can see through to the end this time. Look – sorry old chap, I've got to go, there's someone here with me. It's a hard life being an art superstar you know… 10.00 at the V&A tomorrow."

"That's great could I get your mobile…?"

It was too late, Joe had put the 'phone down and Larry was alone with his inadequacies.

What did he mean; 'see through to the end'…?

He sat down heavily on the couch – it was lower than he expected and he fell into it with the full weight of his body like an old man in a rest home, he tried to cover up his awkwardness despite the fact that no-one was there to see him. He sat and ran through some old ideas, he considered some of the aborted projects that Joe must have been referring to:

II

Pin Drop, *a Science fiction film that never made it beyond the script stage. It was a great concept: In the future a genetic disease has caused the entire human population to lose their sense of hearing. The only humans able to hear are the rich and powerful who have developed an expensive artificial sense of hearing; sound has become power, a commodity available only to those who can afford to hear. Opposed to this system are the audio terrorists who use their own artificial hearing and audio bombs to disrupt and undermine the elite. A battle ensues between the audio terrorists and elite counter-terrorists where* only silence can win *(how's that for a tag-line?). The real beauty of this idea is the opportunity to use sound and silence creatively in the editing – to use the film's soundtrack to tell the story – there would be no dialogue as there is no sound in this future world. The plot and ideology would be communicated visually with harsh and abrasive sounds forcing the viewer to become involved in a battle for silence. It would be the sort of big budget experimental film that was promised but never delivered by the 1960s. Larry had visualised the opening sequence: A camera looks up at a pin as it falls in extreme close-up and slow-motion towards the lens – there is silence and as the pin lands on the lens, it bounces and we hear fractured amplified elements of the sound that it would have made when there was sound...*

II

The Devil's Invention, *a documentary response to the Hungerford massacre: In 1987 sixteen people were murdered by a lone gunmen who allegedly modelled himself on Rambo – a man who appeared to be acting out some kind of American cinematic fantasy. The documentary was to be constructed from talking heads – members of gun clubs talking about what they do and why, talking about their relationship with guns. There was to be no voice-over or commentary – editing and juxtaposition would be used to reveal a fanaticism and madness behind the desire to own and use guns. The message of the film was decided in advance of any filming – it just needed people willing to be interviewed, gun owners who could be convinced that the film would be impartial...*

||

The Call of the Curlew, an idea for a children's book. The concept was to completely re-write a classic work of children's fiction. Each word of the book would be changed, swapped – verb for verb, noun for noun. The structure of the original would remain but the actions and characters would be completely different. *The Call of the Curlew* was a conceptual conversion of *The Wind in the Willows*.

||

None of these ideas had progressed much beyond their initial concept. *Pin Drop* was a half finished script, *The Devil's Invention* remained a proposal and *The Call of the Curlew* didn't quite make it to the second chapter. Perhaps this Godard idea was another dead-end, but he needed to try – to run it by Joe and see if there was some way that fame and fortune could help.

What to do with the rest of the day? He wasn't used to free time – it would have to involve pleasure – a fall back into the butterflies – he would contemplate Sandy, sit in her stylish sofa and watch a film on her large TV. He would drink cups of tea and do nothing – there's always *tonight, tonight, tonight* to look forward to...

▶▶|

The night came. Larry had watched three films; the last one was Hitchcock's *North By Northwest*... each time that he watched it, he picked up something new. Sometimes it was a line of dialogue or concept that he could drop into a meeting at work, other times it was a chat-up line or a put-down. It was anal, and he knew it, but it made him feel clever to quote from movies and compare situations or people to characters from movies, he'd say *"yeah, it was like in..."* or *"you remind me of..."* – everything was referred back to an artificial ninety minute narrative. When he did it, if anyone got the reference, they'd look at him as if to say, "yeah, so what smartarse..." If they didn't get it – it was more of a bemused, blank look and a, *"yeah, anyway..."* He hated blank looks – he wanted everyone to be in on his little world – his little set of references. He expected everyone to know what he was on about –

assuming that his cultural references were universal. But they weren't – that's how the Dark Windows control us, they divide and rule.

Sandy came home late, tired and smelling of tube trains, he kissed her on the cheek and she disappeared for a long, deep bath. She came back into the living room; pink and scented with no make-up and her dark hair tied tightly back in a ponytail. He noticed her soft thighs, slim ankles and narrow feet - she reminded him of Casey – a mysterious Casey from the past – his stomach was in knots of lust, desire, longing.

"Oh Larry, it's been a long day – I'm tired, tired, tired. I was hoping to spend some time with you tonight, you know… catch up on… but, I…" she slowly licked her lips and blushed, avoiding eye contact with him.

"I'd invite you to my bedroom Sandy – if I had a bedroom…"

"C'mon Larry – I'm Casey's sister – remember? Don't get too frisky… *we* were a long, long time ago and I'm a big girl now."

"And in all the right places too…"

"Look – forget it Larry – you're going too too fast…"

"But… there's only one bed Sandy – you know what that means?"

"Yeah, I know exactly what it means Larry – it means that you get to sleep on the couch!"

She slammed the door of her room and disappeared for another night. She *had* got the references but she didn't want to play along. Larry was left with the two glasses of wine that he had poured and a vague feeling that he needed to grow up. He drank both glasses and poured himself another two. When he heard Sandy's light go out, he thought of her lying alone in that warm bed on those crisp white sheets. Then he thought of Casey, Alfie and Lilly and he felt guilt swelling through his drunken body – he savoured the guilt as an indicator of life, as a tonic for those seconds that were slipping away forever – a real emotion for a life that needed to be lived while there was still time.

Chapter 18
Secret Agent

Baden-Powell house is a large hostel and conference centre in the heart of South Kensington's museum district. It was built in 1959, in the same modernist, Le Corbusier style that had influenced the development of Walton-on-Thames town centre. The architect was Ralph Tubbs, who had designed the Dome of Discovery - precursor of the Millennium Dome and highlight of London's Festival of Britain. The Festival was held in 1951 on the South Bank and it was from this that the National Film Theatre and the surrounding cultural quarters slowly grew. There is a crazy myth that the body of Alfred Hitchcock was planted under the foundations of the Dome of Discovery in 1951 after he had completed *Strangers on a Train* - that he was killed and replaced with a look-alike, and that the replacement Hitchcock had created *Rear Window, Vertigo* and *North by Northwest* following Hitchcock's original storyboards with the help of a shadowy organisation. But this was possibly only a myth used to explain another secret that lay buried under the Royal Festival Hall, a secret that was perhaps even less believable.

The first floor of Baden-Powell house overhangs the ground floor – an attempt to free the structure from the ground – a pre-brutist message in brick attempting to point the way to a utopian extra-terrestrial future. The building houses a hostel for scouts when visiting the capital and, on the sixth floor, amongst the conference rooms – with its own private elevator, it houses the London office of the Bland Corporation. This is where Freddie Foulkes deals with British questions – he comes here when a threat to the opacity of his organisation emanates from the British Isles. He was waiting in the meeting room for the arrival of his associate. Magog had recently returned from a second visit to North Wales and was about to receive another dressing-down from his superior. Freddie was pacing around the meeting room, pausing to peer through the Venetian blinds at the traffic on Queen's Gate Mews. He can't quite see the Albert Hall, the Hoop and Toy public house or Dino's Italian Restaurant from here although he was aware that they are only a short walk away. He could quite happily lead a movie tour of Kensington from Baden-Powell house, pointing out the locations used by film-makers who had caused his organisation trouble in the past. He started to mentally run through the narration of his guided tour:

▶

"Good morning and welcome to the first ever movie location tour of Kensington organised by the Dark Windows. If we walk from our office, down towards South Kensington Tube Station we can see where Roman Polanski shot 'Repulsion' in 1965, his film was a portrait of the psychological disintegration of a stunning Belgian beautician, played by Catherine Deneuve. When the extent of his creative power was discovered, we offered him full membership of the Dark Windows and - unfortunately he refused... following this rebuttal, we worked hard to marginalise and criminalise the little fellow. Polanski was replaced by one of our longest serving doppelgangers in 1976 after our brutal campaign to silence him ended in his escape to France and to the production of his final film; 'The Tenant' in which he attempted to codify and describe the conspiracy against him. Polanski played the lead role as the eponymous tenant of a Parisian apartment that appears to hold fantastic secrets. He was murdered after production was complete; the film was then edited by his replacement and, in a bold act typical of the Dark Windows, was transformed and released as an ineffective potboiler.

Let us now head north up Exhibition Row to the Albert Hall... Michael Caine appeared in 'The Ipcress File' at this location. Actors tend to be simpler to deal with and Michael was easy to buy out; all he wanted was the money that he could make from the system, he wasn't an ideologue – money was fine for him. He wasn't even aware of his potential to disrupt the work of the Dark Windows in the 1960s.

Let us now keep travelling North to Holland Park; some of Michelangelo Antonioni's 'Blow-up' was shot here in 1966. The power of a film such as 'Blow-up' can only be guessed at today – the hidden messages in his film nearly fomented revolution forty years ago whereas now they are merely baffling. My predecessor was very proud of the way that he suppressed distribution of Antonioni's films. Some of them might be available for home viewing now - but their ability to affect a mass audience was drowned by our organisation along with the power of cinema in the 1980s. Antonioni wasn't killed; his work was hidden away by the power of vertical integration. 'Zabriskie Point' was his forceful comment on the positive revolutionary potential of the 1960s – made in the USA, it traced the relationship between an Anthropology student and a college drop-out. 'The Red Desert' was his 1964 exposition on alienation, depression and the destruction of eco-systems by post-industrial society. All of these films had an inherent power that was kept from circulation through the simple act of refusing distribution rights. Very few people are likely to want to see these films now and, when they are made available, they will soon be lost in the bloated world of cinephilia..."

II

As he stood, contemplating his cinematic tour of London, the door quietly opened and Magog entered, interrupting his musings. Freddie hadn't had the time to prepare a presentation for today's meeting but the agenda was pretty much the same as last time. Larry Went was a minnow and Freddie didn't like spending time on small fish... it pissed him off to have to deal with minor issues.

"So Maggy – you didn't manage to remedy this problem, this hangover from the Godard swap?" Magog responded with silence, "You were supposed to deal with this no-mark and instead, he's come down here to us – he should be scuttling back into his little cave with his fellow troglodytes... but, no – he's down here hobnobbing with some of our close colleagues..."

"We... I tried to warn him off Freddie – I tried to undermine his confidence, the subtle route usually works with his type."

"When that didn't work, why didn't you try a more direct approach?"

"There were witnesses and – the law – friends, relatives, members of *The Order* – it would have been too messy, they wouldn't have let us get away with it..."

"*The Order*? *The Order* were there – who, I mean how?"

"I was mistaken about someone – someone that I thought could help – they, they let me down... It was a little bit messy..."

"Well it could get messy down here – and it's closer to home. You know of the organisations that would like to see us lose control, you know that *The Order* are active here in London – they might see Went and his interference as an opportunity to wrest control of Dark Windows. I'm already concerned that something is not quite right with the Godard replacement. You know that if they ever get concrete proof of our activities, the whole system could unravel... We need to make contact with the new Godard and I want you to take personal responsibility for the Larry Went issue, you will report back to me in Berne – it's your job now and you have to see it through or..."

Freddie left the final *'or'* hanging – Magog quietly opened the heavy door and left. It was time for him to decide whose side he was on and to who he owed his allegiance. As he left the meeting room, a laugh echoed from one of the hostel bedrooms – a harsh, loud cackle like the Wicked Witch of the West.

⏭

Unbeknown to Freddie and Magog, Larry was within striking distance. He was sitting in the café of the V&A, a short stroll from Baden-Powell House. The Victoria and Albert Museum was well known to Larry. He had worked in the shop there when he was a student and had always had a romantic attachment to the place. The V&A is an imposing edifice in the heart of South Kensington: one of the world's greatest museums, with collections of unrivalled scope and diversity displayed in more than 140 galleries over 7.5 acres. It contains artefacts from around the world, spanning 3000 years of human creativity in applied art and design. It has been statistically proven that, if you studied each object in the museum's collection for five minutes, you would be dead long before you had looked at them all.

Larry had continued to regularly visit the museum over the past few years with his teenage students from North Wales on their annual trip to London. There was a slow but sure leaching of interest each year: The first time that he took them, the students had loved it – they engaged with the immense building and the objects that it contained, but as the years progressed and small interactive screens began to preoccupy them – museums, along with books and cinema seemed to lose their relevance. Never mind that this vast cabinet of curiosities contained the entire history of human creative endeavour – to his students it had become "well boring". Perhaps it was just that he was a year older with each trip, and time, interests, ways of relating to the world move on. He remembered his childhood visits to the V&A being fascinating and exciting – he still got that emotional response walking into the Tate Gallery or the Science Museum, they spoke to him of something bigger – the cathedrals of the atheist. There was a certain smell of climate-controlled galleries – of paint and glue and formaldehyde, the past preserved and displayed. He could gain real joy from an ivory netsuke mouse, a soapstone brick, a naïve wooden Christ or a Utility chair – all of these objects spoke to Larry from the past to the present and spurred him to action – and they were not well… boring.

Take the tiles on the floor of the V&A's William Morris room for example: Industrially fired red earth moulded into two repeating shapes; a large octagon and a smaller square; the octagons but up against each other along four of their sides leaving a space for the small squares... perfect tessellation of two multiples of two simple shapes, human endeavour and design enables these simple shapes to lock together. To Larry the floor of the café where he sat was the epitome of mass-production: Simplicity, Functionality and beauty. He had been sitting in the green gloom of the early morning café – waiting for Joe. He had been served a hot cappuccino and had noticed that the catering staff hailed from across Europe – English appeared to be their common international language. There were no other customers in the room - the staff were hovering, waiting for him to finish so they could clean the table, collect the cup. He was considering the correlation between the tessellation of the tiles and the tessellation of the countries of Europe – the global jigsaw puzzle that is the expanding European Union. He looked up from the floor to see the silhouette of Joe entering the stately space.

"Hello Larry – good to see you again!"

"Joe – you know I always wondered if you really missed me..."

"You're still the same guy – bullet-proof, time-proof... coffee?"

"Got one thanks."

"Had breakfast?"

"No thanks – it's all too glutinous for me."

He called the waiter over with a glance, "I'll have an Americano – make it *very* hot – and a pain au chocolat. You want a banana with that cappuccino Larry?"

"No Joe..."

He sat down on the lightweight aluminium chair that contrasts strongly with the dark William Morris interior "So – you're working in a little Welsh college?"

"You say it like it was hard to comprehend..."

"Well it is…"

"It's very simple: I talk a little, shuffle some paper and each month I take home a small pay-check. I pay the mortgage and buy food – with that; the bank and supermarket make a small profit, which they invest in capital. They call it wage slavery – you may have heard of it somewhere…?"

"I may have, but it wasn't from you!"

"I didn't mean to patronise you Joe – I didn't want to hurt your feelings…"

"My feelings – I hid them somewhere nearly twenty years ago when Sandy left me, I haven't been able to find them since…"

"Join the club – have you looked for them?"

"Only in my wallet Larry – it's a nice room isn't it?"

"Don't know Joe – I'm not sure about William Morris, it's all a bit patronising this Arts and Crafts, Guild stuff… making things with your hands – am I supposed to admire it?"

"I'd like to know what you're down here for…"

"I need your help Joe."

"Just like old times eh? I always liked you and I could use you if you need a job…"

"I always liked you because we were smart together and I could use *you* – but I'm not smart anymore Joe – I'm a teacher…"

"So what do you want from me after all these years? I mean – I know about *your* job, mine is a little precarious but I earn considerably more…"

"So I've heard – you ready to hear me out?"

"I'm all ears…"

"Well Joe, this may sound ridiculous but…" Larry explained the whole story; from the 'photo on the phone to the notebook, the police, the card game, the funeral and the burglary. Joe listened intently, carefully – nothing seemed to disturb his tender but disengaged gaze. When Larry had finished, Joe took the spoon gently from his saucer and stirred his coffee with a slow, determined rotation of the thumb and forefinger. He placed the metal spoon on his bottom lip and winced...

"Have you still got this notebook? I'd like to see it."

Larry took the book from his canvas army-surplus shoulder bag and passed it to Joe. "Look. I'm trusting you - I don't know anyone else with your clout. I want you to look at it – make what you will and then give it back... it's my security blanket."

"You know Larry – I still like you, John does too... and Sandy. We, we want to help you out. This may seem a little odd to you, but we *have* seen stranger things and... and I have an idea. I was expecting to offer you a job this morning, you know – I, I thought that you might be wanting to work for me but I can see another route opening now. I've never met Godard personally but I do have dealings with Switzerland. Juan, my dealer, keeps our finances in order there and he's heard that Godard is involved in something – that he has been collecting money. He's been raising money for a major project... a film project. Apparently, he's always coy about the nature of his planned films – he raises finance on a title alone while maintaining complete creative control. He quite often completely changes the nature of the film once he has the finance; a documentary can become a drama, a drama can become a musical – it's the sort of uncertainty that causes problems for the moneymen. Juan told me that all Godard had was a title and a large sum of money – and now it seems to have gone quiet in Switzerland..."

"What was the title – what was his project called?"

"I don't know – it was something French; *Fenêtres Foncées* – not sure exactly what it means, something to do with windows and fences I suppose..."

"It's not *fences* – it's *dark*, it's Dark Windows Joe!"

"Right – your little conspiracy eh?" Joe started to talk and Larry let him – he started to talk about seemingly disconnected events in the way that artists do… it meant something to Joe but Larry couldn't quite follow it…

"Tarkovsky's *Sacrifice* – have you seen it Larry? It's a powerful film – it speaks directly to the soul Larry and films that speak directly to the soul are a threat to the plutocracy. Tarkovsky was killed for making *Sacrifice* – for explaining in the opening sequence that small acts repeated ritually can change the world – that a system can change the world. From the grave, his Polaroids could change the world – do you know what I mean? It all comes down to the long shot – the rejection of montage as a statement of revolutionary power – it's European Art Cinema Larry, think about *Sacrifice, Satantango, Caché* – think about it Larry! Powerful Art is dangerous to the system – when film becomes poetry it becomes a threat, Buñuel knew this and escaped to Mexico before the Americans could get him – before Franco could get him. And then there was Ingmar Bergman, he escaped to an island and attempted to help Tarkovsky. It's obvious really - Tarkovsky is buried in Paris right? And there's a whole history of Russian émigrés in Paris the place is steeped in treachery and defections: Stravinsky for example – he was reactionary in Europe as an émigré but when he returned to the USSR in 1962 he sang the praises of the Soviets… and Gorky, Maxim Gorky lost his soul to Stalin - he knew about the violence and lived in exile. When he returned, Stalin gave him palaces and Gorky became a champion of the NKVD. He tried to repent in his final years but no one was convinced… What you've got to see Larry is that Soviet Social Realism was a straitjacket. Did you know that Stalin's police once cut the eyes out of a beautiful Russian actress for no reason, except that those eyes had power! Do you understand what I'm getting at Larry?"

"Well I get the general gist of it – but you're throwing too many references at me, and you're not really explaining it…"

"What I'm saying Larry is that your idea about Godard may not be as crazy as it seems... I mean Godard could easily appear to be a threat to someone..."

"Don't you think that Godard was far too obtuse – how could he be a threat to anyone – does anyone listen to him?"

"But what if he was about to make a new film – to re-invigorate Europe? Europe's power is on the rise - it has *Sticky Power* – it has cultural capital and history... and the concept of a powerful Europe would upset many people – many vested interests..."

"So what are you getting at Joe – in relation to this notebook – in relation to helping me?"

"I'd like you to go to Switzerland Larry – to Rolle, investigate your theory about Godard." He looked around the empty café, moved closer to Larry and lowered his voice. "This may sound strange - but I belong to a group of people who are actively planning a revolution, it may be hard to believe but we aim to change, not only the world, but history – we plan to reveal the truth about the past and... and you can help. We want you to attempt to meet up with Godard – find out if he is there and if it's really him. If we can get evidence of Godard's death, it will open up a historical archive that will destroy the Dark Windows: When the world finds out that all of their idols have been killed, replaced or silenced – there *will* be a revolution. Godard may not seem important, but he is the tipping point. Think what happened when they killed Princess Diana – they didn't expect that reaction."

"But that reaction was fuelled by the tabloid press – it wasn't a natural – sociological event..."

"Who's to say that we haven't got powerful people on our side? Now multiply the Diana effect by a hundred, by a thousand – by every cultural icon you can think of..."

"Are you serious? I mean – what if I meet him and he is the real Godard?"

Joe sat back in his chair and smiled inscrutably. "I could be wrong – I can give you a fall-back. It could be an interesting project – a video project, an installation, a series of photographs – let's call it a commission from LockeArts. We'll let you exhibit your findings in our gallery and then see if we can't help you make a living out of it. I'll give you an advance now and you let me know by the end of the week – let me know if you want to go through with it, okay?"

Joe stood slowly and handed Larry an envelope containing a wad of bank notes – Euros - the depth of the wad was measured in centimetres. He started to leave, holding up the Godard notebook and tapping it idly as he left, "sort out your journey and I'll get this back to you before you leave…"

Larry was left alone in the heart of the V&A – an East European waitress smiled at him as she cleared the table, but before he could fall in love again, he stood – put the envelope in his jacket pocket and left. A question was forming in his head – he had taken the money but should he accept the commission?

Chapter 19
I Know Where I'm Going

It was Wednesday now – get through the day and the week will be nearly over, cruising towards the weekend. It felt strange being detached from a job, a nine-to-five routine in a five-day week. It was liberating Larry's soul to be free of the necessity to work... it was an illusion, a pleasant illusion. He hadn't 'phoned work or gone back to speak to Trudy in 'Human Resources', he hadn't 'phoned his publisher about his rejected book and he hadn't even spoken to Casey in the past twenty-four hours. In his pocket he had a wad of Euros and the key to Sandy's apartment, he felt liberated yet he knew that very soon – if he did lose his job in North Wales – very soon he would have to find a way to pay the mortgage and put food on the table. Perhaps he could sign up for Unemployment Benefit if it still existed – he'd never been on the dole under a Labour Government - that would be a new experience.

As he felt himself slipping into negativity, he refocused and started to contemplate the new project – the Godard investigation, the LockeArts commission. There was no time to start worrying about domestic issues; it was time to keep moving on – he had made the break, he now had to forge a new life and whoever wanted to come along for the ride was welcome.

He was sitting on a warm Wednesday evening in West Kensington, staring idly through the window, watching the clouds turn pink and increase in definition as he waited for Sandy to return home. He had been in her apartment for a few hours now and had knocked up a Greek salad with some hummus, tomato salsa, guacamole, crudités, pappadums and nachos. He decided that the time has come for a glass of red and was just extracting the cork when he heard Sandy's key in the lock.

She burst in full of energy – "It's over!" he looked at her and raised an eyebrow, "the start-up… it's over Larry and it looks like we stand to make a fortune! They're selling, selling, selling…"

"So you've got some time – some head-space this evening?"

"Sure Larry – I'm buzzing and I know I've been a little distant but it's all over now… it's time we had a chinwag, a good old one…"

They sat down to their dippy fusion of a meal and between slurps and crunches, they discussed Larry's ideas. He filled her in on the whole Godard story: his trouble at work, his paranoia and self-doubt at home. She listened with a similar intensity to Joe… in itself, this made Larry paranoid as he couldn't see why anyone would be interested in him… but he cast his doubt aside and offloaded the whole affair all over again. When he had finished, Sandy dipped her manicured finger into her glass of red wine and ran it around the rim until the vessel began to sing. She stopped, put the glass slowly to her full, red lips and took a sip… all the while looking directly into Larry's eyes. There was a sudden uncomfortable silence as they both realised how close they had become in a few short, fractured days – how Larry's imagined animosity and Sandy's contrived disinterest had faded to be replaced by a mutual affection. She broke the silence…

"Joe's right you know – we care enough about you to offer you a route out… you've done your time in that pokey dull job – we can help you, I mean, if you're not too proud? I could pay your mortgage for a couple of months while you get started, I mean I'll do it for Casey – she *is* my sister and it's nothing to do with you if I want to give my sister a little windfall. With the money that I've made today from just one little deal – I could pay off your whole mortgage five times over…"

"That just about sums it up – the distribution of wealth in this country, in the world – it just about…"

Sandy cut him off before he could get on his soapbox, "Like I said Larry – if you're not too proud… just forget about money – we'll sort you out, if you can sort yourself out…"

"Sort myself out?"

"You don't need that chip on your shoulder, you don't need to be full of doubt – and paranoia's a waste of time; that's just the result of too much teenage drug abuse. You need to mentally move out of that Welsh backwater – you need to follow this Godard idea through and see what happens. One thing that I can tell you is that this conspiracy stuff might sell books but there's no substance to – there's no point in taking it too seriously…"

"That's not what Joe said…"

"Joe, schmo – he's an artist, he makes money from illusions – from expanding simple concepts into extravagant conceits. To him your idea is just that – it's a good idea, one that might expand the reach of LockeArts, give him some more publicity… it's his roll-up smoking polytechnic mentality coming to the fore…"

"So you think it's just a wind-up – that Joe and John are going to turn me into one of their installations?"

"It's possible, it's possible… I can just see you now - a little tin wind-up Larry. I can see Joe and John winding your little key and sending you scuttling off round a little maze that they've constructed for you – while they stand over like evil puppet-masters! Lighten up Larry - you see conspiracies everywhere. Not everyone is against you – the world isn't as sinister as it might seem."

"But you didn't hear Joe – he was talking about Stalin and people having their eyes plucked out – like, like – who's that guy in the myth?"

"Oh – I know the one you mean – he plucked his own eyes out because he'd killed his dad or his mum or someone… or do you mean King Lear? Someone has their eyes plucked out in that – it's a very common theme…"

"Yeah – but it's not very pleasant…"

They spent the rest of the evening chatting about the past, sitting together on the soft white leather sofa in Sandy's clean, uncluttered living room. Their bodies touched lightly, occasionally. It seemed natural for Sandy to lean on Larry – for their bare feet to touch, for his hand to rest on her knee, for her hair to fall across her face as she smiled and blushed… they felt comfortable together… but before they could get too comfortable, Sandy yawned, stretched, kissed Larry on the cheek and quietly headed off to bed. Leaving him contemplating the scent of her downy neck, the way that her breasts had brushed against him as she gently kissed him and the sight of the back of her knees disappearing into the bathroom. He felt at peace this evening – he didn't feel the need to try and force himself on her with some corny dialogue from a film. He knew that *whatever would be, would be…* and he knew *that* was a corny song from a different Hitchcock film – he hadn't quite liberated himself yet from the Dark Windows and he began to wonder if tonight's dreams would be his own.

▶▶|

The next morning, the ringing 'phone pulled Larry back into consciousness from his dreamless sleep. He woke knowing exactly which sofa he had slept on and that Sandy had already left for work. His eyes seemed to be functioning more effectively and his body didn't ache. It must be the plan – the project… having a clear goal has physical effects, maybe it *was* all psychosomatic; the double-vision, the aching joints, the gluten intolerance – maybe his doctor was right to dismiss it all as the outward signs of an inner entropy. The 'phone kept ringing angrily. He lifted the dark receiver and heard the voice of Chris for the first time since that night at Ian's cottage - the night before the funeral.

"Alright Larry mate – we need to meet up. I understand that you're heading off to Switzerland…"

"What? – How did you know about that?"

"Sandy called me from work – we're early birds mate…"

"I didn't know you and Sandy…"

"We move in the same circles, you know that – I see her around. Anyway - she knows that I know Switzerland and it just happens that I'm heading up to Davos for the weekend to check out the resorts for this year's guide… I've got freebies in the hotels there mate, if you want to buy yourself a flight I'll show you around and take some photos for this project you're working on…"

"What project?"

"I don't know – Sandy said you were working on an exhibition for the Locke Brothers…"

"News travels fast – I mean I hadn't decided what I'm doing yet… I've still got this Surrealist book to sort out…"

"Yeah – it's a small world, you got a pen? Look – Sandy wanted me to encourage you, to get you moving. You need to book a flight – I'll give you the airline's number. I've got to be in Davos on Friday but you'll need to get a flight to Geneva if you want to go to Rolle – that's where you're going isn't it? Then you can get a train to meet me up in the mountains… Okay?"

"Rolle – yeah that's where Godard lives but I didn't say anything to Sandy about Rolle or…"

"Look I'm flying out of Gatwick at 10.15 on Friday - you got a pen?"

Larry took a pen from the pot next to the 'phone – they all seemed to be freebie pens with logos printed on them, the sort that come through the letterbox in an envelope with a picture of a starving child, a frozen old lady or a dead cat.

"Okay Chris – give me the number…" He took an *Oxfam* pen and started to scribble the number but the pen didn't work, "hang on!" he took a *Help the Aged* pen from the pot but it was all dried out, "Just a minute Chris, I can't find a… go on…" the *RSPCA* pen leaked on his hand, in desperation he took the final pen and wrote the number down in one smooth action – he looked at the side of the functioning pen – *Credit Suisse*.

Chapter 20:
Until the End of the World

Switzerland – cheese, chocolate and snowy peaks – perhaps the stereotype hides something, another land that only the Swiss know. In *The Third Man*, Orson Welles famously improvised a description of the country – saying that it had:

"brotherly love... five hundred years of democracy and peace and what did that produce? The cuckoo clock."[10]

This is pretty far from the truth but it has stuck – a chocolate-box vision of a cheesy landscape. It stuck, in spite of the fact that the cuckoo clock originated from Germany's gateau-bearing Black Forest and the federation of Switzerland was formed, not through years of peace, but as a response to centuries of invasions and civil wars. In many ways, the country offers a model for the future of humanity: There is no single language, religion or race – power is decentralised and the people have regular referenda on all issues. Like the European Union (which the people decided *not* to join in 1993), Switzerland has clear regional differences and a range of strong folk traditions based on pre-Christian Celtic festivals. The Swiss Cantons, like the countries of Europe, are fiercely proud of their culture, deeply conservative and tainted by historical claims of collaboration with evil, corrupt forces. However, thanks to its internal coherence, the Swiss federation has managed to remain neutral through two world wars and allowed its people to stay fairly healthy, wealthy and happy. It lies at the heart of Europe harbouring artists,

---

[10] The Third Man (1949)

intellectuals, and international organisations in its cheesy, chocolaty, mountainous cradle. Zürich in the north was home to the Dada anti-artists who, at the height of the First World War, sowed the seeds of Surrealism and contemporary art practice with their nihilistic performances at the Cabaret Voltaire. Larry, however, was heading to southwest Switzerland, to the French-speaking canton of Vaud; the place that Charlie Chaplin escaped to when the American government blacklisted him, the place where Graham Greene is buried and the place where Jean-Luc Godard lived. Like Wales, Vaud is a Protestant region with Celtic roots – it stretches from the Alpine mountains down to the shores of *Lac Léman.* Godard's hometown of Rolle rests on the shores of the lake – it is a prosperous, anonymous, secretive place that registers even less on the world's radar than Colwyn Bay or Penmaenmawr – yet this quiet town contained an artist who has changed the way that the human world represents itself.

▶▶

Larry met his brother at Gatwick on Friday morning and their uneventful British Airways flight, with its tiny tins of fizzy drinks and trolley of chicken wraps, had landed on Geneva's single concrete runway on time. They passed through the uniform international airport facilities – Larry had vaguely recognised the exterior of the building – he'd seem it before somewhere... then it dawned on him: *The Calculus Affair*! This was the airport that Tintin passed through on the trail of Professor Calculus. He recalled how the story involved a device created by Calculus that could destroy cities through the use of ultrasonic sound – a device that had been purloined by the wicked *Bordurian* dictator *Kûrvi-Tasch.* Larry thought about the Balkanised Europe of the 1950s and how the Cold War was becoming a distant memory for this continent, how the weapons and dictators were different in the 21st Century. As he walked out into the crisp Alpine air, he noted that it was cooler than London – it must only be about 3 or 4 degrees centigrade. The world outside the entrance seemed quiet, provincial and underdeveloped – the same

European cars that crushed into the UK's overcrowded road system sat innocently against the terminal's windows. There seemed to be few concerns about terrorist threats here and no dark, American-style trucks driving CORGI registered families to Benidorm. It was all very sedate and sophisticated. In the distance, Larry could make out an electrified train track stretching towards the low-rise buildings of what he assumed to be Geneva city centre. Chris climbed into a Volvo taxi that was waiting attentively in rank.

"See ya later bud! I'll be at the *Belvédère* in Davos – you can't miss it – it's a huge white thing with mountains behind it – on the Promenade – ask for me at reception, you can share my room." His voice faded into the Alpine air as the taxi drifted away. "Good luck in Rolle – remember the *Gai-Remuez*!"

Larry was left alone at the terminal entrance – he turned back into the airport, took the train to Geneva and then jumped on a connection to Rolle. The big Swiss Federal Railway clock with its oversized red second hand was omnipresent - designed by Hans Hilfiker, Larry wore one on his wrist, he had bought it from the Guardian newspaper - a special offer. He liked its clearly articulated, minimal face with no numerals – a big black and white disc of time, of life ticking away.

So far, everything was running like clockwork – he had left Sandy early on Friday morning, happy with his non-specific, non-threatening reconciliation. He hadn't been physically unfaithful to Casey but he felt as if he'd crossed some kind of uncertain moral boundary as he had sat earlier that morning, munching his fruity breakfast - smooching at Sandy in her cream silk pyjamas for possibly the last time. They had made no definite arrangements to meet up again – he knew that he'd be back in London at some point and that maybe they'd get together but... but he was starting to wish that he had forced himself on her one of those nights. He knew that he'd wanted – he'd desired more than anything to sneak into her bedroom at night and make teenage love with her, but something had held him back. He could have argued that it was his moral fibre – he knew that it was the lack of confidence that came with age. He stared out across the clear, still waters of *Lac Léman* towards the Franco/Swiss border as the quiet, clean, smooth train trundled the short distance to Rolle. He pictured his crumbling semi-detached life in Wales as the UK's transport infrastructure. The train he was relaxing in now reminded him of Sandy's smart, organised apartment filled with design classics and sweet perfume.

He was alone in the carriage, he felt independent, free and ready to take on the challenge of the Dark Windows – ready to confront their actions and cast light on the reality of what had happened to Jean-Luc Godard. His paranoid tendencies desperately wanted to believe Joe – to think that there will be a simple solution, that Godard was killed by a secret conspiracy of capitalist organisations. His realist tendencies invested their faith in Sandy's argument – that the answer is far more complex and far less sinister. He wanted to believe her, take hold of his paranoia and laugh in its face – it has no power – he has taken control and will follow this project through, create a work of art that can be installed in a gallery and sold for a large sum of money. He is beginning to think that he might just be clever enough to convince people that the Dark Windows exist – that he will be able to sit back with the ironic, smug look of a successful artist, challenging all with his aloofness and remaining ignorant of the real world. Yet, at the back of his mind, he couldn't shake off the nagging thought that maybe it was all true – that there were Bordurian-style agents following him to Geneva, Dark Windows tracking his every move.

Twenty minutes later, the train pulled into Rolle station. It must have been built at about the same time as Colwyn Bay station – yet it was smart, clean and organised compared to the shabby, grotty, vandalised exterior of Colwyn Bay. He began to muse – what if Britain had remained neutral and allowed the Nazis to take control of Europe? Perhaps, if they had, Britain would be as clean and organised as Switzerland... *stop it, stop it!* He couldn't believe he was having fascist musings – it must be something to do with age and envy – he shook the thoughts back into the Nazi corner of his subconscious and alighted from the train. He stood by the departing engine with his small rucksack and looked along the empty platform. A young boy was the only sign of life, sitting on a bench, reading a brightly coloured magazine and idly attempting to whistle. Larry heard a flapping sound above him and looked up to see the green and white flag of the Vaud Canton shivering in the chill Alpine breeze. The standard was emblazoned with the Vaudois slogan; *Liberté et Patrie*, Liberty and Fatherland.

Larry clutched his map with directions to the hotel recommended by Chris, the *Hôtel Gai-Remuez*, and headed down *Avenue de la Gare*, a more salubrious, tree-lined version of Colwyn Bay's *Station Road*. In the distance, the broad expanse of *Lac Léman* glittered in the mid-morning sun, tranquilly dotted with small white sailing boats; it was not dissimilar to the sea view back home. The streets were quiet, the town had its own by-pass, like North Wales' A55, the Swiss E25 ran behind Rolle - carrying the commuters from Geneva to Lausanne and on to Berne – leaving the small towns along its route to their own secret histories. Unknown to Larry, the E25 was bringing his nemesis to Rolle – Magog was slowly heading into town, ready to carry out the dirty business of the Dark Windows.

Larry soon reached the unassuming hotel - trees shrouded it and he felt that he might have seen it before - in a dream, or a Tintin book, or a Godard film. The whole town was pleasantly bland in an affluent, green, European fashion... he was struggling to imagine the artwork that he might create from this visit - from this calm, quiet lakeside haven. The place oozed with a wealthy suburban stability that many parts of Europe aspired to but few achieved – a futuristic, post-industrial, post-information place of pure existence; of cafés, florists and hairdressers – a pristine secure zone built upon the struggles and deaths of history.

The *Hôtel Gai-Remuez* on the *Promenade des Amoureux* – it sounded a faintly disturbing place for a respectable middle-aged man travelling alone – but a short stroll down the drive revealed a discreet and scrupulous Art Deco construction. The ornately glazed main entrance opened into a small wood-clad reception and bar; to the left an ostentatious white marble fire surround was the only immediate sign of opulence in an otherwise prosaic room. Larry's first impressions of the hotel were that it might have once been gay but now seemed more austere than amorous. Arranged symmetrically around the crackling log fire were a single low table and two Art Deco leather sofas - the bar's sole resident sat on one of these, staring into the flames. He was a withered old Swiss sailor, his white beard stained by nicotine, his tweed suit smartly pressed but showing signs of wear. On the table in front of him lay a small leather cap, an extinguished pipe and glass of ice-cold beer. The room was filled with a reassuring kipper-like aroma; the not-unpleasant smell of fish, wood-smoke and tobacco. The old salt's eyes were fixed on the fireplace, seemingly hypnotised by the crackling log as Larry stepped up to the bar and rang the small bell that sat by the guestbook. A smiling Gallic face appeared from the back room...

"*Bonjour!*" The face looked in its late fifties - had short, neatly cropped grey hair, a broad smile that caused its small bright eyes to shine from within a mass of creases and a rank of brightly ordered teeth to be revealed as the thin top lip disappeared below its long, proud beak.

Larry attempted to reply, "*Ah – je m'excuse – est-ce que vous avez une chambre pour ce soir monsieur?*"

"You are another English *monsieur*? It is very good to welcome you here. My name is Georges Brassey – I am the *hôtelier* – the owner of this fine establishment. I have been speaking my English again after a long time – how may I aid you today?"

"Would you have a room for one person – for one or maybe two nights?"

Georges reinstated his broad smile and looked over towards the man with the yellow whiskers, he lowered his voice, "we are very quiet now getting and the season – she is ending soon – the summer soon starts, after the Easter..." there was a brief pause as Larry returned the smile, "to Switzerland you are new - and are you too from Liverpool?"

Larry searched for the relevance of this comment – he doesn't have a Liverpool accent, he wasn't wearing a Liverpool shirt or a Beatles badge... "Err – no, are you a football fan?"

"*Non, non!*"

"A Beatles fan?" He considered explaining about how he is from Wales, *Le Pays de Gales*, how it isn't England... but he decided it would complicate the conversation.

"*Non, non* – I thought that you may know our other English guest..."

"Do you mean?" Larry looked towards what he had assumed was an old Swiss sailor.

"Non, non – our *other* guest..." He winked at Larry and lowered his voice to a whisper, "this gentleman by the fire is Vaudois – he is having a drink here – all year..."

"But do you have a room?"

"You want a room and a bed and maybe some breakfast? That's fine – this sort of thing I can offer you. But I think that your English friend may be waiting for you..." He looked suddenly grave as he poured a short drink into a small glass and knocked it back, "I really should not be drinking this stuff but *c'est médicinal*... you would like an *apéro*?"

Larry willingly accepted a shot and threw it back – warm, cherry, relaxing – "Kirsch?"

"*Oui* – Kirsch! You like a room for now?"

"*Oui* - yes please – and do you serve lunch?"

"You are here for business with the other Englishman? He has gone to Manigley's restaurant"

"I'm sorry, I don't... *Je ne comprends pas...*"

"*Une carte*? You are here..." Georges starts to draw a small map for Larry – directions to a restaurant.

"Look, I just want to get some food – *manger*"

"You should be careful in a town like this – everybody should be careful. You could choose the wrong café if you do not know the town... some of our cafés are maybe not so good... But this – this is a very good restaurant – five *etoiles* – you meet your friend there? You *could* eat the Fondue but I would be recommending Manigley's *Saucisson Vaudois - beau, fumeux et tendre* – how would you call it? The Sausage Vaudois, she is beautiful, smoky and tender."

Larry was beginning to be confused by this over-familiarity and the mention of this 'English friend'. He sensed that, beneath the surface of Georges' friendly banter, there was an ulterior motive – that, despite the room's homely atmosphere, there was a darker, more oppressive side to the *Hôtel Gai-Remuez*. He turned his back to the fire and looked behind – into the dimly lit other half of the bar and realised from whence this subliminal oppressive atmosphere had originated. While one side of the large ground floor room was sparse and barren, neatly and efficiently organised; the other side of the room was cluttered with a mess of furniture and artefacts. The other side of the bar was like the dark side of the moon, the right side of the brain, the view through Alice's looking glass. Old glass display cases covered the walls, filled with the most incongruous bric-a-brac imaginable. Most prominent were a cohort of stuffed owls dressed in miniature lederhosen who were distributed throughout the curious cabinets that also contained an array of totems, idols and sacrificial objects: Pickled snakes, jars of rusty nails, gas masks, wartime red cross parcels, eggs, seed pods, plastic toys, musical instruments, wood carvings, wire sculptures, bottles, bones, feathers and medical implements. It was as though the contents of a dishevelled, nomadic memory had been extracted, displayed and categorised – it was a vision of the twentieth century that emphasised the fetishistic nature of human civilisation: Objects, objects, objects. Larry turned back to Georges and acknowledged the sight with an exhalation.

"Phew... quite a collection of... quite a collection. I'm sorry but I am travelling alone - *tout seul* – I do not have an English friend waiting for me. My brother – I travelled with my brother, but he has gone... *Je suis tout seul et mon frère a voyagé à Davos...*"

"*Ah oui* – you are all alone in Rolle. This man from Liverpool – I was believing that you may be friends, *Je suis désolé* - we have so few English guests here *monsieur*. But for eating – for eating you should go to Manigley's place; the *Restaurant Vaudois* on *Grand' Rue*"

Larry's bag was taken to his room, he checked in, freshened up and decided that he would take George's advice and head for the Restaurant Vaudois – maybe he'd even try the sausage – and, after a late lunch, he would start to look for Godard – start to search for the truth. Before he left, he caught Georges serving another cold beer to the silent Swiss sailor with the stained beard.

"*Excusez-moi* Georges?"

"*Oui?*"

"*Savez-vous* Godard, Jean-Luc Godard?"

"*Oui, tout le monde connaît Godard monsieur...*"

"Have you seen him here in Rolle recently?"

"*Mais oui*, of course I have seen him in the town – he was at the *fleuriste* – he was buying *Impatiente*, a tray of them on Friday – what is it that you call them... busy... busy?"

"Err – do you mean *Busy Lizzies*? Do you know his address – could you introduce me?"

Georges shrugs his shoulders and taps the side of his beak. "*Monsieur Godard* doesn't like – how should I say? He doesn't like busybodies – you may meet him but... he is a private man, he is Vaudois."

That was the end of it – Larry didn't want to be too pushy and he *was* hungry. Following Georges' map, he strolled up to the *Grand' Rue* noticing those small local, regional differences: Doorbells, door handles, kerbstones, road signs, garden furniture, street lamps, drain covers – the small pleasures of difference and independence – he lost himself briefly in the act of strolling – promenading. He found it difficult to remember his life back home; the students waiting by their desks, the notes on doors announcing his absence, his office full of pointless files – it was all a long way away now.

A few minutes later he was standing outside the Restaurant Vaudois, studying the menu... as he was reading *'Saucisson Vaudois'*, a eurowasp landed on his hand - he brushed it away and entered the quiet, conventional café with it's crisp, white tablecloths on small square tables... and there, sitting in a dark corner, reading a small scuffed paperback, smoking a roll-up and drinking a strong black coffee, sat a familiar figure. It was someone that Larry hadn't seen since the funeral - sitting in the corner looking as comfortable as land-locked Swiss sailor was Mike War.

Chapter 21
Foreign Correspondent

Mike War was an Anarchist from Liverpool – a political agitator from that most radical of British cities. In the 1980s he had been instrumental in setting up the Mutual Aid Directorate: An Anarchist co-operative, whole-food distribution network and publishing organisation based in a four storey squatted house on Fleet Street in Liverpool city centre. Fleet Street is now part of the city's 'cultural quarters'; a bland Euro-pudding of bars, clubs, galleries and offices with expensive loft apartments replacing the rooms where the revolution was once planned. He had kicked against *the system* throughout the 1980s – pirate radio, poll tax riots, flying pickets and Molotov cocktails – all used in the battle against the Conservatives - a response to Thatcher's war against Liverpool, her war on socialism, unions and communities. Mike had been angry about it all: Public utilities were sold off; industries were closed down; whole communities were left to rot and greed became good... but Mike hadn't given up – he was much more radical than the *Militant Tendency*. Pirate radio morphed into community radio, the City of the Left became the City of Culture and the issues slowly became global. He was now part of a loose worldwide resistance movement against the Capitalist hegemony and the destruction of the world – just the sort of person that the Dark Windows might be watching.

Mike knew what he was against: He was against corporate globalisation of the world, he was opposed to trans-national corporations and the international bodies that supported them: The World Bank, the International Monetary

Fund and the World Trade Organisation. He was against free trade, pharmaceutical patents, the destruction of the environment, the oppression of women, the exploitation of labour, genetic modification, inequality, debt and war. He was fighting the forces of conservatism and neo-liberalism. The agenda-setters who control language, dreams and thought were his enemies - Mike was at war with the modern world.

It was harder to define what he was in favour of except in terms of intangible qualities: Equality, freedom of speech, co-operation, fair trade, organic farming, women's rights, animal rights, global resistance, redistribution of wealth, local democracy, peace.

He was an Anarcho-syndicalist, a Situationist, a Lettrist... he had signed up to a range of revolutionary theories over the years – they were pulling together now into a universal field theory of revolution, a manifesto for peace and equality. Nobody had named the theory or written the manifesto yet - it was assembling itself without the need for an author. Mike was hoping that, one day soon, it would formulate itself and challenge the vested interests that were bleeding the world dry.

Mike was a photojournalist and broadcaster, 39 years old and single. His short, slim frame was clad in a leather jacket and jeans – he was a roll-up smoking free agent with an unusual scouse/cockney accent – *Cockouse* or *Scockney*. His mode of transport matched his image but not necessarily his ideology – Cowley's Cortina - a 1986 MG Montego Turbo, a British-built blast from the past. He saw himself as Captain Scarlet fighting the Mysterons or Patrick McGoohan in The Prisoner, trapped in The Global Village – for some reason his frames of reference were themselves trapped in the television programmes that he watched as a child.

Apart from the encounter at the crematorium, Larry had met him only occasionally for brief periods during the making of his documentary film in 2001. They hadn't hit it off. Larry was a middle-class, cynical, soft, southern artist whereas Mike was a working-class, idealistic, hard, northern radical.

The tensions erupted into violence when the documentary was in post-production. Larry had edited the interviews to give the impression that Mike was not to be taken seriously, he had re-ordered statements and excluded key points to create a sarcastic, cynical vision of his ideas. Mike wasn't happy with it and he tried to pull out of the project. When Larry wouldn't let him have the master tapes, he had taken a swing at him and nearly caught him in the post-production facilities. They hadn't spoken since and it had been a great shock when Larry had seen Mike at the funeral. It was even stranger that he should appear now – at the *Restaurant Vaudois* in Rolle – this time Larry didn't feel nauseous, he felt in control. He was sure that Mike's presence could only add weight to his investigations into the Godard affair.

Larry walked directly over to him and held out his hand – Mike's eyes rose slowly from his paperback thriller and scanned the room, his hand gripped Larry's firmly and, as he warmly shook it, guided him into the empty seat at his table. He spoke in a low voice...

"Larry mate, good to see yous again. Don't worry about seeing me here – seeing me at the funeral... we're working together on this one la. I'm gonna explain it all..."

"Are you here because of... are you following me?"

"No mate, I'm on the trail of Godard – you want some scran?"

"What? I mean – you think that was Godard at the funeral?"

"Do you want me to draw you a picture mate? – I *know* that was Godard and I want to find out who is living... who has stepped into his shoes." He stopped abruptly and changed the subject, "The owner of this place speaks good English - do you want to order your scran?"

Mike looked past him towards the proprietor of the *Restaurant Vaudois* who had silently appeared over his shoulder. Larry felt slightly unnerved by the rather intense looking man who was suddenly standing behind him. He had greying hair that was receding slightly, his nose and jowls were large and pitted – on the top of his head were a pair of expensive looking wire-framed spectacles. He slowly raised his dark black eyebrows and looked enquiringly at Larry – his small, sharp pencil was poised precisely over his dark black notebook as his spectacles slipped down onto his nose, controlled by some invisible force.

Larry looked briefly at the menu and then turned to the sinister restaurateur, "errr... I'll have the melted cheese for starters and... the sausage to follow... please, *merci*..."

"*Raclette et Saucisson Vaudois* – very good monsieur, and to drink?"

"Coffee please – black..."

As soon as the man had moved out of earshot, Mike launched into an extended but hushed polemic – allowing little opportunity for Larry to respond. For his own part, Larry was quite happy to listen – he was fascinated by the extent of Mike's dialectic exploration and, as a conspiracy agnostic, he was willing to be converted by the arguments that were being offered to him.

"Okay Larry mate – look, I haven't got much time and I'm running out of allies – I need to convince yous about something... just hear me out and then you can ask questions. We're pretty safe here, there's no cameras and there's no wires..."

Larry settled into his seat, took a notebook and pen from his pocket, "Do you mind if I...?"

"Larry mate, yous can write all you want – just don't put any names down. Do you know what this is all about – do you know what the most deadly weapon in the modern world is? I'll tell you – it's the power of mass-persuasion. Once you've persuaded the population how they should think, you can cook up an excuse for any amount of horror and atrocity – you can convince them that any particular death, torture or sacrifice is reasonable, is natural."

"Okay Mike – I didn't really come here for some sub-Orwellian lecture about Big Brother and I don't need a picture but... Why are you here and what have I got to do with it?"

"Look Larry, I understand that yous have got something – a notebook…"

"How did you…?"

"Never mind how I knew - a process of elimination – have you shown it to anyone? Don't answer that question, you don't even have to confirm that you've got Godard's notebook. The first thing that I learnt in radical politics was 'trust no one' – I need to win your trust so just hear me out okay?" Larry nodded his assent and Mike continued, "You know a little bit about the Dark Windows right? Yous made that little film didn't you? Well let's just think of the Dark Windows as shorthand for the great mass-persuader – the shadowy instigator of the psychological control of society – the one with his finger on the button – the one who owns the dream factory… Now, once someone has control over the way that we think and dream he can't be threatened right?" He looked to Larry for some reassurance.

"Carry on Mike – I'm all ears…"

"The only people, you know this already mate, the only people who can challenge the Dark Windows are individuals with *charisma* – you know what that is? It's an overused word; they used to be called *artists* – people who have a god-given talent to inspire, to create a band of devoted followers and to change the world. In the modern age - terms such as *charisma* and *artist* have been cheapened, destroyed – individual artists have had to gather together into *movements* – brotherhoods of like-minded revolutionaries. It started here mate, in Switzerland, with Dada at the *Cabaret Voltaire*, but it had to go underground when the Dark Windows took hold of Europe in…"

Mike abruptly halted his approaching diatribe as Monsieur Manigley silently encroached with a steaming cup of coffee. He placed it gently on the table and slipped back into the kitchen without a word. Mike continued…

"You've heard of Chomsky's five filters right? – It's probably the best model we've got for the way that Dark Windows works but it's far too naïve, it sees the whole thing as a kind of social accident rather than the full-blooded conspiracy that it is…"

Larry fancied a little lecture so he decided to encourage him. "Remind me about these filters Mike…"

"There's five of them right? And all the information that we get through the Media is filtered before we get it… First you've got these big multinational corporations that own the means of information production and distribution, they don't want to promote freedom or equality do they? Their goal is to make profits – the free market right? Second you've got advertising – information organisations rely on advertising as a means of making money and they can't upset the people who make cheap goods from the exploitation of labour - right? Third – there's where they get their information from, their sources of information – newspapers, magazines, television – they all get information from official sources; the government, the police, the army, universities… and those organisations have got their own filters - right? The fourth filter is fear – media organisations are scared of criticism – they don't want to upset anyone with power, they don't want to lose their license to print money. Let me give yous an example – in the UK, in 1988, Thames Television made a documentary called *'Death on the Rock'* - right? This programme exposed the British government's 'shoot to kill' policy - right? And what happened when Thames TV's license to broadcast came up for renewal? Thatcher's government introduced a new *silent auction* system, where the highest bid got the franchise and Thames TV lost to the big money men – they lost their right to broadcast the truth. Then you've got the final filter: Anti-communism – any planned project with the merest hint of communist, anarchist or radical sympathies would be undermined, removed or mocked… like yous tried with your ironic comments in your little film – but they still wouldn't show it would they?"

"But you're talking about the 1980s – I mean you can watch anything you like now – there are no gatekeepers."

"You're right there Larry mate – new technology – new advanced control mechanisms. That Chomsky stuff is out of date now – it just describes one front in a battle for our minds that has been raging since the birth of cinema. What they use now is the *Monoform*..."

A rattling plate on its route from the kitchen to the table silenced Mike; he paused until the melted cheese had been served and then carried on.

"So yous can watch anything now can you Larry – and what does that mean – do yous think that's democracy? If we take all the films in print, one lifetime wouldn't be enough for you to watch them – the radical messages are hidden in plain view – the secrets are hidden on video, on the Internet – they're all there but no one person can see them. Film is permanent and accessible – digitised and available to all, we're all film-makers and cinephiles – a film is no longer an *event* – its power has been diminished and any truth that surfaces can be buried beneath three hundred thousand lies."

Larry swallowed an extra-chewy piece of cheese before responding, "well thanks for that enlightening talk Mike, can't you just get off your soapbox and tell me what all this has got to do with Godard's disappearance?"

"I've already told you – when someone with charisma appears, the Dark Windows are there to monitor them. Most artists; musicians, writers, filmmakers, have pretty good self-regulatory systems – they want fame or fortune and once they get what they want, they're no threat. If they do become a threat, the Dark Windows have three options: Buy them out, threaten them or kill them. Godard had been warned off and gone ever more esoteric… but he had decided that he was going to make a populist comeback right? So he was killed and replaced, end of story."

"But why not just kill him off instead of replacing him – you know – an accident or something?"

"They used to do a lot of accidents – running people over was their favourite… think about this: *Roland Barthes, Antoni Gaudi, Marc Bolan, Albert Camus, Alexander Dubček, Grace Kelly, Princess Diana, Jayne Mansfield, Jackson Pollock, James Dean, that guy who played The Master in Doctor Who* – what have they got in common?"

"Icons of the twentieth century?"

"Accidents – motor vehicles – car crashes – nothing proven, get it?"

"So why not Godard?"

"He was too important, they had to put a doppelganger in his place – they're worried that we're gaining ground, they need to infiltrate the opposition..."

"The opposition?"

"Yeah – like I said, it's a battle and there's two sides and I want to make sure that you're on my side – right?"

The flow was broken again as Monsieur Manigley silently served the *Sauccison Vaudois*. Larry started eating as Mike continued to expound his theory.

"If you don't believe any of this – if you think that it's all some stupid half-baked fictional conspiracy, just ask yourself this: How many talents have you seen burn-out or disappear? How many artists have started to speak sense and then been snuffed out? How many creative, intelligent, articulate people do you see in positions of power? You may think that it's all coincidence – but I can tell you the Dark Windows do exist and now they've got you down on their little list Larry – they've got yous down because you're interested in cinema and you know about Godard..."

"What makes you think?"

"Eat up your scran mate and I'll tell yous what's going to happen. You're going to show us that notebook, but first go to Godard's office at *13 rue du Nord* and there'll be someone there waiting for you – maybe even more than one..." he winked and passed Larry a slim book, *'The Secret Language of Film'* "You may need our help, they've got Magog on your case..."

"Mag what?"

"The head of Dark Windows right? He's got a right-hand kick called Magog – and he's got his sights set on yous, he's been following yous for a while mate..."

"What does he look like this Magog?"

"Like an owl mate – like an owl; big eyes and a head that can turn all the way around... he's watching yous!" With that Mike stood up and walked purposefully towards the door. He stopped in the entrance and turned – "I'll see you tomorrow night at the *Gai-Remuez* – you'll be there?" and without waiting for an answer, he was gone.

▶▶|

Larry was standing in the entrance of the office of JLG Films at number *13, rue du Nord*, an unassuming apartment block in the centre of Rolle. In one pocket he had the Godard notebook and in the other, he had the *'Secret Language of Film'*. Both collections of words were starting to weigh on his mind in the same way that his collection of books at home used to bother him – he had ownership of them but didn't have the time or the mental faculty to work his way through them – he just knew that some books were important. He wasn't sure what to make of his meeting with Mike either – Mike had spoken at him, given him a lecture that was hardly enlightening but did open up a number of questions. Larry's paranoid tendencies were fully activated now – should he believe Mike? Should he take sides with him? Was it possible that he was winding him up in the same way that Joe Locke might be winding him up...? Just as he was formulating all these unanswerable questions, someone answered the doorbell that he was insistently ringing and his paranoia was swept away by a more powerful emotion.

The door was opened by a woman with an attractive oval face. A pair of light rectangular spectacles rested on the end of her perfect nose, beneath her deep top lip there was a thin mouth of an uncertain expression – half smile, half pout. Her light, wavy hair framed this charming European face, the jewels of which were eyes that burnt with an intense intellect. She was in her early sixties, yet looked much younger – her figure was tall, slim and sexual. Her scent, clothes and make-up were precise and poised – but it was the eyes that took hold of Larry and saw through his bluff professionalism. Before either of them had spoken, they had sized each other up and she was the biggest by far: Like Godard, Joe and Sandy - she had charisma.

Larry stuttered like a love-struck teenager as his cheeks reddened.

"I – *pardon*, err *bonjour… est-ce que…*"

"Hello, how may I help you? Are you from England?"

"No – well, yes… do you, err do you speak English?"

"Can you not guess? Do you wish to speak to Monsieur Godard?"

"Well – I… *je m'excuse*, my name is Went, Larry Went. I was wondering whether…"

Larry was under the spell of this beautiful, stylish woman and was crumbling under the pressure. Luckily, she was in control.

"Mr Went – are you a journalist?"

"No – I'm… I'm a lecturer, I mean an artist – I mean, would it be…?"

"An artist? Perhaps – if you would like to meet Monsieur Godard – you should attend our little *Société de Cinéma* at the *Hôtel Gai-Remuez*, we will meet tomorrow night – do you know the *Gai-Remuez*?"

"Yes – actually I'm staying there…"

"Good – speak to Monsieur Brassey, he will tell you all about our little *Société* and perhaps you will be able to meet Monsieur Godard there?"

As she started to slowly close the door, Larry looked beyond her into the darkened room. The walls were lined with books and, in the darkest corner, two identical and familiar silhouettes were outlined by a dull lamp – one was standing, smoking a cigar and studying a heavy, leather-bound volume – the other was sitting at a desk, tapping away at an electronic typewriter. Larry struggled to see the Godardesque figures as the door continued to close…

"Will you be there *madame*?"

Her eyes burned from the dark room through the narrowing gap as her voice spoke.

"My name is Anne-Marie and I *may* be there tomorrow – *au revoir* Monsieur Went…"

Chapter 22

The Omen

"What have we done - what has Weybridge done? Everything gone - everything destroyed..."[11]

Sandy Banks grew up in Weybridge, a small town – just down the river from Walton-on-Thames. It is another place with links to fame, charisma and Dark Windows; it was destroyed in H.G. Wells' *'War of the Worlds'* and, like Rolle, it is a place that Julius Caesar visited in his short life. In the 1980s, it was upmarket, expensive, semi-rural, green belt commuter-land. A huge British Aerospace factory employed hundreds of well-paid, skilled engineers on the site of the old Brooklands racetrack. There was a tree there with the shape of a pair of goggles indented in the bark – a driver had risked everything on the banked racetrack, he had flown through the air and lost his life as his head collided with the tree. The tree, factory and racetrack are all long-gone now, replaced by a museum and retail complex with hundreds of low-paid, unskilled jobs.

In 1984 there were no hyperstores, multiplexes or retail parks. Films were watched at the local fleapit, television had four channels and music was bought from independent record stores that sold independent records. Revolution was pressed into little black discs and sold at the back of card shops or in dingy basement stores: Rough Trade, Beggars Banquet, the record stall in Kingston market - they sold coloured vinyl, picture discs and, most

---

[11] H.G. Wells, *The War of the Worlds*.

dangerous of all - bootleg records with the whiff of criminality – of something even more independent; live, unprocessed, free from the music business. Secret messages were scratched in the run off groove – secret scary vinyl messages: Crass, Kleenex, The Fall – dark music with oblique references to radical ideas – little three-minute tunes that inspired free thought. Where did they go, why did they disappear and what have replaced them in the collective unconscious of the youth?

It was 1984 and Sandy Banks was alone, driving her red bubble of an Austin Metro from Weybridge to Walton-on-Thames – along the river, along Walton Lane to her hot date with Larry Went. It was night, autumn, cold and wet – the river was rushing to her left, darkness to her right. The long, elegant windscreen wipers calmly attempted to clear the deluge but couldn't quite keep up. The in-car stereo was playing a tape that she had recorded of one of Larry's albums complete with the clicks and rumbles of the original vinyl - *Colossal Youth* by *The Young Marble Giants*. She loved the track *Final Day* and she loved Larry...

> *"When the rich die last*
> *Like the rabbits*
> *Running from a lucky past*
> *Full of shadow cunning*
> *And the world lights up*
> *For the final day*
> *We will all be poor*
> *Having had our say"*[12]

As the night grows darker and the rain heavier, she starts to lose her bearings; the headlights are dimming, the clutch is jumping, she is struggling to control the vehicle – to see where the road ends and the river starts. She

---

[12] Final Day by The Young Marble Giants

senses danger in the contiguous boiling waters. She pulls to a halt – stops in the middle of the narrow road as the sky lights up with a blue flash. Lightning with no thunder illuminates the autumnal trees and the surface of the black river. She pushes the car's door open - the rain whips in through the gap. Another flash - for a second she glimpses something floating on the surface of the rushing river… it's a figure – it looks like Larry struggling for his life in the torrent – but the sky turns black again.

Then there is the pain – emotional, physical, unbearable pain – she is struggling to breathe, slowly blowing the air out of her body that has been taken over by an elemental force that won't allow her to move – that washes waves of pain through her young body – her eyes open wide pleading for help, but she is alone, completely alone and the pain encircles her completely – it contracts from all directions, squeezing her poor young body into spasms of pain. The intensity eventually becomes darkness, unconsciousness, insensitivity. She falls back into the beige seats of her British Leyland Metro and loses consciousness.

She is woken by a bright white light, her body is shaking – tremors – she is wrapped in a silver blanket, still sitting in her car. Through the goldfish bowl of a windscreen, she can see a bright light illuminating the road – a searchlight from a helicopter or a high, high arc light… She is shivering and unable to move from beneath the space-age blanket as a strange scene is played out in front of her…

Three men dressed in white surgical uniforms, with masks and caps hiding their identity, are pulling a small body from the dark river – an inconsequential, disfigured human form – the men silently load the slight body into the back of an innocuous white van and drive away, out of the circle of light – the shaft of light that now illuminates nothing save the rain falling and bouncing off the grey tarmac – the smell of wet roads… Sandy sits there – ossified in the red Metro as she begins to sob uncontrollably – shaking with grief, shivering with fear, pain, cold… She sobs and sobs – the light fades to an orange glow – orange glowing through the tears that were blurring her vision, the tears that were soaking her pillow and she woke in her bedroom, the orange street lamp shining through a gap in her curtains. She awoke sobbing and alone in West Kensington in 2006.

II

She climbed out of bed, it was the middle of the night and her apartment was quiet – very quiet. The only sound - somewhere in the distance, she could hear someone practising piano scales.

That dream again – that pain, grief – what does it mean? Premonition – memory – movie – dream?

At least once every month, for as long as she could remember, Sandy had lived through a version of that same dream. She had never seen Larry in the river before but it was always that road to Cowey Sale; that pain, those spotlights and the scientists with the body. She was always immobile – sometimes standing by the riverbank, sometimes watching from a distant vantage point, occasionally she could see herself unconscious in the car – but she was always alone and cold.

She staggered into the empty kitchen and put the kettle on for a cup of tea, it was three o'clock in the morning and she was making a cup of tea. She opened the fridge to take the milk out and saw the picture of teenage Larry. She felt a yearning for something that she couldn't define – an unhappiness, an uncertainty – dissatisfaction. There was a connection between the dream, her relationship with Larry and a secret that she had kept buried for years. She made a mug of tea and sat silently in her calm apartment – suddenly the yearning swept back over her, she knew what she had to do: She should have told him, warned him - Larry was in danger and she had to go to him.

Chapter 23
Contempt

Larry faced Georges Brassey over the bar of the *Hôtel Gai-Remuez* and enquired about the *Société de Cinéma*.

"*Oui Monsieur* Went, I represent the SDC – it is our little education programme – our re-education programme. We are attempting to put the culture back into *cinéma* here in Rolle. Propaganda is very important in times like these is it not?"

The Swiss sailor had moved from the fireside and was sitting at the bar with another cold beer, mumbling to himself in a slightly disturbing manner – listening to the conversation like a Cold War surveillance device. Georges took a small sip of his large kirsch and continued...

"We have a little talk each month – last month we had *un invité espagnol* – a Spanish guest. The month before we had something... what was it now...?"

The sailor chipped in, "*c'était le pornographe*"

"Ah yes – it was our Danish friend with the DOGME films, *merci* Jules... but this is our first opportunity to make an English lecturer welcome..."

"But I..."

"*Bien sûr Monsieur* Went – tomorrow night *à huit heures* - at eight o'clock, perhaps you could give a little lecture on British Cinema – if there is such a thing!" His face lit up with a broad smile.

"But – they wouldn't know me – I mean, is it a high-brow affair – is it intellectual? *Monsieur* Godard may be there – I wouldn't..."

"*C'est absurde* – your work is well known here… *Monsieur* War is a fan of yours…"

"But he's…" Larry changed the subject as he pulled a handful of Euros from his pocket. "Can I buy a Swiss drink with this toy money?"

"*Bien sûr* – you *will* give the lecture then? It is decided. I will buy you this drink – you would like?"

Larry was just about to order a long cool beer when a man passed swiftly through the bar and out through the ornate Art Deco porch. Even though he had not seen the man's face, Larry felt that he recognised him from somewhere – he turned back to Georges…

"That man – is he?"

"A German fellow called *Herr* Winkle…"

"Winkle?"

"*Oui* – Winkle!"

Larry jumped up from his seat and rushed after *Herr* Winkle – determined to confront him – to grasp this investigation by the neck and see if he can get some results. He was sick of hanging around waiting for things to happen and he was sure that Winkle was the key – Winkle seemed to link it all together, if he could get him on his own – he might be able to get some answers – to make sense from all this. He rushed out onto the darkening *Promenade des Amoureux*… he looked left, right – left, right – *Herr* Winkle had melted into the dusk. He heard footsteps heading down the hill and raced after them towards the lakeside promenade.

The sky was growing gloomy – black clouds specked with orange were reflected in the still waters from where the strange call of the great crested grebe mingled with more familiar shrieks from the gulls circling overhead. He spotted a figure in the distance – disappearing into the shadows. As he started to accelerate towards this dark form, another shadowy outline appeared from behind a tree, held out an unlit cigarette and blocked Larry's path.

The shadow spoke - hoarse and curt...

"*Avez-vous un feu?*"

He tried to get past the man but was restrained by a powerful hand that gripped his shoulder. He looked up at the broad, heavy-set figure – dark trench coat and black peaked cap hiding the face in shadow. He shook himself free of the grip.

"I'm sorry – I don't smoke – *je ne fume pas*..."

"Ah – you are English – you know not this lake... after the dark, things happen here. It is best – if you are a tourist, if you wish to be safe – maybe you should be staying in your hotel *monsieur*?"

"I have nothing to fear here surely? Switzerland is safe – neutral isn't it? Surely I can stroll along the..."

"Some people, they like to do deals – they do things here at night. And... do you know how deep the lake is just over here?"

He gripped Larry's shoulder, guided him to the shadowy lakeside and pointed towards the moon's reflection. Larry had lost his quarry and was uncertain how to deal with this new situation. He sized up his opponent – there was no way he would win in a straight brawl – he had to hope it was just a warning, if they'd wanted to kill him – he wouldn't have seen them coming, he'd be dead by now. He knew now that Mike was right – someone was after him and this character gripping his shoulder could very well be the mysterious Magog. He didn't look much like an owl though – his face in the moonlight was cold, brutal, scarred by a childhood pox.

"Perhaps *Monsieur* Went – you should start smoking while you still can..."

"How do you know my... are you threatening me?"

"*Non*," the man's face crumpled into a half grimace, half smile, "*Non*, soon they will ban cigarettes and then... then there will be no more *Monsieur* Went..."

With that – he loosened his grip, turned and marched abruptly away in the opposite direction. Larry peered into the growing gloom, the moon had disappeared behind the dark clouds – rain was on its way. He realised that he needed to formulate a response – he headed back towards the warm fire and cold beer. Perhaps that thug was right - it might well be safer to confront *Herr* Winkle in the hotel.

But Dewi Winkle did not return to the hotel bar that night, Mike was also missing. It was just Larry, Georges, Jules the sailor and a German Businessman en-route to Lausanne. After a couple of beers, Larry started to feel ill. Like the *Saucisson Vaudois*, the lakeside confrontation hadn't agreed with him - he retired to the safety of his room and half-heartedly wedged a chair under the door handle.

▶▶

Larry woke in the morning after a fitful nights sleep feeling nauseous and bloated – in no fit condition to tackle Winkle and his henchman. He sat back in the hotel bed with the book that Mike had given him – *'The Secret Language of Film'* by Jean-Claude Carrière. He recognised the name… of course – it was one of the names from the Godard notebook! He voraciously digested the book, searching for a clue, convinced that Mike was right – that he was in danger and needed help. As he read, he drew up a mental list of who might be working for the Dark Windows and who might be working to undermine them. When he had finished the book he was none the wiser – he realised that he had abandoned the only people he could trust back home in Colwyn Bay. He 'phoned Casey to check on the family… everyone seemed to be getting on fine without him.

…*school/house/bed/school/house/bed*…

Now that he had abandoned his job, the routine didn't require Larry – he was surplus to requirements. He felt that he *should* miss them, but he had been distanced by the quest and the threats that appeared to be becoming more concrete than a mere suburban paranoid fantasy.

He lay there all day – studying the cracks in the ceiling, damp patches and constellations of mildew – searching for patterns, pictures, solutions, in an alien hotel room. The rain lashed the windows as they rattled in the winds that whipped across the grey lake. By the evening he felt better, his appetite had returned and he staggered downstairs to search for a quiet bar snack. Just as he was about to enter the bar, he was confronted by an over-excited *Monsieur* Brassey...

"*Monsieur* Went – how lovely to see you. I was beginning to think that something had happened to you. Everything's ready for you – we have a projector... you will find the audience most appreciative."

"Could I get something to eat first? I've been feeling..."

"There will be refreshments afterwards – come along *Monsieur* Went..."

Larry entered the bar, it had been rearranged slightly with a projector fixed to the ceiling and trained on a screen in front of the fireplace. A small group of strangers sat in the dark half of the bar – eyes peering out from amongst the stuffed owls and antiques. The only familiar faces were Mike War - smiling in the midst of the audience - and Georges Brassey, who was fussing around Larry, urging him to sit at the table adjacent to the screen. Georges opened the proceedings...

"*Mesdames et messieurs* – tonight's lecture will be conducted through the medium of English. I have much pleasure in introducing *Monsieur* Larry Went from across the water..."

Larry had not prepared a lecture but he was accustomed to public speaking and having classes dropped on him at the last minute. It seemed uncomfortably natural to walk into a room full of strangers and start talking - that was the lot of the lecturer. He considered this a test, an initiation rite that might bring him closer to the secret of Godard's death. He had nothing to lose now and could easily improvise a lecture – improvisation was his default mode. His lectures always pitted the idle ramblings of a man who knew half of nothing against an audience who were half-listening. Tonight's audience applauded politely as Georges took his seat, all eyes were fixed on Larry. He noted the familiar self-conscious awareness his own body, his hair, his posture, his clothes. He could feel the audience summing him up and dismissing him before he had even opened his mouth. He straightened himself, walked into the blank blue light of the data projector, cleared his throat and began…

"Well… I have been asked by our friend *Monsieur* Brassey to give a short talk on British Cinema… but… I, I believe that it was François Truffaut who said that the words *Cinema* and *Britain* were incompatible. Now I'm not going to argue about the nature of British Cinema – I believe that American forms of storytelling, image-making and film production dominate to such an extent that it would be futile nationalism to defend one country's film culture. Let me just say that although the British Isles have produced famous names such as Alfred Hitchcock, Stan Laurel, Cary Grant, Michael Powell and David Lean – none of these have been able to survive by working alone in Britain…"

A challenge fired from the dark, "Do you mean that British cinema is a cinema of *collaboration*?"

"I suppose that is what I meant to say… I mean that rather than talk about film in terms of national identity – I would like to talk about the language of film. I would like to advocate a European cinema of ideas and art that could challenge the *monoform* of Hollywood. Rather than adapt the techniques of Hollywood – we should continue to strive to create an alternative…"

Another voice interrupted from the dark, "What is this *monoform* you mention?"

"I'm glad that you asked: The *monoform* is an concept developed by the British filmmaker, Peter Watkins. It refers to the way that films and television programmes have become repetitive, predictable and closed products. The way that news, history and documentary have become products of effective state propaganda produced to standardised patterns. This extends to the structural patterns of feature films: Editing, narrative structure, use of sound, music and incessant activity is designed to stop reflection – there is no time to think or reflect upon what you are seeing. The *monoform* does not allow cinema to be sublime or transcend the marketplace, it does not allow communication; it transmits fixed ideas. It can reduce any idea – no matter how radical – to a predictable product, sliced up like a sausage. The *monoform* is the most effective form of thought control yet devised by human society..."

The audience remained silent as the wind whistled under the door and Larry pictured tumbleweed blowing down the avenue outside...

"But first, let me return to the potential of cinema, the invention of cinema – the invention of its language... More powerful than the technology of the moving image, is the invention of montage – of editing. The ability of this visual language to educate or indoctrinate is evident from the very early days of cinema: Its use by the Soviets - who sent Kino-trains, Mobile cinemas on tracks, around the country to tell the masses about the political revolution; and the Nazis who used the power of montage to create enduring myths of Fascism. I am sure that you all know *Dziga Vertov* and *Leni Riefenstahl* – if I had the means, I would use these directors to illustrate my point but... let me continue..."

Larry was in full swing now and the audience seemed to be becoming vaguely interested. He could just make out their shadowy forms as they idly looked him up and down whilst sipping their drinks and whispering in each others ears. He took a sip from his glass of water and strained to see if Anne-Marie or Dewi were there before continuing...

"The thing about this new language of film was that it was universal. Silent films could be watched and understood in any country - children can understand film language before they can comprehend the written word, before they can tell the time. The language of film was also in constant flux – new inventions were taken on board: Split screen, close-up, shot/reverse shot, the pulled punch, parallel action – the language was developed in Europe and it took two World Wars before America was able to control its revolutionary power. The European cinematic masters fled to America and their ideas – their dreams - were sucked into the factory production line of the Hollywood studio system. The revolutionary language of film had been adopted by capitalism and accelerated to create an appetite for ever-more frenetic, dislocated movies that sold ideology – an ideology of prostitution and exploitation.

Some artists managed to smuggle their own ideas into the Hollywood machine – they attempted to use the system to subtly undermine the *dream factory*. That's why Hollywood introduced the Hays Production Code in 1930 – everything was carefully codified to suppress sex, humanity and revolution. Artists still tried to gatecrash the party – some were killed, some were threatened and many were blacklisted by McCarthy's witch-hunts in the 1950s." Larry looked over to Mike, who gave him a conspiratorial thumbs-up and a wink. "So... getting back to British cinema – these blacklisted artists escaped back to Europe, full circle, to work on films and television in 1960s Britain. Just take one example: The Adventures of Robin Hood, made for British TV in the 1950s; blacklisted writers used pseudonyms and wrote scripts about the tyranny of Prince John... or Joseph Losey – he went to the same school as Nicholas Ray and they both moved to Europe to escape from *monoform* USA. The more you look into it – the more you see patterns emerge – the power struggle between the forces of reaction and the forces of revolution – between left and right, realism and surrealism..."

Larry was starting to get excited – he was combining his limited knowledge of film theory with Mike's lecture in the café and Carrière's book. He was jumping back and forth in film history – linking, connecting, creating patterns – he felt that he had a thesis here, an idea developing. Just as he was about to continue with his conspiratorial thesis, the door swung open – wind, rain and Jean-Luc Godard swept into the darkened bar. He was with Anne-

Marie who glanced at Larry and smiled as they moved silently over to their reserved table. Godard, dressed in his trademark heavy-framed spectacles with wild grey receding hair and a light coloured mackintosh, pulled up a chair, lit a cigar and looked down at his glass of Cognac – his eyes never once meeting Larry's who acknowledged the new arrivals before continuing with his disjointed and ever-more evangelical narrative…

"I hope that you won't mind me saying that it was the work of the French critics at *Cahiers du Cinéma* that identified this tendency – this theory of the *Auteur*… the concept that the film director was the artist – the author who stamped his mark on the film through control of the camera and *mise-en-scène*. In the 1960s Hollywood took this *Auteur* idea on board as it began to lose its power to the new technology of television. The corporations abandoned cinema and suddenly – individual artists had control of an aging global propaganda system. The *Auteur* concept – developed by, among others, *Monsieur* Godard here, had become a powerful weapon wielded by a small group of radical European and American artists… In the 1960s a second wave of European directors infiltrated the Hollywood system, a window opened – the possibility that cinema could change the world before it died…

But the power of the *Auteur* in Hollywood was short-lived. The clampdown returned with globalisation and the high concept movie. An ever-increasing pace of action – of montage developed in order to conceal the void at the heart of contemporary cinema. A technique that feeds us a constant stream of images yet is designed to stop us seeing, thinking or understanding.

We – as artists, thinkers and humanists – we must take control back from these monolithic global organisations… We must be aware that the moving image is history and that history is the moving image. We live in a time when there are too many images – each one tied down and contextualised. We are given the meanings – we are told what to think and we see nothing – let me give you an example…"

Larry described a lecture that he had given to a group of bored teenagers back in rural Wales about the history of British Cinema: He was using *The Third Man* as a case study – it had been voted the best British film ever by the British Film Institute – yet what makes it British? He had explained to his six students that the director, Carol Reed, was British and that it was set in Vienna in 1949. He had proceeded to show them the famous scene on the Ferris wheel where Orson Welles described Switzerland. He had then asked the students to list the elements of 'Britishness' that they could identify in the sequence. Katie had looked up from her doodling and shuffled about a bit...

"Well, it's in London innit?"

"Interesting observation Katie... what makes you think that this scene is set in London?" It could be an innocent mistake – London was bombed in the war and Katie may not have have been listening, she may not have recognised any landmarks...

"Well, it's the London Eye innit?" Larry had looked carefully to see if she was being ironic – but no, she had genuinely believed that the London Eye existed in a bombed out London/Vienna of the 1940s – she bathed in a daily surfeit of information yet she had no concept of history, geography, technology or national identity.

The audience in Rolle seemed vaguely interested in Larry's anecdote – he tried to contextualise it a little further...

"The past has become homogenised; *Saving Private Ryan* and *Schindlers List* have become the Normandy landings and the Holocaust – Steven Spielberg's films are used in schools to teach the history of the Second World War. Try showing Resnais' *Night and Fog* to a class of teenagers – it will mean nothing to them. The *monoform* has taken over and the sublime has become unintelligible to the majority. But this does not mean that we should give up on the moving image. We must be allowed to tell our own stories using our own language – film *is* reality and we must graft this reality onto our imaginations in order to create the future. We *must* fight against the globalisation of the image and we *must* reclaim European art cinema!"

He looked around the assembled audience and saw that they had heard it all before, that they'd seen through him. He stood intellectually naked as in a dream, awaiting the slow handclap of condescension. He imagined them regarding his wiry frame, taking him by the shoulders and legs and throwing him into a pit of history – an unmarked grave of no-marks in the heart of Europe. He stood and faced them, folded his arms and locked his knees, a loud jet 'plane flew overhead cutting through the engulfing silence. Georges spoke...

"You have finished *Monsieur* Went? Very interesting, perhaps we have some questions for you?"

Larry shuffled his locked legs and glared at the remaining *Société* members – a voice called from the disinterested cabal...

"*Monsieur* Went – do you really believe that all this is the result of... that there is a single, organised conspiracy that controls the film industry?"

"Well, I... err..." Larry started to stumble over his words, he was feeling light-headed, dizzy – he pictured yesterday's *Saucisson Vaudois*... Godard and Anne-Marie stood to leave as another question was fired...

"Which film-maker has chiefly influenced you?"

Larry fielded the question as he attempted to catch Godard's eye – he must speak to him, make some attempt to confirm his identity using the notebook...

"I, err... Jesus Franco."

"But Jess Franco makes cheap German pornographic films..."

Georges saw that Larry needed some support, "That's just *Monsieur* Went's little joke – do we have any more questions?"

Larry watched Godard fade into the dark shadows of the night as the next question arrived,

"*Monsieur* Bela Tarr – now where would you put him? Into which genre?"

"I…"

Just as Larry was about to answer, he noticed that Dewi Winkle had appeared from those same shadows and was standing in the doorway with his friend, the Pockmarked Lakeside Heavy. Dewi asked the next question…

"Can I ask – are you currently engaged on a project yourself *Monsieur* Went?"

Larry took this question as a gauntlet – if this was an initiation, he must rise to the challenge…

"Yes – it's called *The Death of Godard*."

"A feature film?"

"It could be - It's a murder story, about a serial killer – it's based on a real series of murders…"

"Is it about the death of cinema, *Monsieur* Went?"

"In a way…"

"And are you slow to work things out? Such as, perhaps, the plot?"

"Not when I get interested…"

Dewi smiled, enjoying the cryptic exchange… "Are you sure that this isn't dangerous *Monsieur* Went?"

"Dangerous?"

"Mixing fact and fiction in this way?"

"Do you think that I should make it all fact *Monsieur* Winkle?"

"No – I should stick to fiction – straight fiction if I were you…"

"I'm too far along with the script now…"

"Haven't you ever scrapped a project *Monsieur* Went?"

"Often – I could give you a list of abandoned ideas. Perhaps I could just change the names to protect the…"

"…the innocent *Monsieur* Went?"

Leaving his final comment hanging in the otherwise silent bar, Dewi turned back through the door and faded into the shadows, swiftly followed by his trench-coated Heavy.

Chapter 24

The Man Who Knew Too Much

Earlier that morning Magog had swept up to the Berne office, borne on the wings of some dark emotion that lay buried in his subconscious. Like Janus - one face looked to the future with a foul curse, the other looked to the past with pity as he sensed the Machiavellian nature of the mission that he had embarked upon. Freddie had arranged to give one final briefing on the matter of Larry Went - the very mention of this name caused Magog to wince at his own impotence. For a man who was usually proud of his ruthless efficiency, he was damning himself for the affection that he had begun to half-sense growing for Larry's blind, bumbling plight. Why hadn't he snuffed Larry out, leaving him as an instantly forgotten car-crash statistic? His hidden emotional involvement with Larry had doomed his actions with ineffectiveness. He should have known that Godard would have kept a written notebook with detailed, precise information. A man such as Godard would be bound to use a pen and write – transpose his thoughts with wet ink onto a clean, dry white page.

Magog pushed open the heavy door and addressed Freddie, his eyes adjusting to the dark room as the heavy portal silently closed behind him.

"You want to finish with Went then?"

Freddie gripped the table with his manicured talons in response. The mention of Went appeared to bring a hitherto unknown vile manner to the fore...

"Do you want me to tell you what I think about Went? He is a sad specimen of a partially educated pedant - a pointless purveyor of dead theories and outmoded ideas. He serves no use except to keep teenagers off the unemployment statistics. He is a statistical massager of idiot teenagers who counts off his days in dead thirty-minute blocks. He is a crab lying on the seabed who knows nothing but the rocks and sand around him – a spineless crustacean who has seen some bacon on a string and gripped it with the final act of his clumsy engorged hand…"

After this uncharacteristic outburst, Freddie refocused on his bullet points – the organised information that he had prepared for Magog. Freddie had to see it all as a simple set of priorities – a strategy. He had held onto this job as head of the Bland Corporation because he knew how to apply strategies and models to situations. Magog had different but nonetheless required qualities, somehow these qualities conflicted with the Went affair; to Magog it had become an emotional issue – a conflict of loyalties.

The first model of the day was applied as the two men took their standard hierarchical positions in the meeting room. Magog sank silently into the Barcelona Chair as Freddie stood upright in front of him – rigid as he tensed his shoulder blades and gripped his laser pointer. His left profile was illuminated by the black projection as it awaited its first bullet point. There was no need for an introduction – they were both aware of the aims and objectives as Freddie's outburst lingered in the now silent room.

Click:

Freddie listed them regardless.

1: Get the Godard notebook.

"You may wonder why this book is important Maggy – important to us or important to The Order… While Larry remains ignorant of the meaning – alone and isolated – it threatens no one. But if someone gets hold of it who can use the information, if he hooks up with our enemies, then…"

"Could you explain the possible…?"

"Uses? Of course…"

Click

1a: Revelation

"To some the notebook may have a revelatory quality. It may lead them to a clearer understanding of the Dark Windows – what we are doing and what we have done. The book itself could not possibly contain all of the information but it will lead to The Order. The Order have been watching us for many years, watching for a crack – a weakness in the Corporation that they can exploit. They *could* destroy us but they would rather control us. They want to take the franchise from us; they want to take control of the dream factory, the apparatus, for their own ends. They want to convince our ultimate masters that the world should be inculcated with *their* ideas."

Click

1b: Domination

"The notebook is possibly more useful to us. If we can get hold of Godard's book, it may lead us to the Archive of The Order. If we can take control of the Archive, we will be able to dominate the world unchecked by their foolish ideologies. Their brave new European dream factory will disappear. The power that they began to develop in the 1960s, the power that we neutered, will be lost forever. The Keepers of the Archive are dying now – they are getting old and we need to eliminate their threat before the next generation of The Order can organise or take control…"

"I'm lost Freddie" Despite all his years as an assassin in the service of the Dark Windows, this was new to Magog. He had heard of The Order but only as a mysterious threat, an enemy of The Windows.

"Maggy, Maggy… the Dark Windows is a mere mechanism, we use it to control the collective unconscious in the same way that the World Trade Organisation control the economies of the world; we rely on a consensus of ruling elites. We have strategies in place that give an illusion of freedom and maintain a harmonious balance in the cultures of the developed world. The

Order are dangerous – they have Art and Revolution on their side. They are nurturing talent in Turkey, Iran, Senegal, Egypt – across the globe film-makers are creating charismatic works with the power to change the world. If a cinema of freedom were to take hold of the collective subconscious, it would create anarchy Maggy – all of our gains would be lost. But – but - if we can destroy the vestiges of Antonioni, Bergman, Tarkovsky and Godard – then we will continue to control the dreams and lives of the world. We can continue to dominate the collective memory, dreams and history. Humanity will continue to be systematically ordered – organised and arranged to maintain our privileged positions. And with us, with us people are happy Maggy – with dissatisfaction comes revolution, anarchy.

Let me use a metaphor: The Order have developed these cultures in the national Petri dishes of Turkey, Iran, Senegal and so on. In order to release these cultural viruses they need to disrupt our containment techniques - they need to break through our cultural bio-security systems. The only way that they can do this is by exposing our control mechanism…"

Freddie stopped, briefly rubbed his left eye and took a long, slow sip from a glass of cool water as his eyes fixed on Magog's and he continued.

"They have collected evidence together somewhere, a cemetery of dead facts, an ethnographic history of the Dark Windows, a record, an account. From the time of Bataille onwards, they have built a secret museum of evidence that would be catastrophic for us if it were released. The Order have us balanced, continuously balancing, on a knife's edge – at any moment they could use this evidence to stop our work, to wrest control…"

Magog was still uncertain, "Don't they ever…?"

"They test the water, they release evidence occasionally, but we always manage to lose it in our morass of media disinformation. The Order are continuously searching for institutions that will support their ideas. If they could get a media snowball rolling – universities, public or state broadcasting networks, organisations that we struggle to control, may pick up on it and use it to destabilise our system. It's all about the release date, the release pattern – if their revolutionary virus is borne upon a serendipitous wind, it could decimate our finely balanced control mechanism. This archive that *they* keep, this record of *our* actions could be our undoing. We have tried for years to find this archive – the Godard book may lead us there, and when we find it... we will burn it to the ground!"

Magog decided to stoke the rhetorical fire, "But isn't it...?"

"Backed up? Recorded? No. Bataille had this ethnographic notion of collecting evidence in boxes, files, archives, cabinets... The Order continued his work and, like us, they keep no copies, no other records. We both work with word-of-mouth, we don't like to use telephones and our meeting rooms are protected from surveillance. It's all very simple Maggy – we just have to keep the system in balance by preventing any dreams that don't suit our overall goal, that don't suit our ultimate masters, from escaping. But..." Freddie paused and looked into the bright light of the projector, "let me return to my presentation."

Viruses, Petri dishes, museums, balance, scales – the metaphors were blended like a soup - the seeds were sewn into the very fabric of Magog's consciousness. He felt that he just wanted some simple orders to obey, let someone else deal with the politics of it all.

"So Maggy... Point One – we get the notebook and that will lead us to the archive of The Order. Then... then we destroy the archive."

Click

2: Eliminate Larry

"We've been working on this one for a little while haven't we? You are going to eliminate Larry today. Silence him and his family. Any trace, any audit trail that can connect Larry and North Wales to the Death of Godard must be removed by whatever means. If that entails killing Went and his entire family, so be it. It is the smallest people that can destroy the largest empires and I will take no risks. He must be taken out of the picture. Finish him off Maggy and find the archive."

Chapter 25
The Seventh Seal

The *Société de Cinéma* in the bar of the *Hôtel Gai-Remuez* was breaking up. Some of the members were following Godard and Winkle out into the dark night, Larry was struggling to pass Georges and catch them. He almost had to push the hotelier out of the way in order to pursue his quarry. This time he was going to confront Winkle or Godard or Magog or whoever they were... Larry suddenly looked over to Mike who was hanging back, waiting for him to make the first move – their eyes met and Larry bolted for the door, beckoning him to follow. Mike's words were haunting him as he dashed out into the cold night...

The power of mass persuasion... any death could be explained as reasonable... people like Godard were the only ones who could change the world... whose side are you on Larry?

As he stood in the midst of the diminutive dispersing throng, he heard Georges calling after him...

"Monsieur Went – there is no rush – stay for some refreshments..."

For the second time that day he strained to see up and down the *Promenade des Amoureux*. At the foot of the hill, towards the darkening lake, he could just make out the shapes of Godard and Anne-Marie enveloped in a cloud of blue cigar smoke. The wind was slicing clouds across the moon like razor blades across an eye. Larry's hands were itching; he looked down at them, half expecting to see ants crawling from stigmata in his palms. He clenched his fists, enclosing and crushing the imaginary insects, and strode down the hill toward the shapes that were disappearing around the corner onto the dark lakeside promenade. As he turned the corner, he sensed someone was running after him. He looked – but there was no one there: No one behind him on the *Promenade des Amoureux* and no one ahead of him on the lakeside path. The footsteps and the figures had vanished into the mist that was starting to roll off *Lac Léman*.

The mist obscured and disorientated as it started to form halos around the sparsely distributed streetlamps. He was alone with the distant alarm calls of gulls and a lone bat that was flitting through the enveloping misty silence. Suddenly, there was no one. He had moved from that over-warm bar, where all eyes had burned into his ineffective rant. He had moved into the cold, damp night air that wrapped around each strand of his hair and poured into his lungs – cutting from inside with shards of invisible fractured glass as he struggled to catch his breath. He was suddenly alone with his fears: A dark stone alley at night, a wardrobe flying across the floor of a possessed Victorian house, the devil, the antichrist, cloaked figures, red eyes, horns, teeth, leather skin and every conceivable demon from every stupid horror film that he had ever seen swarmed into his subconscious as he stood alone on the misty shores of *Lac Léman*. He stepped further into the dark mist that engulfed and suffocated him like a gloved hand placed over his mouth. He felt sure that the demons were all around him, hiding in the freezing mist; he tried to reassure himself. He couldn't quite shake off the emotions that were borne upon the thousand supernatural narratives lodged in his subconscious…

It's all just a stupid story, there's nothing here – even if you imagine that you have walked through the gates of hell, there is nothing to fear. You are a man standing alone by a lake in Switzerland – there are no ghosts – you've more to fear from the…

He looked around again and listened, there were footsteps coming towards him from out of the mist. He could smell cigars; cigars like those in the bar, like the ones in the offices of JLG Productions... Jean-Luc Godard was coming towards him, materialising from the icy mist. Larry called out...

"*Monsieur Godard*?"

The figure halted and beckoned to him. Larry started towards the Godard apparition, carefully placing his feet one in front of the other as he strained to see the shadowy cultural icon through the mist. Step - grass, step - gravel, step - nothing.

Larry plunged into the icy waters of *Lac Léman*. He tried to swim but struggled as a misty hand pushed him down, down beneath the surface of the ice-cold lake. Dark clouds of water floated before his eyes, the world became as cold as it was dark, he lost any sense of which way was up or down. As he floated into unconsciousness, peaceful at last, there was nothing to breathe, no light – only the sound – the sound of the blood rushing through his body. The slowing pulse in his ear was his last mortal experience before his heart stopped.

II

The cold and the darkness enveloped Larry as he floated down a long spiral tunnel of blackness, enveloping him darker and colder and evermore peaceful. The eternal sleep of death was wrapping her icy fingers around him as a pinprick of white light appeared at the end of the tunnel – he was floating towards the oncoming death train that was about to smash him into a stark new consciousness.

▶

The fluorescent tubes buzzed, flickered – harsh, painful green artificial light – subliminal buzzing, clicking. Larry was standing in a windowless classroom – bare walls, bright magnolia reflecting the green fluorescence. The air was warm, stale, circulated through too many lungs. His arms were folded and legs locked to balance – he was glued to the floor, his legs too heavy or weak to move as he swayed slowly, slightly.

Sitting before him at the rank of neatly organised desks were twelve unknown students, three rows of four – twenty four expectant eyes. Larry didn't recognise the room or the students. He had no notes with him and there were no clues on the walls as to where, when or how he had got there. He looked around the room – there were no windows and no doors. Vacant faces stared at him as the tubes flickered and buzzed.

Is this it? Is this my purgatory – am I going to stay in this room until the day of judgement? Is there someone here accounting for my sins?

All of Larry's indiscretions flashed through his memory as he stood in the ghostly nightmare classroom: Minor shoplifting offences, hurtful comments to his mother, his girlfriends, his wife… smacks that he'd given his children, pointless, pointless arguments with people he loved, road rage, wasted opportunities, abandoned plans, unkept promises. A catalogue of minor sins, but nothing that seemed to warrant this – an eternity in a classroom of strange teenagers. A thumping, throbbing pulse started from somewhere – inside/outside – impossible to tell. He decided to speak.

"So – err… my name's Larry Went and I'm looking after you this morning." The clock on the wall read 9.10 – first session of the day. "Can anyone remember where we were up to last week?"

Larry was fishing for information while pretending to be in control. One of the male students looked up from behind a barren desk, his eyes flashed bright green in the artificial light. He had a huge spot on his top lip, pulsating green/yellow in the bright interior. He looked as if he needed a shave…

"We didn't do nothing last week – this is our first German lesson…"

German? German… in this dreamlike state, Larry remembered: Rhodri had asked him to cover a German class – to teach German first session on a Monday morning. Why had he agreed? Larry hardly spoke a word of German and these kids were doing an advanced course; they already knew the basics. Larry was panicking…

Why am I teaching German?

He decided to start counting, an eternity counting in German. The class joined in parrot fashion, rote fashion...

"ein, zwei, drei, vier, fünf, sechs, sieben, acht, neun..." the cold fingers grip his throat, he can't speak as the students keep counting... "elf, zwölf, dreizehn..."

The icy fingers tightened as he sank back into the hollow darkness of death.

▶▶|

Larry slowly came back to some form of consciousness in a dimly lit bedroom. It was furnished in grey bourgeoise classicism - large, sparse and tidy. He sat up in bed and looked at the alarm clock – 1.00am – death alone in a quiet bedroom. This seemed a superior purgatory; feather pillows and quilt with a pale yellow candlewick bedspread. The dark European-grey bedroom had two baroque doors – one on each side of the foot of the bed. Larry was just starting to drift back into the blackness of his anonymous purgatory, thinking...

who would have believed that death could be so comfortably dull?
When...

The door to the left creaked open and footsteps entered the room – footsteps that materialised into a Flamenco dancer; young, beautiful, voluptuous – her castanets echoed harshly around the room – her pale skin and dark red lips soaked Larry with desire – her long dark hair fell across her pale forehead and bright green eyes glowed through her shining locks. She exited through the right-hand door as mysteriously as she had appeared and Larry drifted back into oblivion.

When...

The alarm clock rang. It was 2.00am, he was still in the grey bourgeoise bedroom. He was looking up at a spider's web moving in the slight breeze as a postman opened the left-hand door and rode his bicycle past the foot of the bed and out through the other door, throwing a postcard onto the candlewick as he passed. Larry sat upright again and leant across to grasp the postcard, reading the large handwritten message:

Mr Went, You are nothing – you no longer exist. J.L.G.

Outside in the darkness, a church bell struck twice. The wall in front of Larry wobbled; it was nothing but a painted stage flat. The once solid barrier slowly toppled to the floor causing a cloud of dust to rise into the brightly lit interior beyond. Suddenly Larry found that he was sitting in the grey bed, looking out through the space where the wall once stood - looking out into a bright, bustling cinema foyer.

There was a queue in the cinema and, standing in the queue was someone that he vaguely recognised... it slowly dawned on him that he was watching himself standing in line. The smell of popcorn and cigarettes swelled into the dark bedroom: It was death; an out-of-body experience where he was watching himself in some distant past/future that never existed – some cinematic vision of a memory outside of time.

The queuing Larry was waiting to buy a ticket for Alain Resnais' *Nuit et Brouillard,* a short film about the Holocaust. Of course – it made sense that up here in heaven or space or a different dimension – outside of the physical experience of life, in the eternal cerebral loop - humanity wouldn't watch the reflection of reality as offered by Hollywood, by Spielberg's redemptive narratives of human holocausts... No, here in heaven, people would want to see what Godard called 'the reality of the reflection' – Resnais' reality - a real response to the horrors of humanity, history and death. It makes perfect sense that the afterlife consists of these reflections – the celluloid record is the collective memory of humanity... of course, it all makes sense...

Sitting in the distant, warm bed, Larry watched an image of himself talking at a blank-faced girl in the cinema queue...

"Of course, I saw *Schindler's List* and I feel that Spielberg is just not sure where he stands on the causes of the Holocaust – I've always felt that he was essentially a cheap populist film-maker, I mean granted that *Close*

Encounters was a great film – good in its use of the conspiracy as a narrative device..."

The queuing Larry wasn't aware that his loud opinions were starting to annoy Vendor Busch, who was standing behind him in the queue. Vendor whispered to his girlfriend,

"This Larry is expressing his opinions far too noisily my dear..."

Larry continued "...I find it all so sentimental, he's sentimental, he really is the most sentimentalist director – I mean, take what he did to Kubrick's *A.I.*..."

"I think that you will find that the key term there is *sentimental*..."

"...it's like Tarantino; I admire his technique but his work just doesn't grab me..."

"...I would like to grab this guy..."

Larry continued... "...the problem with modern cinema is the influence of television, it's what Godard describes as *pure diffusion* - it's the visual exploitation of horror..."

Vendor suddenly lost his temper and tapped Larry on the shoulder, "the funny thing Herr Vent, the funny thing is that you don't know anything about Godard..."

Larry was taken aback... "Really? I happen to teach a class at college called *Godard and the New Wave*. I feel that my insights into Mr Godard's work have a great deal of validity..."

"Do you Herr Vent? Because I just happen to have Monsieur Godard here..."

Vendor swiftly pulled Jean-Luc Godard from the back of the queue to face Larry. Godard took a long draw from his cigar, blew the smoke into Larry's face and caustically addressed him...

"*J'ai entendu ce que vous disiez - vous ne connaissez rien de mon travail. Comment vous avez obtenu d'enseigner un cours de n'importe quoi est totalement étonnant!*"

The queuing Larry turned to Vendor and looked confused. The bedridden Larry watched from beneath his warm bourgeoise candlewick as his reflection disintegrated and faded into a misty damp blackness – he struggled to make out anything at all as strange shadows flickered before his eyes. He was aware of a piano being played in the apartment below – a C scale. The scale morphed into Beethoven's 9th (the choral symphony) – Europe was rising up from the ground floor and filling his blank bedroom. The music ended and, as the choir dissipated into the night, Larry heard a beautiful female voice singing through the deathly evening of a street in East London. His heavenly grey bedroom had become a London squat at the end of the twentieth century complete with 1970s wallpaper and the spirits of its long-dead residents vaguely disturbing his peaceful afterlife. He sat frozen in the bed as the voice reverberated through the empty night.

"I've got you under my skin, I've got you deep in the heart of me…"

Larry climbed out of bed, his head pounding as he drew back the curtains…

"So deep, so deep you're almost a part of me…"

Over the road, he saw a house explode – it burst into flames silently – it was within his grasp, burning and collapsing yet cold and silent…

Is this heaven?

"I have got you under my skin…"

Suddenly cheers flew through the quiet night, thousands of voices in unison expressed anger, excitement and joy…

"Ooh! Aaah! Yes!"

A dark city street at night – no one on the pavements – no cars driving by – yet thousands of voices called out through the orange blackness.

Although he was still in the afterlife, Larry managed to rationalise the disembodied voices – Upton Park, West Ham – there must be a game tonight and thousands of Hammers fans are following the match just yards from this window - a vast body of unified humanity calling out into the night of this ghost city.

The letterbox clattered downstairs and dragged Larry from his contemplation, he stalked down the night stairs to find a padded envelope sitting on his doormat. It contained an unmarked silver disc. He wandered into the living room and placed the disc into the blank television that sat there. The screen flickered to life and displayed what had been etched into the disc: It was the outside of Larry's house. The camera moved towards the front door and entered. There were views of the dimly lit interior as the camera roamed around the ground floor and then up the stairs and into his bedroom. There on the bed, fully clothed and soaking wet, Larry saw himself in grainy video footage - drowned and dead. Someone had filmed him, how could anyone have got in here to film him? Where exactly was he? Who was he and how did he get to be here?

Could hell really be that classroom, that bedroom, that cinema, this house, that video? Is this really my hell or is it someone else's heaven? Death can't be made of mundane visions such as these – surely...

Chapter 26
Close Encounters

The hallucinations parted and somehow Larry realised that he wasn't dead – that this was reality. He wasn't certain how he distinguished between those lucid fantasies and the muggy consciousness that he now found himself in but somehow he knew that this dark room he now inhabited was reality/life – real life.

He was uncomfortable, drenched and cold, as if someone had dragged him from that freezing lake and thrown him onto this lumpy bed. He reached up to touch his hair and then the thin foam cushion that his head rested on. The pillow was soaked through, not with the waters of Lac Léman, but with sweat. His body had left a damp, sweaty imprint on this cheap bed in this dark room. He had had a fever and the fever had broken leaving him shivering under a thin yellow candlewick blanket.

The door at the foot of his bed creaked open and a familiar figure entered.

"Ah! Herr Vent – you are conscious now – you are awake? Do not strain yourself, but you may speak yes?"

He recognised the character from his documentary, funeral and dream. Vendor Busch was tall and wiry, dressed from head to foot in black, a dark wool greatcoat giving him apparent bulk. His short black hair was receding in a straight line that ran parallel with his dark eyebrows and small round spectacles rested on his angular nose. He seemed to have come from the past, his dress had an air of the 1940s and he exuded an odour of mothballs.

"Vendor… how long have I? How did I?"

Larry was confused, he thought back to the lakeside mist, the water and the deathly visions. He had no idea how much time had passed, where he was or how he had got there. He couldn't quite draw a line between the dream of death and the reality of drowning. His body ached and he was finding it difficult to breathe or stop himself from shivering. Vendor spoke in a calm, reassuring tone.

"Don't worry Larry, you are safe now – to the world you are dead, but you are safe here. Maybe it is best if you do not know where you are but rest assured, this is *ein sicheres Haus* – a safe house... They tried to kill you Herr Vent – they pushed you in the lake and left you for dead..."

"But who pulled me out?"

"Our friend Herr Var – Mike, he pulled you out and revived you – he brought you back to life and brought you here. In the mist they could see nothing. The mist killed you and saved you, that is serendipity..."

"But who...?"

"Those who control the Dark Windows Larry – they had to kill you. They know that you have seen something and I believe that they may have discovered your secret..."

"My secret...?"

"Rest Larry, rest and we will speak later."

Vendor lifted Larry's head and placed two pills on his tongue.

"These will help you sleep..."

He swallowed the pills and drifted back into a visionless oblivion.

▶▶

When he woke again, Larry found himself in a blurred and dimly lit room. He had been dressed in freshly laundered clothes and was slumped in a comfortable armchair. He focused and glanced around the dark interior, it seemed like a basement or storeroom. There was a large wooden desk in the corner with a chrome anglepoise lamp casting light across its dusty surface – a surface strewn with books, overflowing ashtrays and glass jars full of pens.

A deep pile of yellow A4 paper lay in the centre of the desk with a large magnifying glass acting as a paperweight.

The room was full of movie projectors and video machines and the walls were covered with shelves. It seemed like some kind of audio-visual archive – an elaborate collection of films and videos categorised on grey metal shelving. On one shelf were rows of green plastic boxes containing 35mm prints of untitled movies, each neatly numbered using Helvetica Letraset. Another shelf held metal tins of 16mm cine film with titles written in broad black pen on white gaffer tape. Behind him he could see video tapes: Half inch reels, Umatic Cassettes, VHS, Betamax, Hi8, Digi8, MiniDV. The tapes were organised chronologically and their size diminished accordingly. Each tape was labelled in the same neat Germanic script – the marker pens becoming ever more fine as the tapes shrunk in size. Finally, close to the door, from floor to ceiling over many shelves, were row upon row of commercially released DVD videos. Larry attempted to get up from his chair to look at the collection but his head started to pound and, as he fell back into the soft upholstery, the door at the far end of the room swung open and Larry's host entered.

"Herr Vent, Larry – do you mind if I…?"

Vendor reached over and flicked a switch on the wall causing a similar green strip-light to the one in Larry's purgatory classroom to flicker to life, illuminating the shabby square acoustic tiles that covered the ceiling - emphasising the smell of damp and musty cigarettes. He glided over to sit at the desk and swivelled around grasping a slim black notebook. Larry squinted at the desk lamp that had turned Vendor into a silhouette.

"You will have many questions Larry… but you should not ask now. We have priorities and I have much to tell you. This…" he held the book aloft, "this is your book – we took it from your wet clothes. I have taken the liberty, you will forgive me, I have taken the liberty of helping you with your code…"

"My code…?"

"The numbers that you have written in this book. The names – it is very simple if you have the key – the knowledge…"

"What do you mean…?"

Larry remembered the list of names that he had written down on the train to London and the codes, the coordinates from the Godard book. He had meant to research them – to investigate them but had become wrapped up in his London past and the mysteries of Rolle.

"Where am I?"

"You are in Lausanne, you are safe – you are in my little archive, my collection. In a minute we'll get you a nice cup of tea and an aspirin and you'll be right as rain. We will move you again soon – you will be safe with us…"

Larry wanted to ask who 'we' were – but he was starting to think about Godard and the notebook again. His family, friends and scrape with death seemed momentarily less important than solving this riddle.

"And the code Vendor… the code – what does it mean?"
Vendor relaxed and leaned back on his creaking, shabby office chair.

"Ah! It is very simple – as soon as I saw your little list of coordinates I realised. Let me show you…"

He reached over to turn on a video monitor next to his desk, the screen hummed and cast a flickering light into a corner of the gloomy space.

"Take this first coordinate *322/00:15:04(1)*. Well the middle part is obviously a video time code – 15 minutes and 4 seconds into a film, yes?"

It may seem obvious now but Larry hadn't worked it out.

"I then assumed that, as it was a specific time code, we would be looking for a digital recording, a DVD video maybe? And this first number, *322* – this may be a catalogue number…"

Larry sat quietly admiring Vendor's archive mentality as he continued to explain.

"I thought of all the commercially released film series and, by a process of elimination, narrowed it down to one collection of DVDs: *The Criterion Collection*. Here in my own little collection, I have all of these films, these American releases of classic cinema…"

He walked over to the shelves and, with ruthless efficiency, extracted a disc and waved it at Larry…

"So here we have Criterion number 322: *Viridiana* directed by Luis Buñuel!"

Vendor played the film and skipped forwards to 15 minutes and 4 seconds. He paused the film – a clear back and white still image flickered before his eyes…

"What do you see Larry?"

"Two men talking?"

"And now?" Vendor pressed a button on his remote.

"English subtitles?"

"Precisely – and how would you say that the last number of your code refers to Herr Vent? The number 1 in parenthesis?"

"The, err – the first letter of the subtitle?"

"Precisely – the letter T!"

"And you have looked all six codes Vendor?"

"Precisely – the next one 139/01:10:22(2) gives us the letter O from Ingmar Bergman's *Wild Strawberries.*"

"To? The code tells us to go *to* somewhere?"

"T.O.L.E.D.O. to Toledo – the code points to Toledo in Spain!"

"But – but it all sounds a bit arbitrary to me – why hide a single word in such a complex way? I mean how do you know that this isn't just a coincidence – how do you that it's important?"

Vendor looked pleased with himself and cast a patronising glance at Larry before continuing…

"The word is significant precisely because it has been encoded, and then, then there are the names in your book: *Luis Buñuel, Jean-Claude Carrière, George Cukor, Alfred Hitchcock, Rouben Mamoulin, Robert Mulligan, Serge Silverman, George Stevens, Billy Wilder, Robert Wise and William Wyler* – do they not mean anything to you?"

Vendor's questions were enabling Larry to empathise with his vacant students back home in Wales as he blurted out his ill-informed response.

"Well Buñuel's film was the first one that we looked at and – and he was from Spain, but there's no Bergman on that list…"

"I thought that you knew about Surrealism Larry – The Order of Toledo Larry – *The Order…* don't you remember your own stupid film? Here – look!"

Vendor brandished a black and white photograph showing eleven men sitting around a glass coffee table in a plush Hollywood apartment. Larry recognised Buñuel, Wilder and Hitchcock but none of the others.

"This photograph shows the last full meeting of the Order before they were forced underground – all of the men on your list are present here in this photograph. And all of these men had access to a secret that could change the world!"

Vendor took a deep breath and reached into the shadows of his desk from where he pulled a tea tray. He proceeded to pour tea into two fine china cups - he passed one to Larry.

"We would like you to join us Larry."

"You want me to join the Order of Toledo?"

Vendor burst into a sudden fit of laughter and then abruptly stopped as his face became deadly serious.

"No Larry – you will join us in our search for The Order. We want to awaken them – to allow them to fulfil their potential before it is too late. Let me explain…"

Larry sat back quietly in the armchair in Lausanne as Vendor helped to elucidate the matter.

"For many centuries Larry, an alien force has been watching the development of humanity from another dimension… a dimension beyond our current perceptions of reality. They watched as we developed a vague understanding that we are different to other life-forms and they watched and waited as these vague feelings were moulded by early charismatic personalities into what we would now call organised religions.

Over the centuries, these relatively benevolent aliens have donated technology to aid the development of human society. When we turned this technology to inhumane and warlike ends, they realised that we needed to be controlled – or rather that we needed to control ourselves. At the end of the nineteenth century, they decided to make direct contact with the ruling elite and offer them tools of mind control that would hopefully save us from our base instincts. Initially, they provided a simple mind-altering technology that we came to know as cinema and, from this, an ever-more sophisticated technology – known collectively as Dark Windows – has been provided to the ruling class of the world."

Larry felt uncomfortable – somehow Vendor's arguments were convincing him that he had a destiny – that he had been somehow chosen to take on The Dark Windows. He felt that he had to say something cynical to break the paranoid, supernatural discomfort of this fantastic notion…

"I'm sorry Vendor – but I still find all this alien stuff a bit far-fetched…"

A subtle anger crept into Vendor's tone – his eyes flashed as he took a sip from his cup of Earl Grey and continued.

"Okay Larry – have you got a better explanation for why we have all this technology – you think that our monkey brains came up with this stuff? Can you explain how *anything* works Larry? Can you explain why cinema and manned flight were miraculously invented in the same year?"

"N… N… No – but you don't expect me to…?"

"I don't need to prove it - you've seen it in action Larry – you have seen how important the fight to control this technology is. We are just little people scrabbling around in the dark and we are afraid of the light. This alien technology is a franchise offered to those groups within our human society who appear to offer the best hope for stability. Unfortunately, humans being humans, a battle has raged for control of this franchise – a battle between the forces of reaction and revolution. It may have been interesting for those disembodied intelligences to watch these subtle shifts in human society in the same way that we might study a colony of ants.

But for us, for us as we live our brief lives on Earth, for us – our mortality gives us a reason to fight for what we believe in. Do you feel your own mortality Larry?"

Vendor's eyes were open wide behind his small round glasses and his thick receding hairline was bristling atop his manic Germanic face.

"The corporations who currently control the Dark Windows have gone to extreme lengths to protect the franchise – you've seen them in action Larry! The only hope – the only alternative to this corporate control – is to allow the humanists, the ideologues, the artists to take over the collective unconscious. Don't you see that The Order of Toledo are our only hope Larry!"

"Okay Vendor – I'll believe you. I'll be your dumb decoy duck. But don't expect me to play the patsy for you. I won't take the fall for you…"

Maybe it was some kind of Stockholm Syndrome… but Larry was starting to feel dizzy – he suddenly realised that this might all be true, that the vague uneasiness in the depth of his soul was caused by the way that his dreams and desires were controlled by the corporate elites who watched over his every move. He suddenly felt a window opening in his subconscious – he felt that he *could* be free – that he *could* liberate himself from the shackles of the corporate world, from quality systems and risk assessments and identity cards and bank accounts. That he could free himself from social networking and the screens that stole his time on Earth. He recognised that all of the technology in the world had the potential for liberation, truth and beauty but instead was being utilised as a series of tools to shackle his desires. As Larry started to focus his waves of paranoia and guilt into a series of possible revolutionary paths of action, Vendor continued with his brief history lesson.

"The first cinematic technology was franchised to humanity at the end of the 19th century, in Europe – the British Empire a place called Walton-on-Thames, to Cecil Hepworth and his friends. The Americans stole Hepworth's ideas in order to develop bland, industrialised, invisible editing techniques. At the same time the Soviet film makers got hold of this technology and used it to develop the art of montage – they were attempting to use film in order to awaken humanity. So, it was no accident that as Stalin tightened his grip, he turned away from avant-garde techniques and towards the same bland social realism and invisible editing that corporate America had developed. As you look deeper into the history you will discover the links between war, weapons and cinema but the main point is this: The battle for control of the universal unconscious continues to this day.

The Order of Toledo hold the unrealised potential of a unified Europe, they have the narratives that can tap into your dreams and touch your subconscious. Godard joined the Order in the 1950s and he once had the means to change the world through the art of cinema. But now… now cinema is losing its power to affect the world – we have one last chance to change the world through film, to save the world from the Bland Corporation. We have to help The Order of Toledo take control of the Dark Windows. We have to convince the world that The Order is the only organisation that should be allowed to control the Dark Windows and you *must* help Larry."

"But I thought the Dark Windows were the bad guys?"

"No Larry – Dark Windows is just the name given to the mechanism that the bad guys use. The Bland Corporation are the guys who control the Dark Windows and they exist to maintain the status quo – to maintain the inequalities in the world. You can help us find the archive of the Order and awaken the sleeping giant, you have to do it – it is your destiny. You have become invisible – you no longer exist, everyone thinks that you are dead.

The Bland Corporation have killed or scared off all of the key members of The Order. I would call them the Leaders but... The Order has no leaders, it is not corporate – it is a syndicate; a loose association of like-minded individuals. These individuals have sworn allegiance to a revolutionary ideal but they do not know who else may belong – they exist in small cells and they wait until the windows open a crack, they wait for access to the technology and this access is nearly always tantalisingly out of their reach.

If you can make direct contact with The Order – if you can get through to the remaining members, we can do the rest. Mike and I have links with Toledo sleeper cells in the major broadcasting networks – we can release the secrets that The Order hold and bring down the Bland Corporation... but we need you to find the remaining members of the Order in Toledo itself. They have something stored there – something that we need - but they, the Keepers, they are not aware of its importance"

"But what about Casey and the kids? What about Chris, Sandy and Joe – can I trust them?"

"First thing I learnt in the conspiracy game: Trust no-one Larry. Casey and the kids will not be safe until they are with us – I have sent Mike back to England to collect them"

"It's Wales..."

"What is whales?"

"Never mind – can I call Mike?"

"Why don't you have a nice warm bath? I could give you a 'phone later – you can call Mike, but don't tell him anything and don't speak to anyone else unless you trust them one hundred percent! You are better off staying dead for the moment, OK?"

"OK Vendor – I'll go along with you. I can't go back now and face Rhodri and all the other pointless, grey men - I'll be your dumb decoy duck."

At the back of Vendor's archive was a small functional bathroom, tiled in white with a single round mirror and no window. After a brief tour of the collection and the hypnotic assertions of Vendor's lecture, Larry was happy to be alone – soaking his chilled body in a hot bath. The mirror was steamed up and condensation ran down the grubby white tiles. Mildew inhabited the grout and sealant around the chipped enamel tub. The smell of damp decay blended with the fresh scent of the orange that he had just eaten and the subtle aroma of the Earl Grey tea that he had taken into the bath. He lay back in the hot water, soaking his aching body – sweating and coughing in equal measure. He felt tired and rough; the brush with death had obviously disagreed with him. He stared idly at the items sitting on the end of the bath: A little pile of orange peel, an empty tea cup and a shampoo bottle. First the power of nature floated across his shallow consciousness:

The orange peel has a natural beauty – humanity would struggle to invent anything as beautiful as an orange...

The simple form of the modernist cup contrasted with the organic form of the orange peel but it too had a power borne of simplicity and abstraction:

A white ceramic vessel from which to drink – ergonomic with no ornamentation – a powerfully simple designed object – designed by an individual as a utopian answer to an ancient question...

Larry was struggling to stay awake as he contemplated the third object – a plastic shampoo bottle:

Again – simple and functional with abstract forms and text printed on the surface – the bottle becomes anchored by signs that devalue its functionality – it turns from a bottle of hair soap into a tool to make you unhappy with your hair, your life, your world... 'Restore your beautifully natural shine'. Who said I lost my shine? Who said I want to shine – what is my natural shine? Why do I feel inadequate? They know that I never had a shine in the first place...

Larry considered this shampoo slogan as the warm bath water trickled into his ears and he drifted off to sleep again. He was obviously more deeply affected by the drowning than he had realised and he wasn't quite ready to take care of himself, let alone take on the might of the Dark Windows.

II

As Vendor and his shadowy colleagues carefully removed the unconscious Larry from the warm and misty bathroom, the Cold War between the Bland Corporation and the Order of Toledo was developing in a darker place outside of the glare of publicity. Little did Larry know that he was being closely watched, that his insignificant form was a key pawn in the ancient battle between the real and the imagined.

Chapter 27
Apocalypse Now

The insistent shrieks of herring gulls drew Larry from his slumber. Somehow he had been transported from the bath to another bed in another bedroom – warmer and brighter this time. Morning sunlight filtered through wooden Venetian blinds. His eyes explored the quiet room, the fan slowly rotating on the ceiling – he spotted his black bag from the Hotel Gai Remeuz sitting by the window.

How did that get here? How did I get here?

The possessions from his pockets were arranged neatly on the bedside table. His Swiss Railway watch and wallet, his wad of Euros, his notebook and keys sat alongside a tumbler of water, some prescription pills, a disposable lighter and a packet of French cigarettes sporting the slogan "*Fumer tue*". He reached over and took a cigarette from the packet; he lit it and inhaled deeply as his bloodshot eyes explored the ceiling, transfixed by the rotating fan – attempting to make sense of his situation. He allowed himself to relax back into the mattress as he slowly savoured the nicotine. When he finally reached the filter, he stubbed it out on the packet and struggled from the bed. He stretched and staggered over to the window, peering through the blinds at the outside world.

Lausanne – shit, I'm still only in Lausanne. Every time I think I'm going to wake up back in Colwyn Bay.

The window of Larry's bedroom commanded a view over the rooftops of Lausanne as they stepped down to the cobalt waters of Lac Léman.

Lausanne – I don't know anything about this place, I thought it was in France...

⏮

Lausanne is another European city founded around a Roman settlement; it is a Swiss university city, capital of the Vaud canton and only a few kilometres from Rolle. It is home to the International Olympic Committee – a quiet, affluent, conservative place. A deep gorge runs through its centre, cutting it in two. The gorge is a useful metaphor for the divisions that, under its calm veneer, rent the city apart. Lausanne is home to one of the most active, powerful and secret recruiting cells of the Order of Toledo; woven into the fabric of the university and the culture of the city – secretly recruiting the young and impressionable to The Order's anarchic and revolutionary ideals. Who knows how many students have left Lausanne as members of The Order – moving on to set up sleeper cells across Europe, across the world?

Apart its share of youthful demonstrations in the 1960s, the only clues to the city's links with the Order of Toledo are its annual Underground Film Festival and the protests that occasionally spill onto its carefully tended streets.

⏭

Larry wandered back to the bedside table, picked up his wallet and studied his damp, smudged photographs of Casey, Lilly and Alfie.

What should I say to Casey about this? I haven't spoken to her about any of this... when I was in Colwyn Bay I wanted to be back in London – back in the past. And now – now I'm here, where am I? I must have been here a week – now I'm getting softer, I can hardly walk. Every minute I stay in this limbo between dream and reality I get weaker... And every minute the Dark Windows send out their messages to the world and they get stronger, they tighten their grip...

⏮

Lausanne is also the place where, in the 1960s, the Polish engineer, Stefan Kudelski, developed his Nagra tape recorder. The Nagra may seem an innocuous machine but its effect on the film industry was revolutionary: It allowed the recording of reality – filmed images and taped sounds could be recorded separately and synchronised in the edit room. It liberated filmmakers from the requirements of heavy audio equipment and allowed them to record Guerrilla-style on the streets. From the 1960s until the 1990s, with support from the Order of Toledo, Kudelski's Nagra was the technology that allowed the ideology of Europe's cinematic New Waves to spread across the world. Kudelski also provided President Kennedy with the SN or Série Noire tape recorder. It is believed that the recordings Kennedy made with his Série Noire machine are what led to his untimely death. What does it all mean: Chaos theory, conspiracy theory, alien technology? Whichever track you trace, the world would be a different place if Kudelski had not manufactured the Nagra.

What does it mean? Nagra is Polish for "it will record" – John Travolta used one in Brian De Palma's *Blow Out* – when he played an audio engineer whose life is endangered by a recording that he accidentally makes of a car crash, a film that references the death of Kennedy and acknowledges Antonioni's 1966 film *Blow-up*, in which a photographer accidentally records an image of a dead body in an East London park, a park that Larry filmed when he was a student in London. Coincidence? Synchronicity?

It will record.

▶▶|

Larry stared through the blinds at the tranquil lake, he turned, and was attempting to loosen his feverish joints with a half-hearted attempt at Tai Chi, when Vendor knocked on the light composite door and swiftly entered. He was still dressed in black and smelling of the twentieth century.

"Larry you are okay? You will see that our friend Herr Brassey has secretly brought your bag here, your things from the hotel? And I have tried to salvage your wet belongings – But your 'phone, it was destroyed by the water. I have a 'phone here for you and I have entered Mike's number only. Perhaps – in the light of events – of our talking yesterday – perhaps it is best if this is the only call you will make?"

He carefully placed the 'phone on the bedside table.

"If you are happy now – we can head for Spain this afternoon. I may drive through the night… and maybe we vill meet up with Mike en-route?"

Vendor left, smiling enthusiastically. Larry remained silent, he felt that this was all an intriguing prospect – that, somehow a plan was coming together. He had made a snap decision that he was with The Order – they would protect him: Sandy, Joe, Mike and Vendor with Casey as his roots and the strength of the Godard revelation… he seemed to have a focus now that was driving him on.

Someone had tried to kill him, Winkle and the Dark Windows were a threat that he couldn't deal with on his own. Somehow he didn't fully believe any of them but he'd left his stupid job behind now – he'd gone too far, and if all that he ends up with is a crazy set of photographs of some eccentric secret organisation, some minimal travelogue or fictional narrative – he felt certain that Joe could spin it into some kind of artwork. Joe and Sandy could help him sell it – whatever it is. He was settled into his discomfort zone now and heading for a new one. It was worth risking his life for some excitement… and Spain, Toledo – it all sounded exotic.

His fixed idea – his certainty in all this was that he couldn't return to another decade of repetitive administrative tautology: He couldn't do another ten years of what passed as teaching, only to find himself having to do a further ten years before retiring to slow death in a bungalow around the corner. No – he had to go to Toledo – unearth The Order and forge a new life. Cinema controlled his conscious and subconscious – it was his obsession and this obsession had grabbed him and thrown him into a narrative more bizarre than any fictional encounter… This was reality.

⏭️

Two hours later Larry found his still-aching body packed into the rear of Vendor's white Renault van, lying on an old mattress with all his possessions crammed in a small black bag. He was still feeling strangely light-headed, more than you would expect from a mere brush with death. He suppressed a nagging doubt that Vendor may be drugging his Earl Grey. As the van set off through the suburbs of Lausanne and towards the Motorway, Larry could not see the black Mercedes that was trailing them from a distance, windows following windows. There were no windows in the white van and the polished Mercedes' windows were dark.

The long pilgrimage to Toledo had begun. As Larry lay in the back of the van, staring at the welded panels on the ceiling, he was reminded of Buñuel's *The Milky Way*: A film about a different pilgrimage to Spain, a story about two tramps and their journey to the tomb of Saint James in Santiago – a pilgrimage to an ultimately empty sarcophagus. *The Milky Way* was the film that Larry had found in *House Bargains* – a film that destroys space and time. Now Larry was setting off on his own pilgrimage, a pilgrimage to the spiritual hometown of the father of cinematic surrealism: Luis Buñuel.

It is 1500 kilometres from Lausanne to Toledo, an overland trek that traces the course of other European pilgrims, scraping a random orthodoxy from a historical mess; piecing together a route, a goal based on the accumulation of chance acts; human, physical and geographical. First they aimed for the Swiss border, into France and the European Union. Droning along with the smell of diesel towards Catalonia and the Franco Spanish border.

Before they set off, Larry had spoken briefly to Mike who was heading North in his Austin Montego, to Wales, to collect Casey and the kids. Although he had no real reason to, he trusted Mike. He was reassured by his apparent sincerity – he felt that Mike was on the side of the poor and downtrodden, that his working class credentials stamped him as realist, reassuring and reliable. In his recumbent and vaguely hallucinatory state,

Larry mulled over the issues and then attempted to shout a question to Vendor in the driving seat.

"Vendor! Where are we going to stay when we get there?"

Vendor couldn't hear, he was playing with the radio, shifting gear and opening cheap packets of French cigarettes. They were on a mission in a shabby white van, cutting a swathe through a new Europe - a quixotic pairing heading to Spain, Toledo, La Mancha. Towards the dust and the heat, the desolate wilderness – ever more Southern, ever more warm. Larry could sense the change from within the white box as he spent hours drifting in and out of consciousness – dreaming his way through Figueras, birthplace of Dali. As they crept along the desolate Spanish motorways, he could see nothing and felt little. In the front, Vendor was singing along with the Euro radio, talking as he ate noisily and flung snacks excitedly into the back of the van.

"Here's a little song I wrote... we will be in Toledo before you know it Larry... you vill never find a more wretched hive of scum and villainy... don't vorry, be happy! I like this song Larry... You would like some more food *ja?"*

Vendor tossed a packet of bear-shaped crisps over his shoulder and whistled along to the radio. Larry was just drifting back to sleep, his half-formed thoughts drifting with him. He knew there was something wrong, that he shouldn't be allowing some crazy German to take him to Spain incognito…

This is some adventure – does Casey know what's happening? What about Sandy and Joe? What about Buñuel? – This is some pilgrimage… perhaps we should be heading to Antwerp – Saint Dymphna, patron saint of mental illness – I don't know much about Toledo – El Greco – the Greek painter what's that big painting – it's divided into two parts – Heaven and Earth, I bet there's a UFO somewhere in that…

Larry was pondering these unhinged ideas and was drifting back to sleep when a packet of bear-shaped crisps hit him in the face and woke him temporarily before he mulled himself back into a convalescent slumber.

II

Vendor stayed wide awake behind the wheel of the white van as it bypassed Barcelona and headed through Zaragoza with the black Mercedes still stalking from a discreet distance.

Not far to Toledo now...

Chapter 28
Out of the Past

"Toledo filled me with wonder, more because of its indefinable atmosphere than for its touristic attractions. I went back many times... until finally, in 1923, on Saint Joseph's Day, I founded the Order of Toledo." [13]

The Order of Toledo was established in 1923 by the Spanish filmmaker, Luis Buñuel, following his mysterious encounter with the providers of cinematic technology in the desert outside Calanda[14]. Initially The Order was established to support and defend human poetry; the written word, against the new machine poetry of the motion-picture industry. Over the next six years he expanded the Order across Europe and into America – coming to a realisation that the only means by which the cinematic machine could be halted in its inexorable spread was to take control of it. He came to understand that technology cannot be un-invented and that it would require a secret international confederation of artists to stop this alien technology being used by the ruling elites to control humanity via the mechanisation of the collective unconscious. Buñuel soon mastered the art of cinema and, in 1929 he made *Un Chien Andalou* with fellow *Caballero* of The Order, Salvador Dali. Their radical exposure of the power of cinema scared the fascists of Europe and the subsequent threats forced Buñuel into exile. First, he traveled

---

[13] Luis Buñuel, *My Last Breath* (1982)
[14] For more details see: Larry Went, *The Dark Windows of Cinema Pt. 1* (unpublished)

to the USA where he established the Hollywood arm of The Order with Charlie Chaplin and Alfred Hitchcock as *Grandes Caballeros*. The American fascists soon ensured Buñuel's exile to Mexico, where he was to remain until the 1960s when the radical Parisian arm of The Order (the *Cinémathèque Française* - the original Archive of The Order) allowed Buñuel to return, triumphant, to Europe where he created revolutionary cinematic masterpieces until his death in 1983. Toledo and its Order of *Cabelleros*, had been the spiritual heart of the battle for control of the Dark Windows since the very early days of cinema and Buñuel was the Order's atheist founder. To Vendor and Larry, the pilgrimage to Toledo was a search for truth – a search for a new God.

Larry liked gods; man created them in the same way that he created mermaids, secret brotherhoods, stories and worlds within worlds. As far as he was concerned, parallel universes and all the other expanding explanations that tie down the inexplicable uncertainties of life: Landscape, sex, seduction, music, the sea of damp air that we inhabit and the stars beyond, were all inventions of mankind and it was all too much for one simian brain to comprehend.

He had been thrashing about in the back of the van for close to seventeen hours, his mind projecting imaginary pictures of Spain onto the white steel panels. Suddenly, the rear doors were flung open to reveal the hot, dry reality of a dusty back street in the heart of the ancient city of Toledo. The world outside the van was like the world outside the cinema - bustling, hyper-real, three-dimensional. Stone, huge hewn blocks piled high into buildings, the city's medieval streets threading organically, creating a labyrinthine form suspended in the Iberian body somewhere just below Madrid like a vital organ of uncertain function - the spleen of Spain. Vendor unloaded Larry from the back of the van, still dreamy and shaking, and led him into the graffiti-covered Toledo safe house. He laid a large, long key in his palm and whispered in his ear,

"Up the stairs Larry, room eight!"

He winked, smiled and drove slowly away. Larry looked around. A little girl wearing an oversized, dirty, hand-knitted, v-neck jumper - about the same age as his Lilly, was kicking a blue football against the worn walls of the safe house. She had been studying Larry and Vendor - taking in their mute exchange and creating from it her own narrative of their relationship. She had watched Vendor guide Larry into the doorway and drive away. Larry became aware of her presence and smiled at her, she looked confused, turned and ran away down the grimy street.

Nobody except Vendor knew where he was now - Vendor was the only link between Larry and his prior life. He was the only one who knew why he was here in the medieval city of Toledo, even he wasn't certain. He had come here to contact The Order and release information that could open the Dark Windows. He had joined a battle between the forces of reaction and revolution. He had become a revolutionary - fighting against those who suppressed art, fighting against those who had killed Godard. Buried in the back of his consciousness, he had a psychological get-out clause: If it all turned out to be some crazy charade, he could turn the whole experience into an artwork, a story, a film; he could go back to Joe and use his history to buy some favours.

He turned into the dim, dank hallway and climbed the dark staircase until he reached the door with a number eight screwed into its rotten wood. He listened - the other rooms in the safe house sounded empty. He turned the large key in the old lock, entered, sat on the steel-framed bed that confronted him and scanned the minimal room. He felt that he should be wistful and homesick – that he *should* feel the absence of his own furniture, his books, his collections of films, photographs and music - that he should be concerned about the loss of his job, his routine. He had dreamt the destruction of all his paraphernalia and, now that he was free of it, it felt good. The ashes of his suburban life had been taken by a northwest wind and scattered across the seas. He had gone, he no longer existed in that other place. Despite this superficial wist, his lack of regret, there was a pain deeper inside Larry's corporeal existence – a dread and a love. Despite his attempt to shed the weight of his personal history and social conditioning, somewhere at his core, he felt a need for Casey, Alfie and Lilly. He knew his ultimate weakness was obvious really - he couldn't just discard his family. Sometime he would have to let them know where he was, how he was. Now he was completely alone in an alien city with no language and no leads, hiding from a fanciful, illusive assassin on a vague mission to make contact with a nebulous organisation – and he was happy.

A light tap on the door threw his thoughts into relief. The landlord of the safe house entered, he spoke near-perfect English with a slight Latin American accent.

"Hi Larry, I'm Tristan – you feeling better?" He didn't wait for a response; his lightness and informality didn't seem to match Larry's perceptions of the gravity of the situation, "Cool... anyway I'll keep out of your way. Vendor told me that you have work to do here – you here on business man is that right?"

Larry stared at the two Tristans in front of him, formed them into one and then focused intently on him before silently nodding his agreement.

"Yeah, right, well, Vendor tells me that you are to go to *Posada de la Sangre* – it's a bar on the *Plaza Colegio Infantes*. You're to go there and meet his friend..."

"Which friend?"

"That's all he said *amigo* – *Posada de la Sangre* in thirty minutes. It's just around the corner from here – give a turn left and you will find it. You want anything later – blow on my door, I'm just over the hall – with the big letter 'A' on my door – OK?"

Larry had just enough time to shower and change into a clean T-shirt. He showered in the joy of freedom, of a change in his life that had taken him from there to here in few days. The energy that he had, for years, invested in an academic Punch and Judy show for a cynical and disinterested audience was now finding a new outlet – he felt refreshed and alert, aware of his own strength again, an independent human.

He exited the Spanish safe house and turned left. A slight sweat formed on his forehead as he attempted to contextualise the next step, did the heat of the afternoon or the thought of meeting Vendor's associate cause it? He wasn't exactly sure how he should act, how he should walk through the streets of Toledo. The only frames of reference that he had for this chicanery were the films that he had seen – he began to consider how Michael Caine's Harry Palmer might act in this situation; wandering through a dusty South European city, heading for a rendezvous with an agent. He started to wish that his brother was with him to photograph this assignment…

What happened to Chris? Does he think I'm dead? Shouldn't I at least let him know where I am? Perhaps I should 'phone Casey again…

Just as his thoughts were drifting into a familial, domestic mode – he was shocked back into the reality of his present predicament on the hot dusty streets of the spleen of Toledo. A few yards ahead of him there was an exotic pastry shop - *una pastelería*. As Larry started to consider the cakes in the encroaching shop window; which ones Casey, Lilly and Alfie would like if they were here; he was confronted by a face from the core of this whole charade. It couldn't be another coincidence; *they* must have followed him here from Rolle…

As Larry approached the *pastelería,* Dewi Winkle was leaving, gently cradling a gold box wrapped in a chocolate-brown ribbon. He appeared to be oblivious to Larry as he headed in the other direction, down the crowded cobbled lane and into a narrow alley on the left hand side of the street. Larry edged slowly down the lane - the few steps to the alley's entrance seemed fraught with danger. He was attempting to be inconspicuous but felt that everyone on that crowded thoroughfare was watching him out of the corner of their collective sliced eye.

When he reached the junction, he surreptitiously glanced up at the street name - *Plaza Colegio Infantes*, he looked down the short, gloomy alley that opened out into a dark square beyond. The only public premises in this narrow *callejón* seemed to be a bar – Larry strolled casually up to the door and looked at the sign: *Posada de la Sangre* – he tried to look the name of the bar up in his cerebral Spanish phrase book – *The Inn of Blood* – it seemed a strange name for a bar, but this was where Tristan had told him to meet someone, surely he can't be meeting Dewi – Vendor would have warned him.

Larry pushed open the ancient wooden door of *Posada de la Sangre* and entered the hushed space of a small, quiet bar. A few old men were sitting in small groups around small tables, drinking cold beer from small glasses and chewing the occasional olive as they drew deeply on dark cigarettes. Nobody looked up at him as he entered and scanned the cramped, dingy, smoky interior. Dewi Winkle was sitting at a table in the shadows of the darkest corner of the room. His bony white hand emerged from the dark into a dusty shaft of sunshine that smoked across the room from some hidden skylight and beckoned to Larry with a swift movement of his index finger. In a daze, Larry floated over to the table and found himself sitting opposite Dewi Winkle. It was Dewi who had threaded through this whole affair; he had mysteriously appeared at and disappeared from the bridge game that night in Penmachno, he had materialised at the funeral and followed Larry to London, it was Dewi who had crept through Larry's subconscious at the *Hôtel Gai-Remuez* and left him for dead in *Lac Léman*. Larry had imagined that Dewi was behind the burglary at his house, the attempt on his life and the death of Godard in Penmaenmawr. Larry had slowly been convinced that the conspiracy was real and that Dewi was the mysterious Magog – agent of the Dark Windows.

Somehow Larry found himself sitting in *Posada de la Sangre* with a small brandy and Dewi Winkle in front of him. Dewi was wearing the same black-zipped outfit and poker face that had stared at him across the bridge table in

Penmachno. Although that now seemed an eternity ago, it had been just a matter of days before. Dewi blinked slowly and turned his head from side to side as his pupils widened and he spoke.

"Hello again Larry, I understand that Vendor has sent you here on a mission to Contact the Order of Toledo – is that so?"

"But are you – I mean did Vendor want me to meet *you* here?"

"You could say that Vendor facilitated this meeting. Would you like a cake Larry? These little custard tarts are exquisite with a brandy…"

Dewi gently untied the brown ribbon and opened the gold box that sat in the centre of the table. As the box fell open, music started to float through the bar, Larry instantly recognized it as Angelo Badalamenti's theme from *Twin Peaks* – a strange choice for a bar in Toledo. He felt a discomforting nostalgia sweeping over him as the music reverberated around the stone walls. Larry bit into a small tart and Dewi continued…

"I am speaking to you now Larry as a friend of your brother – to warn you. To warn you that there has already been one murder and I don't want another one on my conscience…"

"Do you mean Godard?"

"I was at the funeral… Look Larry, you may now consider yourself to be an amateur detective but you're a professional fool and you were born to be murdered. There is something much darker here than your silly game – your project for Joe Locke and your little sojourn with Herr Busch!"

Larry took a sip of his drink and smiled at Dewi, trying to keep his newfound composure, trying to remain cool and avoid the paranoia that the music and the meeting were starting to etch into his flaky self-image. He began to feel dizzy again, he thought about the cake he had just eaten and held his brandy glass up to the light. He thought about Alice in Wonderland - *eat me, drink me* – why had he taken unsolicited snacks from a man who could be – who may be…

"Are you Magog Dewey?"

Dewi laughed beguilingly, "It is Dewi, not Dewey, and no, I don't believe I am who you think I may be…"

Dewi's face shifted and distorted – an owl, a Godard, a Lakeside Heavy – again, again Larry was confusing reality with dreams – again he felt drugged, hypnotised, edgy – he doubted whether he had ever been fully in control of reality as he peered out at the dim Toledo bar from within his fragile human skull. The bar began to spin around, Larry caught fragments of false theories as Dewi talked at him; his eyes and smile fixed – locked on Larry – boring into Larry's slipping, drunken consciousness…

"You have watched too many old films Larry, you compare everything that you encounter in the real world to a film that you have watched. You have bought into simplistic outmoded ideologies – the world has moved on – this is the twenty-first century Larry – you don't have the answers – none of us mere mortals have the answers…"

Larry's fingers were numb – pins and needles toyed with his toes. He was concentrating on the breath – *breathe in, breathe out* – Dewi's corporeal being was disintegrating before his eyes, his voice still rang through the bar, his smile floated in front of Larry's blurring vision…

"You see Larry, this confusion that you feel, this plurality of values, makes you uncomfortable in the contemporary world. It allows the Dark Windows to function effectively; there can be no unity in opposition when there are so many little groups, little individuals that grasp elements of the Dark Windows while never seeing the full picture. There was a time when people glimpsed the truth together, communally – cinema, theatre, live music were places where people gathered to feels things together. Dark Windows is the propaganda arm, the communications department of a broader conspiracy to create The New World Order. The Bland Corporation and their friends are planning a lockdown of humanity; they are farming your subconscious in order to control it. This is why we now have technology that keeps people at home – trapped in their own little worlds typing their deepest thoughts and dreams into electronic consoles. Home cinema is not cinema – everything now is spectacularly bland and significantly trivial. I want to help you Larry but first you must help yourself – you have to act and not just wander along some vague path. You have to ask yourself, do you really care about Godard or Vendor or the people in this bar? Are you interested in anything outside of the flickering images that you see projected onto screens? Do you even care about your own wife and children? What is this fantasy that you are living Larry – is this reality Larry?" His voice, which had risen to a crescendo, fell again to a whisper. "Go to this address and find the Archive of the Order, you must be careful, you must not give too much away. When you have confirmed that this is the place, Vendor will know what to do…"

Dewi thumped the table causing the gold cake box to jump in the air and the remainder of Larry's brandy to spill – drip, drip – on the floor. He studied the drips for seconds that stretched to minutes and when he looked up Dewi was gone. A note sat on the table, weighed down by a small metal flashlight, he read the address: *6 Plaza Colegio Infantes*.

Chapter 29
Tristana

Grasping the directions to the Archive, Larry turned left out of *Posada de la Sangre* and crept into the dark silent stone enclosure of *Plaza Colegio Infantes*. The worn walls and dirty windows of the plaza enclosed him and rose up forming a blue square of sky, that spoke the subtleties of Spanish Surrealism. In amongst the shuttered dirty walls, there was a small, dark shop with the word *antigüedades* painted artlessly on its signboard. The store window was full of faded bric-a-brac: a blue ceramic rabbit, a cheap quartz clock, a few souvenirs of other European cities – a cup from Cologne, an ashtray from Rome. The door was uninviting, coated with a layer of grime that suggested it was seldom used. Larry tried the round door handle, it turned smoothly and an electronic bell chimed like Westminster somewhere in the back as he pushed it open. He heard a body struggle to its feet and slowly approach from the shadows of the back room. He looked around and found himself in a dark and dusty shop. Kitsch ornaments were randomly piled on wooden crates and the floor of the claustrophobic store was covered with cardboard boxes containing what appeared to be house clearances from the 1970s that hadn't been looked at for thirty years. As the shopkeeper appeared from the back, Larry idly turned over some of the china cups on top of one of the boxes, as if to look at the marks, as if he were a collector.

A disheveled old woman stood in front of him, her coarse pale skin and thick black hair suggested that she had spent her life in Toledo, hiding in this dark shop – waiting for something to happen. Larry smiled at her and tried his best Spanish phrase,

"*¿usted habla inglés?*"

"A little, a little…"

"I am a collector, I'm looking for something specific…"

"Specific?"

"Something particular."

"I am sorry, we only sell to dealers, we are commercial."

Looking around the dingy shop, he could see that there was nothing commercial about the premises. They weren't wholesalers and no one would really want any of the trash that seemed to stock there. He tried a more specific approach…

"I collect owls – do you have any owls?"

She looked at him with dark, blank eyes. He continued…

"I'm looking for china owls – *buhos*"

"I am sorry, we are for commercial only."

"You must have some stock here in these unopened boxes – some things that you haven't looked at yet. Do you archive all of your items? I like this, how much is it? *¿cuánto es él?*"

Larry had picked up a small dish from Santiago and was turning it over in his hand, trying to force a response from her. She looked straight at him and repeated her negative sales pitch…

"We are for commercial only, I am sorry sir."

He decided to press her a little; he needed to find out what this place was – whether this anonymous, shabby shop really could be a front for the Archive of The Order.

"Actually, I am commercial – I am a dealer in antiques. I have a small shop in Colwyn Bay, in Wales - *en País de Gales*. I would like to buy some Spanish homeware in bulk - ornaments, collections, anything really. Do you have a large stock out the back – in your storeroom?"

Behind her dull, expressionless eyes, the old lady seemed to understand every word.

"Sorry, we have little stock, very little – just what you may see here. But we close now – only open for commercial. You come back on Saturday and speak to *el jefe*?"

Larry smiled and left, there was nothing in that musty shop that a dealer would want. Even if she sold a full box of tat every day, the profit wouldn't be enough to keep her supplied with cheap *Rioja*. The place was obviously bogus – a front for something. It could be drugs, gambling, stolen goods – he was certain that Vendor and Dewi were right; this address had significance – it was connected to The Order of Toledo. His instincts had started to work, he was relying on them in a way that he hadn't for years – he wasn't thinking too hard, he was ready for action.

▶▶|

Larry paced the streets for an hour or two – merging with the tourists and soaking up the medieval atmosphere. As the sun lowered in the west and evening approached, he returned to *Plaza Colegio Infantes*. The windows of the shop were shuttered now and no light spilled from any of the surrounding buildings. Compared to the bustling city all around, the Plaza was as silent as a tomb. He sat on a stone bench and considered his options as the last rays of sun disappeared and darkness engulfed the square. From the adjoining streets, he could hear the sounds of the city; whining mopeds, pumping music and chatter from the bars and cafes. But here, there was no one – no light, no sound.

This must be it; this square that surrounds me must contain The Archive. These buildings on all four sides must be interconnected. In each room there must be shelves – glass cases full of objects - each with the potential to defeat the Bland Corporation. There must be boxes full of Godard notebooks; evidence linking the Bland Corporation with every dirty deed carried out in the name of maintaining order, in the name of Realism.

When he was certain that no one was moving about or passing through the square, he strolled over to the shop and studied the heavily fortified entrance. The windows were barred and the door appeared to be fastened with two large deadlocks – there seemed to be no way in. He considered attempting to force it with his shoulder. He leant his full weight against the door and gently turned the handle. To his surprise, it swung quietly open and he nearly fell headfirst into the dark interior. There were no Westminster chimes this time and no footsteps, save for Larry's, as he crept in and carefully closed the unlocked door behind him. The shop was as dark as the inside of a coffin. He felt his way to the back of the room, trying hard to avoid the boxes and objects scattered across the floor. Then he remembered the torch that Dewi had left for him, he fumbled in his pocket, flashed the light around the space and headed towards the staircase that appeared to be the only other exit: a steep flight of steps with a closed door at the top. He crept slowly up and was just about to try the handle when he heard heavy footsteps on the other side. He froze and considered his options – he *could* clatter down the wooden stairs, out into the air and life of the Toledo evening. Alternatively, he could stay and confront the approaching footsteps. He was rigid with anticipation – trapped in the narrow stairwell like a rabbit in the headlights. Fear gripped Larry; he stopped his breath and held his body inanimate. The man on the other side of the door tried the handle – he could see a chink of light vibrating at his feet. The man had a torch, was he a fellow burglar? Without warning, the door handle turned abruptly. If he had opened the door, Larry would have had to confront him there and then. But, instead of opening the door, the mysterious man put a key in the lock, turned it and walked away into the silent rooms beyond.

That's it now, there's no way I can force this door without making a noise. Maybe I shouldn't be here anyway – maybe I should escape from this weird environment, just go to the station, buy a ticket and go back home. I don't know why I bought into all this...

Just as he was about to steal back down and escape, he sensed movement in the shop at the foot of the stairs. He looked down and noticed that the front door was ajar and a torch's beam was flickering across the dusty shelves below.

Shit, I'm stuck now. I can't go down and can't go up – they'll get me for breaking and entering – I've got no I.D. and the world thinks I'm dead. I'll rot in a Spanish jail until Magog finds me and finishes the job that he started in Rolle.

In desperation, Larry quietly gripped the door handle at the top of the stairs, unexpectedly he found that it too turned and the door fell open. He regained his focus, slipped through the narrow doorway and carefully, silently closed it behind him as the footsteps started to ascend from below.

Whoever turned that key a minute ago must have been expecting someone and it wasn't me.

He swiftly swept the torch's beam around the upstairs landing, searching for a possible bolt-hole. The hallway was windowless and sparse; save for a worn red wool carpet that stretched ahead to a dark brown door under which another chink of light flickered. From behind him, at the other end of the corridor, slow, light footsteps were climbing the stairs. He had to hide somewhere quick and there wasn't room to hide a woodlouse in this lousy corridor. To the left of the landing were two doors, Larry ducked into the first one and gently closed it behind him, just as the mysterious visitor stepped onto the landing. He held his breath and listened to his pounding heart as the footsteps passed his hiding place and headed onwards to the dark door at the end of the landing.

He breathed a sigh of relief, turned his torch on and glanced around the room that he had hidden himself in. It was an old lady's bedroom - heavy wooden furniture, dressing table with mirror and hairbrush. The room smelt of lavender and talcum – damp and rotten. He began to feel that he had been set-up; that he had blundered into the old shopkeeper's living quarters and that any moment now he would be accosted by her husband or son and accused of burglary. He switched off his torch, opened the door a crack and peered along towards the end of the corridor – searching for signs of life.

He didn't have to wait long before the far door opened and a silhouette flashed onto the back of his eyes. Before he could register the figure, the door shut again and the outline walked towards him carrying a bag. Through the narrow crack, Larry glimpsed a familiar face and sensed his odour – it was Dewi Winkle looking drawn and worried. The sight of his mysterious comrade seemed to affirm that this place was linked to The Order of Toledo, but why was Dewi here and what was his connection to The Order? A few minutes ago, he had felt like a mug, he had felt that Dewi had duped him. But now, with the appearance of Dewi in this dark world of antiquities, now he was back on the track of the Godard mystery – back on the trail of the Dark Windows.

He softly stepped out onto the landing and watched Dewi disappear down the staircase. His first thought was to run after him, to ask him why was here and what he should do next. He realised that he was alone now; that Dewi had his own reasons for being here and that his job now was to awaken The Order, to force them to rise up and challenge the Bland Corporation. Larry resolved to investigate the room from where Dewi had appeared. He crept along the landing, cautiously opened the door and found himself in a peculiar dark room. It was a large, high-ceilinged chamber rendered into a maze by a network of tall metal shelving. Each shelf was piled high with uniform cardboard boxes – it was an archive – The Archive. Just as he had imagined when sitting in the square below, this must be just one of many such rooms. He could sense in this library/museum an extent – a development. The shelves and boxes were clean and organised, free of dust and damp; a contrast to the shabby shop downstairs. The only entrance to The Archive was disheveled and dusty, enough to deter anyone. It was the perfect hiding place. The only way that the Dark Windows would find this place would be if someone from within The Order broke ranks and gave away the location.

He edged through the maze of shelving and found another door. He slipped through into an identical room with the same smell of fresh cardboard and new carpet. He was about to turn back when he heard music somewhere ahead of him, music and laughter. With his torch as the only guide, casting angular shadows through the gaps between boxes, he slowly made his way towards the sound through room upon room of identical, climate controlled shelving. He opened the thirteenth door into a room full of the sound of human pleasure. For a second, he thought that he had stumbled into the heart of the laughter – a familiar tango was playing from an old gramophone down below. The room he now entered was empty; a large square hall with a vaulted ceiling and no shelving. In the centre of the room was a circular pit surrounded by an ornate stone balustrade. From the pit rose flickering lights, tobacco smoke, music and disheveled laughter. He crept to the edge and peered down to the floor below – the image that greeted him both shocked and fascinated him.

A group of men were lounging about in shirtsleeves with loosened ties around their necks and painted courtesans pleasuring them in all manner of contorted positions. The men appeared intoxicated with passion as they writhed and chuckled, some standing and some rolling on the floor. The figures formed a circle of jellified testosterone and, in the centre of the circle, there stood what appeared to be the object of their amusement: A beautiful androgynous blind figure with short, dark hair and a white stick was attempting to find her way out of the crowd that encircled her. The men occasionally stood and jeered at her as she stood, exposed in the harsh beam cast by a lamp suspended over her head from the vaulted ceiling. Larry was directly above her - in the shadows and out of the glare of the lamp. The men would have struggled to see him even if they were interested in looking upwards. He was engrossed by the scene below, it must have been some kind of drinking society, some secret orgiastic clan. Perhaps this was The Order of Toledo – this was the kind of revelry that Buñuel spoke of – a dark poetry of sex and immorality. He leant a little further over the balustrade in order to afford a better view of the proceedings, confident that no one would notice him. He caught sight of an object on the floor – the blind figure was poking it with her white stick. Then it dawned on him - the object on the floor was a severed human hand. He had seen this scenario before somewhere – she was acting out a scene from Buñuel's film *Un Chien Andalou* – the tango, the blind woman, the circle crowding around her – it was the same somnambulistic sequence but played as a floorshow to a group of whoring Spanish businessmen. He slowly examined the beautiful figure at the centre of the scene – her boyish shoes, her tight black jeans that encased long slim legs and a tight, trim rear – her slim figure and erect spine, her broad shoulders and slender arms - this rear view of the blind woman entranced and excited him. As his eyes burned into her back, she swiftly turned and looked up towards him – Larry had a shock that nearly sent him plummeting over the balustrade. The eyes that looked up into the lamp couldn't see him but they weren't blind eyes and the deep red lips that pouted at him formed the mouth of his ex-lover and Casey's sister – in an instant he recognised his desire in the heart of this blind charade – he recognised his Sandy.

II

For a full two minutes that stretched to infinity, he stared at her – her short, dark hair, the gently prominent breasts, the elements that made her whole – fascinating, enchanting, charismatic.

What is she doing here? How can I contact The Order now? There is no one to contact – I can't speak to those men – what am I doing here?

He heard someone approaching from another room, a car screeched to a halt outside – he turned and fled. Back through the thirteen doorways, down the staircase and out into the dark plaza. He inhaled deeply and cast furtive glances around the desolate square; the air was dry, warm and scented with jasmine. He adjusted his gait to affect a relaxed stroll and headed back down the alley and past *Posada de la Sangre*. He slid anonymously onto the main thoroughfare and noticed a crowd standing outside the *pastelería*. They were gathered around a sprawled human form lying prone on the hard cobbled street, a pool of blood; thick and dark in the streetlamps; was forming around the body's recently smashed skull. Some of the crowd were looking up towards an open window above the *pastelería*. Light curtains billowed from the window in the warm evening breeze and a child's voice was calling out...

"*¡Ése es el hombre, él lo hizo!*"

Larry's mind was preoccupied – he was thinking about Sandy standing in that obscene circle of whoring men. It took him a few moments to link the window and the bleeding form. A small girl carrying a blue football continued to cry out...

"*¡Él lo empujó, él lo hizo!*"

The crowd was increasing and Larry found himself safely ensconced in the mob as he managed to shift his thoughts from Sandy to the immediate present and realised that the lifeless form had jumped from the window with the billowing curtains and that the crowd had begun to look away from the dead body, turning their attention towards him...

"*¡Él es el asesino, él lo empujó!*"

As he shifted his attention to the corpse and the small child - he was twice shocked. First, he realized that the body was a familiar figure – the body and the distorted, crushed head belonged to the man who had brought him here: Vendor Busch - his reason for being here, his alibi and escape route was lying dead on the streets of Toledo. Secondly he recognised the small child as the one who had seen him with Vendor – the child had immediately made the link between Larry and the crushed form of Vendor...

"*¡Él le mató, él debe haber empujadolo!*"

He didn't understand what the little girl was saying but he was abruptly aware that the crowd had turned their eyes on him. He realised that he could try and explain – that the child knew nothing and he was a friend of Vendor – but he couldn't get mixed up with the Guardia Civil – he needed to run. He had to find out why Vendor was dead, who The Order were and, most importantly, why Sandy was here with them. Godard was dead, Vendor was dead and Sandy was with The Order – he turned, pushed his way out of the crowd and ran...

"¡Parada! ¡Asesino!"

His feet echoed down narrow alley after narrow alley – shadows pursuing him through the dry, hot evening air. He ducked into a dark doorway and pressed his back against the wall. His heart was running around his eardrums. He struggled to quieten his body and distinguish between the background noise – the sound of Toledo in the distance, like the sea – and the waves of blood coursing through his body.

There was silence and a faint smell of urine in the silent Toledo doorway as he struggled to look at his watch. He waited for exactly five minutes of inaction before stepping out of the shadows. He leant on the chalky stone building, took the last crushed cigarette from his pocket, straightened it and was just searching his pockets for a light when footsteps approached from the distant shadows. A feline figure appeared and spoke in unconvincing Spanish...

"¿usted tienen gusto de un poco de fuego?"

As she struck a match, the hypnotic face of Sandy flickered in front of him. The city's backstreet had become a movie set and they were the only two people on screen. The Order, Dewi and the dead Vendor dissolved. The city was evacuated; the buildings and streets were empty painted images. A warm breeze spiraled around them and pulled them together. Sandy gently took his hand and smiled. Their faces drew close and they inhaled simultaneously – honeysuckle – death that smelt of honeysuckle...

"I think you should come back to my place Larry – we need to talk about this..."

Chapter 30
That Obscure Object of Desire

Sandy was staying in a vast archaic apartment on the hill of Toledo. Larry was gazing out of the window over the city's lights and down to the river Tagus below. He had a vantage point now – a view over the labyrinthine city. He felt contented in the care of Sandy, his wealthy sister-in-law. He had always depended for his security on the kindness of friends. Her hair was short now – the same Louise Brooks bob that he had fallen for at the National Film Theatre in London – but it was still the same Sandy that he had known as a teenager. He turned away from the window to look at her; she was brushing her hair vampishly...

"What's going on here Sandy?"

"We've got to talk Larry..."

He looked into her deep, dark eyes, slinked past her and lay down on the deep, soft bed, stretched and kicked off his shoes. He studied the ceiling intently - a fly was making its final, futile attempt to break free from the web in which it was entangled. Sandy crawled onto the bed and moved her eyes into the path of his gaze, obscuring the web. She kissed him gently on the lips and rolled back onto the mattress next to him. The fly had stopped struggling.

"Do you think we should do this Sandy?"

"Kissing's alright – I'd like to do more, more, more of it..."

She stretched and curled her feline body next to him, ran her fingers through his hair and gently stroked his eyebrows. His gaze stayed fixed on the web as he attempted to restrain his desire. Sandy broke the silence...

"You saw me with The Order didn't you?"

He didn't know where to start, what to think or how to ask her what was going on…

"Vendor's dead Sandy – do you know… did you know him?"

"I saw him in the street – I was in the crowd – I saw you, I followed you…"

Larry was struggling to hide his repressed emotions as he blurted out the thoughts spiraling through his confused consciousness…

"But why were you there Sandy – what were you doing? Someone tried to kill me – I mean it's got complicated since I left you in London, it's not a game anymore – it's not art. You know I went to Rolle with Chris, well not with Chris – he went to Davos and I haven't seen him since and someone tried to drown me but Vendor saved me – well Mike saved me. Do you know Mike – Mike War? And then – I mean now – Vendor's dead. What's going on – why are you here Sandy?"

"What's the matter with you Larry – do you always have to talk about murder?"

Keeping his gaze fixed on the web, he reached out and stroked the soft hair on her forearms – struggling to repress his desire. Sandy purred calmly, reassuringly…

"Mmmm – I came here because I was worried about you Larry…" She rolled over and whispered gently in his ear, "You think you know something don't you? Vendor and Mike told you something about me didn't they?"

"No – are you involved with all this Sandy? Do you – are you?"

"No – I was worried about you – I've been thinking, I don't want anything to come between us. We're old friends, we go back a long, long, long way Larry. We're related aren't we? We should get close, close, close again."

She put her hand gently on his leg – the events of the day had caught up with him, he was suddenly exhausted and bewildered. He stared at the web and tried to resist.

"Don't touch me now Sandy – not like that. I'm tired."

"What did they tell you? What did Vendor tell you? Come on Larry, you're not stupid, you're a clever sort of guy…"

He replied, feigning self-possession, "No one said anything about you…" he thought about the sight of the sightless Sandy, enclosed by the debauchery of The Order of Toledo. Paranoia and fear gripped him, briefly extinguishing his desire.

"Larry, you're a pretty understanding sort of guy – I guess you might have heard some things about me, but you're man of the world enough to overlook them. We've been through this before – you know – with me and Joe. I've been running around since I was seventeen and I guess I've done some pretty stupid things – made some pretty stupid mistakes – nothing serious Larry, just stupid."

He stiffened and turned his back to her. He stared at the grey wall and thought about Sandy and Joe on that mattress in the 1980s, he thought about Sandy in the centre of Toledo's orgy, he saw Vendor's head oozing life. She sensed that his mind was elsewhere.

"Oh Larry now don't start imagining things – don't start fantasising about that little charade I was involved with this evening – it was nothing, really nothing, nothing, nothing."

"But how could you do such things? You're Casey's sister – you're Lilly and Alfie's Auntie Sandy…"

"Oh Larry, Larry, Larry – what do you know? You think you know something don't you? You think you're a clever little artist who knows something but there's so much you don't know, so much." Her mood changed, she seemed to have lost her patience; she was no longer attempting to seduce him. "What do you really know? You're just an ordinary little man living in an ordinary little town. You've spent the prime of your life waking up every morning knowing that there's nothing in the world to trouble you. You have sleepwalked through your ordinary little days, months and years –

and you have slept through your untroubled, ordinary little nights filled with peaceful, stupid dreams..." she turned onto her back and inhaled deeply, "...except that occasionally I brought you nightmares, I haunted you with regret - or did I Larry - was it just your little fantasy of me? You live in a fantasy – you're a dumb, blind sleepwalker. How can you know what the world is like when you've spent all those years in the sheltered isolation of your suburban drudgery?"

He sat up and looked at her as she got up and slinked over to the window. He shouldn't have turned his back on her again, he should have given in to her – fallen into her warm, comforting arms. Now he feared that, in his momentary hesitation, he had lost her again. He studied her back as she stared out of the window at the lights of Toledo glittering below. As he listened to her mounting rage, he knew that she had him in her control and he would do anything to keep hold of her...

"Larry – do you know that the world is a barren desert? Do you know that if you ripped the fronts off those houses down there, you'd find lizards behind each façade - each human a cold-blooded, heartless reptile? The world's a hell – what does it matter what we do in it? Wake up Larry – use your sense – learn something!"

"Sandy – I want to trust you, to be with you – I am with you, but..."

"But, but, but – forget about what you saw, who you were – forget about it all. Get down off that bed and crawl to me Larry – kiss my bare feet – do it now and forget about everything else. This is your reality now – I'm your reality now!"

He crawled down from the bed, his gaze fixed on the floor – he crawled slowly, servant to Sandy's orders. Her soft and beautifully pedicured foot was firm – rooted to the thick wool carpet with the strength of her charisma. He grasped her ankle, pressed his lips against the smooth skin on the top of her foot and submitted to fantasy – to desire.

Chapter 31
Aliens

The mysterious alien beings, known only as *The Dark Windows*, communicate to their franchisees through large telescreens fitted in the boardrooms of the relevant corporate bodies. Sometimes they speak, but, when they need to be precise, they provide written communications. Their written discourse reflects the mechanical translation system that they use and their attempts at linguistic precision have led to the development of an opaque language – a linguistic virus that has been adopted by commercial organisations and cultural critics alike. Overleaf is the transcript of their final message to the Bland Corporation in Switzerland.

▶

MEMORANDUM

    From: Dark Windows

    To: Bland Corp.

    Re: Larry Went

It has come to our attention that the suppression rate for issues relating to our provision of systems to the Bland Corporation has dropped below the 95% benchmark established in the previous review (1968). The quality of information suppression has decreased in tandem with the increase in mortality of human leakage.

We have been undertaking the spadework in a detailed analysis of the robustness and vigour of your ability to manage your own systems. In the light of our commitment to non-commitment, and as a response to these findings, we have instigated an engagement exercise through which we will extend our sources of external reference points to visit each relevant cluster, commencing with artificial dissemination to The Order of Toledo.

This delicate exercise requires that you produce a reflective statement and accept that the outflow of future lifestyle technologies may attach to an alternative franchise. If you are unable to peacefully resolve the Went issue through absorption/merger (see current perfomance indicators) and consolidate stability across the relevant territories (including inclusivity as a cornerstone), then we will be ushered into a position that requires clear accountability. We will re-establish channels on resolution of this issue.

Freddie turned off the telescreen in the Berne office – abruptly aware that he was in danger of losing the franchise. They who provide the Dark Windows were no longer available – they were no longer speaking to Freddie.

The Order's scheme was working – disruption and dissent was being sown. Freddie could see his global capitalist organisation disintegrating before his eyes... and all because of Larry Went. One little man – a patsy – set up by The Order of Toledo to expose the fatal weaknesses of the Bland Corporation. Godard should be dead to the world now – along with all the other cinematic revolutionaries – but somehow his power was operating from beyond the grave through the medium of Larry Went. Freddie had seen The Order's strategy and had thought that it would be simple to subvert their scheme – but death is never simple and somehow, someone had undermined his plan. Magog – Freddie blamed Magog for the whole affair – he had been trusted with the Godard removal and subsequent clean-up – but somehow he had conspired to augment the whole situation and spread the consequences across Europe.

Freddie was squinting with anguish from within his black roll-neck jumper; he had become a control freak who was losing control. He turned on the speakerphone that sat on the Double X table and dialled a number. The speakerphone crackled – dial-tone – speed-dial – Spanish ring-tone – a precise, controlled voice answered...

"Freddie?"

"We've lost contact with the Dark Windows Maggy..."

"Freddie, I have taken Vendor out of the picture and I..."

"Silence! Maggy – I have treated you well – I have trusted you. Vendor's demise may scare Larry, may convince our masters that we are in control again, but you should have quietly taken Larry out in North Wales before any of this happened. It is Larry who has proved that we are not in control. He has been following a trail laid by The Order – his presence in Penmaenmawr,

London, Rolle and Toledo has proved that we are not in control. His presence, and your inability to stop him, has resulted in dead telescreens! We are no longer in contact with the providers – for all I know they may be awarding the next franchise to The Order as we speak. You Maggy – you have caused the problem and you will solve it!"

"I will find him. He did not return to the safe house after Vendor's accident and I have not yet been able to locate him but I…"

"Don't you see Maggy? Larry is nothing and he is everything. I have two tasks for you – two simple, strategic tasks: Firstly, you will destroy The Archive and secondly, you will find where Larry has gone and deal with him – deal with him in a way that demonstrates our control of the situation – and murder may not now be the most effective way. The only answer now is to bring Larry on board – to sign him up."

⏭

The dark windows that looked into the *Plaza Colegio Infantes* cracked and shattered from within. Black smoke poured out, filling the square of sky above and obscuring the rays of the rising sun as flames licked the rafters at the heart of the ancient city. An explosion tore through the antique shop at number 6 - the stairs that Larry had climbed just a few hours before collapsed and crushed the burning bric-a-brac below. The cardboard boxes that he had seen carefully organised on metal shelves smouldered and disintegrated along with their contents in the intense heat.

Magog had achieved task one. The *Plaza Colegio Infantes* would be an empty shell by the time that the first coffee was served at the *Café Toledo*.

Chapter 32

When Worlds Collide

Sandy was staring out of the window as dawn's first rays flecked the rooftops below. Larry was at her feet; his hands caressing her soft calves and smooth shins as he gently kissed her firmly rooted feet. The sky was losing its inky blackness and she struggled to suppress her desire as pink clouds began to distinguish themselves from the dark sky that loomed over the city. The early morning light began to define a black mist that was rising from the old town below. A small section of Toledo appeared to be becoming all wrapped up in black tissue paper with orange flaming ribbons securing the sooty clouds.

"Larry, the Plaza's on fire – come up here…"

He was still on his knees, fixated on her feet - fetishising each toe with gentle kisses.

"Don't you know how to stand up Larry? You just keep your feet on the floor, straighten your legs and your body will rise up on top of your hips – come on – up, up, up!"

Still under her spell, he nuzzled up her soft thigh and appeared from within her loosely tied black silk dressing gown. He stood next to her, his arm gently around her waist; somehow it felt surprising to find that he was taller than her. She had him now – the hook was in and he couldn't get it out.

"That's the Plaza Larry – The Archive is going up in smoke…"

The distant fire temporarily consumed the vapour of his eroticism and, as his head cleared, he wondered about Sandy – how much did she know about

The Order and their Archive? He glanced at her profile silhouetted by a standard lamp and his pulsating desire reasserted itself - he was no longer interested in the years of history, the piles of evidence turned to ashes by a single fascist matchstick. The distant, silent flames brought back the dream that he had had at Vendor's - the house exploding in silence – burning across the street in a somnambulistic 1980s Plaistow – a mute collapsing. He saw his metaphor brought to life in the city below, yet he cared less for the real burning archive than he did for the dream puzzle locked in his subconscious.

"It – it reminds me of a dream I had - in Lausanne, after I drowned. It took me back, the dream took me back to our squat in Plaistow… you know, where you and Joe…"

The intervening twenty years were burning in that inferno in the *Plaza Colegio Infantes*, the distance from 1980s London to 21st Century Toledo was suddenly as brief as a wink, a fraction of a single human's time.

"A dream Larry?"

"Yes – it was…"

"Let me tell you about dreams Larry…"

"Sandy, can I just? - How did you find me here?"

"You're in the 'phone book…"

"What do you m…?"

"I have this dream Larry – for years I've had this dream…"

As he stood transfixed by the distant burning archive, she related her dream to him: The dark, rainy night - heading from Weybridge to Walton-on-Thames, towards the Seven Witches of Cowey Sale where the aliens had planted their cinematic technology for Cecil Hepworth – their experiment with human mind control. In 1905, who would have thought that the Hepworth Manufacturing Company's *Rescued By Rover* would lead, through D.W. Griffith, to modern Hollywood's rise and fall, to Sergio Leonie's *Once Upon a Time in America* – the film that was screening at the Walton Odeon that night in 1984? Tuesday Weld's face projected in an enclosed space to a steaming audience as Sandy drove up that wet dream road – heading towards the eventual end of cinema in the 21st Century… the planned clampdown on humanity – the New World Order – all of this inconsequential trivia was part of the battle. As he listened to Sandy, Larry's absent thoughts wrapped around a song by The Clash. He heard Joe Strummer's voice on the cassette player in his orange Mini Traveller and he drifted away from Sandy's recollection into his own parallel vision of 1980s Walton…

> *"The voices in your head are calling*
> *Stop wasting your time there's nothing coming*
> *Only a fool would think someone could save you"*[15]

Joe Strummer was dead now – just as he was starting to reach an audience of millions again on the BBC World Service. John Lennon, John Peel, Joe Strummer – dead. No one can be allowed to threaten the Dark Windows - but death is not always the first choice for the Bland Corporation - it is better to absorb the threat – to neuter the challenge.

As Sandy narrated her dream and dwelt on the final scene, as she described the scientists removing the alien body from the spotlight, Larry couldn't keep quiet any longer.

"But – Sandy I…"

He held her tightly around the waist, she relaxed and yielded as he pulled her toward him and looked out at the burning archive. For an instant they considered the distant fiery vision together in silence.

"Sandy, I've had that same dream. I've dreamed for years – dreamed of death and regret and that road past the Seven Witches. I've not told anyone… but in my dream, it was me on that road – I killed someone that I hadn't seen, they were lying in the road like a sack…"

It was Larry's turn to recount his dream and describe the emotions that

---

[15] The Clash, "Working For The Clampdown"

had forced him to throw the mutated alien body into the icy boiling Thames one recurring, dark, fantastic night. Sandy and Larry had spent years apart – aware of each other but hardly communicating – dreaming parallel nightmares of guilt, traveling eternally towards each other on the same dark road but never meeting. In the dreams, death and remorse stopped Larry from reaching Weybridge and kept Sandy from making it to Walton-on-Thames. Yet now, as he finished recounting his story – in a reality far-removed from that rainy night in Walton – they had met again and were together again – bound by new deaths – real deaths.

"How do you feel about Casey Larry – I mean in relation to this… to us… to now?"

"Sometimes I feel that she keeps me on a leash so tight, I can't breathe… but it, it's just life – family life…"

"What about the dreams Larry – what do you think they mean?"

He turned to look in her dark eyes and caught her scent…

"What's the name of that perfume?"

"I don't know - I picked it up at Cointrin airport. The dreams Larry…?"

She pulled away from him and lounged back on the large soft bed, one knee raised as she untied the silk belt on her dressing gown.

"Do you like my black lingerie?"

He continued to focus on the smoke and flames that were snaking their way out of the plaza – resting in the still morning air – unhurried as they consumed The Archive – the goal of his journey to Toledo.

"Sandy – the dreams could mean anything or nothing…"

"Synchronicity – there are no coincidences Larry. It must mean something that we've shared this dream. You tell me what you think it means…"

"What do I think it means? Well Sandy, I think that Acetylcholine Neurons have been firing high voltage impulses into our forebrains all these years. These impulses have become pictures and the pictures have become dreams but why we've shared these images through our somatic nervous system is anyone's guess. Let's look at it this way – maybe I did kill someone on that road by the Seven Witches in 1984 and maybe that someone... how about this for a story?" He started to relate the narrative of a film that he'd seen or another dream that he'd had... "There's a gang of bikers in Walton-on-Thames and, in the 1970s, they discovered the secret of eternal youth when they sold their souls to a bloated Toad God in one of those big houses where the City stockbrokers live. It was the son of one of those rich families in Walton – the alienated biker son - you know the type? He killed himself and was re-born as an undead serial killer and then all of his biker gang mates killed themselves too. So there's been this gang of hippy biker zombies roaming the streets of Walton and it just happened that I hit one of these zombie psycho bikers on the road that night in 1984 and it's his spirit that haunts my dream. Only it wasn't really a Toad God that gave him eternal life; it was an alien creature, amphibian-like, who was giving longevity to these rich people... not through magic or fantasy..."

Sandy looked at him, confused by his tangential tale. He realised that he wasn't making sense and changed tack slightly...

"That was just a film that some Australian guy made, trying to give us a message about it all – trying to alert us to the conspiracy. It was alien technology – alien science – what if that were true Sandy? What if the dreams that we had were telling us that there are aliens who can give us eternal life? Maybe one day I stumbled across a dead being on that road, something that had transported down from another dimension. That figure I threw in the water wasn't human – it was too small, too light. What if – what if it *was* real Sandy? I don't know whether that dream happened to me or not – maybe I killed someone on that road and created this story to hide the memory – maybe I just don't remember what happened that night..."

Larry tailed off mid-diatribe and looked at Sandy. The blood had drained from her face, she looked cold and alone. For an instant he no longer recognised her.

"You really don't know do you Larry? You don't know the difference between a dream and a memory. Do you know why? It's not those Acetate Neurons – it's because something in your brain has been re-wired - not just you but everyone, everyone, everyone. We're all victims lover, we've all spent too much time absorbing narratives; seeing stories unfold on screens – whole stories and fragments of stories. We've seen faces repeated endlessly – reproduced until we believe that we know those strangers intimately. We believe that we know these strangers better than we know our families, than we know ourselves. What you don't understand about our dreams is that they're not ours – they've been planted in our subconscious by a machine... an extra-terrestrial invention operated by the ruling elites of the world. These dreams that we've been having for years were put in our heads by the Dark Windows – we shared an experience in 1984 that planted those dreams and remorse has controlled our lives and destinies ever since, in the same way that *they* used to use religion to control the masses."

She stared into his eyes briefly - attempting to match his fantastic polemic with her own crazed conspiratorial theories...

"What I'm talking about Larry is not some silly mixed-up fantasy about alien bikers – what I'm saying is that there *is* an organised system of mind control at work – used by the ruling elite to keep us in place and that system has developed from a technology given to the elite by extra-terrestrial beings. Very soon this system – these Dark Windows will use a global financial crisis to create One World Government and a New World Order in which we won't feature unless... unless we join them... and that's where I aim to be Larry – a member of the New World Order – the Order of Toledo!"

Larry looked shocked. Women don't think like that – he had never heard Sandy speak like that - like a stilted conspiracy theorist automaton. He couldn't tell with his eyes or ears, he couldn't identify the real Sandy anymore - she seemed strange - alien. He reached over and touched her – he ran his index finger around her kneecap and down the outside of her thigh. He laid on the bed next to her, pressing his face into her slim waist and inhaling her scent deeply - the perfume from Cointrin Airport – he spoke into her hip.

"Do you – are you serious about… I mean, you sound like Joe or Mike or Vendor. I thought you were, I mean I thought you didn't believe any of that stuff…"

Sandy smiled as tears welled in her eyes. She suddenly burst into mocking laughter…

"Larry, Larry, Larry – of course I don't believe that crap. I know what our dreams are about, I just can't believe that you don't get it – that you can spout all that incoherent, insensitive nonsense at me. I didn't realise how lost you were Larry – you don't know who you are or what you want and you never have. Something did happen to us in 1984 and you really don't get it do you Larry?"

His pressed his face harder against her hip and gently gripped her warm thigh.

"Get what Sandy? I don't know what happened on that road."

"We had a baby in 1984 Larry. We made love and made a baby and you've spent the last twenty-two years in denial – hiding reality behind your ridiculous fantasies. I had a fucking abortion Larry and you didn't know, you didn't care – you were too fucking immature to even see *why* I couldn't see you for months. You couldn't see why things changed between us and why it all eventually ended. Our baby died somewhere – chopped up in a bucket on that road, burnt in a hospital incinerator… it's a fucking metaphor Larry - it's just too, too obvious. Our relationship was that road and our baby's life that never was – our abortion is what happened to us on that road and I know because I fucking lived it – I felt it and you just fucking dreamed it Larry. You never knew but you must have known really mustn't you? Or you wouldn't have had that same fucking dream for years…"

The tears were streaming down her cheeks and Larry didn't dare to look up at her. He didn't dare say sorry - he didn't know what to say or what to think. He held her as she wept and he tried to piece together his memory of their mutual history in the light of what happened, what really happened. Did the Dark Windows of his soul still fit into this story somehow or was it all just a fiction, something that he'd invented? His perceptions - her story – his story…

Chapter 33

A Married Woman

Mike War had collected Casey, Alfie and Lilly earlier that day and, with a promise of adventure on the open road, was taking them to meet Larry in Spain.

Casey had been pre-warned by Sandy that something was happening and, much as she had wanted to dismiss it as another of Larry's fantasies, she had finally come to the realisation that there was something strange going on. When the 'phone call came through from the Swiss police - the report that Larry was missing, presumed drowned – she was expecting the news, believing Sandy's story that Larry was safe and lying low with some of Joe's friends. At the back of her mind, she was worried that Sandy and Larry might be back together somewhere, but she just had to trust them. Sandy had told her to expect Mike that evening, she had primed the children that they were going to go on an adventure to meet Daddy in Spain.

So... she now found herself sitting in the ferry terminal café waiting for Mike to return. He had kept pretty tight-lipped as he had driven his Montego for six hours down the M5 to Plymouth to catch the twice-weekly ferry to Santander. They had arrived just in time to board but the crossing had been delayed due to industrial action in Spain and she now found herself attempting to calm two fractious infants in a bright 1990s café that smelled of pine disinfectant. A green fire exit sign flickered on the wall in front of her, its faulty fluorescent bulb appeared to be synchronised with the repetitive squeaking of a small baby on the adjacent cream Formica table. Alfie and

Lilly sat opposite her on red plastic seats that were bolted to the table's blue metal frame. They were messily dissecting two *Choc Dips*: Deconstructed chocolate fingers, re-packaged as naked biscuits and chocolate spread in a plastic tub. As she sipped her stewed tea with UHT from a flimsy plastic cup, she began to wish that she'd stayed at home and ignored Sandy's summons. She'd always found it hard to say no to her older sister – she'd always known that she played a secondary role in Sandy's orchestrations.

She looked up at the oversized mother of the squeaking baby as she struggled to stand up. Casey marveled at how this woman had managed to fit her bulk in that fixed gap between the plastic chair and the Formica table, she couldn't help but stare at the woman's non-standard body form. She was wearing a white t-shirt and dark blue tracksuit pants, the height of British sportswear fashion. Her hair was curled in an unflattering tight bunch on the top of her head and she smiled as she searched her pockets for loose change to buy a second packet of buttons for the baby, whose face was already smeared brown from a previous encounter with chocolate. What most fascinated her about this woman were her breasts – they were huge and encased in a bra that was clearly visible through her white shirt. When she faced her, there was a distance of at least 1 metre between her nipples and, when she turned in profile, Casey could see that they drooped so low that they appeared to project from her stomach like a man's potbelly.

On another table, a group of Down's Syndrome adults sat with their carers, getting slowly frustrated with the delay as they drank their cartons of Ribena and fiddled with their wooly football hats. Casey was trying not to be judgemental, she was attempting to think correctly as she matched the image before her with the image created by UK PLC through the media. She looked at her watch and over to the clock on the wall. It was getting late and the adventure was already wearing thin.

I should have stayed at home – coming on a wild chase to meet Larry – he can come home to me instead of swanning off with Joe's money on the trail of some imaginary murderer. I've got other things to do that don't involve crazy conspiracies, he better have somewhere for us to stay when we get there... It's hard enough doing this type of spontaneous journey on your own, but with the kids in tow... why did I let Sandy convince me to come here with this crazy Scouser in his old wreck of a car?

Just then, Mike walked into the crowded café, stepping over a recumbent drunken Englishman who was wearing a football shirt emblazoned with a beer-stained advert for a gambling organisation. He sat down with Casey and the kids and smiled broadly as he spoke,

"Alright la – look, sorry about all this – didn't account for a ferry strike – but, good for them – *up the Diddy workers!* - and all that stuff. Look – I've got yous a room in some shite, sorry, hotel – one of those international corporate chains. They had a family room – it was the only one left. Now - I'll crash here right and yous can sleep in a nice cosy bed – we'll get some scran in the morning and sort out how we're gonna make it to Larry in España – there's always another route, another way - eh kids - you want to see dad in Spain?"

The kids ignored him and Casey replied,

"It's nice of you Mike but – I think we might just go home, give it up as a bad idea. If you don't want to take us, we'll get a train back in the morning..."

"Yous can't do that now, you're not safe if they find you – look I don't want to scare you but..."

"...but?"

"But – look up there – cameras right? Facial recognition software – it won't be long before they find us. I paid cash at the hotel, false names – yous'll be safe there..."

"Never mind the cameras Mike, we're using our passports to go to Spain – I believe that we have barcodes, that we are simply easily traceable numbers on a government database, there's no escape for us mere mortals..."

"*They* don't have full access to government systems yet la. Come the clampdown, come the New World Order – they'll have us bolted down good and proper like these plastic chairs – we'll be sutured good and proper then..."

"I tell you what Mike..." she turned to Lilly who was arguing with her brother "...stop winding him up, he's only little – you're supposed to be looking after him. I tell you what Mike, I'll stay in your crappy Travelodge tonight if you stay with me and tell me everything you know – and I mean everything. Come on kids, we're going to a special hotel with super space beds – come on!"

"Space beds? What are space beds mummy?"

⏭

The four travelers checked into their family room, Casey bathed the kids while Mike watched TV. Lilly and Alfie were dog-tired from the long journey and soon fell asleep in their pull-out corporate sofabed. The room was stuffy and airless – outside the double-glazed window was a huge, noisy extractor fan that precluded any real ventilation. Casey sat on the bed next to Mike. It seemed odd to her to be in a hotel room with a strange man, it was the first time that she had got into this kind of potentially hazardous situation since she was a teenager. There had been student parties back then - crashing at unfamiliar houses and waking slumped across mysterious people - but she had always been careful and faithful. She trusted Mike, he seemed down-to-Earth – he didn't look at her in the way that some of Larry's creepy workmates did – he seemed straight-up, face-value, genuine – maybe a little obsessed with crackpot ideas, but only in the same way that all men seem to get obsessed with music, football, trains, cars, films, politics, conspiracies... Sandy had vouched for him and Larry knew him – he seemed to be a safe bet. She muted the television and addressed him.

"So – Mike – you're from Liverpool are you? Whereabouts?"

"Aigburth..."

"Mmm – nice area…"

She seemed to have touched a raw nerve and Mike launched into a fresh Scouse rant,

"It didn't used to be frigging nice. Lark Lane didn't used to be full of rich kids and posh bars – it used to be full of drunks and doleites – real people. The Albert is still there, yous used to see people there – Ian McCulloch he used to drink there, singing in the back room before they had the big telescreens keeping everyone occupied. He was the singer from *The Bunnymen* – you know them? Ian could have been as big as Lennon but the Dark Windows scared him off - *The Bunnymen's* drummer was killed in a motorbike accident, you know how they like to use accidents to keep people quiet? And, and what about *The Teardrop Explodes*? Julian Cope was done in by drugs and New Age mysticism – he's lost, searching for an answer… Liverpool never got the chance it deserved to become cultural capital of the world… John Lennon, I mean everyone knows what happened to him and it's well documented that Paul McCartney was swapped for a doppelganger – and that was way before the Frog Chorus…"

Casey decided to stop him before he got carried away by his unified conspiracy theory.

"Hold on Mike – what's this got to do with Larry?"

"Well La, it's all to do with Larry's little book and this thing that he stumbled on in Penmaenmawr. You see – Larry found something by accident, something that's not too important really but it started him thinking. The world is set up now to stop people thinking – we're all de-skilled right? Well soon we're all gonna be de-thunk – if you know what I mean? I mean we all spend most of our lives not thinking too much and thinking's pretty rough when yous spent most of your life not thinking… Am I making sense la?"

"Not really…"

"Well Larry's like a fall-guy – there's something going on in Switzerland with Godard right? He's dead – Godard died in Pen' but he didn't – when I was with your Larry in Rolle, I saw two Godards. There were two Godards in Rolle and one dead and buried in Mochdre – that's three Godards, an unholy trinity with at least one ghost. The thing is that Larry doesn't know what he's stumbled on, none of us do, and someone is using him as a patsy – he's being set up and someone's already tried to kill him. Whoever it is will stop at nothing right – and that means that yous are in danger too – right? So what's happening is that I'm working with Vendor – he's my main man – you know Vendor from Larry's film – the guy in Germany? Well he sent me to collect Larry from Rolle – to save him and, well... I did. But the thing is now that I haven't heard from Vendor for a couple of days, he was meant to contact me - I don't know why but he hasn't. So we need to get to Toledo, we need to get to Larry and make contact with The Order of Toledo..."

"What is this 'Order' Mike?"

Mike continued for at least another hour, filling her in on what he knew of The Order, The Dark Windows and The Bland Corporation. His tangential polemic confused Casey but somehow convinced her to stick with him and keep heading for Toledo. As they discussed alternative routes, ways and means of reaching Spain, a news article about the ferry strike appeared on the mute television. Mike turned up the sound and caught the final sentences,

"...the union's leader Juan Torres said that talks to avert strike action between the Comisiones Obreras Union and the state-owned ferry company have broken down. The union is angry over plans by the US-based Bland Corporation to take over the state-owned company's ferry routes. The Spanish Government said there was no other option under European Union competition rules – but the misery continues for Brits waiting at Plymouth..."

Mike switched the screen off,

"Do you see Casey? Do you see the extent of their need to stop us, to stop Larry? Now that makes me feel important, that makes me feel like we're onto something – don't you see they've caused this strike just for us, just to stop us getting to Spain..."

"Mike – don't you think you might be just a teeny little bit paranoid? Can't we just get a little sleep and maybe get some coherence into these wild hallucinations of yours? Maybe in the morning you'll see that we're all little monkeys for the big corporate organ-grinder."

Casey turned her back on Mike and huddled down under the corporate quilt. He lay on top of the covers, looked the other way, considered making a roll-up and settled on sleep instead of stimulation – he was pretty monkey-tired too.

Chapter 34
Deus ex Machina

The sun was rising over Toledo as Sandy and Larry sat 30 centimetres apart on an antique bed, staring out at the thin plume of smoke that was drifting up from the remnants of The Archive. They watched as the world grew light, leaving last night's lamp casting its futile glow over the scene of Larry's dark fetish. He was attempting to slot the events of the past twenty-four hours into separate compartments, trying to organise them so that they made some kind of sense and led somewhere – anywhere – as long is it wasn't back, cap-in-hand to his life of ennui in North Wales. Sandy broke the silence,

"What are you going to do now Larry?"

"About what?"

"This, us, Casey?"

He bit his thumbnail and stared into the distant sky before replying. "I've got, well I had this idea that I could… well it was like a holiday for me really and, and there were two outcomes – well, two possible ways that I could…"

She cut him short. "I mean are you going back to Casey?"

"I can't go back, not now. I thought I'd left you in London and, and she's coming here – shit – where's that 'phone?"

Larry scrabbled through his discarded clothes, found his jacket and pulled out the 'phone that Vendor had given him.

"Look Sandy – there's this guy from Liverpool – Mike… and, and Vendor sent him to collect Casey and bring her here with the kids – to keep us all safe, to hide out together. God knows why I believed we'd be safe – I've got to call Mike, tell him to take them back, that The Archive has gone and it's all over and… I don't know. I'll get in touch with Casey – what I mean to say is that they – whoever they are – have done their job. They've scared me off – I don't give a damn about The Order of Toledo or the Dark Windows. Now that we're – I mean now that I…" He inhaled deeply and briefly turned to face her. "What are *you* going to do now Sandy?"

She watched him in silence as he turned his back on her in uncertain embarrassment and fiddled with his 'phone. He tried to get through to Mike but there was no answer – no connection. He tried to call his home in Colwyn Bay but the 'phone just rang and rang. It dawned on him that he didn't really know who Mike or Vendor were - that, for all he knew, they could have been working for the Dark Windows all along – that they could have kidnapped his family and taken them God knows where – anywhere – there was nothing he could do about it. Sandy seemed to be reading his thoughts.

"You've left them Larry – you left them a long, long time ago – perhaps you were never really with them. Casey will be fine - don't worry. *We* should stay together now, we should see this out – whatever it is."

He fiddled with the phone, desperately trying to find comfort or an answer in a small rectangle of plastic-coated electronics. He found a message – a text sent the night before, just about the time that he was hiding in The Archive. It appeared to make no sense but, in finding it, his fickle concerns about reality and responsibility slipped back into relief. The text was a key, a clue to the next step. He looked round at Sandy who had got up from the bed and was leaning against the tiled wall, her back arched as she attempted to fasten the slim strap of her black bra. For an instant, Larry saw an icon leaning there against the wall – Sandy from his film, Sandy the celebrity – the model for the dozen other dark-haired, pale-skinned, lithe, beautiful women pinned-up above his desk back home. He walked over and touched her gently, caressing her shoulder as he fastened her strap. Casey and his scruffy, pointless British life faded away...

"I've got a message – it's from Vendor but it doesn't seem to make sense."

"Ooh, a posthumous message eh, what does it say lover?"

"*burñ deus' slum* – Do you think it was an instruction? Do you think Vendor wanted *me* to burn The Archive – to set fire to that run-down antique shop? Maybe someone else got the message and..."

"It looks, looks, looks more like an anagram to me, sweetie. Are you any good at them?"

They scrambled onto the bed and, like two excited children, took a pen and paper and scribbled down the message... *burñ deus' slum.* Larry started the textual analysis with an open question...

"Right Sandy – is there anything that stands out to you?"

"Well *deus* is something to do with god isn't it?"

"...*deus ex machina* – God from a machine - that's the film industry alright..."

Sandy continued with her faux innocence "...and the *n* has a little squiggly line over it – it looks like there might be a Spanish word there..."

"That *squiggly line* is a diacritic tilde... If it's an anagram then it's something Spanish..." He concentrated on the letters until realisation dawned on his struggling face, "...Buñuel! – He's somewhere at the heart of this whole thing..."

Sandy crossed out the letters in sequence - b u ñ e u l - "Diegetic tilde eh? I can see you're a lecturer sweetie... that leaves *rdssum – murdss, smurds, ss drum, drums* – it's got to be drums – Buñuel's drums. It's all there lover - Buñuel's drums – you *do* know about the drums of Calanda don't you?"

"Well I guess that I know a little about them."

"What this means Larry - is that we need to go to Buñuel's home town, we need to go to Calanda to find the answer – we've got to do it – like you said, you can't turn back now honey."

He sat back on the bed and lit one of Sandy's menthol cigarettes – inhaled deeply and, as the nicotine swept over him, he thought about the goal of his trip.

"There's only one real reason for all this Sandy – the fraternity of metaphors. I don't know about any of this stuff to do with The Order and the Dark Windows – I don't know anything about Vendor's death or the burning Archive. It could easily all be some fantasy that these Walter Mitty characters have dreamed up and fallen victim to. What I *do* know is that I started to write a book about the Dark Windows that no one wants to publish *and* that I found Jean-Luc Godard's notebook in Penmaenmawr. Now – I'm still pretty cynical about all this but I am willing to believe that, if people are stupid enough to get thrown out of buildings because of their own fantastic conspiracy theories, then people might be stupid enough to want to kill me in the name of some grand illusion that they've constructed. From what I can see, Godard is dead – I saw the picture. I found the book and, when I got close to him, someone tried to kill me. From what I can see, I need to find out who killed Godard – forget about the rest of it – if I can find out who killed Godard – If I can reveal the killers through an exhibition – or a publication… that's where you and Joe come in - if I can get this out in the public domain, if I can get *the people* steamed-up about the Godard execution they might start doing things and then – I'll be safer… and, if they don't want to *kill* me off, maybe they'll *pay* me off. Everyone's got a price – especially me."

Sandy didn't look convinced. "Really Larry? It sounds like you've *seen* a lot… do you think that anyone, apart from you, really cares? Do you think *the people* ever cared about Godard or cinema? Do you think anyone has actually been murdered? Maybe you're the Walter Mitty character, the Billy Liar – maybe what you really want is me, me, me - but maybe you need to give yourself an excuse to leave my lovely sister and start again. Perhaps you need to graft yourself back onto reality honey… but I'll come to Calanda with you – I'll even drive sweetie, I'm having fun with you… for the moment. I just hope you can keep it up…"

"Okay – you drive but we'll have to leave soon and it's a long way. We've got to find out about the town – where to go – what to do when we get there – what did Vendor want us to do?"

From the dark hallway, a light rap on the apartment's exterior door broke his chain of thought.

"You go Larry – I don't want to be seen in the hall when I'm not fully covered…"

He made his way slowly to the door, taking care not to make a noise, pressed his ear against the cool wood and listened to the shuffling movements of a grown man on the other side. He counted to ten and pulled it slowly open. He was confronted by Tristan, the man from the Toledo safe house, looking nervous – much less relaxed than on their previous encounter.

"*Señor Went*? I am sorry – my daughter has caused trouble."

"Your daughter?"

"*Tristana* – she saw you with Vendor and she called out in the crowd, she followed you here yesterday - at night. She said to me that you were here. Do not become to the safe house again – you should go. Vendor, he is *muerto*…"

Sandy called gently from the bedroom. *"Who is it sweetie?"*

"*It's no one*. Look Tristan we're going, it's best if you don't know where. What's happened to The Archive? Why are you here? What do you want?"

Tristan turned his eyes from Larry as if he were hiding a painful memory. He passed a bag through the doorway.

"Your things *Señor Went* – from the apartment. This cell of The Order is gone now – I came to say that now I know no one – I know nothing. He came to find you."

"Who?"

Sandy called again from the bedroom… *"Are you still at the door lover?"*

Tristan lowered his voice to a hoarse whisper… "I know no-one, I know nothing. Magog - a man with a purple jumper and silver hair – do not let him find you. And - *Señor* Went?"

"Yes?"

"Tell no-one about me. Please remember that Tristana – she has no mother – only me – I cannot get involved, *lo siento*."

Larry shut and locked the door, left his bag in the hall and wandered back into the brightly-lit bedroom where Sandy was sitting on the bed, delicately sipping a glass full of lemon juice.

"So lover-boy who was that in the hallway and what do you know about Calanda and the drums?"

"It was Tristan - my bag. It's Easter, the fiesta – the drums - it's this week Sandy. What day is it today?"

"Friday sweetie – Good Friday and the skies have turned black a bit early this year."

"We need to get there today, we need to leave now – all I know is that the drumming starts at midday on Good Friday and carries on all day…"

"And where does Buñuel fit in?"

"He returned to Calanda, his home town, in Holy Week every year, without fail. I mean - I don't know why – I guess he just went home for old-time's sake – but maybe… Maybe there's an ulterior motive – perhaps he went there to meet up with the *caballeros*?"

Sandy became animated. It appeared to dawn on her that something important was happening.

"Oh Larry – it's starting to make sense now! I came up here to perform for The Order – I mean I know these people. I know some of them from the industry but I don't know exactly what they *do* – they just – I mean that place where you saw me *performing* was nothing really. It's just a club; a fun place – a little dancing, a little gambling – some performance and maybe a little sex on the side. People remember me from the old days you know – I get invited to things. They were all going to a convention somewhere nearby - I mean it's just the entertainment industry and I'm a part of it. Just don't ask me how

I fit into it all, I don't like to think too much about the consequences…"

"I know, don't remind me – we've been through all this before - *Letter to Sandy* and all that – I've changed but you haven't, you're still quite a girl aren't you?"

"You think?" Sandy smiled and looked directly into his eyes, tying his stomach into knots of lust with one brief glance.

"Look – I'm not getting into all that history stuff – we're here now, just us – you know the story?"

"Which story? Look – I'm not special Larry, there's plenty of women like me about but, but I'm starting to think that you're all thought and no feeling *Mister Larry Lecturer* – just don't lecture me please…"

"I'm lecturing you now am I?" Larry hung his head, ruminating on the fragility of their relationship.

"Uh huh…" Sandy was lying provocatively back on the bed again, running her finger absent-mindedly around the rim of the lemony glass. "You don't like me hanging around with the international jet-set do you *Mister Radical Lecturer*? That was always your problem – you aspired to the ruling class, you pretended to be a worker… but you never got your hands dirty did you? Do you know why I left you? I went off with Joe because you were suffocating me with your lack of ambition." She ran her tongue around the rim of the acidic glass and shivered. "I thought that it might inspire you to do something with your life. I never for a minute thought that you'd crawl back to Walton and marry my little sister. You don't know how much that hurt me…"

Larry suddenly looked surprised, captivated… "I hurt *you*? Do you mean that you're?"

"Yes I'm flesh and blood – not celluloid. I'm not an image, I'm here with you now – living…"

"…and breathing – you've got tears in your eyes again…"

"No – I'm over that now. I've told you – you know now; you always knew..."

Sirens wailed through the city below and the faint smell of burning drifted on the morning breeze. From a neighbouring apartment, a distant Spanish radio played 1980s Sheffield Electropop...

Everybody needs love and adventure
Everybody needs cash to spend
Everybody needs love and affection
Everybody needs 2 or 3 friends[16]

Larry looked down, carefully unbuckled his belt, slipped out of his trousers and unbuttoned his shirt as he crawled onto the bed...

"We're out of our minds Sandy..."

"And into our hearts, sweetie..."

He crawled up the long, soft mattress – caressing and tasting the length of her thin, pale legs – burying his head deep into her sweet, salty, intoxicating flavours and scents – consummating the desire that had etched a dream cipher into his subconscious twenty-two years ago – tasting and melting into one brief breakfast of pleasure. And then it was all over.

---

[16] 'The Things That Dreams Are Made Of' by Human League

Chapter 35
The Village of the Damned

"Their noise evokes the darkness and the crashing of rocks that shook the world at the moment of Christ's death. And in effect, their sonic conjuring makes the earth shake and the walls shudder; the ground vibrations move through your feet up to your chest. If you put your hand on a wall, you can confirm this incredible phenomenon. In my time, there were hardly two hundred drummers beating the skins. Today there are over a thousand drums."[17]

For most of the year, Calanda is a quiet, anonymous Aragonese town; about six hours drive north east of Toledo. The outside world may be aware of the place for two reasons: Firstly, it is the medieval town into which Luis Buñuel was born and, although he lived most of his life in nomadic exile as he established and developed the fungal strands of the Order of Toledo, the drums of Calanda remained with him at all times – burnt into his own desecrated eardrums. Buñuel created a lifetime's work – an oeuvre of films that dissect and analyse 20th century society. The dreams and illusions created by the histories of cinema are shattered by his quietly revolutionary work. With each viewing, his stark investigations into the dream world that we inhabit expand to explore ideology, religion, love, sex, obsession and the very core of human existence. Despite the universal nature of his work, his exile and his international celebrity, he returned to the small town of Calanda every

---

[17] Luis Buñuel, "Medieval Memories of Lower Aragón"

Easter and joined in the drumming that is the second reason for its notoriety.

Each year at midday on Good Friday, when the first bell of the church tower starts to toll, the *Rompida* commences – the streets of the ancient town reverberate with the continuous drumming of troupes of uniformed *redoblantes* – some dressed as Roman soldiers, others in fascist-style black-shirts and yet more dressed in the Klan-style pointed hoods of *Torquemada* and the Spanish inquisition. All of the groups beat their own improvised rhythms for two solid hours before forming a vast procession that slowly encircles the town, turning the streets into a sonic human particle accelerator. When one group encounters another on the streets, they start to duel – to jam against and with each other until their rhythms cease to collide and become one. For twenty-four hours, without pause or respite, the town drums and their rhythms penetrate every stone until the blood-soaked sticks and skins turn the whole place into a rhythmic symbol of a reality vibrating at one frequency. Communication, communion, rhythm – the drumming is etched into the culture of Calanda – the drumming and the drummers belong to the town, penetrate its fabric and bleed for an experience that lies beyond language. There is a carnal ecstasy in the pounding that liberates the performers from their human skins, their social conditioning and integrates them with the physical world that their mortal souls temporarily inhabit. Every year, Buñuel would join in with the drumming – its visceral imprint would stay with him throughout his life as a barrier that he could use, like the imaginary 'brick wall' in *The Village of the Damned,* in order to isolate himself from the surrounding culture and produce his own personal ideology of liberation. It enabled him to develop a vision of existence outside of the constraints of social conditioning – to tap into and de-tune the collective unconscious.

The drumming had a secondary function for Buñuel – it acted as a smokescreen for the duration of the *Rompida*, beneath which the Order of Toledo could meet. It was at Easter each year that the *Caballeros* of The

Order would meet in Calanda. When the drums took over the town, they could congregate and speak without fear; they could plan their viral attack on the Bland Corporation and all that it stood for. Under the drums they held out a last hope that one day they would control the Dark Windows. Their annual meeting had no published agenda, minutes or action plan – there were no bullet points and no diagrams, The Order met as the eyes of humanity – opposed to governments and commerce, they represented conscience in the abstract – the creative aspect of human nature and they had no need to write reports or publish manifestos.

Sandy's rendezvous in The Archive was just a preamble to the annual Conference of The Order, an initial meeting place for some of the delegates who had flown into Madrid airport. Although positioned in the centre of the crowd, Sandy's role was peripheral and, if Larry had been more astute in his awareness of the cinematic intelligentsia, he may have spotted, from his viewpoint high above the party, among the circle of *Spanish businessmen,* men such as: Jean-Pierre Gorin, Abbas Kiarostami, Jean-Claude Carrière, Chema de la Peña and Roy Andersson. The faces are perhaps marginally less well-known than their faceless works but these men (and they were nearly all men) had escaped from the inferno and were now gathered in Calanda, in the nerve centre of The Order, awaiting the *Grand Caballero*, ready to continue the work of Buñuel.

▶▶

The silver Citroën C3 was making light work of the dusty, dry roads as they wound through the ancient olive groves of Aragon on the final stretch of the brisk drive to Calanda. As Sandy and Larry approached the outskirts, they saw the signs and realised that the town centre was closed to traffic. There was no way in for motorcars – the police had isolated Calanda like Gleneagles for the G8 summit or Davos for the World Economic Forum. As the authorities protected the renewed post-Franco heritage of Aragon, they were unaware that they were also protecting the revolutionary potential of

The Order – nestled in their secret meeting place at the heart of the drumming. Sandy pulled up by a group of policemen in dark glasses on the *Avenue del General Franco*. Larry carefully unfolded himself from the front seat of the *supermini* at the edge of the cordon, just as the *Rompida* was about to commence. She leant over and called to him,

"I'll park up – I'll meet you at the Temple of the Pillar…"

He looked down at her pale body as he struggled to hear her above the noise of the crowds that filled all of the adjoining streets. He looked at her red lips as they repeated the instruction,

"The Temple of the Pillar – you can't miss it – the big bell tower."

He headed into town and was instantly swept into the seething crowds of Calanda. As he turned back to see her driving away, the bell tolled and the drumming commenced. The incessant noise, huge crowds and gathering heat of midday disorientated him as he moved with the purple flow of drummers through the narrow streets. He had no idea where the Temple of the Pillar was, but it was a small town and it seemed as if it would be difficult to get lost here. But, as the drums started to reverberate through his chest, Larry became ever-more confused and the jostling throng made it difficult for him to move freely or identify landmarks as he dissolved deeper into the surrounding mass of humanity that flowed towards the town square. Columns of drummers clad in long purple satin robes were packed into every nook of the *Plaza España*. Over on the far side, he spotted the bell tower of the Temple and attempted to aim towards it through the massed ranks of possessed percussionists. All around him ancient buildings rose three or four stories high, their balconies hung with purple cloth. At his feet small children were dressed in identical purple penitents' outfits – Larry couldn't help but think of Nicholas Roeg's *'Don't Look Now'* – imagining a mad murderous midget behind each pointed hood. He looked up from the mini revelers to be confronted by a tall man in a black cape and hood with pointed devil horns, grinning at him through broken teeth. Then, from somewhere on the other side of the square, he heard a voice call his name – a familiar voice. He squinted into the sun and saw a man heading intently towards him, a silver-haired character in a purple jumper with dark glasses, he couldn't focus on the approaching figure through the jostling crowd but he remembered Tristan's warning, turned and fled.

He pushed his way through the massed anarchy of the drummers, the smell of sweat, coffee and wine – aware of the urgent need to escape from the man pursuing him, the man who had now disappeared into the sea of purple on all sides. High above the square, at the top of a wide flight of stone steps was the large cube of the Temple, constructed from pink-washed ancient stone – a golden light shone from its Romanesque arched entrance and a tall, slender bell-tower rose from its bulk. He headed up the stone steps, navigating around the groups of strangely dressed characters that stood, sat and lay in his path. At the top of the flight, he turned left and sprinted around to the side of the pink stone cube, turning into a narrow trench-like road cut into the breathing, pounding town. The midday sun slanted into the alley – a temporary oasis of quiet amid the building sonic turmoil. The sun cast its golden rays onto the sinister medieval scene that confronted Larry as he rounded the corner. At the far end of the backstreet stood three rows of faceless drummers clad in the white gowns and hoods of the *Cofraternity of Catholic Penitents*. They held drumsticks rigid in their white-gloved hands and, suspended before them, were white-fringed snare drums. The moment he turned into the alley they started, almost imperceptibly, to march towards him. The slow drum-rolls commenced, rebounding from the stone walls, deafening him like the retort of a hand-cranked machine gun.

Back in the square, Magog was pushing his way through the throng, sweating in his purple jumper. A beautiful dark-haired teenager attempted to engage him in a street dance and, when he roughly pushed past her, she tugged at his silver hair and the wig came away in her hand. He snatched it from her and crammed it into his back pocket, looked up and found that he had lost sight of his quarry. He continued his pursuit up the steps in the general direction of Larry's escape route.

Back in the alley, confronted by the sinister white men ahead and the mysterious mauve man behind, Larry was desperately seeking an alternative course. To his right was small, ancient doorway. He pushed open the studded oak door and slipped through into a dimly lit vestry, a cool antechamber of the Temple of the Pillar. He left the dark cloakroom, wandered down the empty nave and sat on a hard wooden pew next to the north transept, affording himself a clear view of the ornate carved altarpiece that, along with the scent of frankincense, dominated the mysteriously empty Temple. He sat and considered the stories unfolding in the carved wood before him – it was here in 1640, that the Virgin Mary interceded to replace the leg of a peasant that had been severed some two years earlier. As Larry considered the feasibility of the miraculous repropagation of human limbs, footsteps from the narthex disturbed his contemplation. Someone was moving slowly down the aisle in his direction – hard heels crisp on the cool stone floor. He dared not turn and determined to bow his head in pseudo-reverie. The purple-clad figure removed the silver wig from his back pocket as he sat on the pew directly behind Larry and quietly whispered his name.

"Larry..."

The voice was instantly recognisable – he turned to check and saw his brother, Chris Went, sitting behind him and they were the only two figures in this cool, sheltered sanctuary. The drums of Calanda traveled through the thick stone walls, spilling into the silence of the Temple of the Pillar, throbbing in the background like some vast ecclesiastical air-conditioning system.

Already flustered by the journey, the crowds and the events of the last few days, Larry was sent into the shock of the familiar by this sudden encounter with his brother – here in Calanda, dressed in a purple jumper.

"Chris? – Wh... wh... what are you doing? I thought you were in Davos –

why are you?"

He struggled to formulate a question, attempting to piece together his perceptions. Who was the silver-haired man pursuing him? Why was Chris here and how did he find him here – of all places? He didn't know where to start or what to ask him. He spotted the silver wig and stared at his brother in disbelief, Chris spoke...

"We've got a lot of catching up to do bud..."

All of a sudden, Larry was distinctly aware of his isolation, alone and alien in a foreign land. His desire to push on with his investigation was disintegrating in the face of the unbelievable events expanding before him.

Why, when there are millions of people in Europe, should I be confronted by my brother in the Temple of the Pillar? Surely there are more interesting characters, more exotic humans with whom I could develop a relationship, more fantastic scenarios than this family reunion. It can't be a coincidence, he must have followed me here -he can only be here because he's in on the conspiracy – he must work for The Order or... surely he can't be...

Chirs spoke again. "You really don't know why I'm here – who I am – do you bud?"

"Chris? I – I – when I left you in Geneva, I..."

"I know everything mate, everything - I've been with you all the way. Look, I am sorry to mess you about but – you don't really know me do you? I mean we did stuff together as kids but you don't know where I went, where I've been... You should never have got involved, you should have let it drop."

"Let what drop?"

Chris looked down as if in prayer and, when he raised his eyes to meet his brother's, the scant sympathy that had previously rested on his features had gone. The face staring at Larry now was hard, strigine, alien. He realised how little he knew about his own brother, how little they shared. Chris's face now seemed to be empty –Buster Keaton stone and the more he looked into

Chris's eyes, the more he saw the owl – the emotionless features of a bird of prey. Larry's face was an open book to his brother who continued in a voice full of mocking scorn.

"Do you want me to spell it out for you brother? M-a-g-o-g! I am Magog – I have always been Magog. It was me that killed Godard and it was me that pushed you into Lake Geneva. I could have killed you at any time – any time. For some reason I felt sorry for you, I felt some kind of phony blood-loyalty to you. I have been following you for some time and the time has now come for you to disappear – I have no option now but to remove you." He took a deep breath and sighed a long sigh of resignation before continuing. "You always thought you were clever didn't you mate? You thought that you were going somewhere but I always knew you were on a road to nowhere – look at what you've got and the life you live – Colwyn fucking Bay – it's a place where people go to die. Just look at the bungalows, the retirement homes, the dirty tearooms, the big coffins on wheels – it's nowhere, nothing – and your 'work' – your stupid lecturing has come to nothing. You're just a pointless, pretentious failure and now, my brother, I expect you to die!"

Larry tried to find some justification for his life choices, tried to bolster his self-belief. "But, but it's not what you've got or where you live that counts…"

"Yeah and you *really* believe that do you? You're nothing but a catalogue of books and films – you are what you've watched – you've never done anything – you're nothing but a spectator."

"I've been teaching for years, helping students to… and I – I've made films – I'm writing a book – you don't understand the determination it takes to do that sort of… it's a vocation"

"Your students don't care about you and you don't care about them. No one's interested in your pathetic book – no one is going to publish your disjointed ramblings."

"You don't understand, you never understood. You've never done anything creative with your life Chris – you've never made films, had exhibitions – you don't have the friends that I have. I've got contacts too – you can't just get rid of me – people will notice, people will care."

"What - like Sandy? Don't make me laugh Larry – why do you think she brought you here? How do you think I knew where to find you? We're *all* in on this bud and you're nobody – you've got no one."

"I've got family – they won't let this go – Casey won't let me go."

"She'll let you go – you've already left her – you've let *her* go – she's gone. What would she think about last night eh – you and Sandy? You're all alone brother, you should end it yourself now - it's better this way."

He pointed his bony finger towards a small door in the north transept. The drums were beating through the walls; resonating through the fabric of the town. He smiled his hypnotic, owl-like grin. "That door leads up, up, up - to the bell tower. You should go through that door now and up the stairs - it's a one-way street – a dead end up there. Now… I haven't got a pearl-handled revolver to give you, but I think you know what to do – I think you know your only option and, if you don't do it yourself, I'll be waiting here… and I have a bullet with your name on that was given to me some time ago – a love-letter straight to your heart brother. Now go!"

Chris snapped his fingers and Larry rose, heading trancelike, for the staircase - his head pounding with paranoia, self-loathing and guilt, placing one foot in front of the other as if driven by clockwork. Turmoil reigned in his shrinking brain as he realised that Godard was dead - Chris, Casey, Sandy, Mike – there was no one left to help him, no one to trust or rely on – he was all alone and the staircase only went in one direction. Inside the bell tower, the drums were amplified as their unified rhythms bounced around the enclosed stone shaft. Subtle timbres resonating through the fabric of the rough wooden staircase that led to the high viewpoint. He gripped the handrail, sweating slightly – somehow he knew that he had only one task left. He had died in Rolle, he had seen death in Penmaenmawr and he had resolved the prosaic mystery of his recurring dream. He had abandoned his pointless job and detached himself from his nuclear family. He had no ability, no skills, no charisma. There seemed to be nothing but emptiness in the cinematic visions that invaded his conscious and subconscious thoughts. The films that had once meant so much to him, and the people that he had attached to this meaning, now seemed to be nothing more than elements - transparent products of a superfluous system of spectacular signs. Godard was just another mortal being, Sandy was just another woman, Joe was just a selfish artist and Mike was just an obsessed anarchist. It was all for nothing, he inhabited a time where there was no ideology – no culture – no relationships – no reality – nothing – blank – blank empty images circulating through a blank empty consciousness.

He carefully climbed the staircase, ascending in synchronicity with the drumming all around, fixed on a complete void, a complete absence. He contemplated James Stewart climbing the tower in *Vertigo*, Orson Welles climbing out of the sewer in *The Third Man*, dead characters, dead actors, dead culture – cinema was aged, fading, pointless, irrelevant and Larry belonged to that redundant past. Above him the bell hung – heavy cast metal, mute amongst the storm of pulsating percussion. He reached the top of the tower of the Temple of the Pillar and looked out across a town alive and throbbing with a cultural significance that meant nothing to him – he looked down on the crowds below, feeling separate, alone and insignificant. The purple throng below was calling him, the drums were demanding that he came, that he dived from the tower into oblivion. For a full five minutes he stood and imagined his body smashing on the stone flags below – he imagined the absence of immortality, he pictured the emptiness that existed before he was born and would continue after he died – he knew that experience was all – existence was all – and he was prepared to end experience and existence for all time. He braced himself on the stone balustrade and closed his eyes – he prepared his body for the impact and was on the verge of leaping from the tower when he heard the voice of Sandy whisper in his ear.

"What are you doing up here honey?"

He kept his eyes closed as he listened to the sound of her voice and felt her warm breath on his cheek. He tried to shut her out, to erase her from his life in the same way that he wanted to erase his own life, he tried to imagine her severed head hanging as the bell's clapper… but it was no use, she had broken the spell of his suicidal determination – he had a reason to live again despite himself.

The incantation of Magog had dissolved, Larry's thoughts of suicide that had seemed so reasonable, so obvious five minutes ago, now seemed vain and pointless. Perhaps all suicides feel that it's reasonable, that there is some use to the act, the power to end the world gives a feeling of omnipotence but it is only the suicide's world that disappears. Sandy gripped his shoulder and a shiver of lust ran through his being, she spoke gently and the last blackness dissipated from his thoughts – it seemed all to easy to flip from one state to the other.

"For a minute, I thought you were going to jump sweetie…"

Larry pulled his fragile perceptions together, he didn't care whether she was with Chris, The Order or The Corporation – she was here with him now, she had become his reason for continuing. He formed a response…

"Why did you bring Chris here? How could you have…?"

"Chris was here sweetie – which Chris?"

"My brother, Chris, he – he – he said he was…"

Tears formed in Larry's eyes – he felt that he was about to cry hysterically so he laughed a manic cackle. His chuckle muscle resonated in tune with the sonic assault of the drums below and the noise all around. The spell of Magog's hypnotic power was broken, perhaps Chris was never there – perhaps Magog had shifted into the form of his brother and pressed the self-destruct button deep in Larry's subconscious. Larry laughed like a lunatic, tears streaming down his sunburned face.

"You look like you need a drink honey – come with me and I'll sort you out…"

Chapter 36
Murder My Sweet

The *Bar Moderno Mínimo* on the *Plaza España* was neither modern nor minimal; Calanda was the kind of place where *moderno* still referred to the start of the 20th Century and *mínimo* just meant small. The walls of the bar were covered with brightly glazed tiles and, behind the dark wood bar with its ornately carved scrolls and ropework, were dark cabinets with polished glass windows that contained bottles: *Colungo, Ratafia, Moscatel, Pazo Pondal, Cariñena, Milenario Brandy, Miura Cherry Liquer, Anissette, Somontano, Ponche Caballero, Crema Caballero* – unfamiliar labels, local brands, intriguing cabinets of alcoholic diversity. Behind the bar, mugs and glasses hung from rusty hooks and the hostelry's narrow windows were draped with discoloured lace curtains. On the stone surface, a basket of ripe plums sat next to an enameled bucket packed with ice - steaming from the freezer. The small, cramped interior was packed with the steaming Easter crowds and the air was filled with the deafening sound of the drums from the street outside. Sandy and Larry had found two seats in the quietest corner of the bar, their conversation protected by the sonic wall of the paschal celebrations. Behind the heavy counter, a dark and earnest young Aragonese barman was preparing two deadly serious dry martinis for them. He took two glasses, a bottle of *Burdon's Gin* and a shaker from the Frigidaire under the bar. He carefully stirred the contents of the enamel bucket with a thermometer, studied the mercury and filled the shaker with ice. He turned and opened a glass cabinet behind the bar, swiftly removing two bottles. He meticulously measured a few drops of *Noilly Prat* and *Angostura Bitters* and poured them over the ice. He stared intently at Sandy and Larry as he placed the lid on the steel canister and shook it gently for exactly 30 seconds before pouring off the excess liquid and refilling the vessel by covering the tainted ice with gin. He replaced the lid, shook and stared for a further 30 seconds before serving the two dry martinis that he had created in the ice-cold glasses that he had prepared earlier.

Larry gently sipped the icy alcohol and his self-doubt dissolved as he watched Sandy's lips confess all to him…

"Well honey, I suppose it's time that I came clean with you – you know – I wasn't sure… I guess I wasn't sure whose side you were on – I really wasn't sure where your allegiances lie… but seeing you just then – seeing Magog hypnotise you and send you off to your death – I guess I kind of knew that you weren't on the same side as the Bland Corporation…"

Larry wasn't sure if he'd heard her clearly, "Magog hypnotised me?"

"Uh huh sweetie – the power of suggestion – some people are more susceptible than others."

"So it wasn't Chris in the Temple? I mean – he just made me believe that it was…"

Sandy cut him short. "Oh no sweetheart, that was your brother alright – that was Chris. Your brother has worked for the Bland Corporation since he was a teenager. That travel photography stuff was a front – he's Magog alright…"

"How long have you…? But he told me that you – you brought me here to…"

"I guess it's his word against mine. Didn't this morning mean anything to you? Can't you tell who's being honest honey? You don't know him – you don't *really* know him – but you've known me for a long, long, long time haven't you? We dream the same dreams - remember?"

Larry was uncertain – if he trusted his senses, he'd go for Sandy every time; she had the kind of face that you wanted to believe in and a body to back it up.

"Look Sandy – I've always – I mean, ever since – oh, I don't know – look, I love… but – but what's it all about?"

The drums drowned out his disjointed thought processes, shattering his confessions and protestations. He sat back and listened as she continued.

"It's all about The Order sweetie. I've been working for The Order – Joe and me, we're like a gang – a teeny little part and, well we had a job to do – we're meant to help take control of the world in the name of love…"

"Yeah?"

"Yeah – in the name of love, liberty, emotion, desire, death, sweat, sex – fucking freedom Larry – that's what it's all about! Do you really want to be tied down all your life baby? Do you want to be force-fed frozen food from poxy printed packages? Do you want to live a life that's all about cars and houses and furniture and *things*? Well – this is not your beautiful house and it never will be. Do you really, really want to feel bad, bad, bad and then drop down dead – or do you want to tear the whole fucking thing up? Do you want to rot in your little mouse hole, saying 'yes' and eating cheese – or do you want to take a gun, kill people and fuck me? What sounds best honey – what are *you* all about?"

The drums and the martini were working their magic on Larry – the thought of killing the bland stuffed managerial shirts; the accountants and resource managers, the systems people who run their little slow death camps, who suck all the creative energy out of every man, woman and child. The marketeers who take the energy and power of revolution, turn it into a t-shirt and manufacture it in a sweatshop. The thought of killing them and fucking Sandy in a surrealist, situationist explosion of anger, suddenly seemed like the best option to Larry… or maybe it was just the gin thinking.

Sandy couldn't read the stupid male thoughts cantering through his mind, but she could see that he was on her side, in her grasp and ready to carry out her commands.

"Now, here's the story sweetie - I'm after Magog – you may not like this, but we need to eliminate your brother. The Order are meeting today and Magog must be here in Calanda to do something extreme... Much as I love you honey, I can't believe that it's just about you. He must have rooted out The Order's annual meeting place and he knows the importance of this year's congregation..."

"The importance?"

"The new *Grand Caballero* – the new head of The Order will be elected today. I shouldn't be here – I'm just an English *Escudero* – but we have to try and do something to stop Magog. Your brother is ruthless – he will stop at nothing to kill the new *Grand Caballero* – and if he does, The Order may never recover and The Bland will triumph."

"But – why can't you just warn them?"

"They don't trust me – we are loose, disparate forces – we trust no-one. I can only trust those in my immediate cell – that's Joe and maybe a couple of others. You see, Chris joined us, he infiltrated us, we trusted him. He knows all about us and, by the time that we found out he was working for the Bland Corporation – that he was Magog - it was too late, he'd already convinced The Order that we were traitors – that it was Me and Joe who worked for the Bland Corporation. The Order still believe that we're turncoats!" She looked around attentively and lowered her voice before continuing. "We've got to go to the congregation this evening at the *Centro Buñuel*. The Order will be meeting and we have to stop Chris – we have to stop Magog before he kills the *Grand Caballero*."

She sat back and sedately sipped her martini as she stared into Larry's eyes. She ran her tongue around her bright red lips and Larry melted like the ice in the barman's steel shaker. He gazed silently at her as she continued...

"Look – this is where Chris is staying in Calanda..."

She handed him a slip of paper and then reached under the table and placed something cold on his leg. He looked down and saw a black metal object on his lap.

"What's this?"

"It's the SIG-Sauer P245 – it's a short recoil operated, locked breech pistol. It's German and it's loaded…"

"Is it real?"

"It's not a toy and this is not a game honey. If we get seperated, if we find nothing at the *Centro Buñuel*, then you must go to the address on that note and kill Chris – kill Magog before he kills you."

"I don't know what to do with this…" Larry put his hand around the rough aluminum handle and stroked the stubby, smooth, steel barrel. The gun was short, less than 20cm long, but heavy – he couldn't believe that it wasn't a toy. He wanted to pass it back to Sandy, but he couldn't – the time had come. He surreptitiously placed it in his inside jacket pocket and took the final sip from his martini.

Sandy continued, "Sure, sure, sure you know what to do – you've always wanted to be in the movies – you've watched enough of them – you've seen people shooting and being shot. Now you've got the gun and you've got the girl – it's what you always wanted sweetie."

"But how do I…?"

"You just point it where you want the bullet to go and squeeze the little trigger – there's no safety catch – it's all *automático para la gente* baby…"

Feedback rang through the bar, electric guitar and female vocals. Someone had put a Euro in the jukebox and Juniper Moon fought with the *Rompida*…

Cuando soy feliz
Mi corazón se para, se para así
Funciona mi cabeza
Que sólo sabe pensar en ti

Sexo intelectual, haremos el amor
Con un cigarrillo en cualquier bar
Besos galácticos
Se sumergen dentro de mí
Me engañas, me siento mejor[18]

---

[18] "Me Siento Mejor", Juniper Moon

Chapter 37
Gun Crazy

At the heart of Calanda lies the *Centro Buñuel*, a renovated 17th Century palace, housing galleries, interactive displays and screening rooms that tell the story of Luis Buñuel's life as a linear narrative. The building has been carefully redesigned as the type of gallery and conference centre that you might find in any European town – a cultural mirage in a world of commerce – an exclusive club for those who understand the language of bourgeois European culture. V&A, TATE, MOMA, MAMCO, FACT, CBC – acronyms, brands, places to buy a quiet cappuccino and sit contemplating postcards and exhibition catalogues.

Sandy and Larry pushed their way through the noisy, crowded streets and down the cobbled slope to the basement entrance of the *Centro Buñuel*. A huge, brightly lit foyer with a large, curved reception desk – the *Centro* was unusually busy today with the crowds from the Easter *Rompida*. Tourists and participants filtered through the cool interior, their excited chatter and the noise of the drums mingled to create an air of fiesta, party, celebration. Larry and Sandy had lost themselves in the crowds and no one noticed as they slipped into the elevator together. He smiled at her and went to put his arm around her waist as he asked…

"Which floor?"

She pulled away from him and, with rapid proficiency, reached up and placed an empty plastic cup over the lift's CCTV camera. She took a key from her pocket, placed it in the keyhole on the control panel, turned it clockwise, looked him in the eye and whispered...

"We haven't got long honey, this place closes to the public in an hour. The Order have private underground meeting rooms in the basement – we're going down, down, down – when the lift doors open, you run across into the room straight ahead. It's the cleaner's store, you hide there and I'll just see if I can't check where this old meeting room is. I'll come back to you and we'll lie low until the building's empty and the party begins – savvy baby?"

Without waiting for Larry's response, she pressed the bottom button and the elevator descended swiftly into the deep basement of the *Centro Buñuel*, down below the crowds and the drums. The doors slid open and Larry dashed across the bright subterranean passageway, hiding himself in the dark, cramped broom cupboard. Sandy strolled slowly out of the elevator and turned right, just as the plastic cup fell from the camera and the doors slid shut.

Upstairs, behind the museum's reception desk, the sleepy security officer had noticed the blank screen, put down his glass of *Somontano* and was trying to work out what was obscuring the lens. As the obscuring cup fell, he had a brief glimpse of svelte Sandy disappearing as the elevator's doors closed. He switched to the basement camera and watched her casually walking towards the secret meeting room of The Order of Toledo. He leant down and quietly radioed for assistance.

▶▶

Larry was perched awkwardly on a cold ceramic sink in the cramped, dark cupboard, his feet resting on a small, folded stepladder. The line of light around the doorframe illuminated ghostly shapes in the inky interior. He fumbled for his flashlight and looked around at the industrial-sized flagons of cleaning fluid, plastic buckets and toilet rolls stacked neatly on shelves.

I guess even secret organisations need cleaners...

He heard footsteps, switched his torch off and held his breath as he listened to the sound of two or three men running down the concrete corridor outside. In the distance, there was some kind of scuffle and Larry felt sure that he heard Sandy's muffled voice as the running men struggled and cursed in Spanish. A door closed and then there was silence punctuated only by his beating heart.

They must have got her – they must have caught Sandy...

He started breathing again – the scent of floral disinfectant filled his head as he sat in the pitch-black cupboard and counted the minutes in vain hope.

She'll be back – she said she'll be back – maybe it was something else out there...

Up above, the *Centro* was closing its doors for the day, the lights were dimming and the tourists were spilling out into the sonic assault on the streets of Calanda. Larry sat underground and waited.

⏮

The Order of Toledo operates as a loose association of small, radical groups. Its clandestine cell structure mirrors the methods of the French Resistance, the Viet Cong and al-Qaeda, with sleeper cells of varying sizes existing across the world and a disparate command structure with the *Grand Caballero* at its head. Below the *Grand Caballero* are the *Caballeros*, or Knights of The Order – these *Caballeros* are an international group of artists, musicians, writers and filmmakers from all corners of the world. Each *Caballero* is responsible for the development of The Order in their own region and for vetting and establishing ground troops known as *Escuderos* or squires. The *Escuderos* organise revolutionary cells across the world and it was Terence Davies, one of the London *Escuderos* who had recruited Joe, Sandy and, later, Chris to The Order. Initially, they had known little of The Order's structure, only being aware of their own recruiter. As they moved through the parties and gatherings of the London cultural elite, they met other members and began to piece together an image of the larger organisation of which they had become a part.

The annual conference of The Order in Calanda is attended only by those ranked as *Caballeros*. The security is provided by an elite unit of Spanish *Escuderos*, who, since the death of Franco in 1975, have been responsible for the development of The Order's secret headquarters, hidden beneath the *Centro Buñuel* which they run as a low-key Aragonese tourist attraction.

Although known to each other, the *Caballeros* keep their identity secret from all others but their own *Escuderos*. They had arrived in Calanda individually, disguised in the purple hoods of the catholic penitents and had gathered deep in the bowels of the *Centro Buñuel*, waiting quietly, patiently in the high security meeting chamber of The Order. They were gathered for one of the most important meetings in the history of The Order of Toledo – for the appointment of the third *Grand Caballero*. *Luis Buñuel* had been the first and *Guillermo Cabrera Infante* had been his successor. *Infante* was a Cuban writer who became director of the *Instituto del Cine* after the Revolution. He eventually fell out of favour with Castro and was forced to live in exile in Madrid and London. Buñuel recruited him to The Order, chiefly because of his radical writings on cinema, but also for his work on the script for the cult Hollywood film, *Vanishing Point*. When *Buñuel* died in 1983, *Infante* was elected as *Grand Caballero* under cover of the 1984 *Rompida* and, following *his* death just prior to the 2005 congregation, a power vacuum had existed in the ranks of The Order. It was in 2006, with Larry hiding like a sardine in the cleaner's cupboard, that the third Grand Caballero was to be elected from the cabal of Knights gathered in their secret bunker. There had been three nominations for the position, all of them European filmmakers of note; members of the European cinematic old guard – the dusty Politburo of powerful image-makers who had mastered the art-form of the twentieth century: Antonioni, Bergman and Godard. There was to be a strict and ordered ceremony during which votes would be cast and no *Caballero* would be allowed to leave the chamber until the new leader was chosen. After the election, the new *Grand Caballero* would lead the knights, in their purple outfits, through the streets of Calanda from where they would disperse, like dark shadows, back to their own spheres of influence.

▶▶

Larry was sitting quite still in his dark cupboard. He had heard no noise since what he had assumed to be Sandy's capture and was starting to consider the reality of the situation that he now found himself in as the tap behind him dripped noisily into the large, white sink on which he was perched. He checked his pockets – he still had a dwindling wad of Euros, a half empty pack of cigarettes from the Bar *Moderno Mínimo*, a mobile 'phone and a loaded pistol. With the skill of someone who had considered and prepared the action for some time, he took a cigarette from his pocket and struck a match. As he lit and inhaled, he noticed a white cleaner's housecoat hanging on the back of the door.

An escape route, a way out – if Sandy's gone, I'd best put that coat on, pretend to be a cleaner and get out of here. I could call Mike and Casey, meet up with them, buy a nice meal, stay in a nice hotel and go home. I could probably apologise to Rhodri and get my job back – maybe it won't be so bad back in North Wales...

Larry inhaled deeply again – suddenly he was scared, weak, beaten into submission. Maybe he was happy that Sandy had gone – it was another escape clause. He couldn't be sure what he wanted – he wanted Sandy, he wanted to escape from the boredom. But without her – on his own with a little bit of money and a gun – without the girl... He decided to make a move, to let fate decide. The great God of Chance would decide his future: Chance, the only potent force in the universe on the side of the insignificant.

He took the white coat from the back of the door and pulled it on. The sleeves were a little short, but it wasn't too small. He took a broom from the cupboard and stepped out into the silent empty corridor, dressed in his working-class cloak of invisibility. He blinked and squinted as the bright artificial light hurt his eyes and headed off in the direction that Sandy had gone, gripping his broom firmly and hanging his head low. The only sounds in the corridor were the gentle humming of the air-conditioning system and the barely audible pounding of the drums in the streets above. He slowly swept down the dust-free corridor with his broom low and his head bent, casting sideways glances at the doorways on both sides as he headed towards the dead end. The doors were silent witnesses to his mounting frustration – his entrapment. There seemed to be no obvious escape route – no stairwell and no open doors. Unknown to Larry, on the other side of one of the locked doors, lay the body of an infamous Danish filmmaker. Dressed in a purple robe, Lars Von Trier lay unconscious on the hard concrete floor, his mouth taped shut and his hands bound tightly behind his back with blue cord.

Larry reached the end of the corridor, a bare white wall with a small white door that barely reached his knees – an access hatch of some kind, about 60cm square with a recessed chrome handle on the left-hand side. He carefully gripped the handle and pulled the door open - it was heavy, insulating the chamber that opened below from the world outside. Bending down to peer through the small portal, he could see a huge, dark, open space. The door allowed access to a narrow gallery that ran around the top of a high chamber. Four grey concrete walls – an underground box the size of a deep, deep Olympic swimming pool. The sheer walls rose to meet the dark grey concrete ceiling above. He crawled through the maintenance hatch, pulling it shut behind him, and made his way along the gallery. The conduit was about 50cm wide, hidden from the room below by a wall 50cm high. It seemed to function as access trunking for the cables and pipes that ran around the perimeter of the room. There were voices below; English, German, Spanish, Danish, Swedish, Italian; mumbling in low tones – reverberating from the concrete walls like the soundtrack of Godard's *Histoire(s) du Cinema*. He crawled further along and dared, from his position in the shadows, to peer over the edge. There was a six metre drop to the floor below and the room seemed to have just one heavy steel door and no windows. It was the archetypal underground bunker. The bunker was lit by tall, flickering candelabras and thirty or so shadowy figures in purple hooded outfits sat muttering on hard concrete benches.

As he peered over the edge, the selection ceremony commenced. One of the hooded men stood and rang a small bell – he spoke in near perfect English with a slight Swedish accent.

"There will be no grand pomp, no wild celebration – the *Grand Caballero* will be selected and announced with unspeakable solemnity." He paused as his words echoed around the candlelit concrete bunker. The hooded men shifted slightly on their cold slabs. "None shall leave except in following the new *Grand Caballero* – no wine or bread shall pass your lips until he is chosen. He will lead us through the streets of Calanda and onwards to take the streets of the world!"

Larry watched in silence as the men below nodded their agreement and the speaker continued...

"Though the world we inhabit may be sordid and dark – the Third Caballero will liberate humanity – will bring down the Bland – will take control of the Dark Windows and shine the light of Toledo across the world. The future is freedom and we elect that freedom today. Speak of your choice!"

Each hooded voice mumbled a name in turn...

"Godard"

"Godard"

"Godard"

"Godard"

The chant repeated again, again, again the name of Godard was spoken. Antonioni was old, immobile, blind, struggling to sit. He leant on the hooded Wim Wenders who cried half-heartedly when his turn to speak came...

"Antonioni"

Bergman had not even attended the meeting, the solidarity was dissolving with the years and he had cancelled at the last minute, preferring to stay in his protestant cinema at home on the island of Faro. He had not welcomed the nomination – he had exiled himself years earlier. It was Godard all the way – the hooded figures were voting for Godard and, before half of the Caballeros had spoken, he claimed victory. He stood, hidden beneath his pointed hood like all the others, encased in the concrete bunker, safe behind the steel door. He stood and, accompanied by his assistant, walked to the front of the congregation. Godard spoke.

"Brothers – brothers of the cofraternity of metaphors - I am aware that you do not all understand the French language and so, I shall speak to you now in the English that I learnt at school. At school I also learnt that, on his deathbed, Goethe called for more light. It was logical, therefore that some years later, cinema would be born in Europe – cinema, *an invention with no future,* they called it… But what is happening right now – tonight - around the world? Millions, billions of human beings are watching screens right now, drinking up images, staring in electronic mirrors, awestruck in the fascination of their drool-inducing screens. And what interest did Buñuel have in these screens? Buñuel was concerned with the revolutionary potential of the ordinary – with super-realism and we, gathered here, we are all film-makers at heart. Whether we use words or images or music – we create the extraordinary from the ordinary – we reveal the revolutionary potential of every single human life. This is why the Bland and their masters want to govern us, to control us, to kill us. I have been quietened, cowed for too long. I have been censored by the Bland Gestapo but, with your support, with The Order of Toledo's support, I feel ready to take control of the Dark Windows – in the name of cinema, of its stories and histories – I would like to thank you." He straightened himself and slowly scanned the assembled *Caballeros* before continuing. "Thirty-eight years after the events of 1968, the Bland Corporation still rules cinema the world over and, to this, we can add the fact that they now control all forms of electronic communication. In our current form, with our current tools, we can do nothing but aim two or three cultural jet planes at the heart of the vast Bland Empire. If cinema does its job properly, then *the people* will organise themselves and together we will continue to struggle on all fronts to take control of the apparatus and to create cinema that is national, free, comradely and bonded in friendship!" He lowered his voice to a hoarse whisper, "I would like to thank you all – but specifically, my supporter and nominator who stands beside me now – Monsieur Von Trier."

The assembled Caballeros applauded and Von Trier spoke in response – only the voice wasn't Von Trier, it was the voice of Magog!

Larry recognised the voice of his brother emanating from behind the purple hood, the voice of the owlish assassin from the Bland Corporation. Anger took hold of Larry - rage, jealousy, determination. Sandy had gone, Godard was here again, the second Godard, about to be killed a second time, but this time it was Chris Went who was about to kill Godard and this time Larry had the means to stop him. Chance had put Larry in this position, chance had allowed him to stumble on the death of the first Godard and chance was giving him the opportunity to save the second Godard. Sandy wanted him to do it, Sandy would reward him, Chris was gone, gone, gone – Chris was in the pay of the killers, a collaborator with the bland. Chris was on the wrong side and he was about to kill Godard – Sandy was right – there was no other possible reason for his presence here and Larry had to act!

He reached into his pocket and drew the loaded P245 out. He grasped it firmly in both hands, rested his elbows on the low wall, pointed it directly at Magog's head and squeezed the trigger.

The sharp crack of a hundred bullets echoed around the concrete bunker as the missile and its sonic shadow ricocheted from the concrete walls below. He watched in horror as Magog looked up at him and Godard crumpled to the ground, blood pouring from his purple heart. Larry had missed; he had missed Magog and killed Godard. Larry had put a bullet through the heart of the second Godard and he had no way out – he had killed - he had killed the wrong man and this time it wasn't a dream!

An alarm began to sound, voices were crying in anger and anguish from the chamber below. Larry got down on his knees and crawled back along the gallery and out of the hatch. The corridor was dark; red lights were flashing on the walls and an alarm was sounding intermittently down the narrow corridor. He walked up to the elevator grasping his broom and pressed the button. He waited for ten long seconds before the doors slid open – the key was still there – he pressed the button and the elevator rose slowly to the foyer. He stepped out into the hubbub of the security alert, feigning ignorance with his demeanour. No one noticed the cleaner who walked unassumingly out of the Centro Buñuel, up the ramp and disappeared silently into the Easter throng.

Down below in the bunker, the Caballeros were attempting to come to terms with the events, struggling to create order from the brutal killing. Magog had unmasked Godard and was kneeling beside him, supporting his head and stroking his rough, sparse, grey hair. Wenders approached, removed his hood and spoke...

"How is he?"

Magog spoke with great solemnity. "He is almost completely bald."

Wenders looked confused. "I don't understand..."

Magog replied slowly. "To put it bluntly – he will soon be dead – dead Mister Wenders"

Wenders answered in stilted English "And your prognoses are seldom wrong Herr Von Trier..."

Magog continued from behind his pointed hood. "By the moustache of Baden Powell, we will catch the killer..."

There was a moment's silence and then, Antonioni's voice spoke from the shadows. "But, no matter how we try, we cannot leave this room without a Grand Caballero. We must rest here – it is the convention..."

Godard coughed and whispered to Magog in a quiet and grating voice.

"Seigneur Elohim soit avec moi – l'empire de la sorcellerie est assemblé ici... Avant que je meure le cher seigneur... Vous n'aurez aucun autre dieu avant moi... venez! venez! venez!"[19]

As the second Godard lay down and breathed his last breath, Magog abandoned the dark panic and left the Centro Buñuel - another shadow in the warm breeze of the April evening.

---

[19] *" Lord Elohim is with me - the empire of sorcery is assembled here... Before I die Dear Lord... You will not have any other god before me... come! come! come!"*

Chapter 38

The Fugitive

It had taken Larry a good hour to find the address that Sandy had given him just prior to her abduction by The Order in the *Centro Buñuel*. He had waved the note in the hooded faces of dozens of evening revelers before finding someone willing to send him down the wrong alley in the wrong direction. When he had almost given up, he stumbled across a short bow-legged Spaniard, sporting a frayed purple robe, stubble and a huge drum. He looked as if he had just dismounted from a Napoleonic steed and was wandering, lost after a rout of some kind. His name was Esteban and he was a friendly Christian soul with no English, who was happy to walk the substantial distance through the clamorous crowd to deliver Larry at Magog's apartment on *Avenue de la Clocha*. Larry thanked Esteban in his best Spanish and watched as he wandered off, the huge drum draped over his shoulder and his purple gown dragging along the dusty cobbles. He looked down at his scrap of paper and up at the number fixed to the wall – 84 – this was the place.

He tried the handle and the heavy oak door swung open into a dark hallway, he sidled in and pulled it closed behind him. The narrow hall was lit by a distant streetlight filtered through a dirty window above the door. His vision adjusted to the gloom as he walked to the end of the hall and opened the single interior door that led into a large, barren living space. The room was completely empty; the grey walls stripped bare, furniture and carpet gone. The parquet flooring was scattered with rubbish; screwed up pages from old newspapers, plastic water bottles and empty cigarette packets. An embroidered cushion and broken standard lamp were the only signs that the room was once furnished, the smell of ashtrays and rising damp pervaded the space that hadn't been aired for some time. The grey walls and high ceiling were ornamented with frames of faded rococo plasterwork and the overwhelming ambience was of desolation and emptiness. Larry walked over to the large double doors that opened into the adjoining room and called into the shadows…

"Chris? … Chris?"

His voice echoed around the dark interior as he moved into what appeared to be an empty library. The next room was decorated in a similar style to the first, one large wall covered with vacant bookshelves and the opposite wall with built-in cupboards from floor to ceiling. He ran his hand along the dusty shelves and opened the cupboards – there was nothing, the room had been stripped, emptied. The noise of the drums still filled the streets outside but the inside of Magog's *Calanda* lair was quiet and dark. He wandered through the empty chambers, reminded of rooms that he had seen – rooms from films and rooms from dreams. He thought of the grey bedroom that he dreamt of in Lausanne, the bedroom at the end of Kubrick's *2001: A Space Odyssey*, the interiors of Buñuel's *Un Chien Andalou*, hotel rooms and stage sets from the hundreds of films swarming in his subconscious merged with the guilt that was rising through his body as he pictured the bleeding body of Godard lying on the floor of the concrete bunker. He took the gun from his pocket and held it ahead of him as he moved through the empty interiors, remembering the kick of the P245's recoil as it pumped a single bullet into the heart of one of the world's most important cultural figures. His head was pounding with noise of the drums; the thrill of the assassin combined with the remorse and anger of a fool. The blood of Godard flowed through his visions of ornate musty interiors and there was no one here. There was no Chris to confront, no Sandy to save and no Mike to meet – he was all alone with the consequences of his actions. He sat down on the floor in the dark shadows, attempting to formulate a plan of action. He placed the gun in front of him, took another cigarette from his pocket and sat smoking in the dark, flicking ash across the antique wooden flooring.

He was just about to light his third cigarette when he heard the outside door open and the light tread of male footsteps carefully approaching. He quietly picked up the P245 and held his breath in the shadows, awaiting the entry of Magog; acutely aware that, in the next few seconds, he may be about to kill his own brother. He held the gun firmly, pointing it directly at the door that gently fell open. A silhouette stood in the doorway, casting a long, dark shadow into the gloomy interior. The shadow inhaled the fresh passive smoke and spoke…

"I telephoned you Mister Went. I telephoned but no one answered…"

He recognised the voice from the bridge game, the funeral and the *Posada de la Sangre* – it was Dewi Winkle. Dewi had followed him throughout this whole masquerade and yet remained a distant shadow. He had appeared at The Archive just before it was burnt and he had drugged Larry in the *Inn of Blood*. He had seemed to be an owl-like malevolent being but… perhaps he was not what he seemed. Larry couldn't bring himself to pull the trigger; he couldn't bring himself to kill again. Dewi appeared to be reading his mind…

"The first death is always the hardest Larry. It is easier from now on – if you want to add me to your tally… please, please squeeze the trigger of the SIG-Sauer P245 that Sandy gave you. But I can assure you that it will not help your predicament to kill me. I may be the only one left on your side."

He walked over and sat next to Larry in the silent empty chamber, lit a cigarette and continued while Larry stared into space, contemplating his guilt.

"It is all true – what Sandy told you about Magog – it's all true. He may have once been your brother but now he is an agent of the Bland Corporation, he has to remove you – it is you or he – there can be only one. You are perhaps wondering who I am – how I fit into this?"

Larry nodded and stared into the middle distance, aware that fate was leading him along a predestined route and that he had to listen to Dewi, whether or not he wanted to. Dewi continued…

"I am a friend of Joe and Sandy – a fellow *Escudero*. They had brought me on board, invited me to join their cell of The Order to investigate your brother and to test your ideological loyalty. We were aware that Godard was killed in Penmaenmawr and that you had discovered something. We were also aware that your brother is Magog, agent of the Dark Windows. It was important to us, it is still important to us that you survive and that you keep that information – you are a living witness, evidence that will allow us to take control of the Dark Windows."

"So – you work for The Order?"

"You could say that I work for the Order – I am a sort of independent *Escudero*; a consultant *Caballero*. I observed your brother infiltrate Joe and Sandy's cell, I saw Magog enter The Order as a double agent and discredit them. I have been following him for some time – I befriended him and he trusts me – and now I have to kill him. I had to test you – to see how you would react in The Archive. I brought Sandy to Toledo, I placed her in the heart of The Archive – none of the *Caballeros* knew that she was an outlaw – but it went wrong. I was hoping that you may have done my job for me today but… I have to stay on the outside, distant, I work for The Order but I mistrust those fanatical, conservative elements who are attempting to take the leadership. Godard was my hope for the future – he was the one who would lead The Order to take control of the Dark Windows and the 21st century… But you killed the wrong man Larry – you killed the wrong person and now they have got your Sandy."

Larry snapped out of his maudlin mood when he realised that other lives were at stake, wider issues than his pathetic guilt.

"Who's got her?"

"Magog – The Bland – they have taken Sandy out of the country and they have infiltrated the heart of The Order. These are desperate times for humanity Larry – soon no one will care, soon they will put their clampdown into action. They will sew-up the planet with their Bland World Order and no one will give a damn. The Order's archive may be destroyed but they cannot destroy the spirit of The Order. Franco, Hitler, McCarthy, Stalin – they failed and The Bland Corporation will fail too. We have to continue the battle for humanity. Forget about the Caballeros gathered here in Calanda, they can no longer help you – we ourselves have to take the fight to the heart of their corporation and I know where that is located. It is a long, long way from here, and we shall go there to find Sandy and destroy their corporate plan. You are wanted for murder my friend, The Order want you, The Bland want you, your friends cannot help you – only I can help you now. But first I must kill Magog – I'm sorry Larry but I must kill your brother. He is waiting in the car outside. He thinks that I am on his side, that I have come to capture you and take you to the Place where they are holding Sandy – to the leader of The Bland. Come - you must come with me now – I will place you in the trunk of the car and kill Magog while he still feels safe and secure in my collaboration."

He was convinced that Dewi was his only hope – there seemed to be no one else to believe in. This new agent of chance was leading him to another place and Larry followed blindly.

"Okay Dewi, I'll go along with your plan – I'll be your dumb decoy prisoner on one condition."

"I cannot agree to conditions Larry – you must put your gun in your pocket and come with me – it is our only hope –it is *the people's* hope…"

"Will you call Mike and Casey – tell them where I am, tell them to go home?"

Dewi nodded his agreement and led Larry out of the house and into the trunk of a waiting black Mercedes. Before he disappeared into the dark boot, he caught sight of Chris's outline sitting quite still in the passenger seat of the executive vehicle. A few seconds later, he heard the muffled thud of a silenced gun amongst the persistent echo of the *Rompida*, a body dragged along the ground and the engine starting first time. The black Mercedes with its dark windows pulled out of town and headed along the *Avenue del General Franco* on the 18 hour journey towards France, Calais, the Channel Tunnel and England. In the dark hallway of *84, Avenue de la Clocha,* the lifeless body of Dewi Winkle lay slumped, face down – waiting for the invisible worm to finish the job that Magog had just started.

⏮

Earlier, back in the bunker of the *Centro Buñuel*, the gathered *Caballeros* were mourning the passing of their new leader – there appeared to be no future for the bickering geniuses who no longer seemed to have a formulated plan, an argument, a theology. Theirs was an organisation based on the power of coincidence and it had been torn apart by a chance act – by Larry's mistake. The alarm continued to sound around the bunker, the red lights flashed and the artists argued over matters of doctrine while Godard's blood flooded the concrete floor. No one had noticed Von Trier leave and no one suspected that Magog had planted an explosive device in the heart of the *Centro*. As Magog drove his shiny Mercedes slowly along the N-211, an explosion tore through the underground headquarters of The Order of Toledo – flames funneled through the basement rooms, incinerating the bickering Caballeros: Wenders, Von Trier and Antonioni turned to ashes in a flash. Innovation, art, the past and all possible futures – melted for all time in a dark concrete bunker under the drums of Calanda. Lying in his hiding place, bumping along with his head resting on a folded jacket, Larry couldn't hear the death of The Order over the rumbling of tyres on tarmac. He was happy in the delusion that it was Dewi taking him home to Sandy, Casey and his life of quiet turpitude.

Chapter 39
Crossfire

Trapped in the dark metal coffin of the Mercedes' trunk, lying on the grey carpet with a folded jacket as his pillow, Larry had time to think, to contemplate. He felt comfortable being smuggled out of Spain in the warm boot of an expensive car. Why did he let himself be pushed into lakes, cupboards and car boots? Why did he let himself be dragged along by other people's stories – other people's designs? He had started to create his own narrative now – a teenage fantasy that had ended in violence, conflagrations and the second death of Godard.

There was no radio playing in the car - no talking, just the constant rumbling and occasional rush of a car passing in the other direction. He began to categorise the slight changes in the nature of his audio experience – the wildtrack: Here a tunnel, there a motorway, lorries, built-up areas, a slight strain in the engine and an incline on the mountains, sharp bends giving way to long, straight stretches of monotony. The darkness of this motorised womb allowed Larry a brief respite from the feverish activities of the past few days. Days in which he had lived, died and killed – days in which the certainties had become uncertain and the indefinite had become defined. He felt that he had taken control of his world – he had become a killer and a fugitive, he had dissolved the possibility of returning to his sedentary life – from sedent to sedition in one foul shot. He drifted off to sleep in the boot of the car – exhausted by his imagined revolutionary potential.

▶▶

He woke some hours later; his mouth was dry and furry. He had smoked too many cigarettes – his clothes were stale and his body ached. He was surprised that his body had coped so well with the events of the past few days – the torn ligament and tendonitis that marked his four decades on the Earth had started to return as he headed back towards the damplands of Britain. The car was swaying, rocking on clicking tracks. There was a slight suffocation in the air; the smell of deep, dark tunnels and electric trains. It must be the channel tunnel – or maybe he was confused by the mental images he had created. Maybe it was an Alpine tunnel, heading back to Switzerland, Austria or Italy. Ten minutes or so later, the car moved slowly down ramps and through some kind of official checkpoint – he briefly heard muffled English voices then acceleration and the familiar, crowded, noisy road system of the United Kingdom. The Mercedes headed northwards towards the M25 and the dark suburbs of London.

Rain was rumbling in the wheel arches and spattering on the metal boot. The black car had driven through the dark Spanish night, the dull French day and returned into the rainy English night. As they crawled along the gridlocked M25 towards junction 10, the sun had set, the owls were waking in the trees of Walton Firs and Larry was desperate to get out of the trunk.

The road was silent and dark as the car drew to a halt. He heard the door open for the first time on that long journey and feet crunched gravel as they approached.

Where am I? I have no idea what I'm going to do next – where I'm going to go. Maybe Dewi will help me find Sandy and Sandy will help me find my future now that Magog is dead...

The boot clicked open; there was little illumination, save the red glow of the taillights under-lighting the demonic face that stared at him from the grim, wet night. The euphoria of fresh oxygen blended with the scent of wet tarmac and the sound of the wind in the broad leaves floating above in the invisible, black night. It took Larry an eternal second to understand what had happened and who was looking down at him. The strigine features of Chris were glaring at him in the red light – Magog – the killer of Vendor, Godard and God-knows who else. Magog had dispatched and discarded Dewi and brought Larry all the way to this dark, wet, English lane – why? Why hadn't he just killed Larry in Calanda and left his corpse to bloat and stink in that dark hallway alongside Dewi's carcass? Maybe Chris was about to offer his brother a deal – send him home – tell him that it's all a big joke. Chris spoke…

"I've brought you home bud…"

"Home?" Larry recognised the air – the smell of affluent, suburban woodland. He could hear a river nearby. The rain was bouncing off the car's black bodywork and dripping in the puddles formed by its tyre-tracks.

"Yeah brother – I thought you'd like to die *here* on this road – on this road that you have dreamt of so many times…"

Suddenly it clicked – he was on the banks of the River Thames - Walton Lane – the towpath by the waterworks. It was the scene of his dream – of Sandy's dream.

How did Chris know about this? How could he possibly know?

The paranoia that he had abandoned in Lausanne – the fear of a conspiracy at which he was a hub – an ideological distribution hub, a focus for fantastic dream-eating zombies. The paranoia that had been lost in the action and desire of the last few days swept back over him, taking hold of his psyche. An owl called from the encroaching darkness – he had seen owls everywhere on his travels: China owls, knitted owls, embroidered owls – the spectre of Magog was everywhere and now there was no escape. His brother was Magog: The symbol of the control mechanisms that restrict freedom, kill charisma, burn books and filter reality.

Chris politely asked Larry to get out of the car boot and they faced each other through the silent, dark rain in the red light of the Mercedes.

II

The silence stretched to infinity, punctuated by the pattering rain and the wind battling in the leaves above. They said nothing as their eyes swallowed each other, as they morphed into one another, their father, the children that they once were. Larry swept back in time to 1984 – to an LSD trip gone wrong. He was in a room, a glue-sniffing squat, Chris was having a bad trip and, as their eyes met, they dissolved into a psychedelic image of each other. Then he was on the banks of the Thames on a long, hot summer afternoon with teenage girls in dungarees, Max Factor and Impulse body spray - the sun burning down on their teenage experience... and then further back, on a beach in Wales, a summer holiday in 1979, the threat of nuclear war in a farm cottage and *Armagideon Time* playing on the radio... mutating into a whining motorbike engine – and then, through the vortex of memory – back to 2006 and a rainy night in Walton. Larry and Chris both reached slowly into their jackets and pulled out guns. The sound of an approaching motorbike cut through the silence like a siren. The single headlamp arced through the night sky, illuminating the leaves overhead, it swung past them and, as it faded away, two shots rang out into the darkness.

Larry stood rigid; the SIG-Sauer P245 held ahead of him, smoke drifting from its short barrel. Chris looked directly into his eyes across the dark expanse that separated them and slowly crumpled to the ground. Larry approached the prone form of his brother, of Magog. His lifeless face was pressed into the sharp gravel and a small Beretta was gripped firmly in his cold, dead hand. He no longer looked like an owl – he looked like Chris, the brother that he wished he'd taken the time to know.

He can't have wanted to live – he could easily have killed me - he must have let me kill him...

Larry leant down and touched the barrel of the Beretta - it was cold. He stood alone on the dark towpath as his dreams spiraled around the space between his body, the trees and the river – settling on reality. He stood in the cold night and grasped the arms of his dead brother. In a trance, he dragged the body of Chris, the body of Magog – face down, the dirt and gravel tearing the dead flesh of his face as it scraped along the ground. He dragged the body the few metres to the bank of the Thames and quietly rolled it into the dark, gently flowing water. The corpse sank under the surface leaving delicate ripples amid the tiny regular pattern of light raindrops. The night was quiet, somewhere in the distance traffic rumbled by, water flowed through the filtration systems of the sewage works and the 21st century continued its inexorable journey away from the previous millennium and into the future. Larry felt part of the past – a fragment from a previous time. The people, places and culture that he knew had drifted away without him even being aware and they had taken his experience, his dreams and identity with them to the bargain basement of human history. He looked into the river and considered stripping down to his dark blue underwear, wrapping himself in chains and throwing himself into the dark, black Thames. He paused again, straightened his body, unlocked his legs, took the Sig-Sauer P245 from his pocket and threw it with all his remaining strength into the centre of the surging river. For a second he imagined a hand rising from the waters to catch the gun – the hand of the owl of the river, the alien lady of the lake – grasping the weapon and storing it safely for future fratricides.

He stood on the dark, abandoned towpath for minutes, waiting for reality to dawn. The rain soaked through his dirty clothes and the cold, damp night finally pulled him from his reverie, forced him to progress onto the next stage of the journey. What was left – who was left? He turned back to the Mercedes and realised that he had thrown the car key into the river with Chris's body. His only options were to wait here for dawn, to wait for chance to deal him the next card or to walk into Walton town centre – to go to the police station and hand himself in – confess all to the Surrey Constabulary.

He headed off down Walton Lane toward the *Seven Witches of Cowey Sale* contemplating memories of this dream lane, of his youth wandering the streets of Walton, imagining a future that bore no resemblance to where he was, to what had happened in the past few days. Back then, he had never imagined that he would live in North Wales with two children and a decade of permanent employment in the same mediocre establishment. The reality of the recent murders, mayhem and incarceration had probably featured more in his youthful imaginings – perhaps this was his destiny – maybe this is what the dreams pointed towards. Someone will have heard the shots and called the police. Any second now a car will quietly pull up and take him away – this must be the end – this must be the end of Larry.

As he placed one sodden foot in front of the other and allowed the thoughts to circulate through his tiny mind, the rain stopped, the moon appeared from behind the clouds and a car approached from the distance along the pale blue moonlit tarmac of Walton Lane. He had come to a halt by the Seven Witches when the car pulled up alongside him and a voice called out...

"Alright mate – I've been trying to bloody track you down all day!"

He squinted at the figure leaning from the window of the bright yellow Ford Capri that had parked next to him – the chiseled features, slight beard and piercing blue eyes. It was a face from the past, a figure from a dream – it was Joe Locke – Joe Locke, his benefactor and commissioner, Sandy's friend and lover – the man who had planted the conspiratorial virus in his subconscious and sent him to Switzerland on the trail of Godard and the Dark Windows. How could he be here, now, by the Seven Witches, five minutes after he had dispatched his own brother into the icy Thames. What did it all mean and where was he going next?

Chapter 40
The Hills Have Eyes

"...the earth was not made purposely for you, to be Lords of it, and we to be your Slaves, Servants, and Beggers; but it was made to be a common Livelihood to all, without respect of persons: And that your buying and selling of Land, and the Fruits of it, one to another, is The cursed thing, and was brought in by War; which hath, and still does establish murder, and theft, In the hands of some branches of Mankinde over others, which is the greatest outward burden, and unrighteous power, that the Creation groans under..." [20]

⏮

In 1649, shortly after King Charles 1st was beheaded, Gerrard Winstanley and his followers, known as *The Diggers*, occupied common land at Saint George's Hill in Weybridge and attempted to claim it as their right. In an early form of Christian Communism, they called for the abolition of private property and the aristocracy, cultivating the commons and distributing the food that they grew. Their concepts of equality and freedom threatened the ideology of the Lords and landowners who sent hired thugs to violently turf *The Diggers* out. Their utopia was short-lived, but the ideals of this charismatic man and his followers still reverberate through the golf course, tennis courts and multi-million pound mansions of Saint George's Hill.

The super-rich now occupy this small enclave on the outskirts of Surrey, it

---

[20] From 'A Declaration from the Poor Oppressed People of England' by Gerrard Winstanley (1649)

was close to where Larry grew up. He had a paper-round in the Hills; delivering rolled-up broadsheets to the servants of film stars, pop stars, sports stars, financiers, arms dealers and gangsters. His brother, Chris, had worked as a caddy at the exclusive golf club – it was where he got his first break, where he first entered the domain of the Bland and the Dark Windows. The private streets of Saint George's Hill are some of the most expensive and exclusive in the UK – it is no surprise that Freddie Foulkes' home, *Black House*, is in the heart of The Hills - at the end of *Yaffle Road*, hidden amongst the descendants of the trees that *The Diggers* had walked through, free men in the 17th century.

This land that, 350 years earlier, had been occupied by Winstanley's *True Levellers* was bought, around the time of the birth of cinema, by Walter George Tarrant, an imposing architect and joiner. He started to develop an enclosed suburban village for the wealthy on The Hill; complete with shops and social facilities. But in 1920, following a trip to Zürich, where he experienced the total pandemonium of *Dada* at the *Cabaret Voltaire* and, galvanised by the devastating effects of the First World War, he switched his focus to the building of council housing for the ordinary men returning from the conflict. His plans for a working class idyll were obliterated by the 1930's financial crisis, he lost control of the company that bore his name and the focus of Tarrant Builders shifted back to the development of houses for the super-rich. Tarrant himself retired to North Wales in 1940, purchasing a large estate near Porthmadog where he died suddenly two years later.

The lands of The Hill had a mysterious resonance, connections to revolutionary tales: What if Winstanley's community had been successful? What if Tarrant had built council houses instead of mansions? Why was the land so important to the rich and powerful? Why did they want to live together in the woods on a hill? This was the place where Chris had been recruited to the Dark Windows as a teenager – it was at the golf club, working as a caddy for Freddie Foulkes' predecessor, that Chris Went became Magog. It was at night, in the green carpeted, wood paneled clubhouse that the late Chris Went's identity was transformed into that of the assassin of the Dark Windows – his conscience was removed and his soul was pared.

▶▶|

Larry bent down and looked at the driver of the Yellow Capri in disbelief, it was Joe Locke dressed as Bodie from *The Professionals*, CI5...

"What are you doing here Joe? How did you find me?"

Joe's powerful presence, his self-confidence, appeared to be momentarily wavering – he seemed uncertain, older and fragile. Although he had the car and clothes of his youth, his face betrayed a weakness and his voice a contradiction that had not been apparent at their last meeting in the V&A museum.

"I didn't mean to find you – I mean, I've been looking for someone else but... You've met Dewi right? He's one of us – one of the gang. I... I had a text from him and, since he came back to England... I mean today... I've, I've been trying to track him down. Dewi had some sort of bug on his Mercedes and I've been following his signal... I just, I just found the car back there and, and – there was no one there. I didn't expect to find... where's Dewi?"

Larry lost all thoughts of giving himself up to the Surrey Constabulary – he decided to confess his crimes to Joe and continue with his commission.

"Dewi's dead – Magog killed him – Chris, my brother - Chris, he was working for the Dark Windows... they called him Magog - he killed Dewi, he killed him in Calanda."

"Calanda? Chris? Magog? What the... where's, I mean if Chris *killed* Dewi - what's happened to him? Did *you* drive back here – is Chris following you?"

Joe appeared to be suppressing a sarcastic grin, Larry couldn't tell whether he was being genuine, he wasn't certain whether it was all a pretense – maybe

Joe knew more than he was letting on. But, on that dark, wet road, Joe seemed to be an ally – a friendly face – he decided to trust him regardless…

"It's like this Joe – I killed Chris – it was him or me. I don't know why, but I think he wanted me to kill him – he brought me back here in the boot of Dewi's car and then he just stood there and let me shoot him straight through the heart – one bullet. He's in the river, dead. I put him in the river."

The facts appeared to click into place in Joe's sharp consciousness; he seemed to grasp the situation, regained his confidence and took control. He leant over and opened the passenger door. Larry's confession of murder seemed unimportant to Joe.

"Get in mate – you're soaked, get in and put the Doyle suit on…"

Larry climbed in and, with a swift wheel-spin, Joe accelerated away from the scene of the crime, talking at the same pace that he drove as Larry struggled to change into the dry clothes that he'd been passed.

"I get it Larry: Sandy, Dewi – the garbled messages – the invitation. It will be some kind of honour thing; Chris must have failed – he must have been ordered to die, Freddie must have ordered it – don't blame yourself… it's destiny. I should have known he'd be here – it's Freddie's neighbourhood – Freddie's party. It's risky, but we've got to do it – she'll be there."

"Who?"

"Sandy – Freddie will have her at his place in the Hills…"

"That's what Dewi said, he said that he was going to take me to the place where they're holding Sandy – who's Freddie?"

"Freddie Foulkes – Unilather, the Bland Corporation – soap, TV, newspapers, movies. He owns the future: Food, fuel, clothes, dreams – he owns the lot. He owns just about every important patent and invention – he even tried to patent rice Larry! He owns part of me: The *Gilgamaze*? Sponsored by Unilather – I'm part of the whole evil system Larry – but we're going to take them on from the inside right?"

"Right?" Larry wasn't at all certain but he sat back and let Joe do the driving and the talking…

"I'm in with the freaking in crowd – you know that mate – you've watched me from a distance – you're not stupid are you pal? There's a party tonight up in Saint George's Hills - Freddie's having a masquerade, a fancy-dress do and Sandy will be there. That's why I'm dressed like this, that's why I'm driving this stupid freaking car – it should be silver but I could only find this canary thing. It's an important event, hush-hush – can't tell you all yet, it's classified but the plan's coming together pal – the plan's coming together…"

The pair of pseudo-cops drove desperately from the banks of the Thames, up the *Seven Hills Road* - tracing the fictional route that Ambassador Thorn made in the final sequence of *The Omen*. They screeched to a halt at the Burwood Road entrance of the private estate. No free man could wander through the streets of The Hills in the 21st century. Larry was impressed by the gated entrance to the vast millionaire's estate with its computer controlled entry-phone system. It had been different when he was a youth – there were no gates on the roads, many of the houses may have had high fences and security systems – but others were easily accessible. Film stars could be seen sweeping their drives and tending their roses – the rich didn't seem scared, they weren't preparing themselves for the clampdown. Now, as the gulf between the inhabitants of the Hills and the rest of the world had widened – now the Bland and their allies were ready for battle. They were building higher walls and retreating into their castles.

He remembered wandering through The Hills at night as a teenager, getting stoned and looking up at the tall trees - peering up the long drives of Tarrant's *Surrey Style* mansions, watching the shadows of the elite flicker by the leaded lights, imagining that it was accessible, that one day, he would live in one of these artisan mansions. As his vague ambitions had entertained vague notions of meritocracy in the early 1980s, he didn't realise that the gulf was widening and the barriers were rising. He didn't realise that the allies of the Bland were getting stronger and preparing the world for a socio-political lockdown. He was oblivious to the concept that history was scientifically predestined or that he would have a minor role in its whimpering endgame.

As he sat next to Joe, in the passenger seat of a yellow Ford Capri, dressed as a fictional 1970s policeman, he became conscious of the levels of security that now invaded every aspect of life. He became aware of the layers of protection that surrounded the real rulers of the world – the bland, anonymous owners of food, fuel and the future. He saw the new high security gate system of The Hill, the minimum wage slaves in yellow vests who controlled the barriers, he recognised that there was no entry now – the land that was once occupied by The Diggers and crossed by public rights of way, was now the village – the village that was home to the global elite. They had purchased the apocalypse and built their luxury bunkers – something was coming and they knew about it.

The rain had stopped, thunder rumbled in the distance and sporadic flashes of lightning sliced the dark night open. They threaded slowly through the silent, deserted streets, to the gated entrance of Freddie's house at the dead end of Yaffle Road. The Capri crept through the automatic gates and down the sweeping drive, headlights illuminating the tall trees that shielded *Black House* from sight. As they rounded the bend, Freddie's monumental Mock Tudor mansion reared into view – raised on a small hill and surrounded by a carefully tended garden, it was subtly lit with bulbs concealed in the neatly clipped bushes. The car crunched across the deep gravel and was directed to a parking space between two large black Range Rovers. Joe's invitation was checked by two burly security guards who proceeded to run metal detectors over the two guests before ushering them across a boggy lawn in the direction of some large, noisy marquees that covered the formal gardens at the rear of the house.

Noise thumped through the thunderous night, the noise of music that Larry didn't recognise. It was something contemporary yet familiar, the whole scenario was disconcerting and Larry was attempting to suppress his rising guilt and paranoia. He looked at Joe, who had donned a black Zorro mask and was offering Larry a similar gold disguise. He accepted it and pulled it over his eyes, concealing his identity. He refocused on the music – there was something of the future in the rhythms, the electronic dance music – it was a remix of something from his past that he couldn't quite define. Concentrating on the music that was seeping from the giant tents helped to steady Larry's nerves - he nodded his head in time to the repetitive electronic beat. As they entered the marquee, the music swelled and the vocals became clear.

"Ov power, Ov power.
Dog power. Dog power.
The secret in a cell.
The freedom of its spell."[21]

The music was different, the drums were just as insistent but the sound was new, clinical, beautiful - like the people that inhabited the dimly lit tent. All around, tall, attractive people danced and swayed in trance-like movements – smiling behind masks and costumes. Joe bent down and whispered in Larry's ear...

"You find Sandy – there's no rush, we've got all night. Over there..." he gestured towards the bar at the back of the marquee. "Over there, behind the bar, you can get into the kitchen. If I disappear, I'll be missed but you can find her Larry – you should be getting good at this sort of thing. When the coast is clear, slip out of the back of the marquee and into the house – you'll be fine mate."

Joe's suggestion somehow filled Larry with confidence, the music swept over him, they separated and Larry drifted effortlessly over to the bar and smiled at the bartender.

---

[21] Psychic TV, 'Ov Power'

"Dry Martini please…"

The loud music and crowds of beautiful people faded into the muted distance as the masked barman smiled and looked directly at Larry. The world around separated and the psychic space between the two strangers contracted, channeling directly into Larry's senses. His attention converged on the strange barman whose hair was slicked back and lips were painted red, he smiled disturbingly and spoke slowly, purposefully… "Sorry my masked friend – only Mr Bond can have that one – I am the cocktail doctor tonight and I prescribe for my clients. You should have maybe a *Charlie Chaplin* or a *Marilyn Monroe* – you choose…"

Larry spoke into the silent space that the barman had created, "I – err – a *Marilyn Monroe* will be fine…"

"Good choice – we've met before haven't we?"

"I don't think so – I…"

"Maybe not…"

The barman turned his back on Larry and the pulsating music reasserted itself in his perceptions of the present moment. Larry watched as the stranger filled a champagne saucer with Dom Pérignon, Calvados and Grenadine, hung a pair of flourescent cocktail cherries over the edge of the glass and passed the bright red drink to Larry, smiling intently. He swiftly knocked back the expensive concoction and the champagne hit him somewhere at the back of his brain, amplifying the echoing music. He became even more aware of glamour that surrounded him, that filled the marquee and diminished his sense of self. The bartender spoke, his voice cut through the ambience…

"Well, well, well - I think that did you some good – will you follow *Marilyn* with a *Charlie* or… maybe I see you more as a *Mary Pickford*?"

"*Charlie Chaplin* will do me fine, do you know that he's buried in…"

Before Larry could finish, the barman swung around and swiftly measured sloe gin, apricot brandy and fresh limejuice into an ice-filled shaker. He strained the Chaplin into a chilled glass, added a slice of lime and turned back to face him…

"Yeah – Switzerland, I know – but I bet you don't know why they stole his body. I think you'll like this one…"

Larry looked slightly bemused, took the sharp, chill drink and carefully sipped it. The barman bent towards him and whispered quietly, his warm breath tickled the hairs in his inner ear… "…they had to swap the bodies. When you've finished that, slip behind the bar – go through the open door on the other side of those red curtains, straight across the kitchen and through the red door. Just look like you know where you're going and no one will stop you."

"Are you?"

"Friend of Joe's – hush-hush…"

The barman tapped the side of his nose and turned to serve another masked guest; a tall, slim woman with long legs in black opaque stockings and high heels. Larry watched her surreptitiously, eyeing her profile - her tanned skin, jewelry and long, manicured fingers. He felt desire arching through his tired frame and slowly sipped the *Charlie Chaplin* as he longed to act upon the lust that was sweeping through him. The lust that was triggered by the dark tent, hard music and elegance that surrounded him. He had never been in a place with so many desirable people before and the alcohol had unbound his ardour. He sighed a long, hard sigh of resolution and headed swiftly behind the bar, through the curtain, a few steps across the boggy lawn and into the bustling kitchen in the east wing of *Black House*. He walked directly through the busy catering throng – directly towards a distant red door. No one appeared to notice him, they were too busy cutting, clacking, burning. He looked straight ahead, taking no notice of the world beyond his gold mask – the door was his focus. He grasped the heavy crystal handle, pushed the door open, shut it behind him and stepped out onto a deep red wool carpet.

The hallway that he had entered was dim and shadowy, lit by high electric candelabra that gently illuminated the dark wood paneled walls. The house seemed deserted and, apart from the muffled mayhem on the other side of the red door, there was no sound save the loud ticking of a grandfather clock. The hallway was bare – there were no pictures on the walls and no objects – just deep red opulent carpet, heavy red velvet curtains and dark wooden walls. Larry walked quietly through the endless corridors of the vast silent house – all of the rooms were either locked or empty and there was no sense that anyone had ever lived there. He stopped at the base of a large, open stairwell and listened – nothing. He climbed slowly up the silent stairway and moved adroitly along the upper corridors, lost in the labyrinth of Freddie's *Black House*. Then, somewhere ahead of him, he heard a crackling sound and smelt wood – burning wood. He crept up to the open doorway. Light from a large fireplace danced into the corridor. He peered around the corner and saw life – fire dancing in a grate – large logs licked by glowing flames. A woman was lying on the black leather couch that faced the fire, lounging back - her short, dark hair moving gently in the draft. She was wearing a red PVC jacket, white roll-neck jumper, black leggings and white knee-high leather boots. Her right arm, which hung limply by her side, ended in a white leather glove. She seemed as if she might be asleep. He walked boldly into the room and faced the recumbent figure. It was Sandy. She seemed drugged, sleepy, high. She looked at him through a haze of half recognition. He instantly fell under her spell again – desire, alcohol, murder – he stared at her as she stared at the roaring fire and spoke softly to him.

"I thought I might see you again honey… but I didn't expect you so soon. I guess, guess, guess that I thought you might have been…" Her voice trailed off as she stared back into the hypnotic flames, her eyes glazed and full of tears.

"Sandy… how did you get here? If they caught you in Calanda – if Magog's men caught you…"

"I guess the *Escuderos* doped me – they bundled me into a car and I woke here – dressed like this. I don't know where or why sweetie – but here I am… It's cosy here isn't it honey?"

"Can you walk? Can we get out of here? I came to – I mean we need to get out of this place…"

"Well I guess we could walk right, right, right out of here honey – but I kind of like it. Why don't you freshen up? – You look rough baby. Clean yourself up and we'll skedaddle. You look familiar – are you supposed to be someone?"

"Yeah – Doyle."

"The Professionals? Mmmm – he was my favourite. We've got time, time, time…"

Sandy seemed spaced out - she didn't move from her reclined position, her eyes stayed fixed on the burning fire as she dangled her white boots sensually over the end of the black couch. She idly waved Larry into the en-suite washroom and he dutifully obeyed. He felt grubby, tarnished and defiled – the time had come to clean himself up before he carried on with the action. It made sense somehow. He walked into the adjoining space, admiring the salubrious washroom with its gold taps, black glazed fittings and walls tiled with tessellating black hexagonal mirrors. He shaved, washed, brushed his teeth and headed back into Sandy's room. He had decided that the best tactic would be to humour her, to get her to quietly leave the room – to head back to the party, out into the yellow Capri and home – wherever that might be.

He took Sandy's hand and pulled her limp body up from the couch. She staggered slightly and fell against him, her warm breasts pressed against him through her tight roll-neck. He put his arm around her PVC jacket, smelt her scent and succumbed to his lust - he pressed his lips against her torpid mouth and held her firmly in his arms. When there was no response, he pulled away and, supporting her drugged weight, turned to lead her out of the room. As they stumbled into the dark passageway outside, they were confronted by a tall, shadowy figure – a ghost from the Rolle lakeside. Larry hadn't seen the

Pockmarked Heavy since their encounter at *Lac Léman* and the *Hotel Gai Remeuz*. The dark shadow in the hallway picked at his teeth and smiled menacingly. A sudden vulnerability quelled Larry's passion as he stared down the barrel of the Heavy's gun.

"Mister Went – we meet again. Have you seen Herr Winkle recently?" He laughed heartily then his face turned to rough granite. "I am now here… and well, there is somebody who would like to meet you. Do you know what Larry? I like you."

Larry inhaled the aroma of the drugged Sandy, held her tightly around the waist and smiled at the Pockmarked Heavy.

"Take me to your new master…"

Chapter 41

When Freddie Met Larry

The Pockmarked Heavy led Sandy and Larry down the dark wooden corridors of *Black House*, across the soft red carpet to Freddie's Surrey meeting room. He pulled the door open and ushered them into the dimly lit space. Freddie was standing behind the *Double X* table, his back to them. Larry glanced around the room, admiring the modern, minimal furniture – it seemed the type of room that middle-class intellectuals aspire to; the Barcelona Pavilion or a scene from a Sunday supplement. Artificial light carefully invaded the interior space through the half-open venetian blinds; this was a chamber awash with style and power – the simple mise-en-scène of desire. He looked over at the exit that was now blocked by The Heavy, standing with his arms folded and his stone face directed towards Freddie.

Sandy immediately slumped down into one of the Barcelona chairs, closed her eyes and relaxed her limp, drugged body. Her mouth formed a fixed pout, red lipstick smudged across her lips, traces tracked along the shoulder of Larry's cream cap-sleeved t-shirt. He glanced at her white roll-neck jumper and long leather boots – he briefly fetishised her slim arms encased in red PVC and her soft hands in their white leather gloves. As a slight déjà-vu tickled his spine, Freddie's voice invaded his private thoughts.

"So Mister Went – Mister Film Studies… you've seen Sandy's costume somewhere before. Do you know who she is this evening? – I don't think that *she* does. Do you know who I am?"

Freddie was wearing a tight black leather jacket, emblazoned on the back with a naïve skull and crossbones design and the words *The Living Dead* painted in white. On the front of his jacket the name *Tom* was painted in green on a red splash of flame. Under the leather jacket he wore a tight white cotton roll neck. Larry looked him up and down before replying.

"You're a comical little geezer…"

"Sorry Larry – wrong film. Sandy and I are *Jane* and *Tom* from *Psychomania* – and, somewhere around here, I've got a toad in a bell jar – *Maximus Leopardis*, the tree-climbing variety… it's only found in graveyards."

"Where are we? Why have you brought us here?"

"I haven't brought you here – you brought yourself. I am part of the establishment and this is my house. We're having a little celebratory party tonight…"

"What are you celebrating?"

"The end of an era – the dawning of a new one…"

It had worked out better than Freddie could have hoped. The Dark Windows could not argue with his ability to manage the situation now. Larry himself had killed the real Godard – that was a bonus in itself, and The Order – The Order had been incinerated in their Aragón bunker. Wenders, Von Trier, Kiarostami – leaving a void to be filled by Bland doppelgangers. Freddie knew that he had the franchise back and he imagined all the lovely new ubiquitous technology arriving from the Dark Windows at an ever-increasing rate; his power doubling every eighteen months. He laughed at this pathetic figure in front of him; he felt pity for him. The time for magnanimity had come, the Dark Windows appreciate a little charitable behaviour – it looks good on the annual report. He couldn't believe that he, Freddie Foulkes of the Bland Corporation, had ever been worried by the Order of Toledo, bothered by Larry Went. He had passed the test set by the Dark Windows and soon they would contact him again, soon the Telescreen would link him to the true rulers of the world and to the conspirators that relied on his tools.

There was a little time to kill first and perhaps he should play with Mister Went for a while.

Far away and muffled by the thick walls of the dark house, thunder rumbled in the distance. Freddie raised a finger to his lips and, with a wave of his gaunt hand, indicated that Larry should sit next to Sandy on the second Barcelona chair. Larry looked round at The Heavy, grinning in his dark suit, and carefully sat down. He had decided to bide his time, to see what Freddie had to say for himself and hope that he could find a way out - maybe he'd even discover what this was all about. Freddie stood behind the desk, silhouetted by the black light that illuminated the large screen on the wall behind him. His lecture commenced.

Larry reclined in the warm leather chair. Exhausted by the events of the past few days, he found immediate pleasure in Freddie's bizarre performance and became absorbed in his presentation – stitched into the philippic that emanated from behind the heavy modern desk.

"Well Mister Went... It is good to meet you at last. Forgive me for lecturing *you*, but I believe that you should understand what you have been involved with over the past few days. Have you seen the news today by the way?"

Click: (News articles appeared on the screen)

"Giants of international cinema die on the same day."

"In a preposterous and uncanny coincidence of fate, uncompromising film directors fade away."

"Cinematic greats in hiding as death stalks the art-house."

Freddie shook his head sadly. "A terrible shame... When things like this happen, It's easy to create a grand conspiracy Larry – I may call you Larry? Maybe these events are real, perhaps they are just imagined – a fantasy. Your memories – your nightmares - are just an alibi for your laziness and stupidity. Do you really believe that anyone would want to kill art in such a systematic fashion? Of course not – evil has more than one face, my friend... maybe a grand conspiracy would not be such a bad thing. A brief history lesson would perhaps help?"

Click: Edison versus Acres.

"Maybe you know this Larry, but I will tell you anyway. Like photography, Cinema was *discovered* – and I choose my words carefully – in many places at the same time. There was *Louis Le Prince* in Leeds, *Edison* in America, The *Lumière Brothers* in France, *Birt Acres* in London and so forth. Film technology was *discovered* but nobody knew what to do with it. Edison wanted films for one person – visual telephony, it will never catch on. Acres wanted to project film on a screen to an audience – a community. For the first 70 years, Acres' vision made sense and the world developed a taste for the communal pleasures of cinema. It became a revolutionary art form, a political tool that could liberate the human psyche. It became a powerful technology, outside the reach of the established world leaders. It was dangerous - someone had to take control of the cinematic apparatus and form it into an arm of the military-industrial complex."

Click: The Counter-revolution. (Images of the 1960s flashed up on Freddie's screen)

"And so there was the 1960s… the hippy counter-culture. You still think that the Sixties were important – the dawning of a new age, an age full of revolutionary potential? All that hope was killed off by brutal assassinations and political bludgeons – and who cares about it now? Even at the time, when the repression was carried out in such a barbaric fashion, in plain view, *the people* didn't care, television kept them occupied – it kept them occupied for decades. They'll believe any story that we tell them - that *you* tell them. Antonioni, Bergman, Godard – the struggle with *The Man* – it's all gone now and no one cares. You don't *really* care do you Larry? What has kept you going on your quest – what has driven you on? Was it your concern for justice - your search for the imagined killers of Godard? Or was it your self-interest, your lust, your liaisons with our friend Sandy here?" He continued without waiting for a response.

Click: Planet Prison. (Images of CCTV cameras, computers, new technology)

"The tools at our command have expanded – developed – and there are more delivered every day at an ever-growing rate: AI, DNA, Biometric scanning, identity cards, retail and banking records, electronic boxes in your living room, your bedroom… networks within networks – ubiquitous technology stitched into the very fabric of our lives. And what is it all for Larry? All of these tools have one end – to maintain the natural order, to access and control the dreams and subconscious of *the people* through the media – simple. These tools that I have stewardship of are the means by which the collective unconscious is manufactured, distributed and controlled. Cinema was an early and relatively unreliable, unscientific method of controlling humanity - it is no longer of importance to the conspiracy of dictators that the Bland Corporation serves."

Click: The Dark Windows. (An image of a human brain appears on the screen)

"This dictatorship conspiracy of which I speak – takes a systematic approach to controlling the future of the planet. First, we control the population via *repetitive transcranial magnetic stimulation*: All audio-visual equipment now has the capacity to stimulate and control the *primary motor cortex* and the *occipital cortex*. We use mobile phone and audio-visual technology to re-wire the human brain, this new technology is ubiquitous – everywhere and invisible. Our *transcranial magnetic stimulation* technique works by suppressing synaptic efficacy in the areas of language and memory – we leave clichés, swear words and fantasy to flourish, but we suppress the brain's faculties for free thought and historical awareness. Our grip is tightening around the world – we are everywhere and you don't even notice us.

Alongside this activity, we have procedures that allow us to pay off or kill any threats to our system – we are quite humane really – the future of humanity is at stake here and we all have to contribute to stability – to sustainability. Don't you agree Larry?" Freddie grinned manically before continuing. "But, where do you fit into all this? *You* are not a major threat, you are not an important person Larry – but you have been used by others in an attempt to undermine us and we therefore feel an obligation towards you, we would like to give you a small payment for your trouble – for your lack of success. And – if you accept, no one will think any less of you. It would be better all round if you took our compensation package and kept quiet."

Larry looked over at Sandy smiling vacantly on the soft chair; he turned his eyes back to Freddie and spoke.

"Is it me who's going mad or the world?"

"Both Larry… your world is in danger. You may think that you are helping to make the world a better place but you have been working with puppets. The real rulers of the world are nameless, invisible figures – they rule in secret and you will never find them." Freddie leant against the wall, looked into the beam from the projector and pressed his button.

Click: Godard.

"You have been chasing an illusive figure, a phantom that once haunted Europe. Godard is dead; you *helped* him to die – don't feel bad about it. Maybe there are others that you can help in the same way. There have always been plots, secrets and revolutions – but cinematic propaganda is impotent now – Godard's films were only ever pastimes for intellectuals. On their own, without the culture of cinema, they mean little – they helped define cinema and cinema defined the twentieth century but now, now I am rambling. What you should understand Mister Went, is that the end is near. This is the greatest conspiracy of all and it operates on a worldwide scale. We are regaining power slowly and systematically and all will soon be sacrificed to the efficiency of the New World Order."

"What if I refuse to cooperate, what if I refuse to help?"

"If you don't help, you will be broken. You will either huddle together with your friends, weathering the coming storm or you will swallow my pill and forget it ever happened. Our organisation has two simple rules, allow me to clarify…"

Click: Rule One: Complete Secrecy

Click: Rule Two: Treason = Death

"Is that why…?"

"Yes Larry – that is why you killed Maggy, he let us down, he let himself down. You helped his 'suicide' and you will be rewarded."

"Was it suicide?"

"Perhaps it was murder…"

Larry searched his recollection of subtitles for an answer; he searched his memory for books that he had read, tracts that might help him know how to act…

Godard was dead – what would Godard have done? How should the intellectual act in a time when there are too many hands but not enough hearts? Was it enough to do nothing, to remain mute? Was the act of non-co-operation resistance? Was refusing to act an act of collaboration? What would Godard have done?

"You see Larry – you have learned a secret, a secret that you cannot escape."

"I didn't want to believe it – I didn't want to… What about The Order?"

"They were all fools Larry – but you - you are an idiot with common sense and you want to *live* with your secret don't you? You have lived and worked in the same place for too long – ten years in one place and stupidity overwhelms you." Freddie smiled; he seemed momentarily concerned – almost human. "How are you feeling today Larry?"

"I'm tired, I've traveled a long way."

"Wouldn't you agree that traveling to Switzerland on the trail of a dead man who wasn't dead was rather an eccentric thing to do?"

"I'd say it was a very practical idea – I'd lost my job and I needed a story."

"If you only wanted a story – why did you go to Spain?"

"I couldn't go home – I can't work at home – I needed to finish the story…"

"You had no other reason to stalk Godard?"

"If I had – I didn't do anything about it…"

"You just wanted a story? Did you find out the ending – did you write it down?"

"I've got the story here…" Larry tapped his forehead.

"Have you had a drink tonight?"

"Yeah - I had a glass of sloe gin with lime juice – I believe it's called a *Charlie Chaplin*. The glass is still in the marquee if you want to check…"

"And you were carrying a gun – quite unusual for a writer…" Freddie moved around to the front of the desk and sat on it, looking intently in Larry's eyes. "Was it a P245?"

"Yes – but don't ask me where it is now."

"And you abandoned your friend here…" he gestured towards Sandy who appeared to have fallen asleep "…you abandoned Sandy in the basement of a museum. You drove home without her?"

"I was trapped in the trunk of a car."

"Why didn't you go back for her – isn't that what a gentleman usually does under the circumstances?"

"I didn't say I was a gentleman, I said I was trapped."

"Did you know that Godard was found dead in the *Centro Buñuel* – a single bullet from a P245 through his heart? And did you know that your brother's dead body has just been found floating in the Thames – his heart pierced by a similar projectile?"

Larry stared calmly at Freddie, assuming that silence was the best policy, he wasn't certain where this was going – he allowed Freddie to continue.

"You're told that your brother is dead and the film-maker you've admired for so long – your hero – was found in Calanda – murdered - shot through the heart with a single bullet. What's your reaction? Shock, horror, sympathy? No – just silence punctuated by feeble jokes. It's puzzling for me Mister Went – I am wondering what we should do with you."

Larry smiled, he recognised the references in Freddie's dialogue and he knew the answer that he was supposed to give…

"I grant you the joke could have been better but I don't see why the rest should worry you – unless you plan to kill me for lack of emotion. You know the story – you don't want to hear my angle on it." Larry looked around the darkened room, searching for an escape route. "How are you recording this Freddie – image or sound?"

Freddie smiled slyly at Larry's response…

"Both – there's the camera…" He pointed into a dark corner of the room "…we have cameras everywhere – do you want to see some pictures? How about the party – shall we see what's happening in the marquee?"

Freddie slid open a wood panel on the wall to reveal a large television monitor.

"Here's the bathroom where you washed."

Click:

"Here's the room where you met Sandy."

Click:

"The kitchen."

Click:

"The bar in the marquee."

Click:

"And look – what do we have here my hard-hearted friend?"

Freddie directed the camera into the shadows at the heart of the dark, pulsating crowd. Larry stood up in shock. It was Casey – Casey Went and Mike War dancing wildly together in the flashing lights of the marquee at *Dark House*. Freddie turned to Larry and smiled…

"Now that's a horse of a different colour…"

Chapter 42

Meet The Parents

The previous day, while Larry was travelling home hidden in the boot of the late Dewi's car, Mike had woken with a start in the stuffy Plymouth Motel room to find Casey's arm draped over his chest. He gently lifted her tired limb and placed it back under the quilt, stood up and stretched. He was engulfed with an urge for a cigarette and the coughing started. Casey woke and looked at him sheepishly, smiled and started to get the kids up and sorted while Mike went outside for a fag.

Thirty minutes later, with little exchanged between their sleepy forms, they were all packed back in Mike's Montego and ready to head for the Channel Tunnel and the long journey to Spain. A further three hours later, as the sun attempted to peep out from behind the grey British sky, they found themselves parked on the hard shoulder of the A303 near Andover. The car's hood was open and steam was billowing from the engine as Lilly and Alfie screamed at each other while articulated lorries screamed past on the other side of the thin glass window.

Casey had just about had enough. She had lost interest in trying to get to Spain in a worn out 'classic' car, she had lost interest in meeting up with Larry and Sandy, she had just about given up on Mike's competence in any regard and she was starting to think that their life was in much more danger, here on the A303, than it would have been back at home in Colwyn Bay. Somehow, as she watched Mike with his head enveloped in steam, cursing at inanimate objects, she had lost all interest in notions of conspiracy, threats and murders. The time had come to take control and get the kids to safety – *sod Larry and his stupid mid-life crisis. It was fine for him, swanning about in Spain with Sandy – the bastard.*

"Look Mike, can't you just call out the AA – you are covered aren't you?"

Mike looked up angrily from under the bonnet, his face smeared with soot from the decrepit engine.

"Yous think I'd subscribe to one of them fascist motoring organisations – lobbyists for the oil industry? They just support the destruction of the world – the tarmaccing of Britain with their stupid frigging pseudo-friendly – *we frigging care* – adverts. Of course I'm not in the frigging AA, RAC or any other fascist lobby group. I can fix this myself; I just need to – Shit!"

A scalding jet of steam shot out of the radiator, he threw his spanner on the floor and hopped about clenching his hand tightly under his worn leather jacket. He sat down on the grass verge, rolled a cigarette and inhaled deeply. Casey watched him through the windscreen and pulled out her 'phone.

"It's okay kiddies – mummy's going to call out the nice man with a van who'll come and take us home…"

Lilly and Alfie carried on scrapping over a toy Thunderbirds figure that Mike had given them while Casey called the AA.

"Hi – yeah… Casey Went – yep – that's right, uh huh. Well we're heading to Dover, to the Channel Tunnel. Yeah sure that's right…"

When Casey had finished on the 'phone she got out of the car and sat next to Mike who had just finished smoking. He flicked the butt out into the path of a speeding Juggernaut and turned to Casey.

"Look La – I'm sorry about all this, yous must think I'm pretty useless – but I've fixed this beast loadsa times. I built her from scratch, just give me a bit of time. Are the kids alright?"

Casey smiled softly at him and reached out to stroke his dishevelled hair.

"Look Mike, it's nothing personal but I'm not going to Spain. I've called the AA and they're coming to get us."

"That's frigging great – why don't you just call the busies as well then?"

"Look we're never going to get to Larry – not with the kids in tow. It'll never work. I've got a better idea."

"What?" Mike looked as if he appreciated Casey's attentions – he wouldn't admit it but he wasn't as self-reliant as he liked to think. He had built walls around himself over the years with his radical dogma – he had disengaged from society to the extent that he had disengaged from people.

"We can go to my folks' place in Weybridge. The AA will tow us there no problem. They're not going to tow us to Toledo are they? Mum'll look after the kids and we can decide what to do – but, to be honest, I might just go home."

"You can't – they'll find you…"

"If *they're* looking for me, I think *they'll* find me wherever I go. There's no escape – you said it – they've got us, what did you say? They've got us bolted down good and proper."

"Well – frig you then Casey – I'm only frigging doing this 'cause Larry asked me to. I'm alright without your frigging AA card and this stupid frigging car. I'm going to Toledo with you or without you. You can wait here for your frigging *nice man* to turn up but I'm going before *they* get me!"

"Who?"

"Yous know who – the *Dark Windows* – the *Bland Corporation* – I bet they frigging own the frigging Automobile Association. Yous can bet they're tracking us right now."

Mike took his rucksack from the back of the car, slammed the boot and marched off down the hard shoulder in the general direction of Dover, his thumb held out hopefully.

▶▶

An hour later, Casey and the kids were sitting in the front seat of a large yellow tow van, Mike's Car hooked up behind them, heading off down the

A303 towards London. They soon passed Mike, his thumb held out in despair. They pulled over, he ran up and climbed in.

"I'm sorry for being an arse Casey – I'll come along with you... but only because yous got my frigging car."

They were soon turning off the A3, heading to Weybridge, to Casey's parents' house in a quiet suburban cul-de-sac.

"We're at Grandma's house kiddies!"

Lilly and Alfie cried out enthusiastically, climbed down and ran into Granddad's carefully tended front garden. The breakdown driver lowered Mike's car onto the quiet road, dripping oil, he got Casey to sign something and then drove off in silence. Mike moped around examining his wrecked Montego while Casey followed the children up the path towards her Mother who was standing in the porch looking slightly put out.

"What on earth is that thing on the road – it's dripping oil on the tarmac – the Neighbourhood Watch won't be happy you know – and who's that dreadful scruffy man over there?"

"Hi mum – nice to see you too. Sorry I couldn't give you any warning – but we broke down. We were going to Spain and we broke down."

Casey's mother looked shocked. "You're were going to Spain with that man over there? Oh Casey don't tell me you've... what's he done to you now? Why have you left him? I mean, I know it's dire up there in the back of beyond, he should never have taken you to that godforsaken place – I mean it's nice for a holiday but it's no place to bring up a family..."

"Mum – I like it there – it's a nice place and I'm not leaving Larry – I'm going to meet him in Spain – or that's what I was trying to do when we..."

"So – who *is* that man?" She waved her hand dismissively at Mike.

"He's one of Larry's friends – he's from Liverpool."

"Oh dear."

"What do you mean *oh dear* – you're such a snob mum – where's dad."

"Oh – that's nice – just because I want the best for you. You should have listened to me before you got married to that man – he was never any good – he nearly destroyed poor Sandy and then he took you about as far away from me as you could get. Your father's in the shed with his new seed catalogue – I doubt if you'll get him out before tea. Come in and have a drink – are you still drinking that funny stuff, I've only got normal tea you know…"

Casey's mother wandered back into the house muttering about not having enough milk for visitors, Casey shrugged her shoulders and beckoned to Mike who waved her away and called back.

"Put the kettle on – I'll see if I can fix this bastard…"

Mother took two mugs with pictures of cats on them from the pine mug tree, stewed two cheap tea bags and poured in some pale skimmed milk, she offered Casey a chocolate bourbon biscuit.

"You're fussy about biscuits aren't you? I'm afraid they're not wholemeal dear."

Casey took a biscuit without rising to the bait. They sat at the work top, looking silently through the kitchen window at Lilly and Alfie playing with empty flowerpots on the flat green lawn. Casey broke the silence.

"Dad's in the shed then?"

"Dear little children aren't they?"

"Have you had an argument?"

"Look – they've got hold of my water feature – do you think they'll damage it dear?"

"Shall I go and knock on the door and speak to him?"

"Oh – I wouldn't do that dear – you know what he's like when he gets the new catalogue. He won't thank you."

"Does he know we're here?"

"I spoke to your sister yesterday…"

"He'll hear the kids anyway won't he?"

"…well, when I say, I spoke to her – she wasn't home, but I left a message on her machine."

"I think I'll pop out and speak to him…"

"Finish your tea first dear. She's very busy Sandy, you know. She's made a lot of money with all this new computer stuff – I think she even has something to do with telephones now. She's very busy you know – has a lot on her plate…"

"I think I'll go and see dad…"

"We had a letter for her – I don't know why it came here, that's why I telephoned her…"

"What sort of letter?"

"I'll try her again later today – I don't know why it came here. Your father thought it might be an invitation from an old school friend – it was something about a Masked Ball I think…"

"I'd better go and keep an eye on the kids…"

"He won't thank you – he's got his new catalogue out there."

"Well I'll need to speak to him sometime before I go."

"I've got the letter somewhere – well it was more of a card than a letter really. It was very nice – all gold-edged. It looked important. It was up in The Hills you know?"

Mother wandered off into the hall and Casey called after her.

"When did you last see Sandy?"

"Here it is dear – it's tonight you see. Fancy dress with a theme; sounds like fun. She'll be a bit late for it now – I don't think I'll be able to get hold of her you know, she's very busy."

"Right – I'm going out in the garden – I'm going to knock on the shed."

"He won't like it dear – it's the one from the Wisley…"

Mother idly placed the gold edged card on the work surface and scuttled out after Casey, intent on defusing the possible conflagration in the potting shed.

By lunchtime Mike, Casey and Mother had become good friends, dad was still in the shed and the children were happily playing underneath a rhododendron bush in the back garden. They were leafing through some old photo albums at the kitchen table and Mike was entertaining Mother with stories of the docks, the overhead railway and how he once met Tammy Wynette. He got up and walked over to the kettle to make yet another cup of tea, he filled it with water and was about to sit down again when he noticed the card on the table.

"*Black House* – what's this then la – a party?"

"Oh yes dear – it's an invitation for Casey's sister – it came through the post…"

"What are you talking about mum?"

"If you were listening – I told you that I telephoned Sandy – weren't you listening to me?"

Mike seemed excited, "It's *Black House* – it's an invitation to the heart of blackness la – it's where Freddie lives – yous know the Levellers, Saint George's Hill?"

Casey replied. "I know the Hill – it's where all the stars live – I expect it's one of Sandy's business contacts…"

Mother chipped in. "Yes dear – it's lovely up there, very exclusive. Sandy's done very well for herself you know. She does work very hard."

Mike continued. "Yous don't understand – this can't be a coincidence – this has been sent to us. It's Freddie Foulkes' place – *Black House*, The Hill – it's the frigging *Dark Windows* Casey. We've got to go – we've got to go to the party tonight. It's our only chance to get in there – to do something about it. The Order of Toledo must have sent it to us – they must have…"

"Oh I don't think you can go dear – the invitation is for your sister. I don't think she'd want *you* to go – I mean you wouldn't get on with those people –

it's a different type up there – you know tennis clubs and golf clubs – bridge and cocktails. It's not really *you* dear."

"Don't be such a snob mum, we're not complete plebs – Larry plays bridge and I like a cocktail – anyway it's fancy dress and I haven't been to a party for years. There might even be people from school there. You'll babysit won't you mum? Please?"

▶▶

Later that evening as the sun set and thunder rumbled in the sky, as Larry pumped a single bullet through his brother's heart, Casey was happily crimping her hair amongst the memories in her childhood bedroom; the room where she and Larry had made love for the first time all those years ago. Casey had discovered a range of tired Eighties clothing in the wardrobe for her and Mike to wear and now they were all dressed up and ready to party. Casey just wanted a good time – a night out. Mike had fixed his car and hatched some vague plan to bring down the military industrial complex by sneaking into *Black House* and revealing a conspiracy. Mother was ready to babysit and father was still in the shed.

Wind was clamouring though the garden as flashes of lightning outlined the ancient trees of Weybridge. The time had come to get the party started, they jumped into Mike's retro car, dressed in their Eighties clothing, and headed off into a darkness that neither of them had quite envisaged.

Chapter 43
Force of Evil

Larry stared intently at the large, flat monitor in the meeting room of *Black House* – admiring the screen's visual qualities and astonished by the image of his wife dancing with Mike War in Freddie's marquee - without a care in the world, as if she didn't know that her husband had killed his own brother, had killed Jean-Luc Godard.

She didn't know.

Freddie turned to the Pockmarked Heavy,

"Get them up here…"

The Heavy spoke quietly into a small radio; Larry couldn't quite identify the language but he got the meaning. He looked over at the green-tinged pixelated image of the dance floor – shadowy figures appeared from the side of the silent screen and grabbed Mike and Casey. They flailed and fought in an all-too-real silent black and white fight sequence before being dragged roughly out of the frame. Reality was hitting home now – Larry's family were being drawn into the battle.

"Okay Freddie – so you've got my attention – you've demonstrated your control. But – but what's it all about? Why have you got me here – Sandy here? Why are Casey and Mike here – what's going on?"

Freddie glanced dismissively over at Larry and Sandy on the Barcelona chairs.

"It's not *about* anything Larry. There is no battle between Surrealism and Realism – there are no *truths*. All of your schemes and dogmas are either elaborate jokes or the constructs of charlatans – nothing is *going on*."

Larry was struggling to make sense of why he was here – in Freddie's *Black House* – why he was alive and Chris dead, why was Godard dead? By what right should he be here and alive?

"Something *must* be going on – why am I here? Why is Casey here?"

"Stop asking me the same stupid questions Mister Went – don't you think that you could just accept that this is the way the world is? You thought that Godard had some sort of mysterious power – you thought that critics and writers had power. Well, maybe once upon a time these people had a little influence... but now - now artists have no power – ideas have no power. Those who create culture know that they have no influence - they merely build careers based an advanced sense of irony. They respond to the demands of the cultural industries. Godard's tired ideas are no longer relevant to the industry - the business. The Bland Corporation have demolished the role of the artist through their marketing strategies and focus groups. Nobody gives a damn about the opinions of the cultural brokers – they are emasculated. What you don't seem to grasp Larry is that advanced art is made by conservative people – your radical artists are reactionaries. Just think of your hero, Godard – a tennis fan who lived in Switzerland and smoked cigars... how radical is that?"

"So what is your vision Freddie – what do you want from all this?"

"Larry – I want you to join us. I have a simple choice for you: Join or die."

Lightning flashed through the venetian blinds and Larry stared blankly into the screen.

"Who, I mean *what* do you want me to join?"

"That flash was a UFO Larry – they've got bases all over the world now you know? They've been coming here ever since 1895 – when the scientists first started projecting moving images. They've been living amongst us ever since and we know all about them."

Larry couldn't quite believe that Freddie Foulkes was talking about little green men. "You want me to join the aliens?"

"They're people just like us Larry – it's just that their society is more highly evolved – they're just testing us. They want us to get to the stage where they are: No wars, no leaders – we'll be able to feed, house, clothe and transport ourselves with no effort – just think of it Larry. We're trying to create the future here. Of course there are too many people here at the moment, we'll need to thin the population down a little but that's all in hand… all in hand."

"I think – do you know what I think Freddie? I think that is just a crackpot idea – that's what I think!"

"You know it's true Larry – you know where all this new technology comes from don't you? And you know that we have to suppress this fact – this information because *the people* couldn't take it – it would cause a panic. *The people* don't want to evolve – they're scared Larry."

"What are they scared of?"

"They're scared of what *you* represent Larry – you represent intellectual freedom – thought free from the constraints of the monoform."

Sandy stirred from her reclined position, sat up and looked Freddie in the eyes, she vocalised one idea before sinking back down into her chair. "What's wrong with free thought – that's what it's all about isn't it?"

Freddie snapped back at her. "Oh yeah Sandy – that's what it's all about alright… But talking about it and thinking it are two different things my dear. It's not easy to have free thoughts when your desires are bought and sold in the marketplace. And if you ever tell anyone that their desires are constructed – created for them by the corporate elite – they're going to get angry. And they'll get busy fucking up the planet just to prove that they are free and that they *own* their desire… and we'll fuck you too Larry – you'll forgive me I'm sure but I'm not just being metaphorical. You see, the idea of individual freedom is noble – it looks good on a t-shirt, it makes a good advertising image or a movie plot but... a free individual – now that's something that our system just isn't quite able to deal with. What has happened Larry is that you developed an over-inflated ego and, for a minute, you thought that you were allowed to express your opinion."

Larry nodded, encouraging Freddie to continue. He decided that silence was the best strategy at the moment, he wasn't quite sure where Freddie was heading – he seemed unstable, dangerous. Freddie carried on with his presentation...

Click: Join or Die

"I'm offering you an opportunity – the chance of a lifetime... Our time on Earth is short Larry. We *need* elites for the betterment of mankind, for our continuity. The Order of Toledo, the Situationists, the Anarcho-Syndicalists and their ilk cause instability, revolution, war – is that what you really want Larry?"

"And don't you want war? Don't the Bland Corporation support war and terror across the world?"

"Of course we do – but ours is instability with a structure – with a goal. Do you really want to support the type of small-town intellect that you deal with at work on a day-to-day basis – do you want *them* to rule? We *need* an elite Larry – you have no other option but to join us. We'll pay you good money for your story..."

"What story?"

"The one you've been working on – the one about the Dark Windows, the one about you and what you have seen – don't be chicken-hearted Larry, write your story..."

The events of the past few days began to pound through Larry's head like a dozen locomotives – he wasn't sure what had happened to him, how he got here and who he was with. He felt that he had had a nightmare and woken up back in the middle of it. Freddie carried on talking at him…

"You're forty Larry, there's nothing tragic about that unless you keep thinking like a teenager. You could write a story about me – about your brother, you know that stories about psychopaths sell like…"

"Like hot cakes…?"

"You're getting the idea Larry – I like it. I mean if you don't want to try and work *me* out – if you don't want to explore your brother's sick mind, how about writing your own story? You know – you could write about lecturers, their threadbare lives, their struggles… Look at it this way Mister Went – you can always go back home to your small town and write your little conspiracy theories but no one will read them. And what if they do? What if people believe your ideas – see them on the Internet and buy into your memories. I mean, maybe by some crazy accident, some Hollywood director makes a movie about it – no one will care and you'll get no money. You'll be stuck – bitter and threadbare in Colwyn Bay…"

Larry looked tired; he'd had enough of Freddie's rambling repetitions. "What exactly are you saying – what do you want me to join?"

"I'll ask you once Mister Went – just once. Take what you've seen and write it down. Change a few names to make it more interesting, maybe add a few more deaths, a car chase and some explosions – and then I'll buy the idea. You sign this contract for me…" he slid a slim document across the table "…and I'll buy the idea. Look – just keep the names of some of these marginal historical characters – especially the dead ones, but you'll have to change the names of some of these guys with power – we'll put the idea out to some agents and get a script made from it – hell we might even get Carrière to write it… – who could direct it now? You could make a fortune, move to the States and join the Corporation. Look at it this way - people are alive for say 70 years if they're lucky, and they're only culturally productive for 50 years tops – individuals don't make much impact on the world… but organisations, systems, corporations – they can survive much longer…"

"No system lasts forever - the British Empire, The Third Reich, The Soviet Union – The Bland won't last forever Freddie."

"There's always continuity somewhere Larry, but I've given you an option – my generosity won't last much longer," Freddie stopped briefly and looked at the seconds ticking by on his watch, exhaling softly and lowering his voice before continuing. "Alternatively you could end up like Godard – dead and gone. Look – no one gives a damn whether you stick to your principles or join us. Casey won't care if you've got a little bit of cash, Sandy won't care, and who's left – who do you care about Larry – what reason could you have not to do it? I'm offering you comfort, fame – life."

Larry looked at Freddie, his aura of precision, his corporate, business-like efficiency and, in a second, with no logic or reason, he responded.

"The answer's *no* Freddie – I won't join the Bland – I won't do it because every part of me wants to do it, because you relied on me to do it in the same way that you relied on Chris to join you. Because you think I'm a poor sap who'll take your money and keep quiet. Maybe Chris was stupid enough to do that – he'd have looked you up and down and bent over backwards for you – for your money – your power. But I won't do it – sure I'll have some bad nights back in Colwyn Bay thinking about you, but I'll get over it. Maybe one day I *will* write my story and maybe you'll still be around to buy it – but it will be on my time and my terms... I've been bullied and victimised for too long – I've been stuck in some backwater taking shit from morons for too long and underneath your casual attire and calmly ordered smiles, you're just another cunt in a suit."

Freddie looked vaguely disappointed; he glanced over at the Pockmarked Heavy standing expressionless by the only exit.

"Brave words, if a little coarse – I expected something more erudite but... Don't worry; you won't be going back to Wales. As it says up there..." Freddie carefully underlined a three-letter word with his flickering laser pointer "...join or *die* – and you have chosen the second option Mister Went –

not the choice that I'd have made; to die for some unspecified cause... oh well, it's probably better this way – it closes the loops."

Freddie turned to address the Pockmarked Heavy...

"Now then – we need to get rid of Larry here, but we also need to remove Sandy, Casey and little Mike the Scouser. They'll be up here in a minute and maybe they should see our friend here with what little life he has taken out of him – and maybe we should humiliate him before he dies... now let me see, I think you should let him watch what we do to Sandy first and then – then we will destroy him."

Larry looked over at the recumbent Sandy, peaceful, beautiful in the Barcelona Chair. "You don't need to do anything to her – to Casey – just leave them alone. Look – I'll sign your contract, you can kill me – just let them go. I can prove what you've done." He suddenly remembered the copy of the notebook – the one that he'd given to Gerard at work. "I have the evidence, the Godard notebook."

"Too late – we don't need your signature and we don't need your silly notebook. I threw you a lifeline and you threw it back. I'm not feeling generous anymore Larry – you killed Godard, you killed Magog – no one would care about your ridiculous theories and I want to see my friend here..." he gestured toward the Pockmarked Heavy "...I want to see him fuck you and Sandy so that you don't recognise each other anymore..."

The Heavy unzipped his trousers and stepped out of them, his erect member standing to a surreal salute in the dark minimal *meeting room*.

"Why are you doing this Freddie? – there's no need to – I don't suppose it would help if I changed my mind..." Larry looked around for options, for places to run, blunt objects to throw. There was nothing, he had no gun and his physical strength was no match for Freddie and The Heavy.

"I do this purely for entertainment Mister Went – for yours and for mine – it will give you something to remember me by before you die. It's my little fetish – call it *scopophilia* – we all suffer from it to some degree."

Larry looked across at the semi-naked heavy and back to Freddie with his *Psychomania* outfit and his grinning face. He looked down at Sandy smiling quietly to herself, her eyes closed – vulnerable and alluring – apparently unaware of the threat that slowly approached her – one heavy step at a time. He imagined her being stripped and abused by The Heavy. An incongruous desire fought against his belief system and the thought of her imminent rape started to excite him. He tried to suppress his desire, his guilt. He imagined himself being stripped and thrown across her naked, abused body. He imagined being held down by Freddie as the heavy attacked him, a soft tip, then rough timber penetrating him, a final ejaculating lubrication followed by the musty scent of penetrated rectum and a brie baguette somewhere in the distance...

How can I imagine this? Why should I think this when we're about to die – shouldn't I be more noble, more powerful? Surely I could have an original thought – a strategy, a plan to get out of here...

Larry looked up from his pathetic taboo fantasies into the eyes of the approaching Heavy. The Heavy winked furtively at him, changed direction, walked over to Freddie and gripped him round the neck with his firm, hairy forearm. Larry watched in shock as Freddie's face began to turn bright red, his throat held tightly by a semi-naked gangster with strong, hairy, bare legs. His eyes bulged as he spluttered, dribbled and collapsed.

Larry looked over at Sandy, still lying quietly oblivious to the threat, Larry's fantasy and the reality of the choking Freddie. He stood up and turned to the door, considering that this may be his only opportunity to escape – he grabbed Sandy's gloved hand and looked back up at the door as it was flung open – and there, silhouetted in the dark doorway, was the unmistakable figure of the man who had sparked this whole quest. Standing in the doorway of the Bland Corporation's *Black House* meeting room stood the outline of a cultural icon...

Jean-Luc Godard.

Chapter 44
The Third Godard

"My world, my world – who would have thought that someone like you could destroy my wickedness?"[22]

Jean-Luc Godard stood in silence for a full minute, surrounded in a halo of smoke, he drew gently on his cigar as Freddie choked and finally collapsed limply in the arms of The Heavy. Despite the despotic nature of Freddie, Larry was shocked by the physicality of the choking – he couldn't be certain if the collapsed man was alive or dead.

"Take *Monsieur Foulkes* to the car, we no longer require him here... and put your trousers on please – I am not happy with the sight of naked men."

Godard stepped out into the light and glanced disdainfully at Larry.

"Monsieur Went, are you not torn by the insurmountable irony that I now control the Bland Corporation – that Godard controls the tools of the Dark Windows?"

He walked with ease across the room; he seemed at least ten years younger than he should as he dismissed The Heavy who carried Freddie past him and out of the meeting room. Larry was alone with Sandy and the third Godard.

"But I thought that you were..."

"Thought? Dead? Thinking *should* be punishable by death – and perhaps then, you would take thinking more seriously. Lakeside magic – the healing

---

[22] The Wizard of Oz (1939)

waters of *Lac Léman* – it happens Monsieur Went. The hand of Godard was created by man – by history - and it is this hand that now controls the mechanism." He held his cigar-holding hand up to Larry - smoke drifted into the shafts of light slicing through the venetian blinds. "It is not the mechanism that is the danger, it is not the tools of the Dark Windows. The danger lies in the hands that control these tools – police, propaganda and the state – all controlled by Godard. I have succeeded where Hitler, Napoleon and Stalin failed. I have already taken control of the universe through the art form of the 20th century - Cinema. Now I will create the 21st century – this century has no art form yet. It has lifestyle, networks and celebrities but no art. Language has become corrupted, speech has been destroyed, human relationships no longer mean anything. We live in a world of fear - fear borne on the death of fraternity. Misery will be the future of humanity unless we create a new means of communication and this new tool will be a New Cinematic Order. The new world will grow from this new form – form that hides form, light that reveals form – faces – bodies – flickering on the wall of a theatre. And when the New Cinema does its job – *the people* will syndicate themselves."

Larry looked over to Sandy who was sitting up, alert and smiling. She winked at Larry and jumped to her feet, saluted Godard and skipped over to the desk from where she addressed the two men present.

"Well Larry sweetie, I suppose you want an explanation – you want to know where you fit into all this? I can tell you the destination but you'll have to map out your own steps honey – make your own decisions. Shall I draw him a diagram Jean-Luc?"

Godard nodded and sat in the chair that she had just vacated, the cigar clenched firmly between his teeth. Sandy plugged a small device into a socket on the desk and clicked. A diagram appeared on the screen.

"You see honey – we had it all mapped out and you were one teeny little part of the whole picture. You may have your little invisible dreams that piece together a reality at which you are the centre; but in my diagram, you're just at the edge sweetie. It's like this..."

Using her laser pointer and a series of flow charts, she explained how there had been three Godards all along.

"You see honey, the real Jean-Luc here stayed in Rolle all along. He got wind of the Bland Corporation's plans to kill him and sent his own doppelganger to Penmaenmawr. Now, I don't need to go into too much detail about where these stand-ins come from, but this little guy came to us via our affiliates in the Order of Toledo and he was a real spitting-image of *Uncle Jean* – isn't that right?"

Godard nodded his agreement and she continued.

"So you see, there were two Godards in Penmaenmawr and they were both Doppelgangers, drones, brainwashed humanoid shells – are you with me on this one honey?"

It was Larry's turn to nod, which he duly did.

"Now this is the clever part sweetie – you know Chris – Magog? Well he was working for The Order – for us – and he swapped the two drones so that the Bland Godard was killed and our Godard drove back to Rolle with Magog..."

Larry interrupted, "...so what – I mean *who* did I shoot in Calanda?"

"Oh – you shot our Godard double, but don't worry because the whole place got blown away and all those avant-garde popcorn salesmen got popped. I mean - you were lucky to get out alive honey."

"You really mean to say that... I mean, isn't that a bit inhumane – I mean I thought you were starting a revolution – something different..."

"We're starting afresh Larry – we're creating a place that doesn't even exist, we can't afford to be humane – if we were humane, we'd just build another archive and keep a little record of the world as it disintegrated..."

"But killing people to create the future isn't creating the future it's... it's..."

"Killing people? – Sure people die, and you've had a little pop yourself honey. You killed your own brother and all he wanted to do was help you…"

"Help me? He tried to kill me – he killed… who was he? What happened to Chris?"

Sandy smiled… "If you'll excuse the pun honey, Chris went a long time ago – he was a void, a cipher that the Bland used and then we used to carry out the work of The Order. He *had* to die - he knew that he had to go. He carried the pain with him and it was best that you killed him – it was what he wanted. Now you can work for us – you can tell your story, you can become a writer – you're an ideal candidate; you know nothing, you've experienced little and you recount the deeds of others."

Larry couldn't quite believe any of this; even the diagram didn't help. "So what about you? What about us?"

"Sorry honey, there is no *us*. I work for Jean-Luc and I've just been stringing, stringing, stringing you along – it's the least I could do after what you did to me. You were useful to us as a means to prove that the Bland had lost the plot. They had lost the ability to silence even a little hollow shell of a man like you. You wanted *us* – you dreamed of becoming two but you will always be one – alone with your popcorn and your dreams of immorality – scratch that - immortality."

Godard stood and silenced Sandy with a glance.

"There is no need to become personal my dear. *Monsieur Went* has been useful to us and maybe he has a quiet, discrete story somewhere within that he wishes to tell. We should allow him to go away and think – one day he could tell the story from his point of view, in the comfort of his island home, while dogs gnaw on human skulls in the heart of our new Europe. There is no change without pain Larry and I can assure you there will be some pain. But our New World Order *will* be more humane than Freddie's and, now that we have the support of the Dark Windows and their dream machines, we will be able to work slowly at creating our utopia. Perhaps you will see it one day before you die." Godard sat back down and looked Larry in the eyes; it was the first time that Godard had directly addressed him. "You must see that it is a privilege to be able to live and work as an artist in Europe – a state that every day, as it grows larger, takes one more step on its inevitable path of decline. Like all states, Europe is run by a self-serving and permanently corrupt regime, a regime that offers justice to the rich and supports the artists that support its ideals. All over Europe the end results of human traffic and human trade sit in doorways collecting coins to feed the habits of their staring children."

Godard settled back in the Barcelona chair and drew thoughtfully on his cigar. "As an artist, I have lived a fugitive life; ever ignored as the mechanical totalitarianism of the Bland became ever more planetary, ever more global. The Bland and their faceless tyrannies attempted to organise and unify time, to eradicate the human face - they imposed a single global ideology of oppression. But, from Rolle, in my small way – with the help of the Order of Toledo – I have opposed this Bland World Order for many years. They attempted to abolish time. They no longer offered us a world with love. But we have removed them now. In this new, young century we will create new forms of art. The state cannot ignore art; it is the only thing that survives the fog of history and extends into the future. Our new art is invisible – it will fear nothing of others or ourselves – we will explode time and from this, forge love. Our New Cinematic Order will climb into your dreams and bring back the flowers that grow there – you will wake and find them on your pillow. The new technology that we now have will turn the world into a poem and a poem into the world. It cannot be imagined in the same way that cinema could not be imagined before it existed and it *will* create the 21st century. Our New Cinema will make current technologies seem as relevant as the *Zoetrope* or the *Leyden jar* - there will be no guns or explosions, games or simulations. It will not be the edge of reality, something approaching reality – it will not be a device or a network – it will be a community that cuts through and reforms reality – it will be a new language. It will be the touch of God and you cannot envisage it because you do not have the vision."

At that point, the door creaked open and The Heavy returned. He was accompanied by some familiar shadows – Larry craned his neck around and saw, standing there in the shadows of the Bland Corporation meeting room, Casey, Joe and Mike.

Chapter 45

Give a Man a Job

Larry Went was standing, leaning against the Double X table. He instinctively hugged Casey and shook hands with Mike and Joe as if in a dream. Sandy was sitting on top of the desk, Godard was in the Barcelona chair and the Heavy was leaning back in the shadows by the entrance. The mood had changed from execution to explication to celebration – Larry was uncertain what to do, where to look or what to say. Everyone seemed to be talking at once and they all had a different perception of where they were and what had happened.

Casey spoke first. "Hi Larry, Sandy – what are you two doing here? It's a great party – these guys just jumped on us and brought us here, I thought they were going to throw us out for using your ticket – it's a nice place. It's not your office is it Sandy? You know Mike don't you? Why aren't you in…"

Mike butted in. "Alright Larry la – what are yous doing – I thought yous was in Spain. Isn't that…" he indicated towards Godard.

"It's a long story Mike – yep that's him alright – well I think it is…"

Mike lowered his voice… "Are yous sure? – He looks a bit young to me mate – he might be the doppelganger – anyway that guy over by the door – is *he* kosher?"

"I think he works for Godard…"

"He's asked me to do a little job for him – help get rid of the boss…"

Joe was leaning over the desk whispering to Sandy. Casey turned from Larry and focused her attention on Godard, "Hi, haven't we met before? Are you Sandy's…"

Godard rose slowly from his chair and quietly addressed Casey. "Yes – I am Sandy's boss, and you must be Larry's wife?" Casey nodded and Godard raised his voice to address the gathering.

"It is good that you could all meet here – come here to our party – the host has changed but the party remains the same. Before we all go our separate ways I'd like to say a few words – to you all. Larry and I were just chatting about the future. I understand that you're looking for a job Monsieur Went – that you've given up on your so-called vocation – that you are writing a book and you are on chapter thirteen?"

"Well I – I don't know if I can go back to the college now – after walking out – leaving like that – I mean I'd have to check my contract, speak to Rhodri… After all this, I just want to live my life."

"You want to live your life Larry? You think your life is your own? You *are* a fool – a bigger fool than I thought. I don't know how you'd feel about working for a living – but if you'd like to have a little crypto-capitalist office here…"

"All to myself?" Larry seemed surprised.

"With his name on the door?" Casey seemed impressed.

"*Naturellement*, with his name on the door – with this young lady…" He gestured to Casey "…as your secretary and a reasonable stipend. Your finished story may be the first step in this New Cinematic Order that we are building. I see no reason why we should not shake upon it now. And you may have tomorrow off to see your children while we get your office ready…"

"But what would I do? I mean where would we live – there's the schools and…"

"Mere details *Monsieur Went*. Of course - if you don't want to work for a better future – if you think that my ideas are bunk… Perhaps you should think it over first. You have seen much in the past few days, it is a lot of information to digest, and perhaps you are not quite ready to understand what has happened to you." Godard broke off suddenly and barked an order at Mike. "*Monsieur War* – I believe that you have a job to do?"

Mike uncharacteristically jumped to attention and left the room with the Lakeside Heavy – glancing at Larry and holding his thumb and finger to form a rough circle in the universal gesture of 'okay'.

Sandy addressed Godard, ignoring her sister and Larry.

"Alright *Mon Oncle* – I'm sure Larry would just love to work here in Black House with you…"

"You think?"

"Yeah and you'd *love* to live in England and water runs uphill and dogs meow and cats bark and water's red hot in winter and freezes over in the summer time. We're off *Oncle* – you call us when you need us again. See you later sis' bye-bye sweetie."

With a quick wink in Larry's direction, Sandy took Joe's hand and headed out of the meeting room, back to the yellow Capri and their London lives.

Godard put his arm around Casey's shoulder and turned to Larry.

"*Monsieur Went,* I will show your new office to your lovely wife here, you relax for a minute and think about your future – perhaps you could give us some information when we return?"

Casey and Godard left through the single heavy door. Larry sat back, alone in the meeting room of Black House – the people had come and gone, they had filled the room with fantastic ideas and ridiculous statements and they had gone. He was alone again with his fantasy, desire and regret.

He sat in silence for a few seconds before he heard the hissing sound. He looked up at the Double X table. Godard's cigar sat in an ashtray, hissing and smoking. The smoke began to billow from the cigar stub, swirling around the dark room, creating beams of light as it engulfed Larry. He choked, coughed and tried to stand. As he staggered towards the door, his vision blurred and he dropped to the deep red carpet, inhaling the dust and fibres of the soft red wool. His head started to pound; there was blackness and the noise of roaring waves as he slowly slipped back into the collective unconscious.

Chapter 46

Psychomania

Mike War parked on the double yellow lines of Hepworth Way in Walton-on-Thames and opened the boot of his Montego. He looked up at the three high-rise blocks on Wellington Close, illuminated by the rising sun, and down at the unconscious Freddie Foulkes, curled in a fetal position in the shadows of his car boot. The Pockmarked Heavy got out of the passenger seat, smiled at Mike and looked up at the third tower.

"This is the place Herr War…"

"So yous really think this Godard bloke will do something radical – something different, now that he controls the collective unconscious – the Dark Windows?"

"As I told you, Monsieur Godard has values – morals. He has four laws, or is it five – I can never remember?[23]"

"Laws – government – it's all about control…"

"I don't know about this – we have got a job to do – a delivery to make."

"And these three tower blocks in Walton-on-Thames – are you really telling me that these are like some sort of portal to the stars? I thought it was them standing stones we passed…"

"No Mike, those stones are just hokum – and these towers? I am just

---

[23] **Godard's Five Laws of Dark Windows**: 1: The Dark Windows should serve all of humanity equally. 2: The Dark Windows may not be used to injure humanity or, through misinformation, allow humanity to come to harm. 3: The Dark Windows must be used to reveal the truth. 4: The Dark Windows must allow each human to discover their own voice. 5: The Dark Windows must allow each human to recognise their own face.

obeying Monsieur Godard's orders. You wait here – when you get the signal, you may go. Okay?"

The Heavy reached into the boot of Mike's Montego and hauled the black bag containing Freddie's limp body over his shoulder. He turned and disappeared into the entrance of the third tower block. Mike leant back on his car and lit a slim roll-up. He stepped forward and looked up at the blue-paneled block with its aluminum-framed windows. He absent-mindedly scanned down the building to the surrounding, carefully tended, grass lawn. His eyes were so focused on the distant building that he stepped into the path of an approaching pedestrian, sending the parcels that she held tumbling to the pavement. He looked up at the pretty blonde woman in the purple patterned dress that he had bumped into – for a second, he thought that he recognised her from somewhere. He picked up the packages and passed them to her, she smiled and looked into his eyes.

"Thanks – is that your car?" She nodded towards the old Austin.

Mike looked directly at her, holding his cigarette behind his back, aware of his smoker's breath. "Yes, I – err… do yous like it?"

"I bet it's fast…" She smiled invitingly at him.

"Do you need a… I mean - would you like me to take you any…?" He paused and looked up at one of the top-floor windows. It slid open and The Heavy looked down at him. He caught Mike's eyes and shook his head, pointing down to the lawn below and indicating that Mike should leave. Mike looked back at the woman… "Sorry love, gotta go."

He climbed into the front seat and started the engine, his eyes longingly following the woman as she disappeared down Hepworth Way and out of his life – a chance encounter that could have… His thoughts were disturbed by a call from the open window at the top of the tall apartment block. A figure was leaning out of the window and calling down to Mike. He strained to see who was calling – it wasn't The Heavy… it was Freddie. Freddie Foulkes, still wearing his leather biker's jacket, was conscious and climbing out of a window on the tenth floor of the concrete block. He called to Mike...

"Shall I come down?"

Mike wound his car window down and leant out in horror to see Freddie plunging in slow motion towards certain death on the lawn below. Before the jumping man hit the floor, a blinding flash lit the sky - the body froze in mid-air and appeared to transmogrify into the frozen silhouette of a reptilian being. For a split second Mike saw a humanoid reptile hanging in space and then, just as quickly, the being and the bright light surrounding it vanished. There was nothing there, nothing on the lawn and nothing in the air. Mike looked up at the net curtains billowing from the open window on the tenth floor, took a deep breath and drove slowly away.

▶▶|

An hour later, Mike was heading towards the M6, back to Liverpool and his radio show. As he rumbled along the crowded motorway, he ruminated on the events of the past few days and the past few hours in particular.

Alien reptilian entities ruling the world for their own pleasure – it can't be real and yet I saw... what did I see? Could I explain it to anyone without them thinking I'm?... And if Freddie Foulkes really was some sort of parahuman serpent – why would he let Godard take over? Was that Godard? Was he just called back to his own dimension – what was that light? Frig it – I'm gonna have to keep this one quiet – no one will believe this. They'll never believe about The Order of Toledo if I start spouting about frigging alien reptiles – the truth is more simple. I bet they put on this whole frigging show to stop me broadcasting the frigging truth – I'll show those bastards. Anarcho-communism or death! They'll have to frigging kill me first.

Mike's Montego headed north up the M6 - back to the real world and real people.

Chapter 47
Arrival

"It appears that art influences the public not by contagion, that's wrong, but through a kind of ethical enlightenment, through one's encounter with the world, with its artists... This has such an impact on the human soul that it changes, and one who's seen or read a work of art can no longer remain the same as before."[24]

Mist swept through Larry's waking mind, the voice of Godard repeating in an endless loop...

It will be a new language, it cannot be imagined.

He slowly came back to consciousness in his own bedroom, his tired old mattress in Colwyn Bay. The room seemed bright; sunlight diffused through the cream roller blind. He looked at his piles of unread books stacked by the bed, the paintings and cheap prints on the walls. Catherine Deneuve looked down at him from a framed poster of *Belle de Jour,* a spider hung from the lampshade – a new lampshade. The room seemed slightly different: different proportions, lower ceiling, smaller window. The mixture of familiarity and difference confused him, his head was hurting and he couldn't remember what had happened. There was the cigar, the smoke and before that... before that he struggled to recollect. It was as if his memory had been erased, veiled in a mist.

He walked over to the window and slowly pulled up the blind. It was a

---

[24] Andrei Tarkovsky

bright summer's morning and a beautiful rural vista. It was his bedroom window but a different view. The golf course and the college had gone; he could no longer see his former workplace. The new view was picturesque: An old ivy-clad telephone pole and a chapel with square twin towers, scattered bungalows in the foreground with grey slate roofs that gave way to a patchwork of blue green fields enclosed by hedgerows and stone walls. A low, distinctive ridge formed the horizon, antenna stood proudly on two distant peaks. He wandered down the stairs and through the empty house. His furniture and belongings were distributed neatly around the spacious, modern downstairs rooms. His old belongings; the books, ornaments and furniture, seemed at odds with the strange modern house. Large blank screens were fixed to the walls of each room. The walls were smooth and clean with modernist, minimal fixtures and fittings. It seemed as if he had arrived at some place in the future – carrying his 20th Century detritus with him. His memory was missing. He didn't feel comfortable. He needed to escape.

He slipped into a pair of striped slippers, slid open the patio doors and stepped out into the large lawned garden that sloped down to a quiet road. He vaguely recognised the location, perhaps it was just the herring gulls and the smell of the sea that were familiar. He sat down at the edge of the lawn and tried to piece together his memory, tried to understand how he had got here and why he was alone. In the distance, chapel bells started to toll, Larry began to shake, his heart started to palpate, lights flashing before his eyes. He stood, staggered and ran to the road. He turned right and down the hill, a few hundred metres to the small, faintly familiar harbour village. The sun was hot but low in the sky – it was morning, Sunday morning. The village was quiet; the only sign of life was the waitress putting chairs out in the front of the village café. Larry approached the woman, a wild look in his eyes, sweat on his forehead, slightly out of breath. The waitress was in her mid thirties with shoulder length brown hair, a black blouse and patterned skirt. She was slim with long legs, a friendly attractive face and light blue eyes. Larry calmed down as she looked up at him and spoke…

"We'll be open in a minute…"

"I'm sorry – I err – what's the name of this place?"

"You're new here are you?"

"Where?"

"Do you want breakfast?"

"Yes – I err – where is this place?"

"The café?"

"Yes…"

She looked a little concerned by Larry's behaviour and started to edge her way back into the café…

"I'll see if the coffee's ready love"

Larry called after her…

"Where's the police station?"

"There's not one near here love…"

"Can I use your 'phone?"

"I've only got me mobile – haven't you got…?"

"Where can I make a call?"

She pointed at a distant red 'phone box, outside the local general store, and swiftly disappeared back into the café. Larry took a few breaths and looked around – why was he here – how did he get here? What had happened to his memory? He thought about Sandy and Casey – why were they his only thoughts – where were they? He had to call Casey; he had to speak to one of them. He approached the 'phone box, he could remember his home number – but where was his home? The red box had a printed sticker in the window…

Na Bathau, Cardiau Ond - No Coins, Cards Only

He pulled open the heavy red door and stood in the musky scent of dried male urine. He picked up the heavy receiver and waited… Dial tone… a female electronic voice purred in his ear…

"Number please."

Larry attempted to dial his home number. The computerised voice interrupted...

"Please press 1 for accounts, 2 to enter your PIN, 3 to return to the main menu."

Larry pressed 1.

"To access your account, please enter your 4 digit PIN number."

Larry pressed 2.

"Please enter your PIN number..." a few seconds of silence *"...no number, no calls."*

The line went dead. Larry left the receiver hanging in the box and started to walk away from his new house – he wasn't certain how he had arrived in this place but he felt an urgent desire to escape. He passed a small empty bus, its door open, engine running. He peered in at the attractive Asian driver - she addressed Larry with a soft local accent...

"*Ble ei?* Where are you going?"

"Where's the nearest town?"

"We're only a local shuttle bus love – for the visitors..."

"Why did you ask me in Welsh – are we in...?"

"It's the local language sir, as a matter of fact I thought you might be Polish..."

Larry realised that he was back home – back in Wales. "We're in Wales? What would Poles be doing here?"

She laughed embarrassedly, "It's very cosmopolitan here – we *are* in Europe you know – are you getting in? I have got a timetable to keep to you know."

"Take me as far as you go."

Larry climbed up into the empty bus and took a seat at the rear. He stared out of the window as they wound down the narrow roads on their short journey. The bright morning sun cut across the blue green fields, glittering on the distant sea and sculpting the mountains to the horizon. The bus edged down a steep, single-track lane to a deserted golden beach. They pulled into a turning space at the bottom of the hill. The driver turned to Larry.

"This is it love, *Porth Oer*, I did tell you, we're only local…"

"*Porth Oer?*" The place was familiar – Larry felt he had been here sometime before. He stood outside the bus in the warm sun, searching his memory.

The driver interrupted his thoughts. "The charge is two Euros."

"Euros?" Larry wondered how much time had passed; there were no Euros in Wales as far as he could remember.

She smiled knowingly at him, "Oh well, never mind – you can pay me later love. Be seeing you."

The bus crawled back up the steep path. Larry wandered down to the empty beach and looked into the distance. It was a small, picturesque curve of a cove with grassy headlands and volcanic rocks bubbling up at either edge. There was a small beach café and shop built into the rocks on his left. He walked over the whistling sands and entered. There was a lone female customer speaking to the rotund proprietor in Welsh. Larry couldn't follow the conversation. The man behind the counter looked furtively over at him and switched to English…

"…will you help yourself to a pineapple madam?"

She put a pineapple in her striped shopping bag and scuttled past Larry, out of the shop, and into the harsh morning light. The man addressed Larry…

"*Bore da* sir – how may I help you?"

"I'd like a map please – a map of this area if you have one…"

The shopkeeper looked a little dubious… "A map eh? I'll see what I've got here…" He turned and shuffled through some papers behind the counter… "Here you are sir – I think that will show you everything."

He opened the map – it was a simple diagrammatic representation of footpaths around the local coastline, a coastline that appeared to be enclosed on all sides by mountains. Larry looked up at the man…

"I mean - do you have a larger one – an Ordnance Survey map?"

"Are you sure? That little one's free, an OS map is much more expensive…"

"That's fine…"

The shopkeeper pulled out an orange-jacketed OS map and laid it on the counter. Larry unfolded and looked – the *Lleyn Peninsula – North Wales* – mountains and the sea all around. Larry looked up and asked the man again…

"Do you have a map that goes beyond these mountains - a larger scale?"

"Sorry sir, we only have local maps sir. There's no real demand for maps… Your first time here?"

Larry looked up at him, panic in his eyes. "Where can I get a taxi – or a car?"

The shopkeeper looked over the counter and down at Larry's slippered feet – he appeared to be questioning Larry's sanity. "Sorry sir, only buses here. I think there are taxis in Abersoch, but that's a little way from here. You'd be best to go home sir."

Larry left the shop and marched back up the slope to the winding road *home*. He decided that it was crazy to try and head off to Colwyn Bay in the hot sun wearing slippers, slacks and a t-shirt. If he was in Wales, he should be able to get back to… get back to where? Get back to who? As he wandered back along the route of the shuttle bus, back to the strange house where he had woken, it all came back to him. He remembered it all: the first dead Godard, the funeral, London, Rolle, Lausanne, The Archive, the Centro Buñuel, the killings, the murders that he had committed and the bodies incinerated, replaced. He remembered shooting Chris with a bullet lost in the rain, the dark past. He recalled Joe, the party, Freddie, Sandy… then he remembered the smoke. He had been gassed, drugged and brought here but how? Why? When?

As he approached the new house, he caught his reflection in the steel-framed windows. He looked older, creased around the eyes, different somehow. He slid open the door and walked in, someone was standing in the kitchen, her back to him. She turned to face him – it was Casey – smiling happy, younger. He didn't know what to say…

"Casey – what are doing here?"

She smiled gently. "I'm your wife…" The sound of a kitchen appliance filled the silence.

"Can't you stop that machine?"

"I can't it's automatic – nearly finished." She smiled placidly again. "Welcome to your new home from home. We've sold the old place in Colwyn Bay and you don't have to work for those people anymore."

"Why are we…? How did I…? I mean who's paying for this place – did you agree to?"

"Sometimes it's better not to ask questions – how are you feeling Larry?"

"Is it Godard? – The Bland? – The Dark Windows?"

"It might take some time to adjust. You had a little breakdown – you were tired – you've been asleep for a long, long time. Godard set this up – we've tried to make it nice for you. You can write here, you can finish your book – there's a little office out the back and…"

"Where are the kids Casey? Where's Lilly and Alfie…?"

"Put yourself in my position Larry – he offered us freedom. It's quiet here – they've closed the local school. It's all holiday homes here now – too expensive for local people."

"But – our kids?"

"They're boarding."

"Boarding?" Larry imagined skateboards, surfboards, snowboards…

"They've paid the fees Larry – Lilly and Alfie love it at the boarding school and we can see them in the holidays. We've got everything here Larry; water, electricity, food… and the village has public meetings, reading groups, a film club. You could even play bridge here…"

Far away, out of view, the world was burning. Cities were reduced to rubble and feral dogs gnawed on the bodies of dead children. Larry looked out of the window across the rolling Welsh landscape to the distant mountains and thought about the last film in the world. There will be a last film that will outlive the last human – what will it be? Will it be distant and just or brutal and fantastic?

The Dark Windows – do they really exist? Is Godard really in control now? How is he going to change the world - what is this new technology – this New Cinematic Order?

He remembered his dreams of death, his fear and guilt. He remembered that he *had* killed now – it wasn't a dream, it was real and yet… this real guilt seemed easier to deal with. Perhaps it was all the result of a lifetime of compromises – an agreeable result but somehow he couldn't help but think that someone, somewhere was suffering for this – that his pleasant rural prison was built on the death of a thousand dreams.

Casey put her arm around Larry's waist and whispered in his ear…

"Beautiful day…"

■

www.darkwindows.co.uk

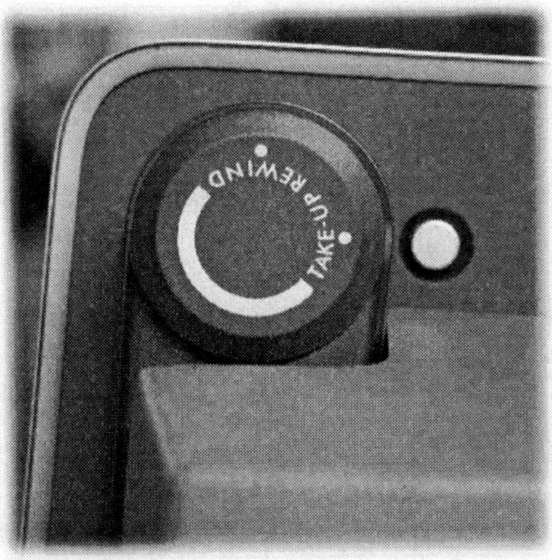
TAKE-UP REWIND